Love is
a time of enchantment:
in it all days are fair and all fields
green. Youth is blest by it,
old age made benign: the eyes of love see
roses blooming in December,
and sunshine through rain. Verily
is the time of true-love
a time of enchantment—and
Oh! how eager is woman
to be bewitched!

BEACON OF GOLD

Against a background of 19th-century South Africa the indomitable Katie O'Neill grapples with life. Twice widowed and with seven children, she is at last reconciled to her soul-mate Paul Van Riebeck, whom she had first met in Ireland. Together they take a leading part in the organisation of the Republic of the Transvaal, are involved in the discovery of gold in the Witwatersrand, and the development of the wine industry of the Cape.

HELGA MORAY

BEACON OF GOLD

Complete and Unabridged

ULVERSCROFT
Leicester

First published in Great Britain in 1980 by
Robert Hale Ltd.,
London

First Large Print Edition
published April 1989

British Library CIP Data

Moray, Helga
    Beacon of gold.—Large print ed.—
Ulverscroft large print series: romance
I. Title
823′.914[F]

ISBN 0-7089-1979-0

Published by
F. A. Thorpe (Publishing) Ltd.
Anstey, Leicestershire
Set by Rowland Phototypesetting Ltd.
Bury St. Edmunds, Suffolk
Printed and bound in Great Britain by
T. J. Press (Padstow) Ltd., Padstow, Cornwall

1

"**D**ON'T shoot him! Don't kill him! Please! Please! I love him! Don't kill him!"

The agonised screams burst into the drawing-room of the Duke of Rotherford's sumptuous London Mansion, where the Duke and Katie Van Riebeck were sipping champagne and talking. Katie jumped to her feet in anguish at her daughter's screams. "That's Mary having another of her nightmares, I must go to her!"

Lifting the hem of her long satin skirts she dashed across the floor—the Duke was beside her opening the double doors—and together they raced across the black-and-white tiled hall and up the great staircase, coming closer to Mary's screams. "Don't shoot him! Don't kill him!"

Reaching Mary's door Katie flung it open calling. "Mary, darling—wake up. Everything's all right—it's all right." She was now beside the big four-poster bed and pulled the red damask curtains aside.

In the glow of a porcelain oil lamp she saw the girl tossing about, her beautiful face white as chalk half hidden by a mass of golden hair. Katie grasped Mary's shoulders as she continued to scream. "Wake up, Mary! Wake up!" Katie shook her forcibly but Mary sobbed in her sleep.

"Don't die, Sannie! Don't die—I love you!"

Then Katie's violent shaking awakened Mary and her grey eyes, distended with horror, stared up at Katie. "Oh, Mama," she gasped, "I was dreaming . . . all about that terrible night . . . of the shooting and Sannie . . . and . . ."

"Sssh—sssh, darling," Katie's arms went around the slim shaking body, gathering Mary to her. "It's all over— over, thank God." Then Katie suddenly remembered the Duke was beside the bed and in panic lest Mary reveal any more she said, "Look, Mary, Cousin Howard is here to see if you're all right, he had heard your screams—I told him that you're affected by these strange nightmares."

Despite her distress Mary realised she must act out the lie of having strange nightmares, so that the cruel truth should never be discovered. She sat up, pushing her long hair back to free her face.

"I'm so sorry, Cousin Howard, that I caused a fuss," she murmured contritely, "I hope Grandmama hasn't been awakened by my screams."

"Don't worry about that, my dear, your grandmama has grown a little deaf." The handsome dark man leaned down to plant a tender kiss on Mary's moist forehead; he surmised that some ugly drama in Mary's native South Africa had sired the nightmares, but to help Katie in her pretence he said, "You were upset, Mary, by seeing *Othello* tonight I suppose. Desdemona's murder is rather blood-chilling."

"Yes, yes, of course, that was it," Katie gladly agreed and the Duke continued.

"Your lovely mother and I were catching up on family news. You must remember that it's years since we met and there's so much to talk about. After all, you two only arrived in England yesterday."

His beautiful cultured voice, his calm manner, added to his likeness to her dead father, all soothed Mary and she held out a slim hand to him which he grasped in both of his own.

"Thank you, Cousin Howard, I'm so glad I haven't been too much trouble." She smiled up at him, then turned to look into her mother's green-gold eyes pouring love and strength into her. "Mama darling, go down and continue your chat. I'll be all right now, but I'll keep the lamp burning beside the bed, because I hate the dark."

"Very well, darling, say some prayers, that will help you to be at peace." Katie stood up and shook out her skirts. "I'll look in on you when I come to bed and I'll leave the connecting door open between our rooms."

"Well, Mary, I'll say this," the Duke said teasingly, "if your singing voice is as good as your professor maintains it is— together with such power as you demonstrated tonight, we'll soon have you performing at Covent Garden."

They were all glad of a chance to laugh, then Katie puffed up Mary's pillows and drew the covers over her shoulders. "Sleep well now, darling, and don't forget we've a wonderful treat coming up. Cousin

4

Howard is taking us to Covent Garden tomorrow to hear *Rigoletto*." She kissed Mary's cheek and left with the Duke.

Back in the drawing-room Katie was still trembling, and asking herself, "when would Mary forget the past?" She took her former chair opposite the Duke's chair, the marble Adam fireplace between them. As Howard poured fresh champagne, Katie was calmed by the beauty around her; the duck-blue silk covered walls with mouldings picked out in gold; the long burgundy-coloured brocatelle curtains; Aubusson carpets in muted shades; two large crystal chandeliers aflame with dozens of wax tapers gave highlights to oil paintings and priceless antique furniture and *objets d'art*.

As she sipped her champagne whilst Howard settled in his chair opposite her, she felt some explanation about Mary was necessary. "Mary's so very emotional, thank goodness my other children are not like that."

"You've borne ten children"—he knew about the little girl who had died—"and it's quite unbelievable, you look so young, and even lovelier than you were—if that's possible—there's a new softness mixed with the fiery spirit."

She smiled tremulously; was it possible that he meant it? "Howard dear, you're the same delightful flatterer you always were." She carefully avoided looking into his splendid dark eyes for they held the old magnetism for her, "But I'm not such a light-headed female as to believe you. Actually I'm looking off colour because I had a brutal dose of malaria, really quite terrible—in Lydenburg." She was talking quickly, hoping to disguise her nervousness at being alone with this most attractive man who years ago had begged her to divorce her husband and marry him, but her entire being was given to the magnificent Paul Van Riebeck. "Yes, and I was stricken at a most impropitious time, can you imagine it—in an ox-wagon on the battlefield when the Boers were fighting thousands of the savage Maporchi tribe. Of course the Boers won." She gave a little laugh. "And after a while I won over the malaria and Paul accompanied me from the Transvaal to the Cape."

"I'm so sorry you were so sick, Katie."

6

"I shouldn't grumble; it was the first serious illness of all my life."

"On Nancy's arrival here from South Africa, she mentioned that you had been ill, but I didn't realize it was so bad." He felt furious at the thought of all the hardships this exquisite lovely Katie had been obliged to endure. "I'm so sorry, my darling."

Katie did not want him to use terms of endearment, though she was gratified by them. She was determined not to permit him to renew his former role of her ardent wooer. But absurd, ridiculous of her! She was no longer the red-haired beauty she had been; time had etched its little trademarks around her eyes and mouth, and now he would feel nothing but fondness for her.

"My beautiful daughter, Nancy, as we both know, is occupied mainly with thoughts of herself. I don't suppose it registered with her that I'd been so ill—anyhow, it's all over now and I'm in Heaven at this chance of being back in England and in the glorious ambience of your town house. You know one really

7

starves for man-made beauty in the Transvaal."

"I should imagine that the Transvaal is rather stark." He smoothed an elegant hand over his thick brown hair.

She nodded, "Vast expanses of unending veld with huge ant heaps, giant rocks concealing lions' caves, the stark sentinel of the great range of the Drakensberg Mountains that stretch across South Africa, shutting out the world. The storms straight from Hell with jagged, forked lightning slashing the black sky, torrential rains, insects, snakes, fevers. Black warriors yelling, *'Bulala!* Kill—kill!' Spears hurtling through the air—blood— death!" She stopped abruptly. "Heavens! I sound like a journalist describing the place—you know, of course, the Cape is not like that."

"It was a most stirring description, I assure you." He realised it had been born out of hate for the place. What courage she had to endure it. His admiring eyes flashed over her red-gold hair piled atop her head, her creamy-skinned face and long throat, big green-gold eyes, the mouth so soft now but that could be so

8

firm when necessary, her full rounded bosom, showing provocatively in the low cut green satin bodice, her tiny waist. He was as much in love with her now as he had ever been. "Really, Katie, when one realizes that you've lived so long in the land you've just described, I can only say you're indomitable and those words are from my heart. How many years, all told, have you been wasted in South Africa?"

She sipped some champagne and her eyes smiled at him over the rim of the glass. "Wasted? Oh no—it's been an exciting challenge but I've been on the so-called Dark Continent almost thirty years —and if I had the time to live all over, I would do it again—I've had a most fulfilled life."

"Yes, yes, you've the spirit of an Empire builder," his elegant hand waved impatiently, "but fighting Zulus and violent elements—digging for diamonds— that's not what God intended a glorious looking, well-born woman like you for." His voice grew bitter. "Van Riebeck should never. . . ."

"Hush, hush, it's unfair to blame Paul; remember I left Ireland after my family's

9

fortune was wiped out by the potato pest
—Van Riebeck was not the reason I
emigrated." She lied as memories flashed
to her. At twenty-one he—the magnificent
looking blond giant, with the exciting
reputation of being one of South Africa's
greatest Kaffir fighters, came to Ireland to
purchase thoroughbred horses to mix with
the colonial strain. He and she, at seventeen and Ireland's foremost beauty, had
fallen tempestuously in love but swearing
he could never marry her, because she was
too delicately raised to withstand the wild-
ness of South African life, he had left her.
Now she went on talking. "I've told you
how I married poetic Sean Kildare and
forced the poor darling to sail for the Cape
hoping we could rebuild our fortunes
there."

"I remember all that, but I've often
wondered why you chose the Cape when
the Irish were leaving in droves for
America and Australia." Howard, with his
intuitive love had always sensed she had
followed Van Riebeck.

"Silly one . . ." she forced a little laugh
". . . it's because it was so ordinary to go
to America or Australia that I chose Africa

—but after months on a sailing ship when we landed at the Cape we found the price of land prohibitively high so again I forced poor Sean to join a trek of forty ox-wagons and Dutch families headed for the North and it was by the most extraordinary chance that I even met Van Riebeck again. He brought his commando to rescue our trek when we were attacked by Zulus. Poor Sean died from a Zulu assegai wound, but I know I've told you this before, I'm only repeating it to show you how wrong you are to blame Van Riebeck for keeping me in Africa."

"It's a fascinating story," he said, wondering why she and Van Riebeck hadn't married after Sean's death. "You've never told me the details of what happened after that and I didn't like to pry."

"Oh, but I'll tell you with pleasure. I settled with the trekkers in Hoffen and tried to make my land pay but storms deluged all my planting so to earn a living I gave lessons to the Boers' children and I also collected gold nuggets from friendly hillside Kaffirs. You see I had my two children to care for." She left unsaid, "the young one was Van Riebeck's but he did not know about him for he and I had quarrelled violently and he had left," "Those were difficult times until I returned to the Cape—sold my collection of nuggets and bought beautiful Abend Bloem." She visualized the great white homestead with acres of vineyards.

"It's all amazing, and at the Cape you met my cousin, Richard Eaton—lucky devil."

She did not answer at once, she was thinking that before marrying Richard she and Van Riebeck had met again and were once more gloriously in love—too much in love—too jealous of each other, their passion had swamped them and again they had quarrelled and parted.

Now she said, "Yes, I married Richard. He was a dear and I was a terror the way I persuaded him to go with our sick children to the Diamond Mines." She burst out laughing at memories of her wilfulness. "Yes, I know Howard, I was a dominating creature but I turned out to be right about the diamond diggings—those two glorious stones we found set us up for years. It was sad though, that Richard died in that terrible conflagration of tents and wagons. Anyhow, once again you can see how wrong you were in blaming Van Riebeck for keeping me in South Africa—after all I only married him when I left the diamond diggings—that's not even ten years ago."

"Only two years before I met her, but two years too late!" Howard fumed inwardly with futile regrets for eight years ago she had arrived in London, after she and Van Riebeck and some of her children had been shipwrecked. It was then that Howard had first met Katie at the home of his cousin Richard's mother. Whilst Van Riebeck was incarcerated in St. George's Hospital with a broken leg, Howard had grabbed at the chance of being Katie's constant escort and had daily fallen more deeply in love with her.

Now he said, "Really, 'pon my soul, darling—if Shakespeare had known a woman such as you, he would have been grateful for a model for his finest heroine."

She laughed with pleasure at the extravagant compliment. "But, Howard, the Transvaal has thousands of remarkable Boer women—much more remarkable than I am." She sipped some champagne.

"Now tell me *your* news—we've not written to each other for years—I missed your letters."

"Did you? I'm glad to hear that. I stopped writing because after my mad trip when I followed you to the Cape, hoping vainly to win your love, I returned here and decided it would be more sensible to stop corresponding with you—it became really too painful. As you know, I tried to fall in love with Nancy because she looks so like you, but—forgive me for saying so —your daughter lacks your character and fire . . . so that was useless. There have been many charming ladies in my life, of course . . ." he gave a shrug of his wide shoulders in the purple velvet jacket . . . "but nothing important."

Embarrassed, yet deeply gratified by the confession, Katie burst out, "You are young still," for Howard was some years her junior, "you will fall in love without doubt and marry. Besides, there's your title to be carried on."

"I told you years ago that I feel no responsibility about that. I've a young cousin on my paternal side who dreams about inheriting the Dukedom."

"Oh, but nevertheless you will surely meet someone you will care for."

He resented her kindly encouragement as if he were a child. "Enough about me." He picked a long cigarette from a jade box. "Bring me up to the moment on all the family."

She was relieved to change the subject of their past relationship and burst out. "I'm very proud of Terence—you remember my eldest son—he's now a successful doctor. And Paul, my second son, married a beautiful Viking-type Boer girl—not quite the girl I would have chosen for him but he seems happy and they are gold mining on the Witwatersrand. Nancy of course you know all about." She thought miserably, except about her incestuous affair with her half-brother Paul.

"Yes," he smiled tolerantly. "She writes to say how she loves Paris and also her hostess' son, Count de la Motte, but of course one doesn't even know how serious the dear girl is."

"Is the Count nice, a good character? Does he wish to marry her?" Oh God,

Katie prayed, that the Frenchman would make Nancy forget Paul.

"He's a splendid fellow, I've known him since he was a child. I only hope he has spirit enough to handle Nancy. How is John progressing, working for Cecil Rhodes? I was very satisfied with his conduct at Eton and Oxford."

"You were wonderful to him, Howard, during all those years and he loves working with Rhodes. Ken is still at the Stellenbosch University slaving to get a law degree; Eileen is fine and Franz and Adrian are too." She laughed. "That's the full roll-call excepting for Mary who, as you know, is over here for voice-training in Italy."

Howard was silent, thinking of Katie's two youngest sons—Franz and Adrian—sired by Van Riebeck. Howard envied the Dutchman almost to hatred. "Well, Katie, that report sounds excellent. Apropos your offspring, I saw my lawyers recently and I want you to know that Richard's offspring are well mentioned in my Will."

"That's very good of you, Howard." She was most grateful to him. "As you know Richard left almost nothing for them."

"Oh, old Richard was rather a spend-thrift, although actually he didn't have much filthy lucre. I suppose he knew his mother or I would always step into the breach. After all he did ask me to be guardian to his children." He pulled on his long cigarette and slowly exhaled. "Now confide in me, my love, what is the trouble with Mary? And who is this Sannie she's so terrified someone is going to kill?"

Katie almost jumped with surprise, she had lulled herself into thinking that he had dismissed the scene with Mary from his thoughts and believed her lies that it was no more than a young girl's nightmare.

"But there's no trouble with Mary. She probably was upset by Desdemona's murder. I'm a little worried about leaving her alone in Milan or Florence, unless you can find a really good, kind family for her to live with." She wanted to drop the dangerous subject of Mary and so introduced a new topic. "I'm almost ashamed to ask you what may be a rather big favour."

"If it's the moon you're after, darling,

17

then that will be rather difficult to obtain." Elbows resting on his knees he leaned over toward her. "But any other wish of yours I assure you I'll move heaven and earth to satisfy."

She laughed over into his teasing eyes; it was such a temptation to flirt with him. "Nothing as difficult as the moon or sending Westminster Abbey stone by stone to the Cape—to be reassembled there—my wish is to meet Lord Derby."

"Good lord—don't tell me you fancy the blighter!"

"Don't be absurd. He's Minister of Colonies, that's why and I thought you being in the House of Lords, you'd be bound to know him."

"I certainly do. Old Edward and I are good friends; we regularly play poker. Fortunately I'll be able to grant your wish this very week-end when we go down to Aunt Cynthia's because Derby will be a week-end guest of Queen Victoria's at Windsor Castle, so tomorrow I'll ask him to come over on Sunday to Aunt Cynthia's for tea—if he can be away that long."

"Oh, Howard! You really are something of a magician! You see I want a chance to present to him the South African Republic's side of the Saint Lucia Bay business. I'll explain quickly in case it hasn't been in your newspapers."

"Don't worry, I think I know about it —correct me if I'm wrong. President Kruger and the Transvaal Boers helped Chief Dinizulu fight some of the Zulu tribes to seize the throne for him."

"Yes, Dinizulu is the legitimate heir, and in return he's given the Boers the right to annex Saint Lucia Bay. An outlet to the sea is essential for the Transvaal to be able to send their produce out to the world, but the Cape Colony Government is fighting against the annexation because they'll lose the Boer's import and export taxes."

"Damn my soul! What a troublesome race the Boers are—always fighting for something."

"Oh, Howard, surely you should admire their courage and tenacity. Paul is in the Cape, as a member of the Transvaal Volksraad; he's fighting to make the Cape Parliament ratify the Zulu agreement."

Howard watched her for a while as she got up and started to wander nervously about the room, lightly picking up

19

beautiful ornaments and putting them down again.

Then he asked, "But if Van Riebeck is coping with the issue, why do you want Lord Derby's help?"

"Because if Lord Derby orders the Cape Government to ratify they'll simply have to! Then Paul will be free to leave. He's needed at the Volksraad; he must go North."

Howard did not give a damn what Van Riebeck did. "I see," he said drily, "so you're still trying to help Van Riebeck in his work?"

"Well—surely any wife would do that," she said with a soft note of reproach in her voice.

"All right then, so we'll set to work on Derby. Now what interests me much more is how long you intend to stay over here?"

"I must return within two weeks to trek North with Paul."

"Oh no! I'll never let you go so soon." He strode to her, his face bent down close to hers. "I know I have no rightful claim over you except the claim of a man who adores you—surely that must bring a little answering pity to your heart?"

A mistake! A mistake! She should not have accepted his hospitality, even though her ex-mother-in-law and Mary were upstairs. Her acceptance had obviously given Howard false hopes. His hands now holding her arms, the fragrance of his delicate pomade—the whole of him was too unnerving, she tried to disengage herself, but his hold tightened.

"Howard dear, of course I'd *love* to stay but the only way Paul consented to my coming was if I promised to return after two weeks."

"Damn my soul, Katie! The years do not stand still and after this visit of yours God knows if we shall ever meet again. Give me two months of your life. Van Riebeck has all of it. Let me love— worship you, that's all I ask, for two small months."

Before she could answer his arms went around her and he was crushing her up against his velvet-covered chest, his mouth was warm, hard on hers and even whilst half of her was despising herself, the other half was joyfully returning his kisses.

In a few moments she forced herself to break out of his arms. "Howard, please—" she said breathlessly, "I must go to bed now—it's very late."

He grasped her arms again, his fingers digging into the flesh. "Two months! I want your promise!"

"Please—let me go now—I'll give you an answer in a day or two."

He smiled ruefully, then let go of her. "Very well, my darling." He went and lit a candle in a silver candlestick to light her on her way up the stairs for the footmen had by now extinguished the tapers in the hall chandelier. He held the door open for her and stood aside to let her pass, cursing the spite of fate that tied him emotionally to this unattainable woman—he, a man sought after by so many beautiful females, not only for his illustrious title and great wealth, but for himself.

2

DRAWN by four handsome, high stepping grey horses, the Duke's shiny black carriage, his coat of arms embossed on the sides, with two footmen in the Rotherford livery of burgundy and grey, riding outside, was moving along the lushly green countryside toward Lady Eaton's home in Windsor. Inside the carriage, Lady Eaton, the Duke, Katie and Mary reclined against the grey suede upholstery.

Katie was relieved to have left Howard's Belgravia mansion for she had been unnerved by the close proximity of the handsome man and by the unbelievable fact that he was still in love with her. For the past three days Howard had driven Katie and Mary around the great city so that Mary, new to London, could see the most famous sights, Westminster Abbey, the Tower of London, the Houses of Parliament, Hyde Park, Hampton Court, a boat trip on the Thames and lastly a view of Buckingham Palace. They had also enjoyed two operas at Covent Garden, where the singing had been a revelation to Mary.

As the carriage drove smartly along the country roads, Katie brought up the question of finding a suitable Italian family for Mary to live with in Italy and the best singing coach to train her voice.

Seated beside Katie, Lady Eaton said, "Why must Mary go to Milan or Florence? Why not let her stay in Windsor with me, Katie, and travel up to London for training? We have excellent professors there."

Katie smiled at the old lady, of whom she was deeply fond and patted her bony hand in a lilac glove. "You're a darling but I think Mary has her heart set on training in Italy. Her teacher in the Cape gave her such glowing accounts of Italian coaches. Isn't that right, Mary?"

Sitting opposite her grandmother and looking into her rheumy grey eyes Mary had not the heart to refuse her so she said, "It doesn't matter, Mama, if I don't go to Italy, it would be lovely to live with Grandmama."

Katie was surprised but also relieved, she would be free of worries if Mary were with Lady Eaton. "Well, if that's what you wish, let us say the matter is decided, but, Lady Eaton, you've been so wonderful in having John to live with you for so long and Nancy, too, as well as my sister's daughter, Marie, you know I don't want to impose upon you.

"Impose, Katie dear—what nonsense!" The old lady loved her former daughter-in-law. "Since I lost Richard, my only child, alas—it's his children's visits that have filled my life. I've missed John since he returned to the Cape and goodness knows how long Nancy will stay. She's bound to marry one of these days and your sister's daughter, Marie, also is undecided whether to return to the Cape or not."

"Aunt Cynthia—I'm very relieved that my little cousin is to stay in the shelter of her dear grandmama's home." Howard spoke with male authority as if convinced his opinion would be respected. "Mary's delicate fair beauty must not be exposed to vulgar stares on the Italian piazzas." He gave Mary a wide smile, for with his strong sense of family responsibility, he felt uneasy about her.

"Oh, Cousin Howard—I'm so glad you think I'm right to stay with Grandmama."

"Indeed I do and I promise you that you won't lack for an artistic life here. Besides Covent Garden, we've twenty theatres in London and I'll arrange for you to see all the suitable plays."

"Oh, thank you, Cousin Howard," Mary said, although some huge trees suddenly reminded her of the Cape and Sannie and she was forced to swallow a sob.

The horses turned down a country road flanked by velvety-green fields and shaded by great spreading trees, then turned into the curving driveway of Clearwater, Lady Eaton's home. The Georgian house of heavy grey stone with heavily carved buttresses was half covered by ivy and beyond the house in the distance were spread out commons where the ancient bulk of Windsor Castle with its Round Tower and buttresses capped a gently rising hill.

"Oh Clearwater is lovely, Grandmama.

Is that the castle where Queen Victoria lives?" Mary excitedly asked.

"Yes," Howard told her, "that's the Queen's main home since Prince Albert, her husband, died many years ago. She's reigned now for forty-seven years but since Prince Albert's death she's never slept at Buckingham Palace."

The carriage pulled up before the charming house; they descended, then went inside to the spacious yellow drawing-room where Katie felt that everything was exactly the same as when she had last been there years ago.

Then Katie caught sight of her niece Marie and went to her. "Marie, I'm so pleased. . . ." She broke off as the darkly handsome girl turned her back on her and went across the room to welcome the others.

Shocked by Marie's rudeness Katie's mind flashed back some years to her home in the Cape when she with her youngest children and eldest son Terence were leaving to trek North. On the wide stoep the family were bidding Katie goodbye.

Near her she overheard her sister Liz trying to comfort a weeping Marie who was muttering, "I don't believe this Catholic rubbish that forbids first cousins to marry! I'm half Dutch like Papa and I'm going to marry Terence!" Suddenly Marie looked up at Katie with murder in her dark eyes. "I hate you!" She spat the words at Katie. "I hate you! You're not my aunt, you're a she-devil! Why are you taking Terence from me? He's mine already and I'll have him back and you won't stop me—I *hate* you!"

Marie rushed wildly into the house and nine months later, Katie heard from Liz that she had given birth to Terence's son. Liz managed to conceal the whole business, putting the child with foster parents for a while and sending Marie to live with Lady Eaton. Had Katie known of Marie's pregnancy she would have sanctioned Terence and Marie's marriage, despite the Catholic Church's ruling. Better to disobey that rather than have an illegitimate child.

Herself incapable of harbouring a grudge, it saddened Katie to discover that Marie still hated her, but she rallied as Lady Eaton asked her, "Would you like to go to your room, my dear. It's the same one you had on your last visit and Mary will be in the adjoining room. Tea will be served in ten minutes."

Relieved to leave the drawing-room to escape Marie's antagonistic presence, Katie went upstairs and in her room pulled long hat pins from her bonnet, then sank into a deep chair.

Damn Marie's impudence! Good God, where had all this rottenness in her niece and her own daughters, Nancy and Mary, come from? Did the heat in South Africa develop early passion in girls? Was it fostered by seeing Kaffirs copulate freely in the bushes? But why had spiritual education failed to check their carnal desires? Bad seed perhaps somewhere in her family? From her father or mother? Never! God rest their souls. In her parents' home in Ireland, she had never heard a murmur about loose morals.

Yet she could not sit in judgement. Hadn't she committed adultery with Paul? But it had been different—though how was it different? She had not been fourteen like Marie for instance, who knew the sin of lying with a first cousin, and Nancy had committed the greatest sin of all short of murder to lie with her half-brother. Then Mary—oh no! Katie could not even think of that. She jumped up, went to the mahogany washstand, poured water from the flowered porcelain jug into the matching basin and washed her face and hands, then unpinned her waist-length hair, combed it out and rolled it into a flat bun on top of her head. She smoothed a rice-powder paper over her face to remove the shine, smoothed some cochineal liquid over her lips and a little Malay kohl on her eyelids. Why was she doing all this? she demanded of herself and knew she wanted to look attractive before Howard and also for Lord Derby if he managed to call. She regretted that her clothes were obviously old-fashioned but she had neither time nor money to have new gowns made such as she had gloried in doing on her last trip to London. With a final glance in the looking-glass she went downstairs.

In the drawing-room she found Lady Eaton seated behind a lace-covered table set with Georgian silver and Royal Worcester china. Beside her stood Dimbleby, the butler whom Katie knew from her previous visit. Mary and Marie were standing by a long window talking and Howard stood near the piano with a tall, sandy-haired man. As soon as Katie entered the room Howard came up to her with the visitor whom she excitedly guessed was the influential Lord Derby. Somehow she must *make* him help the Transvaal to acquire Saint Lucia Bay.

"Mrs. Van Riebeck, may I present my good friend, Lord Derby. As you know he's a most powerful member of Her Majesty's Government."

"His Grace is always charming," Derby said to Katie as he took her proffered hand and bowed low over it.

"But His Grace is very truthful as well." She smiled, gazing fully up into his kindly face and determined to make him like her so he would wish to meet her again. "Your name is very well known, Lord Derby, in South Africa where I live."

"By Jove—you live in South Africa. A beautiful country I believe, but so unfortunate politically, always disputes and wars going on."

"Yes, it's very sad, especially when one considers the size of the country—the whole of France could fit into the

Transvaal alone. With so much land, how stupid of people to still fight over it. Of course with the diamond fields it's understandable. Greedy men come from all over the world to claw out diamonds, but it's unfair that the Boers who trekked from the Cape and suffered unbelievable hardships and dangers still have to struggle to keep possession of their land." She had deliberately set out to pique him in the hope of arousing his interest.

"Mrs. Van Riebeck, you sound very much of a Boer sympathiser, but you're obviously not Dutch."

"No, I was born in Ireland."

"Really, Ireland," Lord Derby said, but he thought to himself—"another trouble spot". "Do let us sit down," he went on aloud.

They settled in three wing chairs near Lady Eaton and Howard said to Lord Derby, "You know, old fellow, Mrs. Van Riebeck was married to my cousin Richard Eaton, your year at Harrow, I believe, and as you can remember, Richard was English to the backbone. Poor fellow, he died in the Colony—so you see, Mrs. Van Riebeck is really no more of a Boer sympathiser than an English one: she calls herself a South African."

"That's true," Katie told Lord Derby, then looked over and, catching Mary's eye, she beckoned her to join the group.

Mary came at once with Marie and both girls being presented to Lord Derby dropped curtsies then sat down.

Katie accepted tea from Dimbleby saying softly, "It's so nice to see you again."

"Thank you, Madam." The elderly man smiled decorously, "and if you'll pardon my boldness it's a pleasure for me to see you back, Madam." He passed on to serve Lord Derby who sipped his tea thoughtfully, then turned to Katie.

"It's very encouraging to hear you call yourself a South African citizen, Mrs. Van Riebeck, but aren't South African citizens very rare? Isn't it mostly a question of Dutch or English citizens?"

"Yes, mainly you're right but I have quite a few relatives in the Cape and they consider themselves South African, as my children do, and they are friendly with English families who've settled in the Cape excepting when the Transvaalers were victorious over the English in the war at Majuba. Then the Cape Dutch rejoiced and the English citizens lamented. They resented the Dutch victory more than the English soldiers who came from England to fight the war."

"That's natural I suppose because the Cape English have to live with the humiliation," Howard remarked, "whereas the soldiers were able to sail for home."

"It's a difficult country to comprehend," Lord Derby spoke thoughtfully and turned his look on Mary and Marie. "And have you two young ladies lived in South Africa?"

"I have, all my life," Mary said.

"Indeed—in the Cape or the Transvaal?"

"Both, though I prefer the Cape, it's so beautiful; but I lived for a while with Mama up in Lydenburg, and sometimes I was terrified. We were giving a party one night when we were attacked by the savage Batlapins waving spears and shouting, 'Kill! Kill!' luckily our forty guests were all crack shots and. . . ."

"Mary! Enough, darling!" Katie was amazed by the force of the girl's outburst.

"Please, you frightened your poor grand-mama." Katie smiled reassuringly at Lady Eaton then glanced at Lord Derby who looked angry.

"But *why* did the tribe attack you, Mrs. Van Riebeck? Were you occupying their land?"

"Oh, no—no! The Dutch always paid herds of cattle to the tribes for their land. It's a peculiar thing but for a while the Kaffirs live at peace with the whites, then suddenly for no reason some devilry rises in them—it's a blood lust and they leave their kraals to go to 'dip their spears in blood' as they call it. It's just another one of the terrible things that make up everyday life for the Transvaalers." She would force Lord Derby to realize something of what the Boers suffered.

"It's shocking, quite shocking," Derby looked at Marie. "I hope you've had a more peaceful life."

"Yes, luckily I lived at the Cape, but on the Colony's borders there were always Basuto uprisings and my brothers and cousins, even as young boys, were called into the Korps to help fight the Basutos,

35

though our homes were never under attack."

"Good and are you going to remain in peaceful England?"

"I'm not sure, you see my father, who is Dutch, wrote to tell me that a new law has just been passed permitting lessons to be taught in Dutch as well as English in the Cape schools so I want to go back to teach. I want to be useful to my people."

"Hmm . . . very commendable." Damn rot, Lord Derby thought, permitting two languages to be taught; it was just another step away from Union.

Katie was determined to arrange another meeting with Lord Derby, for now it was impossible to talk of Saint Lucia Bay.

"Lord Derby," she said, "I simply must hear you address the House of Lords, I'm just longing to."

"Ah, how very flattering, Mrs. Van Riebeck. I shall arrange a seat for you— but I must beg you to allow Howard to bring you to dine with me, not only do I enjoy your society but you can enlighten me on many things in South Africa."

Katie was jubilant but before she could accept Lady Eaton burst out, "You wicked man, you've been tiring my dear Katie with your continuous talk of politics. Howard, pass the cucumber sandwiches, Katie used to love them."

"Of course, Aunt Cynthia." He rose and took the plate with thin, finger-sized sandwiches and proffered them to Katie.

"Oh, thank you, Lady Eaton, I still love them and they never taste as nice outside of England."

"Howard, will you be attending the opening meet of the Whadden Chase in two weeks?" Lord Derby asked as he helped himself to sandwiches.

"I will if I can persuade my beautiful cousin-in-law to join me. Eh, Katie? Even as a girl I believe you were one of Ireland's finest horsewomen."

"Oh," she laughed, "I was raised on devil horses and that's been useful to me in South Africa." She pulled a rueful face. "But unfortunately I cannot join the hunt with you—I'll be on the high seas, bound for the Cape."

"'Pon my soul! You're leaving so soon!" Lord Derby was a little put out for she would be of use to him to explain some of the South African problems. "Now you simply must do me the honour of dining at my London home." He put his cup and saucer down and delved inside his tightly buttoned jacket for his diary. Bringing it out he ruffled through the small pages. "Now when? My evenings are fairly free as Lady Derby is in the North at the moment."

Katie was delighted. "My social engagements are nil, so the choice must be Howard's."

They settled upon the following Tuesday as Katie would be in London with Mary seeing singing coaches.

"Splendid, Tuesday then it is and if you'll agree, we shall be only three, that way we can discuss this vexatious South African problem."

"I should be grateful for that opportunity." She would *make* him help the Boers to be granted rights to Saint Lucia Bay. "There are many things I'd like to tell you."

"Splendid! Splendid!" He stood up and bowing to Lady Eaton he explained, "Regretfully I must return to the castle, His Highness wants me to join a small game of cards before dinner."

After bidding Katie and the girls goodbye, he left with Howard escorting him to his carriage.

"He's nice," Mary said. "Who is he, Mama?"

"One of the most important men in the English Government." Katie enjoyed a small triumph that she was to have a chance to perhaps aid the South African Republic. She longed to tell Van Riebeck about it, but alas six thousand miles separated them. She would write though and tell him before going to bed.

Howard came back, his face all smiles. "Well, Katie, as usual, you made an immediate conquest; you captivated Derby, just as you do all men."

"Oh, what delightful nonsense you talk, Howard," she laughed up at him. "Now, Lady Eaton dear, would it be a good idea if Mary sang a few songs for you? That will give you and Howard an idea of what her voice is like."

"Oh that would be lovely, my dear." Lady Eaton rose and went to sit in a chair near the piano thinking what happiness it was for her to have Richard's beautiful young daughter with her and Katie too who brought such life to any room she was in.

Mary felt a little apprehensive as Katie moved over to the piano, sat on the stool, arranged her wide skirts becomingly around her feet, then opened the piano lid. Then as Howard came to stand right beside her she glanced up enquiringly at him.

"I'm the official page-turner," he teased. "Where are the music sheets?"

"Oh, *that's* why you're here," she laughed, "but there's nothing to turn, I accompany Mary from memory." She looked at Mary. "What will you start with, darling?" She gave the pale-faced girl an encouraging smile. "Mary sings in four languages—French, English, German and Italian," she went on turning to Lady Eaton whose face lit with a proud smile.

Feeling rather sick and giddy with nervousness Mary murmured, "I'll start with an English song, 'The Shepherdess' please, Mama."

3

THE next morning Mary begged to be allowed to remain in bed because of a sick headache, so Katie went down to breakfast with the family and found a telegram beside her plate. Asking Lady Eaton's permission she opened it, then read the contents aloud.

"Hurrah you have arrived stop leaving Paris and joining you on Tuesday at Howard's Belgrave house all love. Nancy."

"Good! So she's decided to put in an appearance," Howard said drily.

"She's none too soon." Lady Eaton gave a little disapproving sniff. "I really expected her to return in time to meet your ship, Katie dear."

"Well—yes, I was a little disappointed not finding her there, but I suppose something very exciting detained her in Paris." She glanced across the snowy white tablecloth at Howard who looked so impeccable in a light-grey suit, the tightly buttoned jacket showing a high stiff white collar.

"Have you given Nancy permission to use your Belgravia home just whenever she wishes—I do hope that she doesn't impose upon you."

"Nonsense," he laughed easily showing his strong white teeth. "My home is open to all of my family and that applies to you, too, Marie, although you've seldom accepted my invitations."

"Thank you, but I've been very content at Clearwater, I'm not infatuated with London life like Cousin Nancy."

"Marie has been studying very hard, Katie, at the seminary in Windsor," Lady Eaton said. "For some time she's been preparing herself to be a teacher."

"That's excellent," Katie said as politely as she could manage but still upset by Marie's rudeness to her. She put her knife and fork together, unable to finish the grilled kidneys on her plate. English breakfasts with a dozen or more different dishes did not agree with her. "If you'd excuse me for a few minutes I'd like to go up and persuade Mary to have a cup of tea. I think she's exhausted actually; London is quite overpowering when it's all so new to one." She pushed her chair back and stood up and Howard immediately rose to his feet.

"Of course, Katie dear," Lady Eaton nodded, "go and see how the poor child is and ring for whatever you wish."

Katie found Mary with her head hanging over the side of the bed, while she vomited into the porcelain chamber-pot on the floor beside the bed. Katie rushed to her. "Oh, my poor darling."

She supported Mary's head with one hand and held the chamber-pot up to make vomiting easier for Mary. After a couple of minutes Mary spewed convulsively but only bile appeared.

"I think it's over, darling, your poor stomach must be utterly empty." Katie eased Mary back to lie against the pillows. "There—just rest and I'll bathe your face and hands to refresh you."

"Oh, Mama—I feel terrible, the bed and the whole room seem to be swinging around."

"It sounds like a spell of vertigo." Katie went to the mahogany washstand and poured water from a porcelain jug into a matching basin, grabbed a sponge and towel then carried them to the bed. She started to sponge Mary's ashen face, then her neck and arms. "You've probably eaten something that disagreed with you, so I'll ask your grandmother to send for a doctor and he'll give you some powders to put your liver and stomach right." After she had dried Mary, who was already falling asleep, Katie put the chamber-pot in her adjoining room then ran down to Lady Eaton and asked her to send for a doctor.

"But immediately, my dear, we still have nice old Doctor Trevor who's taken care of both Nancy and John." She turned to the butler. "Dimbleby, send a boy on a fast horse to Windsor and ask Doctor Trevor to come at once."

The family left the dining-room to go to the morning-room, cheerful with bowls of flowers and chirping canaries in brass cages.

Howard went to look over the daily newspapers spread out on a table, then said to Katie, "Mary was nervous last night and having to sing such a long repertoire probably upset her, but I was most impressed with the quality of her voice and her talent to sing in three foreign languages."

"She had an excellent teacher in the Cape, but I'm so glad you approve of her voice, that makes me feel vindicated for the expense I incurred in bringing her to Europe."

"I'm sure your judgement was right, dear," Lady Eaton said as she accepted *The Times* from Howard.

Within a few moments they were all reading newspapers until the clip-clop sound of horses' hooves made them look up and Dimbleby came in and announced to Lady Eaton, "Doctor Trevor has just arrived, my lady."

Katie jumped up from the chintz-covered chair, "I'll come at once."

Upstairs, in the shadowy bedroom, Mary was sleeping and Katie said, "She had a terrible fit of vomiting, Doctor Trevor. I'll raise the blinds and awaken her. We've only been in England a few days but during the three weeks at sea, Mary was in excellent health."

The old grey-haired doctor nodded. "So this is Miss Mary Eaton, eh? I've treated Miss Nancy Eaton and also your son John.

Well, we'll soon take care of Miss Mary."
He touched Mary's shoulder. "Wake up,
Miss Mary—I'm Doctor Trevor come to
make you well."

Her lids rolled back to show her big
grey eyes and she stared up at the
fresh-faced, grey-whiskered man. "Good
morning, Doctor," she murmured, then
he sat on the side of the bed and took her
pulse.

After a moment he turned to Katie and
said gently, "Perhaps, Mrs. Van Riebeck,
you would like to leave me with Miss
Mary?"

"Yes, of course, Doctor, my room
adjoins this one; I'll wait for you there."

In her room Katie stood at the tall
window staring out at the lush green fields
and suddenly she felt stricken. Oh God!
Vomiting like that in the morning! Could
it be morning sickness? Oh no! "Mother
of God—I beg Thee—don't let Mary be
with child!" But she had been lying with
Sannie for months—she had admitted
that. If she were with child—what in
God's name could be done?

It seemed eternity plodded by as her
agonised thoughts raced through her

tormented mind. She was moist with perspiration, her fingers digging into the window-frame when at last she heard Doctor Trevor's knock. She sprang to open the door connecting with Mary's room. One look at the Doctor's grave face and she knew that stark tragedy was ahead for Mary.

"Sit down, my dear Mrs. Van Riebeck —I can see by your expression that you suspect the unhappy truth."

"Yes," she whispered, sinking tremblingly into a chair.

Doctor Trevor sat opposite her saying, "She has no idea she is with child. She's such a shy, innocent girl that I had trouble in persuading her to allow me to examine her. So I thought it would be easier for her if you told her the truth. I think she'll be shocked because like many women she's been menstruating regularly. I told her she has an upset stomach and to go back to sleep."

Katie just nodded. Seeing she could not speak Doctor Trevor continued, "Do you know the man responsible? Can you persuade him to marry her?"

Katie slowly shook her head, "He's

dead," she muttered stonily. "Tell me, Doctor, how many months . . . is she with child?"

"Still in her second month—she's so slim she won't show her condition for quite a while."

"Yes—that could somehow be a help." She suddenly sprang to her feet feeling more distraught than she had ever been in her life, for all the other problems she had hitherto faced she had found solutions—to this one she could think of nothing to combat it. "I must beg you, Doctor, not to let Lady Eaton or anyone know about Mary's condition."

He rose swiftly. "But of course I should never divulge the truth, but I'm worried about you, you seem in a state of shock. I've sal volatile in my bag, let me give you a dose—it will help you." From his bulging bag he pulled out a blue paper packet and shook the powder into a glass on the washstand, poured water from the glass waterbottle and handed the mixture to Katie. "Drink this it will help to calm you."

She swallowed the mixture and put the glass down. "Thank you, Doctor, you're very kind. I suppose I should have suspected this but God knows why—I didn't until a few minutes ago and the shock . . . well . . ." She fought to gain control of herself. "I'll have to think of a plan to save Mary from disgrace . . . and the child too."

"You will, you will. This type of thing is happening every day, believe me, and even in some of the finest families. Well, I'll leave you now."

"I'll come down with you. I don't want to see my daughter yet—not until I've thought out a way of saving her."

"'Pon my soul, you're a splendid mother—no recriminations nor blame to heap on the poor girl. I admire you."

"She's human." Katie's voice broke on a sob that was half choking her.

Downstairs she managed to be outwardly calm and saw the doctor into his waiting carriage then she went inside to tell Lady Eaton and Howard, "As I suspected, Mary's got a slight dose of food poisoning; the doctor left me some powder for her." As she was talking her agitated mind made a swift decision, "Howard is the sole person to help me. I must confide in him at once."

49

"You look rather pale yourself, my dear Katie," he said with concern in his dark eyes. "Are you feeling all right?"

"Oh, quite well, but you know I believe I'd like to ride for a little through Windsor Great Park. Could we?"

"Just what I'd love," he said. "I keep a couple of good mounts in Aunt Cynthia's stable."

"I'll loan you a riding habit, Katie dear," Lady Eaton volunteered.

"Don't worry, I'll pretend I'm in Africa and ride as I am—if you don't mind, Howard?"

"You could ride in the robes of a Magi priest and I'd still be delighted to be beside you—also it's unlikely that we'll meet many riders—it's still too early."

At first they rode slowly over grassy paths with velvet-like softness, passing beneath great oaks and lime trees with their leaves turning in places to rich gold. Reaching an open space in the lush parklands, with Windsor Castle on their left, Katie spurred her horse and galloped off madly with warm tears running down her cheeks. She needed to feel the air brushing her cheeks, needed to be a part of the horse's great extending and contracting muscles, to inhale the scent of damp earth: it all helped to strengthen her and galloping along beside her Howard, without seeing the tears, intuitively sensed her desperate mood.

After five minutes she reined in and called over to him. "Shall we dismount for a while?"

He pulled up immediately, threw a leg over his horse's back and sprang to the earth, then he lifted her off her horse. He took the reins of both animals, tethering them to the branch of a nearby tree whilst Katie walked a few feet to settle down at the base of a giant cedar, leaning back against the comfort of its trunk. All her life she had drawn strength from great trees.

Howard unbuttoned his jacket, took it off and said, "You must sit on it—I insist, the grass is damp." She shook her head but he placed the jacket on the grass and caught her under an arm and moved her to sit on the jacket. She did not trust herself to murmur her thanks, she was too close to weeping out loud.

Saying nothing, he settled beside her,

elegant in a grey brocade waistcoat and wide-sleeved white shirt. After a few moments he gently asked, "Whatever is this thing that's upsetting you so much, my darling?"

She hesitated, it was hard to tell him, then in a few seconds she burst out. "I'm going to confide in you—you are the only human being I can divulge this to and I won't insult you by asking you never to repeat it. Mary is with child, Doctor Trevor has just told me."

"Damn my soul! Well, whoever the rotter is I'll make him marry her and. . . ."

"He's dead, Howard," Katie said flatly.

"The devil he is!" No wonder Katie was so upset. "Well, we'll have to find someone else to marry her—she just can't give birth to an illegitimate child!" He felt furiously enraged with this unknown man for dying and leaving Mary in this state. "I'll find a decent fellow—settle money on him and after the child's birth, Mary can divorce him, if she wants to. Don't worry, my love. I'll take care of it all, it's not an insoluble problem." He expected to see relief come to her face but it did not nor the agony leave her eyes. "You are so good, Howard, but God help us—it's not as easy as that."

"But in God's name, why not? She's a lovely girl and I'll settle money on her. There will be no complications, I promise you; I can arrange the whole thing through my most discreet lawyers and. . . ."

"Howard—Howard—Howard! The terrible tragedy is," she half-moaned, "Mary's baby—is likely to be—black."

"Holy Christ, Katie—what are you saying?"

"SANNIE! The name you heard her scream out in her nightmare—he was a big, handsome Zulu—black—black—black!" Katie stopped, then recovered some strength to go on. "He was born on our estate—we were all so fond of him, he and the other black children used to play with my children when they were all small. I'll tell you about it. A few months ago Mary was mooning about the place like a love-sick calf and I couldn't get it out of her—if she were in love or not. She told me nothing, so I spoke to Kenneth—he's two years her senior and he started to watch her. I wondered if it was a married man she'd fallen in love with because that might be why she was so secretive. Then one night Ken hid in the bushes under her window . . ." Katie hesitated to draw breath then went on. "Mary let a rope ladder down from her window to the ground and Ken saw a big man come silently out of the bushes, climb the ladder and go into her room. Ken was furious. He rushed into the house, got his gun and blew the lock off Mary's door—he found Sannie—black as night—naked with Mary —in bed. They of course sprang up in amazement." Katie was suddenly too grieved and dejected to continue.

"Finish it, Katie—I must know it all."

"Well, Mary screamed to Ken, 'Don't shoot him! Don't!' and at the same time Sannie sprang at Ken and taking him unawares he wrested the gun from him, pointed it at his own heart and shot himself. He collapsed at Ken's feet murmuring, 'Master Kenneth . . . I glad . . . I saved you . . . from murder.'"

"Damn my soul! Good God! But in his fashion this Sannie was not too bad—I mean saving Ken from killing him." Howard felt he had never heard such a harrowing story and by God, with members of his family.

"I rushed in at that point," Katie went on, "and found Mary sprawled over Sannie's naked body." Never would she forget Mary's white nakedness over Sannie's black body. "She had fainted—so while she was unconscious I rallied Ken to carry Sannie's body downstairs. Then we dressed Sannie and left the gun beside him in such a position that when he was found the next day everyone thought it was an accidental shooting or suicide." Katie's heart was palpitating uncomfortably. "When Mary regained consciousness she was in such a terrible state I told her Sannie was badly wounded but not dead. Then I whisked her on to a ship for Europe—for her voice training."

"Does she know now that Sannie's dead?"

Katie shook her head. "I was hoping that with the change of scene—coming to England and meeting young Englishmen —with time she'd forget Sannie and then I could tell her."

"My poor darling Katie, what an

unspeakably hideous mess for you and Van Riebeck. What did he feel about it?"

"He knows nothing about it, thank God! When it happened he was away seeing the Governor in Cape Town. If he ever found out about it, I'm afraid he might kill Mary. Certainly he would disown her, never speak to her again or have her in our house."

"Surely you're imagining that he would be so severe—I can't believe he would be, once the first shock had passed."

"Howard, you don't understand how fanatically the Dutch feel about such things. Years ago he gave Paul a most dreadful thrashing when they were elephant hunting near the Zambesi and he caught Paul lying with a black girl under the wagon. Paul and Van Riebeck didn't speak to each other for three years but it's a thousand times more of a disgrace for a white girl to be bedded by a black—it's cause for murder with the Dutch."

Despite the sinister circumstances Howard felt a strange triumph—so Van Riebeck had failed her in this one of her greatest dilemmas and she was turning to him, Howard. By God he would not fail her. "What a devilishly cruel race the Dutch are."

"Not really cruel. They have their own standards and remember that Kenneth— one of your own family—was going to kill Sannie and he had loved the Zulu since they were children. Oh God," she beat the heels of her palms against her temples. "If Mary's baby is black she can never come home; she'd be ostracized by the whites as well as the decent blacks. It's the worst tragedy that's happened in our family. I feel a curse has been laid on us."

"It would be stupid to deny the seriousness of it all. Have you considered that Mary could be operated upon," Howard said very gently, "so that Sannie's child need never be born? That's the kindest solution for Mary and the child."

Katie shut her eyes and shook her head violently so that her tears splashed out. "That's murder in another form. I'd never be a party to it and I'm sure Mary wouldn't do it. She's so ridiculously romantic that when she learns Sannie is dead she'll believe she's being some kind of a heroine by bearing his child."

"It's the devil's own mess!" He felt for

his cigarette case. "May I smoke, Katie? Will it worry you?"

"Of course not. I feel I could smoke Dacca—as the Kaffirs do—it's a drug that helps you forget the pain—anything to ease this mental torture."

As his mind pulled the problem about he lit his cigarette with a wax match and inhaled deeply, then he said, "Perhaps a solution would be to find the darkest-skinned European we can—Spanish or Italian—as a husband for Mary, then if she has a near black baby it would not be so extraordinary to everyone."

"Yes . . . you're right, it is the *only* solution. Although crinkly negro hair is a palpable sign of negro blood, still with the mixture of Mary's blood, the child's hair could be straight. Of course we'll have to tell the man—whoever he is—that she's with child but not say anything about Sannie's colour."

"Absolutely not, but events now make it essential that she goes to study in Italy. I think Florence would be advisable, because I've an old aunt there whom Mary could live with."

"Oh thank God for your help,

Howard!" She caught at his upper arm with both hands. "I could not cope without you. Could we return to London on Monday instead of Tuesday to start making arrangements to go to Florence?"

"We shall do anything you wish, my beloved Katie." He was grateful to Fate that he could aid her, for this sordid business would forever be a strong link between Katie and himself. "I shall explain to Aunt Cynthia that after hearing Mary sing last night I'm convinced she must go to Florence for coaching."

"I hate to disappoint dear Lady Eaton, but there's no choice. Shouldn't we go back to Clearwater now? We've been gone quite a while. I dread the task ahead of me, but Mary must learn the truth."

He sprang up then leaned down, extending both his hands to help her up. With all of his being he longed to pull her into his arms, to kiss her mouth twisted with grief, her eyes heavy with sorrow, but he knew that at such a time it would be a flagrant intrusion on her.

She got shakily to her feet and picked up his light-grey jacket. "I hope it's not grass-stained." She held it out for him to slip his arms into the sleeves. As he eased his wide shoulders into the jacket she said, "I haven't said thank you for everything, Howard—but. . . ."

"It's quite unnecessary, my darling—as you well know." They started for the horses. "With all this trouble to contend with you'll probably wish me to cancel the dinner with Derby."

"No—no! It's a Godsent opportunity for me to help the South African Republic. I can't think of Mary, there's my entire family to think of and they'll all benefit if I can help the Republic take possession of Saint Lucia Bay."

Howard stared at her with an amazement he did not try to hide, then he smiled widely. "I told you—you are indomitable and by God, you *are!*"

Before mounting they stood for a second looking deeply into each other's eyes and she thanked God for the love of this wonderful man that was such a strong crutch at this dreadful time. Then he said.

"I'll ride into Windsor after lunch and telegraph my old aunt in Florence to announce our arrival at the end of the week. She has a passion for saving all the stray cats in Florence, but her little Pallazio has plenty of space for us as long as we're polite to the cats."

Katie knew he was trying to lighten her grief so she forced a smile for him and said, "I quite like cats." She was thinking his aunt won't have the heartaches with cats that she would have had with children.

4

"I'LL do whatever you want me to do, Mama." White-faced from shock, eyes wounded-looking with grief, Mary murmured brokenly. "Now that I know Sannie is dead—nothing really matters. I'm just glad that I'm going to have his child."

Katie paced the floor of Mary's bedroom in Howard's Belgravia mansion. Oh God, she thought in exasperation, it's exactly what I expected from her. "I'm amazed at you, most girls would be shattered at the very thought of having an illegitimate baby."

"All that matters to me is that a part of Sannie will always be with me."

"That's not being very fair to your child; you've a responsibility to make the child legitimate and Cousin Howard, whom I was forced to confide in, has a clever plan." Then she told Mary about the proposed trip to Florence and finding an Italian husband for her.

"But I couldn't bear a man to touch me —especially whilst I'm carrying Sannie's child," Mary burst out. "It would be like being unfaithful to him." Her slim hands were held protectively over her stomach.

"Don't worry, Howard will arrange matters so that this man will be your husband in name only—just there to protect you and to give your child a legitimate name. At the birth I'll tell the family you've had a seven-month child. That way no shadow will fall on your name or your child's."

"Then I can leave this so-called husband and live alone with Sannie's baby, but . . . if the baby looks like Sannie I know I can never come home . . ." her voice broke into sobs . . . "that's true, isn't it, Mama?"

"Yes, darling—that is true, but don't let's think about that now. The child might look just like you—with all your golden beauty." Katie felt such intense pain for this fragile daughter whom she had given birth to and raised that she berated herself for somehow having failed Mary as a mother. Now she rallied herself to try to cheer her. "But God has blessed you with a lovely voice and I know you'll be a great singer, that will compensate you for much of your sorrow."

She moved across the room and swept Mary into her arms, hugging her to her heart. "Don't worry, my love—everything will turn out all right and I'll come to Europe for your child's birth. You just devote yourself to training your voice. But when I leave you in Florence you must be brave! Remember, everyone has to fight in life in some form or other. You must become a great artist—that could help your child, if he or she is suspiciously dark —you understand, darling?"

Mary clung to Katie sobbing, "Ah, Mama, Mama—I'm sorry for all the trouble I'm being to you, but please believe I tried not to love Sannie . . . but I couldn't help it . . . he was such a wonderful man . . . it's very important for me that you believe that."

"I do, darling—I do. What a tragedy for you both that he was black. God help us, someday surely this dreadful prejudice about colour must change. Now, do you want to rest or do you want to come to

Victoria Station with us to meet Nancy's boat-train?"

Mary gulped back her sobs; she must be courageous about her life and try to be like her wonderful mother. "I'll come with you, Mama. From this day on I'm going to try to be happy so you will stop worrying about me. Are we going to tell Nancy about me?"

"No! Not Nancy or anyone. Not even Ken when I go home. The secret of Sannie's baby must remain only with you, Howard and myself. Please *swear* to that."

"I *do* swear to it, Mama." Mary pronounced the words as solemnly as a religious vow. "Even the man I have to marry must never know about Sannie's colour."

"Now, darling, you are being sensible. Hurry up and bathe your eyes and put on your bonnet, the carriage will soon be here. Now I'm going to freshen up to be ready to leave."

In the crowded railway station, on the platform Howard stood between Katie and Mary. He was pleasantly amused by the admiring glances that their beauty evoked

from nearby people awaiting the big loco-
motive which was now advancing belching
smoke and looking like some prehistoric
monster. Red uniformed porters rolled up
heavy trolleys and called out, "Porter,
porter. Take your baggage." One of
Howard's footmen in attendance behind
him engaged two porters for he recalled
that His Grace's beautiful relative always
had a mountain of baggage.

As the long train started to slide along
the platform and then came to a stop, passengers' heads were poking out of windows
as people tried to recognize friends and
relatives in the waiting throng.

"There's Nancy! There she is!" Mary
cried excitedly as steps were put out and
first off the train stepped Nancy looking
like an artist's dream. Red-gold hair piled
high with a tricky little green hat held on
by long pins, a green figure-hugging
bodice, tiny waist and full skirts.

The family rushed to greet her and
Howard was on time to lift her down the
last high step, but she barely thanked him
and threw her arms around Katie.

"Mama—Mama darling—oh, darling
Mama!" She planted kisses on her

mother's cheeks. "It's so wonderful to see you again." Then she kissed and hugged Mary, and finally kissed Howard's cheeks. Looking up at him flirtatiously she smilingly said, "Don't scold me, but I've brought loads and loads of luggage, with the most divine gowns, also a wonderful French maid—Annette." She pointed to an elderly stiff-backed woman in black taffeta standing near the train. "There she is."

"Well," Howard smiled benignly, "recently you've taken to travelling like an Oriental potentate. Rogers is here and he'll bring Annette and all your luggage in a cab. Let us go home for some peace and tea—shall we?"

Seated in the carriage whilst admiring Nancy's beautiful Parisian clothes, Katie was also worrying about where the money came from for a French maid and all the luggage, but as the carriage moved through the traffic of horse-drawn omnibuses, smart carriages and landaus, high-stepping horses and riders, with streets filled with hand-carts and pedestrians, Nancy entertained the family by relating amusing anecdotes about incidents at the Parisian parties and balls she had attended.

It was not until Katie was in Nancy's bedroom at the Duke's Belgravia home that she could say, "You look beautiful and your costume is superb but, darling, where does all your wealth come from?"

In answer, Nancy rolled her lavender-coloured gloves off and held out her slim white hands. A huge diamond glittered on her right hand.

"No," she laughed, "I haven't got an engagement ring, although the Count has proposed, but this diamond," and she held her right hand out to Katie, "this is one of a pair I was given in Kimberley when I was working in that faro club. I sold one for a small fortune so don't worry—it's all my own money that I'm spending."

"That's splendid." Katie suddenly recalled that her sister had told her about the gems. "Yes of course, Aunt Liz told me about the diamonds but however did you get them? You weren't digging on a claim."

"Don't look so suspicious, Mother, you know that I engaged a bodyguard to keep the disgusting men from pawing me when working in the club." She burst out laughing and threw herself into a deep chair. "But my two gems were *presents* and all I gave for them were smiles and half-promises in my eyes. Then you sent brother Paul to bring me home and that was the end of my diamond collecting."

Nancy sprang up and went to the dressing-table and whilst she pulled long hatpins from her hat, memories almost smothered her—Paul, her magnificent looking half-brother, the devil-storm whipping in from the veld blowing away the tents and tin shacks. She and Paul clinging to each other to maintain a footing. The black night, slashing rain, jagged forked lightning. The two of them sheltering in Paul's brick-constructed rooming house.

Soaking wet clothes clinging to them, he giving her his dressing-gown and pulling a dry shirt over his magnificent body. The candle flame fluttering, hail battering at the corrugated iron roof. Paul giving her the brandy bottle, she gulping brandy then he doing the same.

Within minutes they were in each other's arms, then on the bed making savage love—releasing years of stifled longing for each other. Oh Lord, what unutterable joy it had all been and for all the months that had followed at the Cape. Then it went wrong and Paul married Herta.

Her mother's voice came as a cruel slashing intrusion into her memories of her marvellous lover.

"Nancy! Nancy! What on earth's the matter with you? I've asked you three times if you intend marrying this Frenchman?"

"Oh, did you, Mama—I'm sorry." She busied herself with tidying her hair before the mirror. "Yes, why not?" she asked with bitterness. "He's wealthy, handsome and adores me slavishly and I love the life in Paris—the pavement cafés, the theatres," she laughed, "which I don't understand properly, but the general gaiety of the beautiful city appeals to me —Yes! I think I'll marry Jean-Claude."

Relief washed through Katie, although instinctively she felt Nancy's love for Paul was not dead. "The Count sounds most desirable, darling. Is he coming over to meet me, to tell me of his intentions?"

"Oh, certainly, he's most correct,

although I must warn you that as I am a divorced woman his family is against our marriage."

"Poor Nancy, and I suppose it was almost impossible for you to explain that your husband turned out to be a pederast —but I can explain it all to the Count."

"Thank you, Mama, but Jean-Claude is very modern so I've told him about Eric and he's engaged ecclesiastical lawyers to put my case before the Pope and plead for an annulment of my marriage. I believe it may be granted because of Eric's pedastry, but Jean-Claude says if the Pope refuses an annulment he'll defy his family and we'll be married anyhow."

"But they may cut him off, deny him his wealth."

"No, no, they can't do that, since his father's death he has inherited the title and most of the fortune." She got to her feet and shook out her taffeta skirts and started wandering restlessly about the room. "It might be fun for me, being the Countess de la Motte. Although titles are now wholly accepted in France, the Revolution was only sixty years ago. Jean-Claude was telling me about balls in Bonaparte's reign

71

—only people who could count a member of the family as a victim of the guillotine in the Reign of Terror were invited, then they laughingly made signs to each other of chopping with their hands at the back of their necks and then dropping their heads forward as though they were decapitated."

"How macabre! How terribly callous."

"Yes, horrible. Tell me, Mama, what is Paul's wife like?" How bitter were those words to her. "It was such a surprise to us when the telegram arrived at Abend Bloem saying Paul had married."

"I suppose so, it was all very sudden." Katie spoke casually. "I think you may have met her on one of your stays up at Lydenburg. She is Herta Vostler. Do you recall the family? Their farm isn't too far from Papa Paul's."

"I don't remember her." Nancy almost spat the words out. "Most of these Boer girls all look alike to me. Golden-haired, with white skins, which they madly protect from the sun with goats' masks, and bodies that soon grow fat—they really are like cows and hopelessly uneducated. How could that suit Paul?"

Nancy's jealously was painfully transparent. "Yes, I know what you mean but Herta is only seventeen so her body is still beautiful. Papa Paul thinks she'll make Paul a fine wife—especially for his life in the Transvaal."

"Oh yes," Nancy sneered, "but Papa Paul didn't marry a 'cow', he stayed a bachelor until he could marry *you*. Surely Paul was not in love with Herta?" The imploring sound in Nancy's voice almost frightened Katie for it convinced her that Nancy was still in love with Paul.

"I don't know really, the whole thing happened so fast . . . after a dance we gave on the farm and about forty wagon-loads of Transvaalers came. I think Paul realized he needed a woman—a wife, I mean—where he was going on the Witwatersrand and decided upon Herta."

"Yes, yes, I suppose that was it, but. . . ." Nancy broke off and went to answer a knock on the door and to admit her French maid. "Ah, here's Annette and the houseboys are bringing my luggage up too." She pulled a guilty grimace at sight of all the heavy leather trunks that were arriving.

"I must leave you," Katie got to her

feet, "I have to change, Howard is taking me to dine at Lord Derby's."

On her way to her room, Katie was filled with the unhappy conviction that Nancy had been talking so rapidly about the French Revolution so that Katie could not question her about her true feelings for Count de la Motte, but Katie sadly knew Nancy was not really in love with him but still hankered after Paul. Thank God he was now safely married.

Katie was glad to be alone in her room; it had a soothing effect upon her with its pale pink walls and matching damask curtains now drawn across the ten foot high windows closing out the great trees in Belgravia Square. The furniture of satin and rosewood in Louis V style was exquisite. With a flush of pleasure she smiled at the three silver bowls filled with hothouse talisman roses—her favourites and, just as he had done years ago, Howard again showered them upon her.

She decided not to ring for a maid—she preferred to be alone with her thoughts—and started to unbutton her bodice while her mind was still occupied with recollections of Nancy. At fourteen, finding her bed empty, Katie had searched for her and found her asleep after a ball in Abend Bloem on the beach lying in a boy's arms. Nancy had believed she was devoted to him, but a few weeks later aboard ship bound for London she fell in love with a young midshipman who was drowned when the ship caught fire and sank and for a few days Nancy was inconsolable. Soon afterwards, she was "in love" with the gifted pianist, Howard's godson, Eric Preston, and had eloped to Florence with him and married him. Next it was Howard himself she was "in love" with and was so devastated to discover he was in love with Katie that she ran off to the diamond fields and unluckily Katie sent Paul to bring her back. Ah yes, unluckily, for, Katie surmised, it was there they must have first committed their grievous sin. Amazing how Nancy did not realize that Katie suspected the truth.

Stepping out of her wide skirts Katie laid them over the back of a chair, then she glanced at her little clock beside the bed; she had only half an hour left to dress in. She must hurry and rehearse again to herself what she was going to say to Lord

Derby. It was an important meeting for her so she must forget about her sons and daughters and their worries and summon all her thoughts to aid her to succeed in her mission.

How proud of her and relieved her beloved husband would be should she succeed in swaying Lord Derby towards favouring the South African Republic's claim to Saint Lucia Bay.

5

LORD DERBY'S residence was one of a row of magnificent mansions in an elegantly curved road in Regent's Park, a triumph of architecture of the great John Nash.

As Katie sat beside Howard in his shiny carriage, she said a little caustically. "It's almost impossible that a man of Lord Derby's wealth could understand and sympathise with what the Transvaal Boers lived through trekking from the Cape to the Transvaal. I don't suppose he's ever seen the interior of one of the fourteen foot wagons they lived in for months on end, but heaven help me . . ." she gave a little chuckle . . . "I'm going to try to explain things to him although I may not be as effective as Paul Kruger, the Transvaal President."

"Believe me, darling Katie—you have all the cards stacked in your favour. I hear that Kruger is a rather uncouth brute."

"Well, he's no Adonis or Greek scholar

77

but he is shrewd and in his way he's a great man. Certainly very capable of dealing with the Transvaalers, many of whom are uneducated, people. The only book they read is the Bible . . ." she gave a little laugh . . . "and they are convinced that *they*—not the Jews—are God's chosen People."

As the carriage drew up before the mansion, a footman jumped down to lower the steps and Howard descended to offer his white-gloved hand to Katie to help her down. As she placed her fingers in his, she smiled up at him, thinking that from their very first meeting years ago he had rendered services to her. How fortunate she was to have his love—a different type of love from Van Riebeck's, who as a pioneer rightly expected his wife to serve continually.

Silent, impeccably groomed footmen in green livery ushered them into the sumptuous mansion and into a small, luxuriously furnished drawing-room where Lord Derby, elegantly attired in deep blue velvet knee-length jacket, white frilled shirt and tight trousers, welcomed them. The greetings over he said.

"As we agreed we three are dining alone so we may talk freely, and I'm using this small drawing-room; it's so much cosier than the big one which is more of a ball-room so I keep it closed when my wife's away."

As sherry was served they immediately started to discuss South Africa with Lord Derby questioning Katie about conditions and she explaining the struggles and hardships the Dutch had endured to form a civilization out of the wilderness of the South African Republic, then as they moved into the luxuriously appointed dining-room lit by dozens of tapers in silver candelabra, she continued to relate the Boers' difficulties and achievements and throughout the impeccable dinner of oysters followed by grouse and served by three footmen, one behind each diner's chair, Katie held Lord Derby's and Howard's complete attention.

When she would finish on some aspect of the Transvaal, Lord Derby would then astutely question her further so that she could explain even more. With flushed cheeks and great green-gold eyes brimming with a righteous light she cleverly fought for her husband's cause.

"Really, Mrs. Van Riebeck," Lord Derby said admiringly, "you've given me the clearest picture I've ever had of some of the problems. Were it possible for a woman to be an ambassador you would make an excellent one."

She smiled. "Thank you," she said as with a golden spoon engraved with the Derby crest she toyed with a lemon sorbet, "but I've merely tried to explain the true nature of the Boer people to you. They are very insular, only interested in their farms and cattle. They're unique because they are not ambitious for gold or diamonds, in fact, Pretorius, the first President, passed a law forbidding a man to let anyone know if he found minerals on his land. You see they wanted to keep foreigners out of the Republic. They count their wealth in the size of their lands and vast herds of cattle and above all they treasure freedom."

"They seem a stubborn, pigheaded lot to me," Howard said, "I can't understand why they don't see the wisdom of joining up with the Cape Colony, the Orange Free

State and Natal. After all there are plenty of Dutch there."

"That's true, Howard, but there are also a great many English settlers in those places and frankly most Transvaalers don't like them. They are bitter because England forced them into Confederation some years ago and they had to go to war with her to regain their Republic."

"Yes, yes, it's my opinion that Confederation was forced upon them too soon," Lord Derby said, "but I have been told there are quite a number of German nationals and Belgians too in the Transvaal."

"There are a few schoolteachers and lawyers and a sprinkling of doctors, but it's overwhelmingly Dutch, not like the Cape Colony where even the Parliament is predominantly English. Another grievance the Transvaalers have is that Natal and the Cape Colony have clamped iniquitous taxes on Transvaal produce going through their ports and goods coming in. It's impoverishing the country: that's why they're determined they must have their own port." She turned her eyes compellingly on Lord Derby. "It's only fair that they should occupy Saint Lucia Bay; they fought three quarters of the Zulu tribe for it."

"But by doing so President Kruger broke the Pretoria Convention with England." Derby looked severe. "The Convention said there was to be no fighting with Kaffir tribes over territory disputes. You see England is obliged to protect the tribes in her possessions."

"But it was the best thing for Zululand to have one king instead of the nation being broken up into many little kingdoms which the English had instigated after their war with Zululand. It's the Republic's right to occupy Saint Lucia Bay; surely you won't let them be cheated of it."

"I'm inclined to favour the Transvaalers in this and I'll certainly do my utmost to see justice done, but over here there's a great deal of ill-feeling for the Republic since they were victorious over our soldiers at Majuba, and another thing, there's the fear that Bismarck will start pouring his Germans into Africa."

"Surely that's a good reason, Edward, to grant the Bay to the Transvaalers,"

Howard said. "Mrs. Van Riebeck assures me that the Transvaal is ready to move settlers in immediately and establish their claims so that would certainly oust the Germans along that bit of coastline."

Katie was grateful to Howard for his help and she swiftly added, "Howard is right; you should let the Transvaal occupy Saint Lucia Bay before the Germans send some 'supposed traders' to settle there and then immediately appeal to Germany for protection, so Bismarck has an excuse to send a gunboat in to take military possession, as he did at the harbour of Angra-Pequena."

"I agree—I agree, but such a decision does not rest only with me and as I've told you English public opinion since Majuba is very anti the Transvaal Republic at the moment. It's a delicate business, I cannot rush it but I promise you, Mrs. Van Riebeck, I shall do my best to advance your cause."

"Oh, thank you so much." It was not a victory, but at least Lord Derby was an ally. "May I write and tell my husband you are sympathetic to the Republic's demand for Saint Lucia Bay?"

"You may indeed." He nodded emphatically.

They went on then to talk of the way that Germany, France, Portugal and King Leopold of Belgium were all trying to carve up the African Continent and to discuss the gold findings on the Witwatersrand forty miles from Pretoria, capital of the Republic.

When Katie left for the drawing-room and the men remained for their port Lord Derby said, "'Pon my soul, Howard, Mrs. Van Riebeck is a most remarkable woman —what beauty together with such intelligence. Easy to see why you're so obviously enamoured by her, but why the deuce didn't you propose marriage after Richard's death?"

"Damn my blood! I most certainly would have if I'd known her, but she was in Africa and I here. When we met it was too late—she was married to Van Riebeck."

"I've heard he's a splendid fellow in his way, but hardly right for her I should think."

Howard shrugged widely. "He's reputed to be something of a wonder in everything

84

he touches—you know the type—a born leader." Howard spoke sarcastically. "At his name the Kaffir tribes tremble; he was a foremost commander at Majuba when the Boers disgraced us with a damned good trouncing. He's also a leader in Transvaal politics, an important member of the Volksraad. I'll confide in you, Edward. I tried with all my power to make her leave him and marry me." He held his port up to the candlelight as though studying the colour. "But it was quite useless—she was so in love with him, still is I'm afraid."

"Well, keep trying, old man. 'Pon my soul you're a deuced good-looking blighter and you can lay the world at her feet. A refined brilliant woman like that—it's a bloody disgrace that she's wasted in Africa. Don't give up—is my advice, she may come around one day and accept you."

"I wish to God you were right. Anyhow thanks for the encouragement, old boy. I'll follow your advice, I won't give up."

Katie and Howard left soon after coffee in the drawing-room, and while they were riding back to Belgravia Square she excitedly discussed the evening with Howard who agreed with her that in Lord Derby she had gained a valuable ally for the South African Republic.

Once in bed, she said her night prayers and thanked God for her seeming success with Lord Derby, then she started to fall asleep, her elation claiming her almost to the exclusion of worries over Mary.

Four days later, thanks to Howard's efficient arrangements, they were ready to leave for Florence. To act as chaperone to Katie upon her return journey to England alone with him, he had engaged an elderly impoverished gentlewoman to join them later in Florence.

Katie was spared the necessity of finding an excuse to prevent Nancy from accompanying them for Nancy said, "I was so unhappy in Florence when I discovered Eric was really a pedarist, and later when cholera killed my baby boy, that I simply couldn't go back to Florence."

Now as Nancy sat at the dressing-table in Katie's bedroom supposedly to help with her packing Katie asked her, "What will you do if Count de la Motte arrives whilst we're away? You can't receive him here alone."

"Don't worry, I'll go to grandmother's and he can come to Clearwater. You'll only be gone a week or so, I imagine; it can't take long to find a good singing coach and Mary will soon feel at home with Howard's aunt, she's a dear old soul."

"Oh, I hope finding a coach will be easy," Katie said, thinking desperately— but what about finding a husband for Mary?—and went on, "I promised Papa Paul I'd only be two weeks in Europe. Of course it may have to be much longer."

As Nancy played with Katie's ivory glove-stretcher, inserting it into the fingers of some gloves, opening and shutting it to stretch the suede she said, "Oh Mama, you owe it to yourself to stay awhile now that you're here. Have fun, go to balls, the theatre and opera with Howard as you did the last time you were in London."

"Heavens! That's the last thing I'd do. The papers wrote so much gossip about us then, they almost broke up my marriage. Papa Paul was so furious."

"But I hate the thought of you going

back to Lydenburg—you're wasting your life up there."

Lifting some dresses out of an armoire for packing Katie burst out laughing. "You silly girl, surely you know how I love Papa Paul; not a moment of my life is wasted whilst I'm with him. I'll tell you something you don't know: I married Sean Kildare, then later your father when all the time I was aching to be Van Riebeck's wife." She started to lay the dresses on the bed for folding. "You see we were such fools—always quarelling violently then parting. It's only ten years ago that I got my wish—so every moment with him is precious."

Nancy stared enviously at her mother's beautiful face with the green-gold eyes fiery with defensive love and she said, "Oh yes, of course I knew something of your turbulent love history. I think you're right —to live with a man like Papa Paul any woman in her right senses would forget the gaiety of Paris and London."

She pulled the glove-stretcher from a finger and clicked it aimlessly, just staring at it and thinking, Oh God, let me be with my beloved Paul, and diamonds and gold could gather dust in the gutters for all I'd care. She looked over at Katie folding a dress and laying it in her trunk on the floor. "Mama, you must borrow some of my new gowns; yours are hopelessly out of fashion."

"Of course they are. I had them made here seven years ago, but you don't realize that rinderpest wiped out our Lydenburg herds and it cost a good deal to build them up again, then Papa Paul's money and mine from the ostrich farm in the Cape went to buy guns and ammunition to help in the Majuba battle. I just managed to bring enough funds to finance Mary's trip."

"All right, Mama," Nancy sprang to her feet feeling suddenly protective towards her mother. "I'll go and bring some of my gowns. We're about the same size since you lost a little weight with malaria."

As she rushed out of the room Katie prayed: Oh God, please give her happiness with the right man. She's a kind, generous girl; don't judge her too harshly for her heavy sin with Paul.

The party's arrival in Florence to outward

appearance was a happy affair, for despite Mary's apprehensions of marriage to a stranger and Katie's fears about it all, they were overwhelmed by the beauty of the ancient city dating from the first century. The carriage drove along a narrow road at the base of hills lavishly covered by dark cypresses and silvery olive trees. Surrounding the city the hills provided a gentle framework for Renaissance edifices with towers and terracotta rooftops and medieval buildings painted in ochre and burnt sienna.

As they travelled alongside the blue-green waters of the Arno the grey stone bridges spanning the river grew rosy from the glow of the afternoon sun.

Nearing the Vecchio Bridge, Howard said, "That's Aunt Gertrude's palazzo just ahead," and pointed to a squat square building with a crenellated wall running around the top.

The carriage pulled up at the entrance and as they were descending, heavy double doors studded by huge nail heads, were swung open and smiling servants ushered them in, and then up a shallow flight of stone steps to a big studio-like room, where Lady Dobson, in a dramatic flowing gown of red velvet, but of no particular period, came forward to meet them, accompanied by half a dozen cats at her heels.

She was a handsome woman with piled up white hair and an aquiline—almost bony—face with deepset penetrating black eyes. She held out both hands to Howard who grasped them and kissed her cheeks.

"Dear Aunt Gertrude, you look splendid."

"My beloved nephew, what a benediction for me that you are back again, in the City of Flowers." She kissed him lingeringly on both cheeks then turning to Katie and Mary with a wide smile she flung out her arms to give a hand to each of them. "My dears—my beautiful dears, welcome, welcome—I must paint you almost immediately, you are both so, so lovely."

When introductions and greetings were over they all sat down in Renaissance type velvet and brocaded chairs, then servants in soft shoes padded in to serve coffee and liqueurs with small gold plates of delicately flavoured honey cakes.

Katie was enchanted by Lady Dobson

and the splendid chamber with long windows showing a view of the Arno's green-blue waters. Paintings of all sizes and of various subjects were crowded together covering the stone walls; the furniture was of heavy dark wood, handsomely carved; exquisite Persian carpets were strewn over stone floors. The air was scented by incense which Katie presumed was to disguise the smell of cats. Both Lady Dobson and her home were wonderfully reassuring to Katie, she felt that Mary could not feel lonely for long with this warm, demonstrative woman.

"Lady Dobson, Howard has told us you are an artist. Are these" . . . Katie nodded to pictures on the walls . . . "some of your works?"

"Yes indeed, but alas, they are not good," Lady Dobson chuckled. "You see I was widowed at seventeen and I was determined to learn to paint so I came here and stayed on. Oh what a scandal I created in our most illustrious family because I would not return to England but you see I had fallen in love with the city. How could one help it: here one is surrounded by the genius of Michelangelo, Leonardo da Vinci, Donatello, Galileo, the great scientist, Machiavelli, the great philosopher and the divine Dante! You must remember there were twenty-eight great Tuscans." She looked directly at Mary. "Ah, dear child, you will love it here for Florence feeds the soul; it held me so that I never returned to England."

"That was naughty of you, dear Aunt Gertrude," Howard scolded affectionately, thinking the old darling is beginning to look like her cats. "All the family had to come to Florence so as not to lose you completely."

"And how educational for them, instead of spending their lives fox-hunting, fishing and shooting, they learned something—for instance that it was in Florence the Renaissance started out with Alberti, Brunelleschi, Botticelli and Savonarola and following these giants came Michelangelo, Leonardo, Machiavelli and Galileo and so many, many more. Oh, the city is well named 'the Athens of Italy' and for you, Mary, who've come to study here—the city will open its arms."

She leaned towards Mary. "Do you know that opera was born here at the end of the sixteenth century and the first piano was built here for the Medici court. Lulli and Cherubini were native Florentines, oh you lucky, lucky girl to be given the opportunity to study here and I shall take you to concerts in the Medici chapel and I shall enjoy showing you some of the treasures, the paintings and sculpture that the great artists bestowed upon the world."

"Oh, thank you, Lady Dobson." Mary had been warmed by the old woman's enthusiastic recital. "I'm longing to visit the art treasures with you and the concerts and I'm also longing to begin my voice training." Already she felt she had known Howard's aunt all her life and was less afraid of the time when her mother must leave her.

"There's only one thing against the City of Flowers." Lady Dobson lowered her voice and confidentially told Katie, "They neglect the cats—yes," she nodded, "so I've made it my duty to care for them. I keep them in their quarters, just a few special friends stay with me."

She then escorted Katie and Mary to their chambers whilst Howard went off with his valet to install themselves in the Albergo Dante near Lady Dobson's palazzo. His reason for staying at the hotel was his need for freedom of movement to work on his plans for Mary's future. From the Italian Embassy in London he had obtained addresses where most of the poor artists gathered and he went there first, and wandered like a tourist through the shabby squares and narrow streets, examining the paintings on show, but more particularly looking at the artists, hunting for extremely dark-complexioned and black-haired young men. He found half a dozen who were suitable in looks, so saying he was a novelist looking for local colour he got into conversation with them as best he could in his broken Italian, and plied them with strong wine, then watched their behaviour.

Some he immediately eliminated for coarse manners; some who behaved well he saw again, and wining and dining them he questioned them about their homes and families. On the third day he had made a choice of a well born, well educated young man with a true talent to paint, an ambition to become famous, and who spoke some English. Cosimo Urbino was penniless and Howard thought he had found his man, but he must know something of Cosimo's background so Howard visited a reputable firm of lawyers and asked for an urgent report on the Urbino family in Venice. Within a few days he received a favourable reply. Then he called at his aunt's palazzo and privately saw Katie.

"Darling, I believe I've arranged everything."

She crossed her arms tightly over her breasts as if to ward off pain, then she said softly, "Tell me . . . about him."

"He's twenty-one, from a good but impoverished Venetian family, as dark as a European can possibly be. He's decently educated and a fine painter. I got him drunk, but he remained a gentleman: that's a very good test of what a man's like."

Howard pulled on his cigarette, he disliked the whole business but he must get on with it.

"Well, I made a proposition about the marriage to him, explaining that I was not trying to arrange an ordinary marriage which is quite a usual thing to do, but that we wanted a man to give his name to someone's unborn child and the mother. This annoyed him immensely so I quickly explained that a handsome 'gift' went with the arrangement, but that stung his pride and he informed me he was not for sale, so I apologised and tried a new tack, I enlisted his sympathy and won him that way."

"So then you arranged it?" Katie asked in a hoarse whisper.

"Not at once; he wanted to see Mary first. As I knew Aunt Gertrude was taking you both to the Uffizi Gallery to see the famous twenty-eight Tuscans set in the niches there we followed you keeping a distance behind you, and I pointed Mary out to Cosimo—that's his name, Cosimo Urbino. Mary was standing before the statue of Leonardo da Vinci, and Cosimo exclaimed, 'She's beautiful!' and then we followed you past Galileo, Machiavelli, Boccaccio and, by the time you reached Cellini, Cosimo was pulling on my sleeve muttering, 'She's as beautiful and delicate as a Botticelli painting. I will accept your offer to marry her but I refuse a sou for payment. It is I who shall be indebted and

I swear to you that I will never touch her unless she wishes it.'"

"Oh thank God, Howard—he sounds like a decent character." Katie suddenly felt calmer now that a suitable man had been found.

"I'd swear that he *is* a decent character."

Katie smothered a sigh, "Now how are we going to explain this rushed marriage to your aunt?"

"Don't worry about the old darling. I'll just say that Mary knew Cosimo from before and you've sanctioned the marriage and want it at once so you can attend the ceremony. Fortunately Aunt Gertrude is so obsessed with cats, her twenty-eight Tuscans and her 'City of Flowers' that she's not much interested in anyone's affairs."

"But if Cosimo comes to live here . . . I mean . . . I swore to Mary that whoever she married would be a husband only in name."

"I'll care for that. I'll tell Aunt Gertrude that Mary's very shy and would prefer her own room; a freedom lover like my darling old aunt will think that's quite natural."

"Oh dear God, Howard, I'll never be able to thank you enough—I must go or I'll break down and cry like a fool." She sprang out of the chair and dashed to her room, her balled handkerchief pressed against her mouth.

That evening Howard and Katie took Mary for a stroll along the banks of the moon-flooded Arno, and holding Mary's arm Howard told her about Cosimo. Feeling she was trapped Mary wanted to run away from Howard and her mother, but she told herself it was all inevitable— she must marry this stranger.

"Could I . . . start my singing lessons at once?" she blurted out, "I mean before the . . . the. . . ."

"Yes, yes," Howard assured her. "I'll take you to Signor Cantelli in the morning. He's the finest coach in the city. You may commence at once."

"Thank you . . . Cousin Howard, please . . . I don't wish to meet . . . this Cosimo Urbino until the day of the . . ." She could not voice the word, it was choking her.

A few days later, in the thirteenth century

Church of Santa Cruz, at a small side altar, Mary stood trembling all over. She wore a white, full-skirted satin dress and tight bodice, a white net hat on her pale golden hair piled on top of her head, for Katie had tried to make the wedding at least visually beautiful. Mary kept her eyes glued to the priest saying the nuptual Mass, not once did she glance beside her at the tallish, slim Cosimo Urbino, wearing a pale grey suit of Howard's. His head capped by black hair curling tightly to his scalp, Cosimo was praying for the future but his soulful black eyes kept darting sideways to enjoy Mary's delicate profile. Soon he would paint this angel and after her child came in seven months she would become the most beautiful model of a Madonna and the world would proclaim his painting of her and her babe as the work of a genius.

Behind the bride and groom, Lady Dobson, Howard and Katie knelt in the first pew. Impossible for Katie to deny her tears: they were tears of regret for the past, but also tears of gratitude that Mary's name would be protected. Katie liked Cosimo instinctively, felt he would watch over Mary. His curly black hair would be a help to Mary's child, although Cosimo's was shiny and silky, not crinkly and woolly like poor Sannie's had been.

When the ceremony reached the stage of the exchange of rings Katie glimpsed Mary's ashen face. It looked like marble and pity surged through Katie. How sad that what should have been one of the happiest days of Mary's life was reduced to an exercise in self-control. But with her own first two marriages—had she not forced herself to sensibly endure them when she had been aching for Van Riebeck?

Lady Dobson had arranged for a small wedding breakfast at the palazzo and Mary was obliged to maintain the pretence that she and Cosimo were in love so she forced herself to smile and talk to him. He seemed so respectful, so gentle, that her fear of this strange man started to abate and after drinking some champagne she decided that his beautiful pointed white teeth were rather like Sannie's, but that made her so miserable she had to turn away from Cosimo.

Later Howard insisted that Cosimo go in

a carriage to bring some of his paintings, together with his personal belongings to the palazzo. When he returned there was a lively commotion as Lady Dobson examined Cosimo's canvases in the red light.

"Cosimo has enormous talent," she pronounced, "I wish I had a tenth of it."

Then he and Lady Dobson indulged in a long discourse in rapid Italian about painting.

While Mary went to change, Katie murmured to Howard, "I believe the worst is over, thank God."

"I agree and I'm really rather pleased with Cosimo; I think we chose well. I'll talk to him again later and tell him I'm going to give him and Mary a liberal monthly allowance to be paid through the attorneys I used here. I'll explain that Mary must be properly cared for and he, poor fellow, must buy some new clothes."

"It's so very, very good of you, Howard. You're a remarkably fine man."

"Mary's a very fine girl, and one mistake mustn't be allowed to count against her."

"Thank God you're so merciful. Well, I suppose there's no reason to worry about her for another seven months—then—God help us! I've got to come back for the birth, because I must see about the child's colour, but don't let's talk of it now. I think she'll be all right if we were to leave in a couple of days, don't you?"

"Certainly, she's delighted with her singing coach and she's very much at home with Aunt Gertrude," he smiled, "and I feel she'll be able to tolerate poor Cosimo."

"Good, so perhaps we might plan to leave the day after tomorrow?"

He nodded, thinking unhappily, she's so damned anxious to return to Van Riebeck.

6

RELIEVED to have returned to Howard's London home, Katie settled in her favourite wing chair in the drawing-room and from a small stack of letters that had been awaiting her she opened one from Nancy, then with dismay clouding her eyes she looked up at Howard who stood a few feet from her.

"Whatever is Nancy doing this for, Howard? She's written from Clearwater saying she's postponed her official engagement to the Count and she intends returning to South Africa with me! Why in God's name?"

With an elegant hand he smoothed over his thick brown hair as if the answer lay there. "Most extraordinary girl. When we left here for Florence three weeks ago I understood that she had settled on marrying him."

"So did I. Of course I'd like her companionship on board, but I feel so emotionally weary I was cherishing the idea of three weeks alone."

"God knows, our beautiful Nancy is a creature of change, but you've only just arrived after this affair with Mary, so for heaven's sake don't start worrying over Nancy. Does she say when she's returning from Aunt Cynthia's?"

Katie scanned the letter. "Yes, tomorrow. Oh damn, that means I'll have to go down to Clearwater tonight."

"Good heavens! But why?"

"Well, I expected to find Nancy here—and I know it seems too absurd . . ." she was embarrassed at having to explain . . . "but Paul would be most annoyed if I stayed here with you alone."

"Alone—the deuce take it—there are twenty servants sleeping below stairs."

"But they are hardly chaperones and you are not aware of it, but Paul is very jealous of you, ever since those wretched columnists linked our names together."

"Predicting that I hoped to marry you and damn my soul, how right they were, but I would think Van Riebeck is so deuced sure of you," he spoke bitterly, "that he's convinced you'd never give

105

another man as much as an affectionate glance—anyhow if you wish it, I'll sleep at my club. The St. James' is no distance away."

Katie jumped up. "Oh, of course not! I simply won't turn you out of your own home!"

He caught at both of her hands. "You could turn me out of Paradise and send me off to Dante's Inferno if it would give you any pleasure—Oh Katie. . .!" With a quick movement his arms went around her and he crushed her to him.

She did not fight against him for her entire being surged with gratitude for the wonderful man and the way he was caring for Mary, and, his personal appeal weakening her, her head sank on to his shoulder and she felt him bury his lips in her hair, then on her neck. This little amount of affection she was giving him was not robbing Paul of anything. She owed it to him for it was Howard, not Paul, who had saved Mary. Van Riebeck would have made an outcast of her, perhaps in his first rage even killed her. With stored up emotional gratitude bursting from her, she lifted her face up to

Howard's and as he kissed her she joyously returned his kisses.

His arms became like bands of steel around her as he covered her eyes, her cheeks, her mouth with kisses. He was like a ravenous man at last being fed. When she felt his excitement mounting to a danger point she pulled her head back and struggled to be free of his embrace but he held her close.

"Don't, don't darling—for God's sake," he begged.

"But we must stop, dearest Howard—you know we must."

He held her a moment longer, then reluctantly let her go. "I don't wish to *impose* my love-making on you," he said stiffly.

"Oh you know it's not that—you know very well it's because I'm not a free woman." Her hands went up tremblingly to tidy her hair as she started to walk toward the fire, then she said, "Tell me, are you as active as ever in the House of Lords?"

He gave a dry little laugh. "Well, darling, that should be a safe ground for discussion." He opened a green Sèvres cigarette box. "May I smoke?" She nodded and he lit the long monogrammed cigarette. He was still feeling excited by having held her so close, by her response to his kisses. "Yes, in fact, I'm more active than ever. I'm very occupied in advancing plans for the establishment of the telephone system. You see since 1877 the Post Office have refused to grant a licence to any of the eight companies excepting Edison and Bell, but when they applied for permission to dig up the streets to lay down the necessary wires, the Government refused it."

"It's really a disgrace to withhold such a wonderful invention from public use."

"'Pon my soul it is! Now Bell and Edison are trying to bring the telephone to the public by the erection of poles with wires, and this is the moment that the Post Office suddenly decide to install telephones themselves, but by God, we squashed that nonsense in Lords!"

"That sounds only fair, but whenever will this miracle talking-machine be available to the public?"

Howard shrugged elaborately. "God knows, already the struggle is eight years old, but I've also another great interest. I'm trying to improve working conditions in factories—the North in particular. In fact I've travelled around the country a good deal to see for myself what's going on. I'm sorry to say there are a great many abuses which I'm determined to have corrected." It was a small relief to the pain of his vain longing for her, to share his interests with her.

"That's splendid of you, Howard, but you were always a champion of the labouring classes, weren't you?"

"So much so," he laughed, "that my enemies stupidly accuse me of being a bit of a radical, but let me tell you of my favourite hobby. I'm creating a vast garden, occupying about 120 acres, all planted with rare trees and plants collected from all over the world."

"How lovely! What a delightful hobby!"

"It is indeed. I suppose you could call it a dream-garden. For the last five years I've been searching for rare specimens in Australia, China, India, Japan, Turkey, Russia and shipping back a variety of plants and trees to my place in Cumberland. Of course having 62,000 acres it means nothing to turn 120 acres into a garden. The site is on a hill so as to catch the most sunlight. I've built big, heated conservatories to preserve equatorial specimens, then at the height of our summer we plant them out."

"Howard, it all sounds absolutely fascinating." She stared at him with wide admiring eyes. Talking of his dream-garden made him look as carefree as a boy.

"It's all most interesting. I've got thirty gardeners of mixed nationalities to care for plants and trees from their particular corner of the world. You see, Katie, it's not just a hobby, I feel I'm doing a service to mankind in preserving types of flora that could otherwise become extinct." He uncrossed his long legs and leaned toward her. "I was hoping to take you up there, Katie, but as you *insist* upon sailing on Friday . . . there's no time."

"I'm obliged to leave—otherwise I'd love to visit your dream-garden." She was sad that she could not. "Perhaps I'll find some rare plants and trees in the Transvaal to send to you." Her eyes shone with the anticipated pleasure of sharing this living interest with Howard.

"I look forward to having you collecting for me. Tell me, did you mean what you said in Florence that you'll be back in seven months for the advent of Mary's baby?"

"Yes, I must be there." She had to know if the child were black.

"Good, that gives me something wonderful to wait for."

"Dear, dear Howard, whilst I'm terribly flattered, I really wish you would not remain alone. I'm sad about you, it's such a waste of a most marvellous man."

He shook his head, "I'm selfish, I'm a lover of perfection and as I can't have you, I'll stay alone with the memory of what you said to me once. 'If I did not love Paul —I would have loved you.' Tell me—is that still true?"

She did not answer but nodded her head.

"*Tell* me—please say the words."

He had been a blessed angel to her and Mary so she did not find it difficult to murmur, "If I did not love Paul—I would have loved you."

"Thank you, darling," he murmured.

They stared into each other's eyes and

for a flash of a second her mind envisioned life as the Duchess of Rotherford—this handsome, Byronic-looking man as her adoring husband, all Europe's culture to indulge in, untold wealth for herself and children, then came a vision of scorching veld, a magnificent-looking great blond man, thighs gripping the back of a madly galloping stallion as he fired from the saddle into a black mass of insanely screaming Zulus, spears raised to kill. She on the back of a wagon slashing with a long knife at savages trying to drag her to the ground. Straight through the black wave Van Riebeck fought his way to her wagon.

She lowered her eyes from Howard's and bent to the table beside her chair gathering up her letters. "I think I'll lie down for a while and read the rest of my post; there are letters here from the other children."

"Of course you must rest before dinner." He went over to the double doors to open them for her. "I'll go to the club after dinner."

"I do apologize for the inconvenience I'm causing you—forgive me," she added softly, "and for all the grief I've unwittingly caused you."

"Katie, darling, no need to ever apologize to me, just knowing that the world holds you, and that sometimes you must think of me—is a compensation."

"I will share your dream-garden with you—in my thoughts from thousands of miles away." As she went through the door, she purposely did not look up at him and he forced himself not to touch her.

Katie's last three days in London were fully occupied; there were the reservations to be made on the steamship *Athena Castle*, a call at the telegraph office to cable to Van Riebeck giving him the date of her arrival, and Lady Eaton came up to spend a little time with her "dear Katie and Nancy".

Katie also arranged to pay some important business calls. Now, riding in a carriage of Howard's along Picccadilly crowded with horse-drawn traffic, she composed in her mind what she would say to the manager of Fortnum and Mason. The carriage pulled up before the luxurious store, for over one hundred years one

113

of London's finest suppliers of delicacies, amongst other articles.

Stepping into the thickly carpeted emporium, where assistants wore frock coats and tight trousers, she sent her name by one of them to the manager who immediately had her ushered into his panelled office where he rose to greet her.

"Mrs. Van Riebeck, this is indeed a pleasure, Ma'am. We've not seen you for some years—alas not since you stopped shipping us your splendid Cape wines."

In his black tailed coat, high white collar and tightly fitting trousers, Katie thought he looked and behaved like an Earl. She graciously gave him her hand and he bowed over it.

"Mr. Danton, how very nice to see you." She settled in the chair he held ready for her and he seated himself on the other side of his big desk.

"I trust, Mrs. Van Riebeck, you are here to tell me that your Stellenbosch vineyards will again be supplying us with wines. It must have been a frightful blow to you when your vineyards were wiped out by phylloxera."

"It was a near-disaster for my family,

but fortunately we were able to switch to ostrich farming and we've done extraordinarily well on ostrich plumes."

"Ah yes, some years ago when your sister was in London, I believe she told me how brilliant you'd been in inventing special incubators to hatch the giant eggs."

Katie's mind flashed back to her struggle to raise money for the giant-sized incubators. "Yes, we were lucky, Mr. Danton, and of course we've planted new French vines and, thank God, they are developing fast. Not too long now and you'll be receiving Abend Bloem wines."

"Excellent, excellent! It can't be soon enough for us."

"You're very kind, but in the meantime we're involved in a new venture—it's called Konfyt—a great delicacy."

"You must help me, Ma'am, I'm afraid I'm quite in the dark."

"I believe it's not known outside South Africa. It's a special old method of drying fruits, apricots in particular, also peaches and watermelon rind. All soaked in sugar and dried in the sun, it's delicious I assure you."

"Indeed? Konfyt—it sounds quite

succulent, Fortnum and Mason must certainly try it."

"Indeed you must, I shall ship you a sample box. Transportation will be expensive because it can't go by sail boat, it takes too long and the fruit, although dried, might spoil, so it must go by steam."

Then they went on to discuss possible quantities and prices and when Katie was satisfied that Mr. Danton would be a heavy buyer, she shook hands and left. She then drove to several other stores dealing in luxurious foods, and returned to Belgrave Square, well satisfied with the responses she had aroused for Konfyt.

Lady Eaton and Nancy were having an early lunch in Aldwych then going on to the Playhouse to a matinée to see the famous Sarah Bernhardt perform.

Lunching alone with Howard, Katie told him about Abend Bloem's latest enterprise. "You see, although we've been so successful with ostrich plumes, there's always the danger that they could go out of fashion. After all they've been popular for so many years that people might suddenly be bored with them and we would be left with a great loss, like when the vines were diseased and our vines are still too young to bear grapes, so we are producing Konfyt." She explained what it was.

"What a clever idea; I think you'll do well on that. You're marvellous, Katie, I drink to you." He raised his champagne glass in a silent toast then sipped the topaz-coloured liquid. "And whilst you were laying the foundation for another fortune, I checked on your double cabin on the *Athena Castle*. All is well and you sail at four on Friday from Southampton —unfortunately for me."

She avoided looking into his dark eyes; the sadness in them hurt her. With her fork she toyed with the Sole Veronique on her plate and murmured, "Thank you again—Howard—thank you for everything."

The cabin on the steam and sail ship *Athena Castle* was so filled with flowers the scent was like a conservatory. There were several boxes of Talisman roses from Howard for Katie and flowers of every description for Nancy from Count de la Motte.

Katie and Nancy were exclaiming with delight and untying ribbons on cardboard boxes when over the excitement peculiar to a ship readying for departure came a dominant sound, the beating of a gong and a man's cockney voice crying.

"All ashore whot's going ashore!"

"So soon!" Howard exclaimed and Katie, relieved that the goodbyes would not be prolonged, said, "Nancy, you go up on deck with Howard and I'll wait here for the luggage to be brought in."

"Oh, no—Mama—you go! Go on!"

Howard pulled at Katie's hand. "Yes, yes, at least wave to me from deck." He planted two kisses on Nancy's cheeks and told her, "Take care of your wonderful mother and come back soon to marry la Motte, and I'll arrange to have your maid sent back to Paris."

"Poor Annette but I think she'll be pleased to go."

Howard picked up his grey top hat and settled it aslant his head and left, pulling Katie right behind him.

They had to manoeuvre adroitly a path

between throngs of people, some rushing down the companionway, some rushing up until they burst out on to the deck, where already people were making for the head of the gangplank as the cry, now with an added warning tone, was called out.

"All—ashore—whot's—going—ashore!"

The ship's orchestra was playing *Auld Lang Syne* and some drunken voices were sentimentally bawling out,

"Should auld acquaintance be forgot
    and never brought to mind
We'll take a cup of kindness yet
    for the sake of Auld Lang Syne."

The music and singing, added a false emotion to an already highly charged atmosphere and Katie thought, "Oh Lord, it's so upsetting, this business of a ship setting out to sea."

Reaching the head of the gangway Howard turned to her. "The cruel word 'goodbye' should be dropped from the vocabulary." Then he grasped her in his arms and crushed her to him, he didn't give a damn for nearby passengers or their departing friends; he kissed this woman he

119

loved with all of his being and she was returning some of his warmth. He felt her tears on his face, the parting was hurting her too.

"Best be 'orf, sir, we're taking up the gangplank any minute," the warning came from an impatient sailor standing beside him.

Then Howard released Katie. "I'll watch over Mary—I'll visit her, so don't worry, darling. I'll live for your return in seven months—for God's sake don't change your mind."

"I won't—I won't." Her tear-filled eyes looked up into his dear face and she gave him a twisted smile. "Better go—the sailors are waiting for you to be off."

He started down the gangplank, cherishing the fragrance of her still clinging to him and her tears wet on his cheeks—they were a little comfort to him, they surely must mean that he had a place in her heart.

7

IN the Cape Colony, in the lushly green countryside of Stellenbosch beneath the Jongkerhoek Mountains, two big men rode their horses slowly. They were descendants of the earliest settlers, lawyers and bankers from Holland, and being fifth generation born in the Cape, they were automatically classed as Colonial aristocracy. Both were inheritors of great homesteads and vineyards in the district and both of them loved South Africa with a fierce pride.

Paul Van Riebeck, who stood 6ft 4, sat absolutely straight in the saddle, golden-haired and clean-shaven, his face like a bronze carving beneath his wide-brimmed hat pulled low on his forehead against the sun's glare.

His companion, Jan Hofmeyer, was a big man with dark hair and beard. He and Van Riebeck had been friends from childhood although Van Riebeck, as a boy, had left the Cape when his family trekked

North after the English occupation when they emancipated the black slaves. The English offer of financial compensation to be collected in London was an insult to the Dutch who angrily demanded, "Who wants to waste three or four months sailing to England and another three or four months sailing home? Better to go North and be free of the detested English and all their new laws." So they trekked eleven hundred miles and established the Transvaal.

About half of the Cape Dutch remained and tried to live as contentedly as was possible alongside the new English settlers. Jan Hofmeyer's parents had been amongst those who had stayed on.

Over the years when Van Riebeck had returned to the Cape to be properly educated he had seen much of Jan. Then Van Riebeck sailed for Holland to attend University there and upon his return had gone back to the Transvaal to work with his people, for he respected them and wished to help the courageous settlers who were battling to exist in a harsh land of alien Kaffir tribes.

Now, as a member of the Transvaal

Volksraad he and Hofmeyer, for some years a prominent member of the Cape Parliament, editor of a newspaper, the *Volksvriend*, and leader of the Afrikaner Bond, spent many hours discussing South African politics. They had just left a meeting of the Afrikaner Bond and rode borrowed horses.

Now as they turned their horses into an avenue of giant Van den Stel oaks that led to a scenic spot, long a favourite of theirs Van Riebeck said, "Jan, I don't agree with how you are trying to change the Bond. I believe that it should return to its original militant attitude when it encouraged national feeling, protection for farmers, the spread of our Afrikaans language, and a claim for an educational system suitable for rural whites. Let it take up its original cry. 'Africa for the Afrikaners!'"

Hofmeyer was annoyed by what he considered was Van Riebeck's backward thinking. "The Bond is an organization of Dutch farmers who make up the largest electors of members for Parliament—we both know that, which means they have a voice in affairs. When du Troit created the Bond he nurtured it on anti-English hatred and I'm trying to stamp it out. Good God man, you can't build any type of security on hatred—and I know damn well that no Government in the Cape can succeed without the Bond's support so I'm aiming to point the Bond toward conciliation and eventual Union with all South Africa's people."

"Ach man, it's nothing but a pleasant dream. Look what the Transvaal suffered when England forcibly brought us into Confederation—such bloody injustices, we had to go to war."

"Of course I was naturally against England's forcing Confederation on the Transvaal, yet—as I've told you—I was against your fighting England."

"*Magtig!*" Van Riebeck exclaimed. "You're not going to say you were against our trouncing the British at Majuba!" Van Riebeck's deep voice was heavy with challenge.

"Don't be *voordamnt* man, like all Afrikaners I rejoiced in your victory, but I'm against open hostilities, against the white races fighting each other when we are so heavily outnumbered by blacks. A funny thing is I was discussing the war with Cecil

Rhodes—I know you don't like him, nor did I to begin with. I thought he was a regular beefsteak John Bull Englishman but he's more than that and about the war, he surprised me, he said, 'I think it was a good thing.'"

"He's a bloody liar, Jan! Why should he think the war was a good thing when the English were beaten?"

"Yes, it's surprising until you hear his reason, he said, 'It's made the English respect the Transvaalers and made the Dutchmen respect one another.' Now when an Englishman speaks like that to a Dutchman, I think it's a damned good sign."

"It may look like that now, but I feel like our President Kruger, who says, 'It would be better if Rhodes concentrated on the diamond fields instead of politics or he'll give us trouble, but though the race-horse is swifter than the ox, the ox can draw heavier loads.' Kruger insists that Rhodes is our enemy."

"Kruger might be right—he might be wrong."

"Of course Kruger's right! Rhodes is disputing our rights to occupy Saint Lucia

Bay. The bastard wants to deny us a Port —an outlet to the sea. Thank God the final decision doesn't rest with the Cape Parliament."

"You think you'll fare better with the English Government?" Jan asked caustically, as the horses stepped out of a leafy tunnel on to a shelf of land that gave a vast vista of blue sparkling ocean.

"We might have fairer treatment in England—my wife wrote me from London that she dined with Lord Derby and presented our case to him and he was definitely sympathetic to our cause. Thank God Katje's ship docks tomorrow." He had always called Katie by the Dutch version of her name. Excitement surged through him at the anticipation of soon holding her in his arms; he was on fire to bed her.

The men dismounted, throwing the reins over the horses' heads so they could crop the thick grass sprinkled with tiny white daisies. Seating themselves cross-legged in the shade of a clump of red flowering eucalyptus trees, they took off their wide-brimmed hats, mopped their foreheads, then pulled pipes and pouches from their pockets.

"How long has Katje been gone?" Jan asked, tamping tobacco into the bowl of his pipe.

"Too long, man. Ten weeks. But in Florence she had difficulty finding the right singing coach and she stayed on until Mary settled down."

"That's understandable. It's splendid the way Katje accepted the hard life in the Transvaal."

"Well, she's a fine strong woman who has the good of the South African Republic at heart." Van Riebeck drew happily on his pipe.

"But it still must be difficult for a woman like Katje, and a man like you Paul —you could have served South Africa well in the Cape Parliament, there's no need to stay in the Transvaal."

"Hell and damnation, Jan! This is an old bone of contention between us and I repeat, if all the educated Dutch had chosen to remain in the Cape and left the Transvaal to the doppers—most of whom are illiterate—where would our Republic be?" He pulled on his pipe. "Besides I like the smell of freedom, it suits me. I'd be no good in your shoes, I could never placate the English, although God knows I admire you and ask myself where would the Cape Colony be without Dutchmen of your ilk?"

Hofmeyer nodded heavily. "We all need each other, that's the truth; that's why I'm body and soul for a united South Africa, with the Cape, Transvaal, Natal, Orange Free State. All under one flag—a South Africa Federation flag—but . . ." and he paused to add dramatically and in slow deliberate speech, "*not* under President Paul Kruger or the Transvaal Volksraad."

"Just what's wrong with Kruger and the Volksraad?" Van Riebeck demanded flaming with anger at Hofmeyer's words and superior tone.

"It's composed of unworldly men—I won't say ignorant men because there's you and some others like you."

"What the hell is so bloody well superior in the Cape Parliament, I'd like to know?"

"If you weren't so damned stubborn you'd attend some of our sessions, instead of spending all your time trying to talk our farmers into quitting the Cape to settle in the Transvaal. In our Parliament you'd find a high standard of debate. Latin quotations are quite usual and. . . ."

Van Riebeck burst out laughing, "*Magtig*, Jan—that's really too funny. Isn't there enough trouble deciding who speaks English and who speaks Dutch— must you bring Latin in to confuse the situation?"

Hofmeyer could not help laughing at himself. "Oh well, have your joke but tell me does your President Kruger still hold Parliamentary sessions on his front stoep, wearing his black stove pipe hat?"

"He does and the Transvaalers love it and also, he still has his spitoon beside him to spit into, but who cares? He's a wise old fox who guided us back to freedom and victory at Majuba."

"*Magtig*! Majuba! Majuba! The word will become almost a prayer with the Transvaalers. It's done you harm as well as good. It's inflated your opinions of your strength but be that as it may, join me at a Parliamentary session tomorrow after- noon."

"Sorry, but I'm meeting Katje's ship."

Good words, but the hours would be heavy until he saw her.

"Then in the morning, come with me to call on Cecil Rhodes. You may alter your opinion of him when you get a personal view of him."

"I don't like the rumours about the man. Why won't he employ a female in his business or any of his homes? Why does he dislike women?"

"*Ach*—whose business is that?" Hofmeyer knocked the bowl of his pipe out on his heel. "I suppose you also believe the talk that he used some kind of witchcraft to make a million pounds in no time on the diamond diggings."

"I'm not that *voordamnt*, Jan, I know he must have a brilliant mind and I think I told you that I have met him personally —a stepson of mine, John Eaton, is a secretary of Rhodes, and through John I lunched at Rhodes' home." He would go with Jan, it would help to fill the waiting time for Katje. "Thanks, Jan, I'll come with you to Rhodes." He pulled a heavy gold watch from an antelope-skin, waist-coat pocket. "Ten past five, we'd better be starting back if we want to catch that train for Capetown."

"Right. The ride was good; fresh air always clears my mind after a stormy session with the Bond's members. We can turn the horses in at the railway station. The station master will see they're returned to Van der Meer."

As Van Riebeck got to his feet he leaned on his arm and winced.

"What's the matter, Paul?" Hofmeyer frowned.

"A damned rhino gored my shoulder to the bone on the trek down from Lydenburg and it still hurts sometimes."

Hofmeyer's solemn face broke into a taunting grin. "But you Transvaal fellows who fought at Majuba were reputed to be magical shots. Did you lose your magic?"

"No, I was hunting with a Cape Colonist." Van Riebeck swung a long leg over his horse's back and settling in the saddle caught up the reins. "The silly bastard couldn't shoot straight, he winged the rhino and it came at me. As she pinned me down and gored me I knifed the great cow in the heart." Laughing to himself he

131

touched a heel to his horse and started moving off.

In the office of Cecil Rhodes' house on the Herengracht, Capetown's most important thoroughfare, Van Riebeck and Hofmeyer sat in comfortable chairs while the loose-limbed, untidy-looking Rhodes walked the floor. Watching the Englishman Van Riebeck thought, He doesn't look like a genius who so swiftly became a millionaire and gained a seat in Parliament.

"You know, Commandant Van Riebeck," Rhodes was saying in his high-pitched voice, "I enjoyed our meeting some months ago because I like you Dutch people, I like your homely courtesy and your tenacity of purpose."

Liar, Van Riebeck thought but met deception with deception. "I'm glad to hear that, Mr. Rhodes."

"Indeed yes. Now for example, when I first met Mr. Hofmeyer I was in doubts about him." He turned his rather bulbous blue-grey eyes on Jan and smiled ingratiatingly. "But before long I saw that he was a realist and not an adversary who would balk all my plans in Parliament and we soon became friends."

Van Riebeck hated the way Hofmeyer was smiling at Rhodes as he said, "Well, Rhodes, we became friends because we share a dream—the Union of South Africa." He left unsaid, "but under a Dutch, not English, flag."

Rhodes tossed a strand of auburn hair off his forehead. "Yes, yes, Union is essential." He looked at Van Riebeck and said, "Both Hofmeyer and I want no truck with the Westminster Government, I can't tolerate their vacillation and Hofmeyer resents their interference; he wants South Africa to govern herself. Now I sympathise with this and also Hofmeyer's desire to protect Cape farmers from foreign competition so we've come to an understanding. I aid him in every way I can and in return I have his promise to help me keep the road to the North open."

"I want protection for all of South Africa," Hofmeyer swiftly explained to Van Riebeck. "It's not love for the British that makes me malleable to them but I know too well how vulnerable we are. Any independence we have is dependent upon which world power rules the seas. A blind man could see that."

"But a united Dutch Republic could beat off intruders as we beat back the English at Majuba."

"That's bloody rubbish, man!" Hofmeyer jumped angrily to his feet. "Our country is connected only by ox wagon. We don't have great railways to speed help to each other! If the Cape or Natal were invaded and I swear the Germans would try it if the English weren't here, then how the hell could the Transvaalers get here in time to help us push the invaders back into the sea? Just tell me that."

"But, Jan, you don't seriously believe any power wishes to invade us?" Van Riebeck thought Hofmeyer was dramatically exaggerating.

"But I *do* believe it!" Hofmeyer pulled irritably on his black beard. "I'd rather be under the English than Germany or France or America for that matter."

"The Americans have all the land and natural wealth they'll ever need and they know what it is to fight for independence. Instead of invading us they're more likely to aid us fight for independence. . . ."

Rhodes' high-pitched voice interrupted, "Ah, what an error Britain made in allowing the American colonies to become independent—we must win America back! That will make an even vaster British Empire: it will be the salvation of the world." He thumped his chest whilst his eyes stared strangely. "I am an Empire builder and it shall be my life's work to hand Britain a United South Africa."

"Christ Almighty, Rhodes!" Van Riebeck jumped to his feet to closely confront the mad Englishman. "Do you forget that I am a member of the South African Republic's Volksraad?" He had to force himself not to pick Rhodes up by the scruff of his neck and shake him. "Now listen to me—we shall *never*, by God, let the British flag fly over the Transvaal again!"

Rhodes stared up at Van Riebeck, who seemed to be rising like a tower above him. "Commandant Van Riebeck, you must not be angry with me, I beg you, my friend. After all every man has a dream. Now sit down please, and you too, Hofmeyer. Do let us sit down and behave like friends."

Hofmeyer caught Van Riebeck's eye and sent him a message of caution. "Yes, come on, Paul. We've all become too tense."

Warning himself to accept Hofmeyer's counsel and not break contact with Rhodes, Van Riebeck sat down, crossing one long leg over the other whilst he was wondering if there could be a touch of madness in Rhodes.

Then brandy arrived and as the three men sipped it, they all seemed to grow calm and spoke of casual matters but in a few minutes Rhodes looked at Van Riebeck and said, "Well, as I said, Commandant, all men have their dreams and I know yours is to occupy the land around Saint Lucia Bay—ah, I'm right, am I not?"

"It's certainly more than a dream—it's justice that we should occupy it." Van Riebeck's temper was starting up again and his deep blue eyes blazed at Rhodes.

"Yes, yes, then I suggest a pact between us. You persuade President Kruger to cease putting obstacles in my way to the road North and in return I'll help you as much as I can to occupy Saint Lucia Bay."

What a bastard Rhodes was! Van

Riebeck loathed him but suddenly decided to play him like a fish. "Your ideas interest me, Mr. Rhodes."

"They should do, Van Riebeck," Hofmeyer muttered meaningly. "You'll learn a lot if you just listen."

Van Riebeck nodded, suddenly thinking, Hofmeyer too is playing Rhodes like a big catch. "Go on, Rhodes, explain what you want about the Northern Road."

"Well, it's terribly important because it leads up to the great plateau of the African Continent." He suddenly waved his heavy arms about wildly. "Up to the Equatorial Lakes, the Sudan—just think of all the white men who can settle there—and create fine cities and towns and all connected by railways." His voice was racing with an almost breathless excitement and by the strange look in his eyes it seemed he had forgotten the presence of the Dutchmen. "Africa can become as big and flourishing as America—British from the Cape to Cairo. This would compensate England for losing her American colonies."

Van Riebeck decided the Englishman was mad so he said quietly, "But you've made no provision for the millions of Kaffirs occupying all that land."

"Kaffirs!" Rhodes gave an impatient wave of his hand. "We can deal with all that once we hold the North—then the balance of the map will be ours and all the riches—the gold!"

"Ah yes, the gold," Van Riebeck nodded, thinking that Kruger's dream like Rhodes' was also to spread North to the Zambesi, but not for gold. Kruger wanted land to put more space between the Transvaalers and the ever encroaching English. He said, "But the question of gold is still very much debated. Don't rely upon it to bring you the fortunes you grabbed from the diamond mines."

"Zimbabwe! What of the ancient Zimbabwe ruins? Where did the gold from there come from? Learned men believe that the Zimbabwe ruins was the source of gold for Sheba and Solomon." In his excitement Rhodes grasped Van Riebeck's arm. "The mountain of 'Fura' or 'Afura' or 'Aufur' could well be interpreted as 'Ophir'—gold dust has been found there in the ashes. Just think of it: there could be untold riches in the earth just waiting to be mined."

"It's a fascinating conjecture," Hofmeyer remarked as he glanced enquiringly at Van Riebeck. "You know more about it than I do."

Van Riebeck forced a little laugh. "Yes, from time to time absurd stories come out of Matabeleland that there's gold growing into the bark of trees but you know what lies the Kaffirs tell." Paul knew Rhodes had sent emissaries to King Lobengula trying to obtain concessions to mine in Matabeleland but had failed because the Transvaalers had warned Lobengula that the Englishman would swallow him and his people. Van Riebeck told himself that he must try to put Rhodes off Matabeleland.

"You're making a mistake believing there's gold in Matabeleland or Zimbabwe," he said. "You know I've spoken to quite a few prospectors who've been there and come through Pretoria and they've been convinced that there is nothing worth mining in Matabeleland and Zimbabwe is utterly played out."

"Well I can't help but wonder if it's not

the home of King Solomon's mines? Be that as it may be, do we have a pact between ourselves? You work on Kruger not to block my attempts to keep the road to the North open from the Cape and I'll do everything I can to help you occupy Saint Lucia Bay."

For a moment Van Riebeck loathed himself, he was a fighter not a politician, but the Transvaal *must* have Saint Lucia Bay, so he said, "But where exactly do you feel Kruger would be blocking you on your way North?"

"At the small Boer settlements, Goshen and Stellaland, he wants them brought into the South African Republic which would automatically block the Northern Road."

Van Riebeck's mind raced, to relinquish the two small settlements in return for powerful help with gaining the Bay was worth the price. He could persuade Kruger of this. "I'll do my best, you have my word on it and when will you commence to work on the Saint Lucia problem?"

"It will have to wait until I return from Kimberley. I'll be away for about ten days, but when I return I'll address Parliament and say I've changed my mind and I recommend that you have the Bay. Of course I'll have to push the project from then on. Anyhow, Hofmeyer, will be in the house, he can keep you informed of what happens."

"Good, then I'll show you a copy of my letter to Kruger telling him of our arrangement about the road North and persuading him to relinquish our claim to Goshen and Stellaland."

They shook hands then and the Dutchmen left. When they were back on the Herengracht, Van Riebeck asked Hofmeyer, "Will Rhodes be able to sway Parliament in our favour?"

"My answer is—I think he will. He's very popular and the members trust his judgement, there's no doubt he's a growing force."

"Well I hope to God he can help us."

Van Riebeck was unreasonably elated by the meeting but he knew he was being optimistic; Rhodes might fail to push the Bay project through and Kruger might refuse to relinquish the two settlements.

The tinny chimes of a clock in a tall, wooden tower rang out. "One o'clock!"

Van Riebeck sighed, "*Magtig*, two more hours before Katje's ship docks. Come and have lunch with me at Pooles hotel."

Hofmeyer gave him an amused look. "All right, but, man—you look as excited as a 'teenager going to meet his sweetheart," Jan teased, "and you're wearing all cream clothes—all done up in your Sunday best. *Ja*, just like a 'teenager."

"I'm much more excited than any 'teenager could be," Van Riebeck laughed, giving Hofmeyer an enthusiastic slap on the shoulder that made him wince.

8

HER heart thumping with excitement Katie stood with Nancy and a throng of eager passengers on the deck of the *Athena Castle* as the ship approached land. How lovely the 3500 foot high Table Mountain was, Katie rejoiced to herself. It was indeed the sentinel of the Cape of Good Hope; its huge flat-topped bulk seemed to be pushing at the blue dome of the heavens, its base was rooted in white frothy surf. The sea, green with tiny white capped wavelets was decorated by the Malay fishing fleet with its small sails in many colours.

"This is the third time that I've sailed in here," Katie said to Nancy, "and it all looks lovelier than ever."

"Yes, Mama, it's so glorious to see all the sunlight but Cape Town's houses spread out over the mountain's base do look a little suburban and. . . ."

The ship's guns booming a salute to Cape Town drowned out Nancy's words.

Then the *Athena Castle* edged closer to land, there was a gentle bump, the engines died and the vessel was alongside the dock where a mass of white, black, brown and coffee-coloured people pressed forward against a wooden barrier, as they stared up at the ship.

Katie's eyes searched frantically amongst the crowd for sight of Van Riebeck. Then she saw him. "There he is!" She cried to Nancy and waved toward the huge man in cream-coloured clothes, his head and shoulders above everyone. "Oh, there he is!" she repeated joyously as tears burned her eyes; she had not realized until this moment how much she had longed for him.

People were calling out to each other from ship to shore and navvies were manoeuvring the gangplank into place and on board sailors swung back the barrier and made the gangplank fast. Hours earlier Katie had stationed herself beside this spot so that now she was the first passenger to rush down, one hand lifting the hem of her flowered patterned skirts to avoid tripping, the other clamped to the top of her straw bonnet.

144

"Paul! Paul!" she cried for he had not yet seen her, his eyes were eagerly searching the crowd, then he spotted her and he started for her pulling people out of the way to reach her. Then his arms grabbed her and crushed her against his hard body in a bear's hug.

"Darling, darling!" She laughed up into his handsome grinning face and he bent and kissed her until she could hardly breathe.

"Hey, Papa Paul, I'm here too." Nancy tapped his shoulder.

Then he let go of Katie and turned to plant a kiss on Nancy's cheek. "Hello, Nancy, what in God's name brought you back? Your mother's cable said you were coming but no explanations."

"But aren't you glad I'm here? Aren't you glad to see me?" She pouted prettily.

"Of course I am—just surprised that the joys of Europe didn't hold you. But let's get out of this crush." Throwing an arm around Katie and Nancy's shoulders he started to manoeuvre them through the jostling throng to a long line of waiting carriages and carts. "You both look beautiful, Katje. . . ." His blue eyes poured love down on her. "You're more like sisters than mother and daughter."

"Wicked flattery, darling, but the voyage really did me good." His remark delighted her for he scorned to pay fatuous compliments. "But wherever is the family?"

"They haven't come, excepting for Franz and Adrian and they're waiting in the carriage with Maarje."

"But why on earth didn't the others come too?"

"Well—Terence is on call at the hospital, John is working with Rhodes, Ken's at the University and your sister Liz is knee-deep in dried fruits supervising the coloured women's packing. In any case you and I aren't going to Abend Bloem until tomorrow, I've appointments in Cape Town this evening so we'll spend the night here."

"Oh, Papa Paul—may I stay in town with you and Mama?" Nancy called up to him.

"No!" he thundered down at her but with a smile. "You've been with your mother for three weeks on board. Now it's my turn to have her."

They had reached their carriage, and the second Van Riebeck handed Katie up little Franz and Adrian jumped on to her, knocking her back on to the seat, half suffocating her with stranglehold hugs, kissing her cheeks, pushing her hat off, but she revelled in it all and her arms were tight around their strong little bodies. A wonderful, joyous reunion.

"Missus, I am glad—so glad to see Missus." Maarje's voice broke with emotion and as Katie turned to the coloured nursemaid she was touched to see tears in the big brown eyes.

"I'm so very glad to see you too, Maarje." Katie gave her arm an affectionate squeeze.

"Katje, I'll go with Nancy to collect the baggage . . . Van Riebeck looked into the carriage . . . "whilst you and the boys wrestle with each other. They missed you badly."

"Yes, yes," Katie answered breathlessly, "and I missed them—oh, my dressing-case will be all I need for one night, darling."

"Good. Nancy, Maarje and the boys can

drive back to Stellenbosch with the baggage."

"Oh, Papa Paul, we'll have to hire a Capecart to follow us with my baggage." Nancy laughed as if she knew she was troublesome but everyone enjoyed indulging her. "I've half a dozen trunks as well as all my portmanteaux."

"Same silly Nancy, eh? Come on." He grasped her arm to lead her back into the mass of people.

A little later when Nancy and the others moved off in the carriage, followed by the high-wheeled Capecart, Katie and Van Riebeck settled into a hired cab, its driver a yellow-skinned Malay, clean looking in blue blouse and pants faded by many washings, with a wide brimmed, peaked straw hat on his oiled black hair.

"Drive up to the Kloof Jong," Van Riebeck ordered in Dutch. "*Ja, Baas*," and the Malay flicked his whip over the horse's back and the cab moved off.

"Darling, whyever are we going up there?" Katie was surprised. "I thought we were going to an hotel?"

"No, the Van der Merwes loaned us their house; they've gone over to Robbin

Island, as it's his time to examine the prisons there, but don't worry, they've left servants in the house and I thought you'd like it—because it's cooler up there." He caught and held her gloved hand.

"Darling!" She twined her fingers through his. "I'm so happy to be back with you I don't mind where we go—although of course I'm longing to see the rest of the family."

Leaving the docks the cab turned in Bree Street which was crowded with vehicles and pedestrians. There was suddenly so much noise, of creaking wheels, cries of street hawkers and protesting animals, that conversation became difficult so Katie and Van Riebeck sat back just enjoying being together. The colourful street of red earth never failed to fascinate Katie, flanked by pepper trees it was sliced in the centre by a canal where black children were having fun, floating fruit peelings down the dark water. On both sides of the street were squat buildings—offices and shops—painted in coral, white and yellow.

The pedestrians were made up of various colours and races; tall, blue-black

Zulus moved in groups, the men wearing only loin cloths, the women, their pendulous breasts naked, babies slung across their backs in rag hammocks, wore calico tied around big swaying bottoms. Indian women were swathed in brilliantly coloured saris, their men wearing red and black fezzes, with billowy white cotton shirts and trousers; Malay and Hindu pilgrims returned from Mecca wore flowing garments and clip-clopped along on topless wooden shoes held on by a knob between their toes. Little brown men, Bushmen and Hottentots, lolled against buildings smoking and gossiping. Malay fruit hawkers, poles slung across their shoulders, with baskets of exotic looking fruits dangling from both ends cried their wares and the fishmonger shouted through a horn, "*Kopplejoe! Snoek!* Fresh fish!"

"It's just like my first landing at the Cape, even the pungent scents are the same," Katie said loudly into Van Riebeck's ear.

He nodded and answered, "The improvements that have been made are all on the Herrengracht—but we'll soon be out of this bedlam."

A few minutes later the cab was climbing a rise toward the base of Table Mountain, the business district was left behind and they entered the residential quarter. Lush gardens with flowering acacia and camphor trees, half concealed big white houses with heavy gables, green shutters and red tiled stoeps where women sat chatting as children crawled around or played about their feet.

"Oh, Paul, darling, all this makes me so nostalgic, you know I haven't driven up here for heaven knows how long."

They turned to stare into each other's eyes. How she had always loved his eyes —from their first meeting their vivid blueness, like the blue that so often surrounds a flame, had excited her.

Staring into her green eyes, flecked with gold like a leopard's eyes, at the creamy skin of her neck and throat he was madly impatient to lie with her, to see the whole of her creamy skinned nakedness. He murmured, "We'll soon be at the house, my Katje—soon be there."

Then he directed the driver up a lonely road newly made, until they reached an isolated clearing where a pretty pink bungalow sprawled. Paul stopped the driver, then jumped down and lifted Katie to the ground.

"It's a wonderful spot, darling—not another dwelling in sight."

He grinned as if at his own cleverness and turned to pay the driver and collect their small bags as she walked up a shingle path flanked by pink and white flowering oleander bushes to the open door where a smiling coloured boy in stiff white jacket and knee-length pants bowed her in.

Minutes later she and Van Riebeck were in a spacious chamber with white walls, red tile floor and wide windows showing the blue Atlantic far below. The satinwood four-poster bed, the antique armoire and chests with silver trappings were of exquisite Malay workmanship shipped a century before from Batavia.

Loving it all, Katie turned joyously to the huge Van Riebeck. "It's all beautiful —beautiful! Darling, how clever you are to have arranged it."

He spun his wide-brimmed straw hat on to a chair and caught her in his arms. "I'm always sharing you, my beloved, with your offspring—that's including my own sons

—so this time I was determined I'd have you to myself, if only for a few hours."

"Dar . . . ling." Her eyes stretched wide in mock surprise. "So it wasn't *true* that you had appointments in Cape Town?"

"No, it wasn't true." His sunbronzed fingers pulled her straw hat off then went to undo her high collar. "Do you mind the lie?"

Suddenly she started to tremble with longing for him and reached up to loosen his cravat. "Oh, my beloved—of course I don't—I missed you so much."

He was on fire to cover her and ripped open her lawn bodice, sending the buttons flying, then he dragged her skirts off and sweeping her up in his arms he carried her to the huge bed. Seconds later he was stripped and lying beside her dragging off her camisole and long drawers.

"By God," he muttered hoarsely, "how I've waited for this minute."

His mouth was on her breasts, kissing, sucking at them with a half-wild passion.

Her hands in his thick hair pulled his head up for him to kiss her mouth and he climbed on to her, his embrace shifting to her buttocks, fingers digging into the flesh. With a groan he entered her and climaxed almost immediately. For a minute or two he sprawled over her, then conscious that his size and weight could crush her, he rolled off her.

"Sorry, darling, that I behaved like a callow boy—but for ten weeks I've been going insane to make love to you. Ten weeks is too bloody long for a man to wait to enjoy his wife."

Triumphant that at her age she still had such power to arouse him she murmured, "Beloved, just to be with you like this—is heaven for me. You've no idea how I've longed for you."

"So the handsome Duke of Rotherford didn't steal you from me—I damn well wager he tried to."

"Silly darling." She turned her head to smile at him and her eyes rejoiced in the sight of his magnificent body. The great shoulders, the broad chest merging into slim hips, the long powerful legs. It wasn't just this man who lay beside her whom she saw but many other visions of him flashed to her. The magnificent young arrogant brute with his impudent all-over glances, his impertinent remarks, "Yes, she's beautiful, a blind man could see that. Notice how her eyes go from gold to green when she's angry. Like a lioness about to spring, a man must strike first or go to his doom at her claws."

Then another vision. "Lovely, lovely," his mouth against her throat, his hands caressing her breasts, "Did you know that in my country your name is Katje?"

Yet another vision, lying with him on the wild veld, under the leafless Kaffirboom tree with its scarlet blossoms. "Katje, Katje—my lovely Katje. With your breasts like ripe melons. Your flaming hair—young skin white as magnolias. My God, I've wanted you—all of you. . . ."

Now his hands were moving lingeringly over her body, caressing her, playing with her, sending her into a rapturous delight.

"Paul . . . oh, Paul . . . it feels as if the years have dropped away and we're almost new again to each other."

"Hmm . . . I know what you mean . . ."

Then her hands reached out to touch his manhood; he was ready again and a longing for him made her move up against him, pressing herself against the hardness of his body. "Now—now, darling . . ." she whispered.

Then he swiftly covered her and together they reached a summit of ecstasy.

More wonderful hours of love-play followed until sated they fell asleep. Hours later Katie awoke with moonlight silvering the room. She lay listening to Paul's deep breathing, then gently releasing his arm from around her waist she slowly left the bed, careful not to make a noticeable movement to awaken him.

Bare feet tiptoeing over the tiles, waist-length hair her sole covering, she went to the wide open window and revelled in the scents of night blooming flowers and the view before her—a purple-blue sky with a full moon floating across it as though blown by a baby's breath; the mountains of Devil's Peak and The Lion's Head were black against the heavens, their deep kloofs dark with closely packed trees dropped down into a shiny sheet of dark blue glass that was the Atlantic.

The ocean was calm now but Katie recalled a time when whipped up by wild winds it was cruel and savage, with demons in control—that night when her beloved mother and sisters had been arriving from Ireland aboard the sailing ship *Nottingham* that was struggling to gain the land. But the vessel struck hidden treacherous rocks and swiftly began to sink. On the beach she and Van Riebeck, amidst a desperate throng, had watched the ship disintegrate, heard the drowning peoples' voices singing "Nearer my God to Thee". Now Katie shivered at the memory and then another vision of Paul came to her.

Stripped to the waist on a rearing, screaming horse he flashed past her on the beach summoning the men to the passengers' rescue and calling, "Tie ropes to your saddles and wrists." His voice fought to rise above the screeching wind. "Other men on shore—hold fast to the rope ends —play out the ropes slowly. Now in God's name let's ride!"

Horsemen followed him as he forced his protesting horse into the boiling surf, forced it to swim toward the wreck. Then he was rescuing people, then turning his horse to swim back with terrified people clinging to the ropes, his legs, the horse's tail and mane.

Van Riebeck was magnificent, a creature out of a Greek classic as time and again he and other men went back to rescue the drowning.

Three of Katie's sisters had been saved, a fourth with her beloved mother—drowned. Even after all these years, it hurt her.

Now suddenly Paul was behind her; his arms catching her around the waist, he pulled her to lean back against him. "What are those deep, deep thoughts about, beloved?"

She leant her head back against his chest. "You, my darling." She made no reference to the shipwreck. "Being up here seems to have sprung open a lid in my memory-box and all sorts of memories are popping back. How beautiful it is up here —wait! Listen to that bird."

They were silent, listening to the almost eerie cry of a night bird, then when it ceased Paul answered with a perfect imitation of a bird cry and the bird replied.

For a few minutes they enjoyed the

game of "talking" to the bird then Paul said, "Do you realize it's past midnight and you haven't eaten anything since you left the ship. Aren't you hungry, darling?"

She turned around to face him. "No, I'm too happy. But you must be hungry."

"I am a little; making love always gives me an appetite. Yesterday I told the cook to roast a chicken stuffed with white grapes and we'd eat it cold and I brought champagne up. Now I'll just light the lamp." He went to the bedside table, raised the glass chimney on an oil lamp and put a match to the wick. "There, now I'll get the supper." He started for the door.

"But, darling, you can't go like that, you haven't a stitch on."

"Doesn't matter, the servants are asleep outside in their hut so I'll pop into the pantry and bring our supper in."

"I'll come and help you—just let me dress."

In a stride he was before her, catching her by the shoulders. "Don't you dare dress," he chuckled, "I intend to keep you naked until we have to leave here tomorrow afternoon."

She reached her arms up and clasped his neck. "Have we got to leave tomorrow afternoon? Couldn't we stay here for an extra day? It's bliss to be ourselves up here, I feel so free—so—well—untrammelled. Oh why haven't we ever thought of doing this before?"

"Yes, of course we can stay. By Heaven, that's what I want. I'll send a messenger to Abend Bloem saying I'm held up in town with appointments." He grinned teasingly in a way she loved. "But I've a provision to make—You don't dress. For years I've wanted to be able to look at your beautiful naked body walking around during the day and at last I can. I'll send the servants off for the day. It's so damned marvellous to be utterly alone! We can be as mad and wicked as we like and no offspring will come knocking at the door to interrupt us. Now I'm off to fetch our supper."

She watched him go, thinking how lucky she was that after having suckled ten children her breasts had remained firm and attractive so that Paul was still so enamoured with her body.

9

WITH a towel twisted around his hips, Paul stood at the table opening the champagne bottle that he had brought in on a tray with the chicken. "We must make a pact not to discuss family affairs or politics whilst we're up in the pink bungalow."

The cork came out of the bottle with a pop and he started to pour the topaz-coloured liquid into glasses. He handed Katie a glass. "Do you agree?" He raised his glass to her in a toast.

"Yes, I do agree, darling." She held her glass up to him. "To the pink bungalow —may we come back to it some day."

"I'll drink to that."

She took a big gulp of champagne. "Hmm—lovely. Quite my favourite drink," Katie chuckled and drank a couple more mouthfuls. "But we aren't dressed for the part." She grabbed at one of her frilly petticoats and draped it sideways about herself.

"That's cheating, darling—you promised 'no clothes'." He reached over to pull the petticoat away but she stepped back. "No, please—I feel better, especially with the carved chicken staring at me." She emptied her glass and held it out to him playfully. "More please."

"Whew! That was quick." He filled her glass. "Watch out, darling, it will go to your head on an empty stomach."

"I don't care, I feel free and wonderfully wicked." She drank again. "I don't think I've ever felt like this in my life before." She again swallowed some champagne, then giggled. "Drink up, Commandant."

He laughed at her. "Don't worry, I am keeping pace with you. Lucky there are two more bottles in the pantry, but you'd better have some chicken, come on there's chutney and guava jelly for flavouring."

"All right, I'll be good—but just a little more champagne to go with it."

Shaking his head good-humouredly he poured champagne out and the towel around his waist fell off. His muscular body with sunbronzed, shiny skin was so magnificent—like Michelangelo's David that she had seen in Florence—that she suddenly wanted him to be making love to her all over again.

"Let's leave the chicken, darling." She tossed her petticoat on to a chair. "We can always eat."

With a deep chuckle he lifted her in his arms and carried her to bed. As they started love-play she murmured, "Put the lamp out, there's a horde of moths around it."

"They won't annoy you and I want to see you. We always have to make love in the dark so none of the family spy light under the door and barge in." His hands were smoothing over her breasts and down her body. "Now I can look at you to my heart's content, I can enjoy you in every kind of pose."

For hours they made love, both being driven by an unsatisfied hunger for each other. It was their custom to make love wildly but tonight she was different—so abandoned that for the first time he dared to try tricks with her, learned in his University days in Holland from upper class whores. Nothing shocked her, instead, everything he did to her titillated her and her responses were marvellously wild.

At last they lay back panting for breath; then suddenly he realized the room was bright with sunlight. "*Magtig*, Katje—it's day."

But she had fallen asleep. Smiling he put the lamp out, arose, closed the shutters and went back to bed to sleep.

They awoke some hours later and he got up and brought her some champagne. "It's good for you," he grinned down at her. "Such hours of love-making are a strain on the heart you know."

She rose on an elbow, took the glass from him and sipped champagne but she was feeling miserably embarrassed as she thought of the hours of love-making. But Paul was her husband—absurd to be embarrassed with him, yet this new facet of love-making had revealed something of her that she had never imagined she possessed.

He knew her so well that he guessed her thoughts and fetching his own glass he came back to the bed and said, "Bloody marvellous that after all the wonderful love-making we've known—last night we reached a new summit." He raised his glass to her. "I toast the most glorious, unbelievable woman—my wife."

"Paul . . . oh, Paul." Her eyes gazed up at him with a wondering and troubled look. Was he perhaps disgusted with her? But she saw only adoration in his wonderful eyes. They both sipped their champagne, then she asked a little diffidently, "What happened to us, darling—we've never done such things before."

"But you loved it all—I know that."

She nodded. "Why did it only happen last night? Why never before?"

"Because it's the very first chance we've ever had of being entirely alone—without people around us. You didn't feel like anyone's mother; you had no pretences to keep up," he laughed teasingly. "You could release everything and get back to nature and be a savage woman and on my blood—I *like* it that way."

"I loved it all—but it's still difficult to understand—I mean that being free makes such a difference to people. I suppose that's why newly marrieds keep the place of their honeymoon a secret—to get away where they can lose their identities."

"Their identities and their inhibitions." He nodded. "And we're going to make a habit of going off alone from now on. I feel I've only been allowed a half of my wife all this time."

With almost physical pain she suddenly wondered if she had disappointed him in love-making for all these years? Then a rapier of suspicion pierced her mind. Had he been making love to some woman— knowledgeable in these things—whilst she had been gone? Is that what had aroused him so passionately that last night he decided to impart all he had learned to her?

"Paul, I. . . ." she began, then swallowed the terrible question, "Have you been unfaithful?" She could not insult him that way.

"Yes, my love," his eyes narrowed with interest, "what did you start to say—then decided not to?"

"It was too silly."

"You know somehow I don't think it was. I know you, my beautiful Katje, better than you think I do. What were you going to say?"

For no real reason she was annoyed with

him and blurted out. "Well, if you insist —I was wondering after last night—well I was wondering if you'd been unfaithful to me because where did you suddenly. . . ." Her sentence died away.

"Ah ha! You were wondering if some new woman had awoken me?" Annoyed by her lack of faith in him he laughed a little grimly. "No, I haven't betrayed you —not even in my thoughts! It's funny but I was wondering about you—wondering at your responses to me last night and I asked myself did his Grace the Duke succeed in climbing into your bed?"

She flung her champagne up into his insulting face. "How dare you! Damn you to hell! To say such a thing!"

He sprang up and reached for a towel off the end of the bed, then slowly wiped his face. "Same Katje—as always—you resort to violence if I annoy you. Anyhow, there's no one to see this performance, not like in Hoffen when you slapped my face before the forty men of my commando."

"Oh God—why bring that old story up? I'm sorry I just threw the champagne at you, but you were damned insulting." She saw that his eyes had gone from flame blue to ice blue, it was the danger signal. They must not quarrel! Whatever happened, they must not! "You surely believe in me when I swear that Howard's never been anything but a kind cousin-in-law?"

"Good, let's keep it like that." He tossed off the rest of his champagne. "Now I'm going out to wash at the pump —you should eat some of that chicken, it will steady your nerves."

She watched him flick a towel up and leave the room. Damn him! He hadn't changed with the years—not even an apology for his insult. She left the bed and ate some chicken, then she went to the washstand, poured cold water from an enamelled jug into a basin and washed. Feeling a little sick she went back to bed and lay on the edge of the mattress. She did not want to touch him if he came back to bed.

A few minutes later he came in and lay on the other side of the bed so as not to touch her. Exhausted they fell asleep immediately. Hours later he awoke, dressed and went out to send one of the coloured servants with letters to Abend Bloem and Hofmeyer's office saying he was detained. Angry as he had been with her now that he was rested he told himself to dismiss the whole subject from his mind. He wasn't such a fool as to allow it to spoil the rest of his stay up here when he could wallow in bed with this highly passionate wife of his.

Katie was entirely refreshed when she awakened and determined that the angry scene with Paul was due to their fatigue. Nothing was going to be allowed to spoil this wonderful unexpected "honeymoon" of theirs. When he returned from a walk they were both eager to renew the spirit in which they had arrived at the pink bungalow so that night was as passionately wild as the first night.

Christopher Van der Byl, tall, golden-haired husband of Katie's younger sister Elizabeth, met the train when it pulled into Stellenbosch railway station. He kissed Katie's cheeks and told her how well she looked, then shook hands with Van Riebeck.

"Liz didn't come, Katie, because she's knee-deep in dried fruit and had to supervise the coloured women. She said she knew you would understand." He led the way back to the carriage.

Katie settled back against the black leather seat and tucked her full skirts in around her feet to make way for Van Riebeck and Chris as they climbed up and settled opposite her.

"It's lovely to be back!" Katie smiled across at Chris.

"We all missed you, Katje." He turned to Paul with a laugh, "and this man was counting the days for your return."

The coloured driver wiggled his reins, clucked to the horses and the carriage moved off through a long tree-lined street of mighty oaks, planted centuries ago by the original governor of the Cape, Simon Van der Stel. They were soon passing along roads with white gabled houses and in a grassy square, a painted white church with wooden tower, clean as newly baked bread. Katie glimpsed Stellenbosch's greatest pride—the university where her darling son Kenneth was reading for a law degree. Then the carriage rolled along out to beautiful open countryside where high purple heather brushed the horses' bellies.

Whilst Van Riebeck and Van der Byl,

friends since childhood, chatted about politics, Katie sat back half listening and thinking. Everything looks as somnolent as ever, it doesn't seem possible that I have travelled thousands of miles to England and Italy, it seems as if I never left Stellenbosch. The heat, the blue Jongerhoek mountains, the tall trees, the slowly moving horses, the black and coloured workers in the corn fields.

In about fifteen minutes she grew excited as the carriage travelled along a long familiar country lane and then turned into a wide avenue of oak trees and there at the end was Abend Bloem. As always at sight of the great spreading white homestead with fancy gables, green shutters, wide red-tiled stoep, Katie's heart sang; the gallant spirit of the old house seemed to be welcoming her. She loved her Cape home as much as she loved some human beings.

As the horses clip-clopped down the avenue, several people emerged from long glass doors of the house on to the stoep— her family coming to welcome her. Dogs came rushing along to run barking at the horses' heels and coloured boys came to hold the horses' heads. As the carriage drew up before the shallow steps, Kenneth sprang down from the stoep and lifted Katie to the ground.

"Jumping Jerusalem! Am I glad you're back, Mother." He planted a kiss on her cheek and she whispered in his ear, "Mary's fine," and went up the steps to meet the family.

Thank God, Kenneth thought, for since the hellish night when Sannie had shot himself, Kenneth had worried often about his sister.

Now Katie was being kissed and embraced by her sister Elizabeth, so serene-looking with her black hair swept up off her unlined forehead and her grey eyes bathing Katie with love.

"Mama! Mama!" Eileen threw her plumpish young body into Katie's arms. "Hurrah—you're home!"

They hugged and kissed, then Nancy claimed Katie for a moment with a swift kiss, then Franz and Adrian were insisting upon having her attention.

"I didn't have the domestics line up to welcome you, Katie," Liz explained. "I thought you'd be tired."

"Exactly and I haven't been gone long."

Laughing and talking the family all swept into the house with its wide hallway and on into the spacious drawing-room, Katie's favourite room in Abend Bloem. She loved its tiled floor, red shading into rose, and polished to shine almost like glass, the painted grey walls, Adam green satin curtains, Belgian crystal chandeliers, the tapestry-covered sofas and chairs—lovely room. What happiness and sorrow she had known here.

She settled in an armchair near her sister, who cuddled little David in her lap. The lovely looking child with curly black hair and dark eyes was Liz and Katie's grandchild, born of Katie's son Terence and Liz's daughter Marie's sinful love. But the grandmothers had arranged to foist David on to the world as Nancy's little boy who had actually died in the Italian cholera plague. That deception had worked well.

Now Katie leaned over and kissed David's fat cheeks whilst Liz said, "I'm longing to know how Mary has settled down in Florence."

Katie braced herself to tell the necessary lies.

173

"She's settled down wonderfully; she absolutely loves it; all the art and beauty is like a fairy story to her," she lied smoothly. "She's met the nicest young painter and you'll hardly believe this, but I think it was love at first sight for both of them."

"Oh, Mother," Kenneth burst out, "that's splendid news!" What a relief, Kenneth thought, that so soon she has forgotten Sannie.

"I simply couldn't believe it when Mother told me on the ship," Nancy exclaimed. "It's so unlike placid Mary."

"I think it's lovely—just lovely." Eileen clapped her hands together. "I do hope they'll be married, Mary's *so* beautiful." Eileen had always resented that Nancy had been the most admired in the family and Mary seemed to go unnoticed.

"But Katie, that's splendid news," Liz said enthusiastically.

"Yes indeed it is." Katie hated having to lie to Liz. Then, "Is there any word from Paul on the gold fields?" she anxiously asked her sister.

"No—nothing, but don't be worried, you know how difficult communications are up there. We are bound to hear from him soon, anyhow if anything's gone wrong, Paul's wife would write and tell us."

Nancy suddenly jumped up and flounced out of the room; she could not endure to hear of "Paul's wife". It seemed to Katie that only she noticed Nancy's departure, God help us, Katie thought desperately. Is she still in love with Paul? Could she be hoping to see him? Is that the answer to why she's returned here?

Liz's voice cut across her fears. "Katie darling, John and Terence will be home from town for dinner and I'm hoping my brood will also be here."

"Oh, I hope so, I wrote to tell you, of course, that Marie contemplates coming home?"

"Yes, you did." Liz's eyes went misty with longing. "That would be an answer to my prayers, but she hasn't written to me about it."

Katie leaned over and squeezed Liz's hand. "Marie looked beautiful and is studying very seriously to be a teacher." She said nothing about Marie's rudeness to her. "Well, darling, I think I'll go up and unpack." She got to her feet.

"We've done it, Mama," Eileen cried. "You see Nancy had your keys on the bunch with hers so we opened your trunk."

"Oh, that's lovely, thank you darling, so I'll go up and quickly change and be down for tea."

"Can I go with you, Mama?" Adrian pulled at her skirts and she leaned down and grasped his chubby, sticky hand, "Of course, my precious pet, come on." She turned to little David. "Do you want to come, too, my love?"

"No, no," he half hid his face in Liz's bosom, "David stay with Grans."

Liz was his great love, for Nancy, supposedly his mother, was often away from Abend Bloem and when she was there she gave him only spasmodic attention. Natural enough, Katie mused, Nancy was in reality his aunt. His own mother, Marie, had never even seen him, insisting at his birth that she did not wish to.

"Mama, may I go with you?" Eileen jumped up eagerly. "I'll undo your hair

176

for you and brush it with long strokes. You always love that."

"Of course I do, darling, come on." Katie noticed that Eileen's breasts were developing so fast her lawn bodice was much too tight; she must have new dresses made by the Malay dressmaker. "Liz, when you have a chance, could you send a message into Stellenbosch to Sheraz's house and tell her I want her."

"Actually, she's coming tomorrow to make nightshirts for the children."

"Good. Have we any flowered cotton left in our kist?"

"Yes, I recently replenished our stock; I bought up a lot of bolts at bargain price from an Indian in town—it was salvage from a shipwreck and there's hardly any waste except cutting off the seawater stains near the selvedge."

Katie smiled approvingly at her sister's wise frugality. "You really are a clever one, Liz!" Then with Eileen and Adrian clinging to her, she went upstairs.

10

THOUGH slavery had long been abolished, the centuries-old bell was still in use and now the sound of its peals rang out across the fields announcing to the coloured workers that their day's labour was done and they were free to return to their huts and families. It was an especially magical time before sunset, when the evening blossoms started to open in welcome to approaching night, when the blue sky had paled and was tinged by pink.

On the wide red-tiled stoep the family was gathered sipping Cape sherry as they reclined in wicker armchairs skilfully plaited by local Malay artisans and made more comfortable by chintz-covered cushions.

Katie's children, Van Riebeck, Chris, Katie and Liz's children were all happily chatting, and Katie revelled in one of her rare chances of having so many of her loved ones assembled at the same time. Of her ten children she had tucked the two youngest into bed upstairs, five were on the stoep, Mary in Florence, Paul in the gold fields—alas, little Helen years ago had been buried in the Transvaal.

Brushing aside the sad memories Katie looked at Terence, her first-born, tall, slim, dark-haired, he had inherited his father's aristocratic bony features, his almost spaniel-type velvety eyes but not Sean's mouth; Terence's mouth and chin were firm, determined-looking. Katie was proud of his success as a doctor after only a few years in practice. When would he fall in love again or had that wretch of a girl of Huguenot stock hurt him so deeply that he feared women? Louise had severed their engagement when phylloxera had wiped out Abend Bloem's vineyards and she considered the family financially ruined.

Katie's look passed to John, eldest son of her second husband Richard, with pale blond hair, steel-grey eyes, fresh complexion, disciplined mouth and determined jawline—he was unmistakably a well-born Englishman. Katie thought with a critical amusement that John wore the invisible badge of Eton and Oxford, an hauteur that irritated many people. He had been a difficult child and as a youth had the effrontery to criticize her for marrying Van Riebeck.

Of course she loved John, but he was so unlike Kenneth seated beside him. Of middle height with mousy fair hair for ever tossed looking, with merry green-blue eyes, a mouth smiling even when in repose, Ken was like the Irish side of the family. He had always adored her; for Ken she could do no wrong and he held a special place in her heart. Poor Ken, terrible for him, being dragged into the sordid tragedy of Mary and Sannie.

"Katie darling—Katie!" Liz's persistent voice broke into her musings. "You're frowning so—whatever are you thinking of?"

"Oh, am I, Liz?" Katie forced a little laugh, "I was doing my usual mental rollcall of my offspring, but perhaps I was frowning at the sound of so much chatter going on."

"There is indeed," Liz looked around at the group, "and I hear mainly the words

'Witwatersrand' and 'Gold' from Chris and Paul."

It was true. The two men were disputing the wisdom of President Kruger's determination not to develop the Witwatersrand gold mines.

Van Riebeck was saying, "Kruger is convinced that if once the South African Republic opens up the Witwatersrand the big English fortunes will come in, then we'll be swamped by the English arriving from England. Just look what happened in the diamond fields."

"*Ja, ja*, it's a difficult thing to decide upon." Chris mopped his suntanned forehead with a big cream silk handkerchief. "But you've got to be sensible, man, your government hasn't the money required to develop the gold themselves and your exchequer is in difficulties."

"Kruger is being painfully shortsighted," John arrogantly burst out talking to Van Riebeck and his uncle. "He should go on his old knees and beg a great man like Cecil Rhodes to come and develop the Transvaal's wealth for him—look what miracles Rhodes did for the diamond fields."

As anger flashed in Van Riebeck's eyes at John's impertinence Kenneth swiftly joked, "'Emperor' Rhodes, that's what we must call him. Since John's been working for the great man I now dub him 'Emperor' Rhodes."

The young in the family burst out laughing at John's discomfort, for his hero-worship of Rhodes aggravated them; then Kenneth went on teasingly, "After all, Rhodes is no ordinary mortal as far as John's concerned."

John sipped his sherry as the muscles in his cheeks twitched, but he ignored Kenneth.

"John, you must present Rhodes to me," Nancy said, "and if I find him appealing I'll encourage him." She looked provocatively beautiful in a low cut lilac satin gown which Katie considered too much for a family dinner. "I'll help him to spend some of his great fortune," Nancy laughed, "I'll make him develop the telephone—all the way across South Africa." Then she could talk to her beloved Paul.

"I'm afraid, my dear sister, that you're in for a disappointment. All your beauty and wiles would fall very flat with

Rhodes." John's mouth curled with an unpleasant smile. "You see Rhodes is not made of common clay, he is absolutely a cerebral creature, he's not like ordinary men who need women around—he's a genius."

Katie burst out laughing. "But, John, do you mean to imply that men who fall in love and marry are all mentally inferior to Rhodes?"

At the ridiculous idea everyone laughed and John tugged at the points of his high wing collar that were digging at his under jaw. "Well, Mother, it's easy to make fun of what I said, but remember Rhodes is not the first great man who considers women a deterrent in their lives—for example take Alexander the Great—as a young man studying in the groves of Aristotle's Academy—females were not permitted within miles of the place."

Van Riebeck and Van der Byl exchanged meaningful glances which Katie caught and a surge of anxiety rose in her; she did not like the fact that John was so much under Rhodes' influence.

Nancy indignantly burst out, "Honestly, John, you sound like my effete husband;

he was always citing the Greeks in self-defence after I discovered he liked men." She had always quarrelled with John; his superior manner irritated her.

"I don't know much about Eric, excepting he has the potentials of a great pianist," John answered with contempt. "Perhaps he found your wild disposition a drawback to his career."

"That's enough, John!" Van Riebeck spoke with quiet authority. "You and Nancy sound as ridiculous as when you were children—always quarrelling. It's boring for other people. But about Rhodes and the Witwatersrand gold fields—I had a meeting with him recently and he indicated that it's Zimbabwe he's interested in, not the Transvaal gold fields."

"Oh no! He's *most* interested in the Tran. . . ." John stopped and clamped his mouth shut, furious with himself for almost betraying Rhodes' schemes.

Van Riebeck was amused by John's lapse; it revealed to him that the foxy Rhodes had been deceiving him, but to save face for John he swiftly addressed Terence. "What's been decided at the hospital?"

"Good news, Father." Terence, since a small boy, had loved Van Riebeck and the word "Father" came easily to him. "They've invited me on to the board as a consultant."

"Oh darling, how wonderful!" Katie cried amongst the general noise of congratulations and Eileen jumped up to come and plant kisses on Terence's cheeks.

"Clever—clever brother. I always knew since I was little and you used to stuff straw back into my dolls' bodies and mend the china heads that you'd be a marvellous doctor." She half perched on the arm of his wicker chair.

"Now—now," Terence laughed and gave her long hair a playful tug. "Don't make too much of this appointment."

"*Ja*, but at your young age, man, it's quite an honour," Chris insisted.

"Well, Uncle Chris, naturally I'm very pleased, but sometimes I regret not accepting Mother and Father's offer for me to finish my studies in England and Germany. Anyhow, I subscribe to their medical journals and I glean quite a bit from them."

"I'm so glad that you love your work, Terry," Katie said.

"Oh a doctor should be dedicated to his calling, but later on I'd like to devote myself to research. When I think of the good Pasteur's done with his innoculation to immunize animals against anthrax—I am inspired."

"What's anthrax?" Eileen asked still perched on his chair arm.

"It's a carbuncle—a malignant boil."

"Might Pasteur's immunisation have saved our herds in Lydenburg when rinderpest wiped them out?" Van Riebeck asked anxiously.

Terence slowly shook his head, "No, Father, rinderpest is a diphtheritic inflammation of the mucous membranes, especially of the intestines. There's no cure for it yet. But Pasteur's immunisation has already saved millions of animals all over the world. Some people say its monetary value adds up to more than France's war indemnity to Germany in 1870."

"I think medical research would suit you very well, Terry," Liz said. "As it is, your entire life is given to your work."

"Thank you, Aunt Liz." Terence was

devoted to his unselfish aunt who for years had kept Abend Bloem going during his mother's compulsory absence in the Transvaal. Now, embarrassed by everyone's attention on himself he asked, "By the way, any news of Paul?"

"Nothing yet," Van Riebeck answered, "but we'll soon be hearing from him, and when we're back in the Republic your mother and I will visit him. The Volksraad want me to have a good look at what's happening on the Witwatersrand. We receive such contrary reports."

At that moment the boom of the old brass gong came from the house and the family moved inside for dinner.

In the big dining-room dozens of candles in silver candelabra gently lit the yellow painted walls, the Brussels lace tablecloth, crystal goblets and silver baskets of exotic fruits. Katie thought appreciatively that her sister maintained the good standard which years ago Katie had commenced.

Fourteen of the family stood behind allotted chairs, their heads bent as Van Riebeck said "Grace", and, as he finished, chairs were scraped back and everyone sat down. Then in came coloured maids in shapeless white dresses, their bare feet slap-slapping over the tile floor as they carried big platters of Dutch blue delft piled high with rice and fish kedgeree.

Then everyone started talking, asking questions and not waiting for replies but Katie revelled in the vocal chaos created by the dearly loved voices.

As always Liz had arranged a splendid dinner: following the rice and fish kedgeree came *babootie* and suckling lamb baked in herbs, sweet potatoes, bananas baked in honey, cabbage stuffed with mince-meat and *mosbolletjies*, the spongy buns flavoured with wine.

The wine was good, preserved by Chris before phylloxera had devastated their vineyards. It was a delicious meal and everyone seemed happy.

After dinner coffee followed in the drawing-room, then card tables were set up and whist and poker games arranged for everyone except Katie and Liz, who valued a chance to talk. In answer to Katie's enquiry about the progress of their ostrich feather business, Liz assured her that although Cape exports had generally fallen off, Abend Bloem had been very little affected.

Katie thanked God, for her family and Liz's family were mainly supported by the hideous birds' feathers and so were a hundred coloured workers, many of whom had been born and bred in their huts on the Abend Bloem land.

Van Riebeck's estate bordering Abend Bloem had also gone over to ostrich farming and, as on Abend Bloem's land, Chris, who ran both estates, had planted young French vines which were doing well.

In addition, fearing a time when ostrich plumes would become unfashionable, Katie had started the dried fruit project.

Now she said to Liz, "I haven't had a chance to tell you, but just before I left London I saw the manager of Fortnum and Mason and all the shops selling delicacies and they were most enthusiastic and want to handle our product. I promised we'd send them a couple of sample cases and they can order on those."

"Splendid, Katie! I'm delighted to say in the ten weeks you've been gone, the new trees have shot up and I've been able to train some of our coloured women to be really reliable at drying the fruit, but I'll show you everything in the morning. I think Jan will be able to run the project later; he's very interested in it." She glanced across the room where her young son was playing whist. "It will be wonderful if we can gradually hand over most of our interests to our sons—won't it?"

"It would be ideal."

"Cornelius has been a great help on the ostrich farm since Paul left for the gold mines and Ken's been studying so hard for his final law degree."

Katie looked over at the golden-haired Cornelius, Liz's third son, heavily built like his father; he was lost to everything in a poker game. "And what about Stephan? Does he still want to be a priest?" The aesthetic-looking young man was playing whist with Nancy as his partner.

"More than ever he wishes to take Holy Orders." Liz's voice quavered with satisfaction.

"Oh Liz!" Katie turned wonder-filled eyes on her sister. "How lucky you are to have a son with a vocation to God."

"Yes, I know that," Liz answered humbly, "yet I can't help feeling sorry for Chris to have to relinquish his eldest son to the Church—after all, Chris is not a Roman Catholic—he can't feel as we do about it. My prayer is that Stephan can go to study in Rome, if sending him there and supporting him for years isn't too great an expense."

"But he *must* go to the Sacred College in Rome!" Katie exclaimed. "There's no question about it; we'll manage his expenses. His religious education is more important than the education of any of our other boys." She sighed with deep satisfaction. "Just think of how proud our beloved father would be to have a grandson who's a priest. Oh, I almost envy you."

"Katie! Don't say that, when you've a son like Terence who does so much good in the world caring for the sick."

"I suppose I shouldn't have said that."

"Tell me something about Howard." Liz lowered her voice so that it would not carry. "Still not married?"

Katie shook her head, "No and it's such a shame—a waste of a wonderful man."

"Is he still in love with you, darling?"

Liz knew how deeply in love Howard had been with her glorious sister. "It wouldn't surprise me at all—he's that kind of man."

"Well," Katie flipped her ivory and satin fan open and started to fan her face, hoping to conceal her expression, "he's such a flatterer, he says his feelings for me haven't changed."

"I believe him—poor man."

A ridiculous surge of longing to see Howard, if only for a few moments, swept through Katie, but she swiftly crushed it. "He has a most original new hobby." She explained about Howard's garden and how he collected rare plants from all over the world.

"What a beautiful idea—but it sounds just like him."

"I promised I'd send him some original specimens from the Cape or Lydenburg— what about chincherinchee? I'm sure he hasn't got that kind of everlasting plant, they are unique to the Cape."

"Oh, we must send those and also silver leaves, which grow only in the Cape."

"Yes, yes, but we'll have to have a small tree dug up and have it balled, then despatch it by steamer not by sailing ship."

"That will be quite expensive."

"I don't care, Howard has been so good to my children; it will be a small repayment." She suddenly felt at peace about Howard. In sending the tree with its beautiful velvet-like silvery leaves and the chincherinchee plant with its white paper-like flowers, she would be maintaining the spiritual link with Howard and surely she owed him that much comfort.

11

KATIE and Terence strolled down the wide avenue with moonlight sifting through the oak trees' branches, forming pretty patterns on the ground, and the air sweet with the scent of the evening bloom, the waxy, bell-shaped flowers that opened only at night named Abend Bloem—after which the estate got its name.

"I asked you to walk with me, Terry, because there's no chance for us to chat with all the family around." Katie tucked her hand into the crook of his arm. "After hearing what you said before dinner tonight I wanted to suggest that you go to Europe to further your studies—if you wish to. I'm sorry I didn't *insist* upon it before you began practising."

He patted her hand on his arm. "Mother dear, for heaven's sake, it's absurd to sound as if you've something to reproach yourself with because you certainly have not and I love what I'm doing."

"But, darling, the family exchequer can afford to send you to Europe." She would somehow manage to finance him.

"You're wonderfully generous, but I know the exchequer is not too full: you and Father spent a fortune on guns and ammunition for the Majuba war. Then there's all the expense with Mary. Don't worry about me, I'm very content with my work, believe me."

"I'm so glad, but I hope you leave yourself some time to enjoy life—to have fun. Don't keep your head always in books and let life go by. Aren't there any nice girls in Cape Town?"

"Hundreds, I'm sure." He laughed.

"Well then. . . ?"

"I've been waiting to tell you—there *is* a special girl, but I didn't talk of her before you went to Europe because I wanted to be certain we were right for each other." His voice shook with fervour. "Now I am."

"Oh darling, I'm delighted!" No need now to dread Marie's return; Terence would not be tempted by her presence. "Tell me about her—when can I meet

195

her?" She stopped walking and in a pool of moonlight stared eagerly up at him.

"The sooner the better, but I don't want to bring Elaine here just yet—you know I love Nancy and John of course but they might be a bit overpowering for Elaine. I hope you understand what I mean? Nancy's so absorbed with herself, her jewellery and clothes and John's absurd worship of this rotter Rhodes can be so irritating."

"Don't be too hard on Nancy. I know she seems silly and flighty but don't forget how willingly she fell in with my plan to pretend your little David was her child."

Guilt flushed through him. "God knows I'll always be grateful to her for that and I didn't intend to be critical of her but . . . well, she's so unlike Elaine."

"I understand. Later Elaine can meet all the family. Meanwhile I'll go into Cape Town to meet her, but tell me something about her."

"Well, she's beautiful in the quiet way that Aunt Liz is; she's an only child of Irish-English stock. Her father, Sir Daniel Musgrove, is head of the hospital, a brilliant doctor. When he was in London he accepted the post out here because Lady Musgrove was suffering with TB and he hoped the climate might cure her."

"And it has, I hope?"

"No alas . . . Elaine nursed her devotedly but she died a year ago."

"How terribly sad, I'm so sorry . . . poor Elaine. So she's alone with her father."

"Yes, he's a splendid man and they're Roman Catholics—which pleases you of course." He gave a little chuckle. "Elaine now acts as his secretary; she's also devoted to medicine."

"She sounds like a self-sacrificing girl as well as intelligent. Have you asked her to marry you?"

"Yes," he murmured, his voice trembling with emotion, "and she has accepted me."

"This is wonderful news, darling. I thank God. What a blessing that you will be happily married, but I must meet Elaine as soon as possible, *please* . . ." she gave a tender little laugh . . . "and I promise you, I'll be as quiet and gentle as Aunt Liz is."

"Mother! Stop teasing me—just be my own wonderful beautiful mother—that's what Elaine is expecting. But you know I have a problem—my little son—I must tell Elaine about David."

"But must you? Would it be wise I wonder?"

"But I couldn't marry her without telling her. I only hope she won't judge me harshly."

Katie was immediately ready to fight Elaine. How dare she judge! How dare anyone! "You were shattered emotionally at the time by the cruelty of that wretched Louise, and Marie put herself out to comfort you." She bit at her lip thinking it was not an easy step for him to tell Elaine so she added, "And don't forget, you were very young at the time."

"It's all true what you say, but I was weak and I've never forgiven myself for it, though I've worked up my courage to tell Elaine. Being the kind of girl she is, I think she'll understand and not let it make any difference between us."

They started strolling again. "She'll probably be upset to begin with, but after a little while I think she'll accept it." Katie added encouragingly, "and even love you more for your honesty."

"I'm daring to think that way myself, anyhow by Monday I shall know, so if you don't receive a message to the contrary from me, will you come to town on Tuesday to meet Elaine and Sir Daniel?"

"Gladly—gladly, darling. I'm longing to meet them. You know—to touch on other things—I'm a little worried about John being so close to Rhodes."

"You needn't be; John's absolutely normal. He and I see quite a bit of each other in town and I assure you he also enjoys plenty of feminine companionship."

"Well, I'm relieved to know that." Katie's mind now thrust forward a question she was aching to ask him, though she thought miserably that she already knew the answer. "Darling, I'm enquiring about this for a friend—although I suppose it's a stupid question, but if a black and white lie together and a child is the result is there more chance that it will be white or black?"

"An equal chance. Tell your friend the child might be black, white or mixed looking like a Cape-coloured person and if that boy or girl, when an adult, is white for example and lies with a white, the offspring could be black. The negro strain could appear for three or four generations and of course equally a white child could be born to blacks."

She had not known for certain that the negro strain could reappear for generations. Terrifying Biblical words suddenly flashed to her mind, "I the Lord thy God am a jealous God and visit the sins of the fathers upon the children unto the third and fourth generation."

She started to shiver from head to foot and noticing it Terence asked, "Are you cold, Mother? Shall we go in?"

"Yes, yes." Death had brushed her soul by what Terence had told her. "I think I'd better go to bed, Terry dear, I feel a little feverish."

"Not going down with another attack of malaria, I hope. I'd better dose you with arsenic, I've got some in my bag."

Later as Katie lay beside an already sleeping Van Riebeck in the great four-poster bed she dreamed that black babies were crawling all over her—she could not escape them, wherever she went they followed her with incredible speed their hands dragging at the hem of her skirts as they called, "Grandmama—grandmama."

She awoke wet with perspiration but grateful that Paul slept heavily. Thank God the nightmare had not made her cry out. Now she gently left the bed and by moonlight coming through the half-closed shutters she made her way into the adjoining little dressing-room and at the open window she sank on to a stool. Ashamed of her weakness, she upbraided herself, then faced a challenge: what if Mary's child be black as Sannie was? Must she not learn to live with the fact that God had created blacks as well as whites, all were His creatures. She should accept and love the child.

But in her agitated mind she argued, yes, she could accept the child but what of her other daughters, her sons and the rest of the family? They would be disgraced, ostracized. Terence the doctor would suffer; fingers would point accusingly at him, voices would hiss; his sister fornicated with a Kaffir. Never would she allow him and the rest of the family to be victimized because of Mary's folly. She would protect them; if once back in Florence for Mary's confinement she found the infant showed plainly to be sired by a black, Katie would make Mary swear never to bring the child to South Africa.

But contrary to all her upbringing Mary had loved Sannie's blackness and she was so strange that in the emotional flush of new motherhood and on fire with false heroics she might decide to blaze a trail for half-castes and return to the Cape with her child determined to defy all prejudice.

If this should be Mary's decision, Katie would somehow spirit the child away, and Howard would help her. They would place the boy or girl in a convent with nuns and Mary would be told the child was dead.

Having made her vow Katie grew calmer. Six months must pass before Mary's confinement so until then Katie told herself to forget Mary's tragedy and the part she might have to act in it. She returned to bed and with her indomitable courage she made herself think of the happy event of Terence and Elaine and their future marriage.

The following morning the scent of coffee drifting up from the kitchens awoke her. Van Riebeck had already left. It was one of the many things she loved about him that he never disturbed her in the mornings, if she were sleeping. She jumped up and went to open the shutters and sunlight streamed into the room.

In this room that she loved so much, in that same bed six of her ten children had first opened their eyes to the world. Wonderful old bed, how much loving and lusting it had been a party to. She smiled as happy remembrances flashed through her mind.

At the double mahogany washstand she poured cold water from the porcelain flowered jug into the matching basin. She washed and dressed hurriedly, deciding on a dress of pink cotton sprigged with small blue flowers. By the sounds of activity in the house she guessed she was the last one up.

Downstairs she popped into the big kitchens where she always enjoyed the scent of spices. Strings of vegetables and hams hung from hooks on the rafters. Sara, the coloured cook, busy at the huge wooden range smiled, "Good morning, Missus. It is good Missus is back."

"Good morning, Sara. It is good to be back and is your family all well?"

"*Ja, ja,* Missus," Sara nodded and laughed. "My daughters have three more babies since Missus was away." She went back to stirring a mixture in a large copper pot. "I send Missus coffee and *mosbolletjies* to Missus Liz's office?"

"Yes please, Sara." Katie threw smiles at the coloured maids who were peeling vegetables and as she was leaving her eyes flashed over big iron rings embedded in the stone floor. Long ago, the then mistress of Abend Bloem had chained Hottentot slaves to the rings during the night to prevent them from running away. Thank God, Katie thought, slavery was completely over.

In the corridor she heard the murmurings of subdued voices coming from the back stoep and went a few paces to look out at a couple of dozen coloured field workers wearing their cleanest clothes standing in a group. The men swiftly pulled old straw hats off and with the women they gave her wide smiles.

"Good morning, Missus. It is good

Missus is home." They all said as if they had been rehearsed.

"Thank you, I'm very glad to see all of you, but why are you here?"

"We wait for Massa Terence," a little man with grey peppercorn hair said. "He take care of all our sickness—every Saturday—you remember, Missus, like Missus did long ago."

"Ah yes, of course, I forgot it was Saturday. Doctor Terence will make you all well, I'm sure."

Back inside the house, loving its familiar scent of wax and polish, she went to a room and opened the door a little way. For a moment she peered in unobserved. Terence was examining a coloured woman's arm with a serious-looking Eileen beside him holding a tray ready for him with implements and bandages.

Katie stepped quietly inside, "Good morning, please don't let me disturb you."

Terence and Eileen looked up with swift smiles and he said, "We'll soon have Lotte fixed up," then spoke encouragingly to his patient. "Her cut is nice and clean and healing well. I'm just going to bandage it."

In a few minutes the grateful woman left

205

and Katie asked Eileen, "Since when have you been assisting Terence?"

"Since you went to Europe, Mama. You see, Aunt Liz can't do it any more she's too busy seeing to the dried fruit."

"Eileen's an excellent assistant, Mother," Terence said.

"I told you, Terry, when I was small in Lydenburg I used to help Mama treat the workers of all sorts of things, snake bites and ringworm."

"Indeed you did and what a great help you were. I was thinking, darling, that you might come up to Lydenburg when we go. You wanted to last time I left, do you still. . . ?"

"Oh Mama!" Eileen plonked the tray on a table and rushed to give Katie a bear hug. "I've been praying you'd take me because you've no excuse to leave me here any more. I'm educated at last."

They all laughed. "Well, you've had a good groundwork of schooling which wasn't possible in Lydenburg," Katie said, "and I can give you further education." After the terrible experiences of Nancy and Mary, Katie had decided Eileen must be under her eye. Liz had too many other responsibilities to keep a close check upon her.

"It's wonderful, Mama." Eileen gave Katie another huge hug, "I can wash your hair and brush it and oh—just take care of you."

"Well, well, that's a good resolution," Terence laughed, but his dark eyes searched Katie's face. "How's the fever?"

"All gone, Doctor, thank you, I feel splendid this morning." She longed to give him one of Eileen's bear hugs but such luxury of affection was denied to mothers with their grown sons. "Now I won't disturb you any further. I'm going to have coffee then join Aunt Liz in the fruit shed and afterwards ride out to see if the ostriches are as hideous as ever, then I'll have my great treat and see how our baby vines have grown."

Terence opened the door for her and as he released it, Eileen said thoughtfully, "Mama's so marvellous, I wish she would never be old; I don't want her face to wrinkle or the red-gold of her hair to go grey."

Terence felt his eyes grow moist. This little pixie sister of his often surprised him with her strange thoughts. "What's wrong with growing old, silly? Mother will always be wonderful, even when she's a hundred."

"But I don't *want* her to alter. You're a brilliant doctor, can't you give her some medicine so she'll stay just as she is for always?"

"You've been reading *Alice's Adventures in Wonderland*, but no Doctor can make people small or large, or keep them young." He spoke gently, looking into her upturned trusting blue eyes. "Don't you think God might object to people interfering in His design for His creatures? You must learn to see beauty of the soul, Eileen, not just beauty of the body." He tousled her hair, "Now come on, we've got all those poor people outside waiting for our help. Kindly show the next patient in, Nurse Eaton." He assumed a deep pompous tone which always amused her. "If you please, Nurse Eaton, my time is valuable."

She giggled delightedly, "Yes, yes, Doctor, immediately," and she dropped him a mock curtsey.

Liz proudly showed Katie into the shed

where newly picked fruit was stacked into piles and the air was filled with its scent. Coloured women were sorting out the best of the apricots and peaches and other women were stoning them, preparing them for drying. The sisters passed into an open space where on roughly hewn platforms big trays were set out and generously lined with sugar on which apricots, peaches and cut-up water melon rinds were placed to dry in the sun. As the juice ran out of the fruit into the sugar beneath, they mixed together so they became as one.

"Liz, you've worked marvels since I was away, I'm amazed—the new sheds, the platforms and trays. And you've trained the women well; they seem quite efficient."

"Yes, but they have to be supervised, or they'll let bruised fruit be dried and the flavour is not the same. Now come and see the packing shed."

They walked into the connecting shed, with roughly hewn waist-high tables, where coloured women were carefully packing the fruit in rows on to white paper inside wooden-slat boxes.

"What organization, Liz! You've

arranged about paper, boxes, wire—oh just everything."

"Well, darling, I've merely tried to emulate your energies, but like you, I long for Abend Bloem to return to wine-making."

"Oh yes, that's my wish also; still we must hang on to the ostrich farm as long as there's a market for the feathers. But where is all my brood? I came down so late I've missed everyone except Terence and Eileen caring for the sick."

"The men have ridden over to Hofmeyer's place; John's calling on 'Emperor Rhodes'," Liz smiled. "Ken is on the ostrich farm and Nancy is queening it over the Coetzee sisters, displaying her Parisian gowns in her room."

"The Coetzee girls are old friends of Nancy's, aren't they?"

"Yes, and they still come early every Saturday and stay for lunch. I think Josephine, the younger one, is mooning over Kenneth."

"And he?"

"Doesn't even notice that she's there—poor girl."

"And the very young I suppose are in the playground?"

"Yes, Franz is trying to teach some of the coloured infants the alphabet, I know Paul doesn't approve of his children playing so much with the coloured and black children."

"Yes, he's so very prejudiced like most Transvaalers." Perhaps he is right, Katie thought, Mary's familiarity with Sannie started in childhood. "Tell me, has Sannie's mother recovered from his death?"

Liz did not answer. She was correcting a packer. "No, no, don't squeeze the apricots against each other; leave a little space between them."

"*Ja, ja*, Missus."

The sisters walked out of the shed and over to the shade of a pepper tree. "About Sannie's mother, you know what it is with these people. She's got ten other sons and daughters so she hasn't much time to grieve over him. But I miss Sannie; he was the nicest stable-boy we ever had."

"Yes, he was a good boy."

"His sister, Cillie, one of our best

211

parlour maids, won't come back to the house since his death."

"Oh, why not?"

"She told one of the other maids, it upsets her too much because she swears Sannie was in love with a girl in the house and a jealous lover murdered him."

Katie's heart hammered so violently against her bodice, she feared Liz would see it. If Cillie were left to gossip with the maids, one of them might stumble on the truth. Cillie must leave Abend Bloem!

"Poor girl, she's trying to find someone to blame for Sannie's death, but it was obviously an accident or suicide. I think it would be a good idea if I take Cillie to Lydenburg with me, the change will make her forget her silly suspicions." Settling her wide-brimmed straw hat on her head she said, "I'm off to the stables now to ride to the new incubator sheds to see Ken."

12

TO begin with Nancy enjoyed showing off her glorious Parisian gowns to the Coetzee sisters; their exclamations amused her.

"Oh, how beautiful—the satin skirt is pleated like a fan," Josephine exclaimed and Fleur went on, "And those darling little gold birds embroidered on the bodice! It's the loveliest dress I've ever seen, Nancy! Oh, do show us all of them."

Nancy continued pulling out the Alençon laces and satins in glorious shades, the point-de-Venice bodices with skirts in the latest "organ shape" pleats, but in a short while she grew bored with the girls' purrs of delight, their envious sighs and she wanted to be rid of them.

Why in the devil's name had she forgotten how dull Abend Bloem was without her magnificent half-brother? On this, her fifth day home, she was silently cursing herself. She missed Paul with almost a physical pain. When she passed his bedroom where for six months of glorious nights they had made love, she wanted to scream with frustration. The front stoep, the dining-room, the drawing-room, she visualized him everywhere—it was exquisite agony she was suffering. She cursed her impetuosity which had made her suddenly decide to return here. She was a fool—she had been well aware that a three month trek by ox-wagon separated her from him.

And how could she ever reach him? Her stepfather to whom she had idiotically confessed her affair with Paul, would never permit her to travel in the family wagon when it went North. God! She wanted to be back in London or Paris, where at least she met young men. She burst out to the pretty fair-haired sisters.

"Don't you feel terribly closed-in? Nothing exciting happens here."

"Oh, do you feel like that?" Fleur's bright blue eyes flashed a chiding look at Nancy, "but we have lots of fun in Stellenbosch, there are plenty of parties with dancing on the various homesteads and Mama sometimes takes us in to Cape Town to the theatre."

"Yes, I liked it well enough when I was growing up but after Europe it all seems so dull."

"But it needn't be, Nancy," Josephine assured her. "There are lots of dashing officers in the regiments stationed at the Castle. Let's give a ball! You ask your mother to give one and we'll ask our mother to give another and we'll have all the handsome young men out. The trouble is they're nearly all English and Papa being Dutch like your stepfather doesn't like the English much."

"What's the matter with the older people?" Nancy demanded. "And what about your brothers at the Stellenbosch University, they must know men who feel like we do—not Dutch or English, but just South African."

"Yes, they do." Fleur clapped her hands with excitement. "Come on, let's start writing a list out. Let's start with your brother Terence. Now he's on the hospital board he must know lots of nice young doctors we can invite."

"A good idea." Nancy went to a drawer for pen, ink and paper—even planning a ball was a help to her. She must—must—

must meet some man to make her forget Paul. The French Jean-Claude had not done so. But then where was there a man to equal Paul? Golden-haired, golden-skinned giant. Easy enough to find men to love her, but it seemed impossible for her to love them. "Here we are, girls." She waved a sheet of paper, then found an inkwell and quill pen. "Let's sit here and start."

The three of them sat close together, and Fleur suggested, "Let's do it as if we were in a Dutch Church, you know, men on one side, women on the other."

"Of course! Well, we'll start with my brothers." Nancy commenced writing, "Terence, John, Kenneth . . ."

"Oh Kenneth," Josephine cooed, "he's my favourite of all your family." She felt herself blushing, "He should bring some friends from the University."

When they had listed the suitable brothers, sisters and cousins in their own families, they had twenty names and Fleur said, "No more family, now we need outsiders."

"Exactly," Nancy agreed, "but just how are we going to meet the dashing officers you spoke of who're stationed at the Castle?"

"That's a problem," Fleur sat back in her chair, "what about your brother John? He must know them."

"I don't think so; he is entirely wrapped up in Cecil Rhodes' clique."

"Well, let's invite them," Fleur giggled. "Aren't they all diamond millionaires? I just *adore* diamonds."

"You're a horribly mercenary girl," Josephine chided her sister.

"I admit it, I want to travel as Nancy does and have beautiful clothes like hers. Well, back to our list."

As the Coetzee girls discussed between themselves if they should invite young men living in districts a fair distance from Stellenbosch, Nancy was occupied with her own thoughts. She would find some way to meet the officers stationed at the Castle! When she was a child and her father was an aide-de-camp to the Governor, lots of dashing officers in scarlet tunics came frequently to Abend Bloem, but since her mother had married Papa Paul, the guests were usually Dutch and Aunt Liz's friends were mainly from the

Stellenbosch district. She reached a swift decision: she would present herself at Government House, saying she brought a personal message from the Duke of Rotherford for the Governor. It was bold—but no matter. The illustrious Rotherford name would open the doors of Government House to her; there she would meet some officers from regiments stationed at the Castle.

"Nancy, shall we send some of our coloured boys with invitations to our friends in Swellendam, Tulbagh and Worcester or shall we send invitations by post?" Fleur asked excitedly.

"Oh, of course by special messengers who must take the invitations and bring back replies." What stupid oafs the girls were! "We can't wait all year to know who's coming."

"But we don't even know what *date* to give in our invitations, you haven't even asked your mother yet if you can hold the ball."

"Don't worry about that," Nancy said airily, "she'll say 'Yes', in fact I'll go and find her and arrange the date. Will you

218

two hang up my gowns, please, whilst I'm gone."

"Could we try them on?" Josephine begged, "Oh, please, let's."

"If you like," Nancy answered unwillingly, "but be very careful of the lace and all the beading." The Coetzee sisters were more heavily built than she was, her waist was much smaller than theirs. "Don't stretch them around the waist."

"We won't—we won't," they assured her as she grabbed a hat and left.

She found Katie just as she was entering the stables. "Mama, where are you riding to?"

"To see Ken at the incubator shed. Join me?"

"No, *thank you.*" Nancy gave a little grimace, "Just the smell of the ostriches makes me feel sick, but, Mama darling, I want to give a ball, may I?"

Nancy's green-gold eyes glowed with excitement; her lips were parted showing the tips of her pointed teeth. Once had she really been as beautiful as Nancy? Katie wondered.

"Well, darling, I want to say 'Yes', but

first I must discuss our finances with Aunt Liz."

"But I'll pay the expenses, Mama. I've still plenty of money in the Standard Bank and I've also got my second big diamond."

"No, no, I don't like you to pay for a party in your own home—but if I could find some way to invite the damned parliamentarians who are blocking Papa Paul's efforts about Saint Lucia Bay, and we can influence them in helping him, then I could stretch our finances."

"That sounds wonderful, Mama, but I'll gladly bear the costs. Shall we set the date for two weeks from today?"

"Why not?" Katie was thinking the ball could also be an engagement party for Terence and Elaine, but she must wait to tell Nancy this.

"Marvellous, Mama!" Nancy kissed Katie's cheek. "You *are* marvellous you know." She seemed as excited as a child as she smiled into Katie's eyes so like her own. "I'll go and tell Fleur and Josie." She raced down the path flanked by scarlet gladioli and purple irises.

Watching Nancy's beautiful figure in the full-skirted white dress, skimming over the chalky earth, both hands holding the wide brim of her pale straw hat, Katie enjoyed the lovely picture she made against the Jongerhoek mountains. Then Katie felt a surge of protective love for her eldest daughter and she prayed, "Dear God, cure her of this terrible incestuous love for Paul. Oh God, p-l-e-a-s-e let her meet some man she can fall in love with."

"Mama says we can have the party in two weeks," Nancy cried as she burst into her room.

"Hurrah! Hurrah!"

"So you two had better start writing your invitations for those guests in the far-off districts." Nancy was quite indifferent to these young sheep farmers who would be invited. "Have you thought about where all the guests from distant places will stay? We can take quite a few here and also at my stepfather's estate—Aunt Liz and Uncle Chris always stay there when Mama comes to Abend Bloem."

"And we can take a dozen or more." Fleur looked questioningly at Josephine who said, "Yes, we'll move into truckle beds, the boys won't mind that. Oh, isn't it exciting! Nancy, have you got a plan to get to know some officers?"

"Yes, yes, but don't ask me about it yet; I'll let you know in a few days' time what's happening."

They continued to discuss arrangements for the ball and the Coetzees asked what was the latest music in Europe? What new dances Nancy knew from Paris and would she teach them to the Coetzees? What should they wear? Would Nancy allow a Cape Town dressmaker to copy two of her gowns? She unwillingly agreed. Then they discussed the supper menu but Nancy told the girls her mother and aunt were expert at all that.

Still very excited they eventually went downstairs to join the family for before-luncheon sherry on the big front stoep.

On Sunday morning Katie accompanied by seven of her offspring, with Franz and Adrian on their brothers' knees, all squeezed into the big carriage drawn by four horses and left to attend Mass at Stellenbosch's small Catholic church.

Later, on her return to Abend Bloem, Katie was delighted to find her younger sisters, Sheila and Moira, with their families. Liz had arranged for them to come as a surprise to Katie. There was much hugging, kissing and laughing between the four beautiful sisters, then Katie's cheeks were kissed by her brothers-in-law.

Sheila's husband was an Englishman, Captain Lawrence, who held a fine position in the Government, and Moira's husband was a German, Sarel Van Rienfeld, engineer in charge of road works.

Amidst excited chatter from the grown-ups and laughter from the children of the four families, everyone sat down for lunch. Liz had arranged for two tables to be set up, one for the grown-ups, the other for the small children.

After lunch Kenneth rounded up his cricket team which he laughingly called "Abend Bloem's First Eleven" which consisted of the four married men, Katie's three sons, Liz's three sons, and Malcolm, Sheila's son in his early 'teens.

The opposing team was made up of friends from the district. The young ones galloped down the wide oak avenue making the dust fly, the older players arrived circumspectly with their women-folk in carriages.

The pitch was in a clearing of several acres, especially set aside for cricket. Under the shade of pepper and acacia trees, the ladies sat in wicker chairs, chatting and watching the game. Katie and Liz found these Sunday cricket matches the easiest way of entertaining their feminine neighbours. They found it less boring than being closeted with them in a drawing-room drinking coffee.

At four o'clock the game stopped and refreshments were served, then play continued until late afternoon when sherry and brandy were served on the big front stoep, then the visitors, including Sheila, Moira and their families, departed.

After supper in the drawing-room, Katie said to Liz, "Oh what a happy day it's been. Thank you, darling, for arranging it all."

Van Riebeck put an arm around Liz's shoulders. "You are quite a marvel. You take such good care of all of us and I don't know what Katje and I would have done without you and Chris running the estates."

"*Ach*, come on, man," Chris laughed, "it's not like you to make pretty speeches. You need another brandy."

The men went down to the end of the room where a silver tray held brandy and glasses and John came up to Katie and Liz.

"Well, we're leaving, Mother. Terence is already on the stoep. Coming to see us off?"

Katie and Liz went out to the steps where the Capecart was waiting, a coloured boy took Terence's bag and put it in the trunk, then climbed up on the driver's seat.

"See you Tuesday, Mother, at 4.30 in my consulting rooms," Terence murmured to Katie and she nodded understandingly, then they kissed each other's cheeks and he climbed into the Capecart.

"Well, cheerio, Mother and Aunt Liz, it's been a deuced pleasant week-end. See you next Friday evening." John kissed Katie and Liz's cheeks, then climbed into the Capecart, but his smart top-hat hit the white canvas hood and toppled into the cart, giving them all a little laugh. John quickly retrieved it and settled down beside Terence and the horses moved off down the long oak avenue.

13

THERE was no sound in the house when, early in the morning, in her room Nancy pulled out a sheet of her father's crested writing paper which her mother had scrupulously saved for the use of Richard Eaton's children. Nancy wrote the address and date, then she began.

"Your Excellency,
    This letter is being written at the request of my guardian and late father's cousin, His Grace The Duke of Rotherford, with whom I recently stayed in England. His Grace regrets that he cannot personally present me to you, but bade me write to introduce myself in his name.

I am
Yours sincerely
Nancy Eaton

PS. My late father, Captain Richard

Eaton, had the honour to serve Sir George Gray as aide-de-camp."

She re-read the letter and felt it would serve her purpose. Then she dressed and quietly went downstairs, as she did not wish to see any of the family and explain her reasons for going to Cape Town. She heard servants' voices in the kitchen but relinquished thought of breakfast and left the house. At the stables she instructed a boy to drive her in the carriage to the railway station at Stellenbosch. There she bought a ticket, then boarded the early morning train to Cape Town.

She sat down and, satisfied to have left home unobserved, she leaned back against the green plush upholstery. As the train started she glanced at the handful of passengers, decided they were uninteresting so she enjoyed the familiar countryside slipping by. Oh Lord, if only the railway-line planned to connect the Cape with Kimberley were finished and then from there the Natal line were started, that would cut the journey to a third to the Transvaal and her beloved Paul. Once she saw him, he would explain what extraordinary circumstances had occurred to force him into marrying Herta, for Nancy knew in her bones that he still loved her.

She was weary of beseeching God to release her from the bondage of loving Paul because God ignored her prayers.

When the train arrived at Cape Town railway station which boasted of its modernity by its electric lights, Nancy gave up her ticket and went out into sunlight and the Heerengracht, the town's fashionable thoroughfare.

Nancy smiled to herself as she watched women who proudly wore gowns and bonnets that five years ago had gone out of fashion in Europe. She stood for a moment looking at people boarding a six horse omnibus, then she quickly spotted a group of English officers, especially smart in tightly-fitting red tunics and black trousers. She wanted to talk to them now; it would save her the bother of calling on the Governor. Though tempted to smile at them she dare not and pretending to ignore their obviously admiring glances, she opened her lace parasol, placed it on her shoulder and started to saunter toward the Standard Bank's new building.

How sleepy and provincial looking Cape Town was, Nancy thought irritably compared with the bustle of Paris and London, with their great buildings and monuments. Here was only natural beauty, the purple blueness of Table Mountain, towering above the town, the oak trees, the zinc tubs stuffed with brilliant flowers, the coloured sellers beside them seated on the pavement kerbs, and at the street's end the jetty and blue sea beyond. Well, Nancy told herself, she alone was to blame for being in South Africa.

Suddenly she felt so wretched that she changed her mind about going to the Bank and crossed over to the shipping-office where she enquired about an early booking for England, but the four ships leaving during the next month were filled. Well, that settled that, she told herself and as the clock on the wooden tower struck eleven she decided to hire a cab and go directly to Government House. Arriving at the imposing looking building she leaned out of the cab and handed her letter addressed to Sir Hercules Robinson to a sentry, then ordered the driver to take her to the railway station. She hated Cape Town today.

At the station she learned that the next train to Stellenbosch was in an hour. Irritated at having to wait in the gloomy station where coloured sweepers were releasing the dust with their big straw brooms she left and went to a nearby tavern she knew. "The Jolly Sailor" sported a notice: "Coffee served as early as morning gun fire." It was almost empty now for the customary hour to drink mid-morning coffee was eleven o'clock. Nancy sat down in a corner and told the coloured waiter to bring her coffee and hot milk. Then she picked up a much used copy of *The Cape Argus* attached to a band of wood so that customers should not purloin it. Without real interest she scanned the front page and read.

"During the last few years we have made fine progress and all has gone well financially in the Colony, troops and contractors are everywhere and our exports, mainly of wool and wheat have risen. The diamond production and sales at Kimberley have mounted beyond anyone's dreams. Building has been resumed on the Cape Houses of Parliament; Cape Town now proudly owns a large reservoir and its breakwater shelters large vessels. Passage to England has been reduced to three weeks and the most important point of our progress is the work on the railway going to the diamond fields."

Nancy slammed the paper down with disgust, thinking, But no railway has been started to connect with the Transvaal. She suddenly was sick to her soul of everything. Without Paul's presence South Africa was intolerable to her. Life had treated her rottenly: the first boy she had fallen in love with, a midshipman, Harold Best, had been drowned at sea. The second man she fell in love with and married turned out to be a pederast and suddenly loathed to touch her; when she started to undress a sort of disgust drove him from the room. Then her infant son had died of plague. Not content to torture her with all this, God had let her believe that the Duke of Rotherford was in love with her and she had revelled in the thought of being his wife. Then she discovered it was her mother whom he loved. Later had come the stark knowledge that she and Paul were wildly and incestuously in love.

The waiter broke into her miserable reverie as he put coffee and hot milk before her and she suddenly said, "I don't feel well. Bring me a *big* brandy—please."

"Yes, Missus," he said and went to obey.

She had discovered in Paris that half a dozen brandies helped her over the agony of wanting Paul and half a dozen more helped her to return the Count's affection. With one hand she poured hot milk into the cup and simultaneously with the other she poured coffee and made a good mixture. She started to sip it when the brandy came, then put the cup down and took two mouthfuls of brandy. She spluttered and coughed; Cape brandy was harsh, not like the velvet-smooth Courvoisier the Count had plied her with in Paris.

"Boy, bring me another big brandy," she called to the waiter and when it came she finished it in a couple of swallows. It went tingling through her and almost immediately she felt less miserable. Then she drank the coffee, paid and left.

On the way to the railway station, she decided to buy a bottle of brandy to keep secretly in her room, and in the bottle store she asked the salesman to draw the cork, as she had no corkscrew in her room. Brandy was very helpful upon occasions but she must be careful not to drink too much as she once did in Paris.

Alone in her part of the train, she opened the bottle and drank three full mouthfuls then replaced the cork and pushed the bottle way down in her reticule so that no-one would notice it. Afterwards she dozed until the train stopped at Stellenbosch.

When she got out, she saw her mother, seated in a train that was just pulling out, so Nancy had no time to try to attract her attention.

Arriving in Cape Town, Katie did some small shopping, then took a cab to Terence's consulting rooms and as soon as he greeted her with a wide smile she knew all was well about Elaine.

Kissing her cheek he led her to a chair

saying, "Thank God, Elaine was wonderful when I told her about little David."

"Terry—praise God! I must admit I was a little afraid she might be upset."

"She was surprised, of course, but there was no question of her being shocked or . . . well . . . disgusted. She just said, 'What happened in your life before we met isn't my business, Terence, but I admire you for telling me.' Then she added, 'When we're married, I think David should live with us. You'd surely want your son with you'."

"What an angel of a girl! You've been blessed, really blessed." Katie glanced with satisfaction at Terence's new knee-length well cut jacket and tight fitting trousers. "That's the finest suit I've ever seen you in. Elaine's influence?"

He nodded. "She made me go to the English tailor instead of the Malay who always used to make my clothes. Elaine thought I should have this suit to wear at the hospital board meetings."

"She's absolutely right about that."

Katie was ashamed that she had not insisted upon Terence using the English tailor months ago when she had compared his clothes with John's impeccable London suits when John had returned from England.

"Come on, Mother, I've ordered a carriage to take us to Sir Daniel's home."

"Yes, I'm ready, but just let me give you this." She drew open the cords of her black silk reticule and her fingers dug down to the bottom to close over a small heart-shaped box. She pulled it out and handed it to Terence. "This is for you, darling, to give to Elaine."

He looked astonished and taking the little red plush box from her he pressed the clasp, the lid snapped open and he exclaimed delightedly at sight of a heart-shaped sapphire, the size of his little fingernail, surrounded by small diamonds.

"It's beautiful, Mother, but it's *your* ring."

"No, no, your father's grandmother bequeathed it to him when he was a child to someday give to his fiancée. Later, with great love he gave it to me. Now, darling, with great love I give it to Sean's son." She smiled up at him with trembling lips, her great eyes grown misty. "I know very well that a young doctor can't afford to buy an engagement ring."

"Mother," Terence's dark eyes glowed with love for her, "you are the *best* mother a fellow ever had. I'll put it on Elaine's finger as soon as we get there."

Sir Daniel Musgrove's home at Sea Point, a short distance from Cape Town, was built high off the beach road, as if tucked into the rocks by magic. He had bought it after his wife's death for he and his daughter loved the close proximity of the sea.

Katie and Terence climbed a long flight of steep rock steps to the open hall-door where Sir Daniel and Elaine, having heard their voices, stood waiting for them.

Elaine's appearance immediately delighted Katie. She was above middle height, with a slight figure, dressed in pale grey half-mourning for her mother. A lovely long throat supported her pale oval face, like a flower on a stem; her eyes were large and a golden-hazel; a cloudy mass of chestnut-coloured hair stood out almost like a halo around her head.

Her voice was low and soft, as she said, "We're delighted you've come, Mrs. Van

Riebeck," and Sir Daniel joined in, "So very good of you. Come in, come in."

Sir Daniel was a small, thin man, with a lean face and tender eyes that Katie associated with aesthetics—his thick untidy grey hair added to a priest-like effect.

Seated in the drawing-room, with wide windows showing unlimited sea, Katie's swift glance approved of everything she saw; exquisite antique furniture in a mixture of rare applewood and walnut; oil paintings—obviously family portraits, for two of the women resembled Elaine; a Viennese carpet of flowers and leaves in muted shades; all was in excellent taste and obviously the Musgroves had shipped everything from England.

"What a lovely home you have up here." The enthusiastic words spilled from Katie and Sir Daniel chuckled, "You're very kind, but it's rather an eagle's eyrie, isn't it—I mean having to climb all those steps?"

"It's well worth it, sir," Terence said. "Up here you feel close to heaven—and I love the sound of the sea pounding the rocks."

As Elaine shot him an affectionate glance, Katie felt deeply satisfied; then Elaine looked at Katie. "After that climb up seventy steps I should imagine you'd like tea now."

"Yes, thank you." As Elaine tinkled a little brass handbell beside her, Katie said to Sir Daniel, "The sea looks very inviting. Do you swim much?"

"Oh yes, we both do. The swimming and the view is why we bought the house. I suppose you know that at a certain point down there you can sit on a rock and dangle one foot in the Atlantic and the other in the Indian Ocean?" He seemed as delighted as a child by the phenomenon.

At that moment a coloured maid in white entered in answer to the bell and Elaine ordered tea.

"At Abend Bloem we're some miles from the beach but the countryside is lovely," Katie said. "I hope you and your daughter will visit us for a week-end?"

"We should like that very much, shouldn't we, Papa?"

Sir Daniel nodded. "Indeed yes, Terence is always extolling the beauty of Abend Bloem. You know, Mrs. Van

Riebeck, your son is a very capable doctor, I'm proud to have him on the hospital staff."

"Not half as proud as I am to be there, sir."

Katie felt this was a propitious time to talk of the betrothal. "Sir Daniel, I'm so happy that you and your daughter have done Terence the honour of accepting his proposal of marriage."

Elaine's pale face flushed with shyness and Sir Daniel said, "I couldn't ask for a finer son-in-law than Terence."

"Or I for a finer husband," Elaine murmured glancing at Terence with love-filled eyes.

Terence felt his throat go dry and tighten. "I'm luckier than any man alive."

"Oh—it's lovely," Katie cried joyously, wondering why on earth Terence didn't give Elaine the ring? "Elaine, you're a daughter-in-law most women dream of having; Terence has told me you'd like to be a doctor yourself."

"I'd like to specialize in children's illnesses—but now I'll be content to care for my two splendid Doctors—Papa and Terry."

"You'd make a fine doctor, my pet," her father said, "but I wouldn't like you to confront all the opposition there is against women studying medicine." Sir Daniel turned to Katie. "I'm thinking of the First Doctor of Modern Times—Elizabeth Blackwell. Forty years ago in Philadelphia she was stoned by the public for studying medicine and for working in an anatomical laboratory. People considered her a freak."

"Poor girl, how disgraceful!" Katie remembered having heard about Elizabeth Blackwell.

"She had to disguise herself as a man," Elaine said, "then later she went to study in Paris—as a woman—and she was accepted at the Maternelle. But at the great hospital she was incarcerated for four months at a time and given only one free day to go out." Elaine's eyes flashed with indignation. "Still at Maternelle 3000 babies were born per month so she learned a great deal."

"Didn't she later become friendly with Florence Nightingale?" Katie was beginning to remember the story. "Once I gave some talks in London to aid the suffragettes and some of them were upset because Doctor Blackwell had refused to help the American Women's Rights Movement."

"Ah yes," Sir Daniel laughed, "when the Movement invited her to join them she replied, 'I do not sympathise with an anti-man movement; many men have been too kind to me and women's freedom may be gained in another way. The object of education is not concerned with men or women's rights but with development of the human soul and body'."

"Well, I don't think she should have refused to join the Women's Rights Movement, Papa. After all it was born of necessity. Do you agree, Mrs. Van Riebeck?"

"Most decidedly. Someone has to help improve conditions for women. For example, take the divorce laws and inheritance laws, men have all the rights and as for women ever being given the right to vote—heaven only knows if that will ever come."

"Mother—Mother," Terence laughingly remonstrated, "really you shouldn't become so upset about it."

"Oh, Terry, I'm *glad* your mother feels

like that. My Mama did too." Her lovely face grave with indignation, Elaine turned to Katie. "When I wanted to read History at Oxford, Papa had great difficulty having me accepted at Lady Margaret Hall. It was founded only four years ago and though women may attend lectures and university examinations, they may *not* have degrees."

"But that's infamously unfair and. . . ." Katie broke off as the maid carried in a large silver tray set with silver tea pot, kettle and delicate Crown Derby china.

As Elaine poured tea then Terence handed it around, Katie told herself that in his excitement Terence had forgotten about the ring.

Hoping to prompt him, she cried, "Without wishing to appear as an interfering mother, I must ask about your plans for the wedding, because, alas, I'll have to return to the Transvaal before too long." She surreptitiously held up a finger to Terence and toyed with her ring.

"Oh heavens, Elaine!" Terence burst out. "I haven't given you your engagement ring." He swiftly brought the case from his pocket, snapped it open, took the ring out, grasped Elaine's left hand and slipped the sapphire heart on to her engagement finger.

She looked down at it with joy surging through her, wishing that her mother were alive to share this moment with her. Eyes swimming with tears she looked up at a blushing Terence. "It's the loveliest ring I've ever seen, Terry," she murmured.

"I'm glad you like it, Elaine." He longed to crush her in his arms, to tell her he would adore her until his last breath but instead he held out the jewel case. "Look, it's from Shannon, Limerick."

Elaine gazed at the red satin-lined lid with a small label, "O'Connors, fine jewellery, Shannon". "Fancy, Papa, my engagement ring is from Ireland."

"It's a family ring," Terence explained. "My great-great-grandmother gave it to my father."

Sir Daniel rose to look at the jewel case. "What an extraordinary coincidence," he said in a hushed voice. "I bought your mother's betrothal ring from O'Connors in Shannon."

They were all stirred by the coincidence as if it were a good omen, then excited words burst from Elaine.

"Oh, we must put engagement announcements in *The Times* and the *Cape Argus*—don't worry, Terry, I'll see to that, you haven't the time, and about the wedding date, it must be soon. When do you leave, dear Mrs. Van Riebeck?" Already she loved Terence's mother.

"In about a month, I should think."

"That will give us plenty of time, but, please, I think we should be married very quietly—because I'm still in half-mourning for Mama."

"Of course," Terence swiftly agreed.

"I've a suggestion," Katie said. "We've a darling little Catholic Church in Stellenbosch that Terence has attended since he was about five. Why not be married there and have a quiet wedding breakfast at Abend Bloem?"

"Oh, but as Father of the Bride it's my job to care for that." Sir Daniel looked almost indignant as he pulled at his grey hair.

"Oh, please, sir, let Mother care for it," Terence said. "She's an absolute expert at such things."

So it was agreed and when Sir Daniel went for champagne so that they could drink a toast to the betrothed pair, Elaine asked Katie, "I can't be married in white with a veil when I'm still in half-mourning, can I?"

Katie suffered for Elaine in her grief over her mother's loss but she said, "I truly believe your mother would want you to be married in white and not mauve or grey."

"I don't care what you wear!" Terence burst out.

"What's all this? What's all this?" Sir Daniel asked as he came in carrying a tray with a champagne bottle and glasses. Elaine told him the problem and as he held the bottle to uncork it with both hands he said, "You will definitely be married in white! Why ever do you think your mother cherished her Chantilly lace wedding veil for all those years? And you'll wear the wax orange blossoms too."

When they had drunk toasts and enjoyed the champagne, Sir Daniel suddenly said, "Now what about a swim for all of us, Mrs. Van Riebeck, you too my dear. Elaine can loan you a bathing dress. Come on now." He thought Katie was a splendid woman who would not mind his bossiness. "Come on, doctor's orders, for the health."

Katie laughed, "I always obey doctor's orders," and she went off with Elaine, thinking Sir Daniel, with his Irish charm, was nostalgically reminiscent of her father when she had been a child. She easily fitted into a pair of Elaine's long black baggy trousers that gathered in around her ankles, and into the long matching tunic, with pleated skirt, high neck and elbow length sleeves. With Elaine wearing a similar bathing dress, scarves tying up their hair, they joined Sir Daniel and Terence, their bodies enveloped in long bathing suits.

Laughingly descending the seventy steps, they reached the beach and splashed into the sunlit sea. Sir Daniel, a strong swimmer, was soon a distance ahead of the others and Katie veered away from Terence and Elaine to give them a chance to chat alone.

Katie was content to float on her back, arms outstretched beside her. She felt at one with the sea as she drifted quietly, her eyes on the blue dome of the heavens and listened to the nearby laughter of Terence and Elaine. She sent a prayer of thankfulness up to God, for the wonderful girl Terence would be blessed with for a wife. Then she added, "Dear Sean, if you can see your son now, be happy in his good fortune."

At last one of her children would be married decently and happily, unlike the runaway wedding of Nancy and Eric; the crude wedding of Paul's in a magistrate's office to Herta, a Transvaal farm girl, whom Katie sensed was only good for bedding. And the last wedding of Mary, already two months' pregnant, with a paid man for a groom. But with Terence and Elaine, Katie encouraged herself, God was relenting toward her and turning His face back to her.

14

"OH, how lovely!" Nancy cried triumphantly as she rushed into the little den where Liz and Katie sat heads bent over the estate's accounts.

"What's happened?" Katie looked up from a ledger at Nancy waving a stiff cream, gold-edged card above her head.

"An invitation for dinner at Government House. Just come by special messenger." She handed the card to Katie who read aloud. "Sir Hercules and Lady Robinson request the pleasure of the company of Miss Nancy Eaton and chaperone to dinner on. . . ."

"I didn't know you knew Sir Hercules, darling." Katie handed the card back.

"I didn't, Mama." Nancy flung herself into an easy chair and laughingly told her mother and aunt of how she had sent the letter to the Governor. "Of course I knew that even if Sir Hercules didn't know Howard, the very name—Duke of

Rotherford—would open all doors. Wasn't I clever?"

Liz made a little disapproving sound. "Clever, but not truthful, Nancy."

"Oh, Aunt Liz—what does it matter? I've not hurt anyone." Nancy's green-gold eyes sparkled with fun. "Mama, you must be my chaperone."

Katie did not hesitate for a second. The dinner might provide her with a chance to somehow advance Paul's cause with the Governor about Saint Lucia Bay. "Yes, I will, darling."

"Wonderful!" Nancy jumped up, "I'll send a stable boy off with my reply at once," and she rushed from the room.

"Really, Nancy has inherited a lot of your spirit, darling," Liz smiled affectionately at Katie, "but still, I don't think she should have written an untruth to the Governor."

"Liz, my love, Nancy realizes we no longer have any connections with Government House so she's made some in her own way. I don't really blame her; she wants more amusement out of life." Katie was relieved that Nancy would enlarge her acquaintanceship in the Cape lest secretly she was nursing an idea of going to the gold fields to see young Paul. "The dinner is tomorrow night so, as Van Riebeck will be visiting Hofmeyer and his 'Afrikander Bond' meeting, I'll be free to go." She changed the subject. "Oh, I'm so happy about Terence's engagement."

"Indeed, yes—but when you told me about it last night I could hardly believe it. He's never breathed a word about Elaine."

"I think that's because he wanted to make sure first that she'd accept him. She's a wonderful person, Liz, you'll like her. Well, I suppose it's back to slavery for us," she chuckled as she turned a page of the big ledger before her. "Heavens, how I hate paper work, I think I'd rather help to pluck the ostriches, despite the smell and all those little feathers that float up my nose."

Liz laughed understandingly. "And I certainly prefer working on our fruit project. Darling, I hope that Van Riebeck's work will keep him here so you can attend Terence and Elaine's wedding."

"Oh, Liz—I pray so but I swear— nothing will make me miss *this* wedding, it will be a compensation for Mary's and Paul's weddings—both of which I hated."

The dinner at which Katie and Nancy were guests at Government House was a disappointment to Katie, although she knew she looked beautiful in one of Nancy's Parisian gowns of green satin trimmed with gold, for once her beauty failed to interest a man, for Sir Hercules was coldly polite—nothing more. Then it flashed to her. Was she not the wife of the famous Commandant Van Riebeck, a hero of the Majuba battle? Sir Hercules, like every Englishman, could not stomach such a defeat by an enemy less than a quarter its size.

But for Nancy, daughter of an Englishman, second cousin to the Duke of Rotherford, the Governor was all charm and presented to her the most eligible of the dashing-looking officers.

After dinner when dancing began in the ballroom, for Katie as well as Nancy there was a plethora of partners but this meant nothing to Katie; she had come to influence the Governor but he did not invite her to dance, for there were many titled ladies present to whom he must give homage but it meant Katie had no opportunity to talk to him.

When the party ended and she and Nancy were settled in their carriage Nancy was exuberant. "I've met some wonderful officers and they are all coming to our ball —I'm delighted."

Katie was worried by Nancy's blurred speech. Surely she had not drunk too much? Katie decided not to remark upon it now and so spoil Nancy's happy mood. Instead she said, "I'm glad, darling, but I'm afraid I wasn't able to help Papa Paul. I wanted to invite Sir Hercules to Abend Bloem, as years ago I was able to invite Sir George Grey, who was Governor, to a ball at Abend Bloem and it turned out to be very beneficial to Papa Paul."

Nancy was not listening; she was aglow with her triumphs with this new group of men; life was going to be different for her.

Katie and Nancy spent the night at Saint George's Hotel for it was too late to take the journey to Stellenbosch, and at dawn, still in evening dress, they returned home to find that Van Riebeck and Van der Byl were back from Swellendam. Nancy was suffering with a thumping headache and sick stomach; she had drunk far too much champagne at Government House, not only during dinner but because each of her dancing partners had brought her a glass to drink with him when he toasted her beauty. Now she slipped away from the family, went to the huge kitchens and ordered the maids to bring a copper bath to her room, with jugs of hot water. After the bath she intended to go to bed.

When Van Riebeck was alone with Katie in their bedroom, he angrily demanded, "Why in the name of hell did you go to Government House? That bastard Sir Hercules for weeks has been serving me with excuses not to see me! Then you go to the bloody man's dinner party!"

They stood confronting each other. "I'm terribly sorry, Paul darling, but I didn't know that or naturally I wouldn't have gone. Damn Sir Hercules for his discourtesy to you!" She turned her back to him saying, "Unbutton this bodice please, darling."

His big fingers fumbled over the tiny satin buttons and loops. "Perhaps it's spite, because of our victory at Majuba, but perhaps he actually is not able to reach a decision about Saint Lucia Bay; after all, the real government comes from Westminster."

He finished unbuttoning the last button. "There you are. Well, Lord Derby might yet help, God knows." He watched her stepping out of the wide pleated skirt and she swiftly told him all about Terence and Elaine, ending with, "I'm sure you'll like her and her father. I hope they'll come out soon to meet all the family. He's Irish," she smiled, "like your mad wife."

"Well, if Elaine has a hundredth part of your character, darling, Terence is a lucky man."

"Oh, she's lovely and the wedding is arranged for a month from now."

She was at the mahogany dressing-table taking hairpins from her hair and to him she looked so appealing, so soft and desirable in her calico long drawers and frilled camisole that he longed to lie with her at this moment, so he strode to her and caught her in his arms. "But we may not be here another month, my Katje." Seeing the distress on her face he said, "Poor

Katje, you certainly created your own type of hell when you married me. It's so often a toss-up for you, isn't it? Where does your devotion call you? What is your duty? Oh, don't deny it—it's always cropping up —the children or the. . . ."

"The man I love. Remember I have loved you before even Terence was born and long before others were born, or thought of—*you* are my first love."

His blue eyes grew almost dark with love for her, but then a questioning look lightened them. "Yes, I know that beloved, but your children naturally have an immense pull on you."

"Would you have me love them less? What about Paul—our love child? My heart is aching to see him on the Witwatersrand. And our little sons Franz and Adrian, don't you think I longed to hold their little bodies in my arms during the time I was away? I love all of my children—but for you—I have a different— an all-absorbing love."

He crushed her to him, kissing her with all of his being. God had been good to him with this woman even though she had dragged him through Hell's fires and by marrying her, instead of a Boer woman, he had flung away all chance of being President of the South African Republic—but life with her had been recompense for it. Then as his hand began to caress her breast there came a thumping on the door, then Franz and Adrian's voices cried, "Mama—Mama, may we come in?"

She smiled teasingly up at Van Riebeck, left his arms and started pulling on a cotton gown. "This time it's 'our' children, darling, who are interrupting us."

He gave a good-tempered chuckle as she called out, "Come in, my loves," then the door burst open and the golden-haired boys threw themselves on their parents.

"Papa, come and show us some tricks," Franz demanded. "Flick some birds from the sky with the long whip."

"Yes, Papa, and I want you to bend an ox's head down to touch the ground." Adrian caught at Van Riebeck's hand and started pulling him toward the door. "Come on—you too, Mama, come and play with us."

Some hours later as the family sat on the front stoep drinking after-luncheon coffee they lazily watched some of the children chasing butterflies with nets whilst others threw sticks for the dogs to catch, then a coloured rider cantered down the wide avenue and around the back of the house.

A few seconds later a barefoot coloured maid brought a small silver tray with a cable on it—and handed it to Liz who picked it up, then said, "It's for you, Katie. Of course the maids can't read." Liz handed the grey envelope to Katie.

With a quickening heart, for she sensed the cable's message, Katie slit the envelope open, read the words, then exclaimed with false amazement. "Heavens! Just listen to this—it's from Howard and says, 'I gave permission for Mary's marriage to Cosimo Urbino in a Catholic Church in Florence stop hope you will approve stop she very happy stop love to all family Howard'."

"Good Lord!" Kenneth whistled in surprise and Nancy laughed, "That's fast work for our quiet Mary."

"It seems extraordinarily quick," Liz said looking with bewilderment at the others.

"Isn't Rotherford being rather presumptuous?" Van Riebeck asked annoyed by

Howard's intervention, "By what right does 'he' give permission?"

"But he *is* Richard's children's supposed guardian," Katie said placatingly, "I'm surprised by the marriage, of course, but I told you it was love at first sight when Mary and Cosimo met. I pray they'll be happy."

"Who is this fellow, Cosimo Urbino?" Chris asked, "I don't think you told me, Katje."

"He's a very promising young painter. I must say I liked him. He's of good family and quite insane about Mary's delicate type of beauty. I suppose we should consider this as good news."

"Well, they are two artists together, between her singing and his painting I suppose they'll have plenty in common," Kenneth said but he was astounded by the marriage, for Mary had been so insanely in love with Sannie. He was impatient to talk privately to his mother but was obliged to wait.

"Yes, perhaps the marriage is a good thing," Van Riebeck said reflectively thinking that Mary seemed hardly worldly enough to be alone in a strange city with only Rotherford's old aunt. "It must take a load off your mind, Katje."

She nodded, "Yes, it does. I've a feeling that it will all turn out well. I'll write to Mary tonight. Well, well, my brood seem suddenly marriage minded, Paul, Terence and now Mary."

Nancy got to her feet. "Well, Aunt Liz, as you've given me the job of arranging the menu for the party with old Sara I'd better go to the kitchens and start." She went into the house but not to the kitchens —she went to her room; she needed brandy.

"Mother, how would you like to ride with me around the ostrich farm?" Kenneth asked, "I want to show you some little changes I've made."

"Why I'd love to—by the way, *you're* not being married at any second, are you?" Katie asked with a laugh and the others joined in.

A little later as Katie and Kenneth were in the stables he said, "I suggested the ostrich farm because I wanted to drag you away to talk to you."

"I guessed that. You're of course astonished about Mary."

"Jumping Jerusalem! Am I!" He lifted Katie into the saddle then swung a leg across his own horse and they rode out of the stables.

Choosing a favourite route they passed under the shade of a long row of acacia trees where honeysuckle had climbed and dripped from their branches, perfuming the air.

"How could Mary have married so quickly, Mother?" Kenneth muttered. "She *must* have loved Sannie, otherwise how could she have been so mad as to lie with him?"

Kenneth must never know Mary was pregnant by Sannie. "She's unpredictable, but to be fair to her, I tried to make her transfer her affections from Sannie to the artist and thank God, my plan succeeded. Now at least we won't have her coming back here and crying on Sannie's mother's bosom and disgracing our entire family."

"Yes, I think perhaps you were wise."

"Sometimes I think that she's a better Christian than we are in that she considers blacks and whites as equals."

"That's fine to talk of but if she'd

married Sannie she would have soon found out what the world thinks."

"That reminds me, Ken darling: Aunt Liz told me Sannie's sister, Cillie, is convinced that a jealous lover murdered Sannie over one of our parlourmaids. I'm afraid of the maids' gossip; if they keep it up they might somehow stumble on the truth. I don't think Cillie should stay at Abend Bloem. I considered taking her to Lydenburg but, as we shan't be leaving until after Terence's wedding, it means she'll be around to gossip for another month. I'm sure Aunt Sheila would be glad to take her as she's such a good parlourmaid."

"That's a damned good idea. You know ever since the night that Sannie shot himself I've felt that something might get out. So far we've been lucky, but a girl like Cillie could start up a thread of suspicion that could end up with the truth coming out about Sannie being Mary's lover and point at me as the one who killed him."

"My God, Ken!" Katie reined her horse in and he did the same as she stared over at him with terror weakening her. "I've never thought of that."

He took his wide-brimmed hat off and mopped his perspiring forehead with a white silk handkerchief. "I'm glad that you *didn't!* But the truth is I was *ready* to kill him—luckily for me, he saved me from it. But don't worry; no court would convict me if I *had* killed him—though we still don't want the exposure. Come on, let's go home and I'll drive Cillie off this afternoon. I'll feel better when she's away from Abend Bloem and starts to forget the whole rotten business."

The following afternoon Katie was lying down when Van Riebeck brought letters out from Cape Town's Post Office and handed one to Katie. "This will please you, Katje—from Paul." He sat on the edge of the bed as her eyes flew over the pages covered by the big bold handwriting.

> Camp 3
> Witwatersrand
> (Not sure of the date, up
> here, all days merge together)

Dearest Parents,

Hope all is well with you and the family. This letter is long overdue so forgive me but when we first arrived here and "settled down" there was so much to do the days were not long enough, also I delayed writing because I wanted to give a cheerful report.

Alas, I'm still not able to. My land undoubtedly has gold on it but the difficulty of retrieving it is enormous. Digging is in rock ground and the mining of the diamond fields which we did in Kimberley was child's play compared with this. It appears to me, and to friends I have made here, that a man will go nowhere without machinery and this is expensive. Also water must somehow be piped in. I have of course learned the technique of crushing a sample of the ore with pestle and mortar, then panning it to show a "tail" of gold. Doing this by hand is a wearisome business.

Yet I intend to remain here, for I feel instinctively that I shall succeed and find wealth eventually.

There are hundreds of speculators here and all feel like I do. There are a thousand diggers alone on Moddies Farm.

It's hot, dusty and windy. The nights can be very cold. Herta seems content and works hard at cooking and going around to buy food which is snapped up very quickly.

That's all for now, hope you'll soon be back in Lydenburg and that we can meet.

Much love to all
Paul.

Katie looked up at Van Riebeck with worried eyes, "What do you think about it?"

"Think? I think pretty much as all Dutchmen do, that wealth is in land and cattle." He held up a silencing hand. "Oh, I know, I know—fortunes were made in diamonds and I suppose will be made in gold, too, but for the few who grow wealthy, there are thousands and *thousands* who break their backs and their hearts. It's not the life I would have chosen for Paul."

She felt guilty because it was she who was instrumental in Paul being at the gold fields. "He certainly has more hope of gaining wealth on the gold mines than elephant hunting on the Zambesi, and he wasted three years on that."

"If that's a reproach for me, I accept it. After having sent him to the University in Holland to study law I made a grave mistake by taking him away, but you know that I believed he'd continue his studies in Pretoria." He shrugged his wide shoulders. "Unfortunately that did not appeal to him."

Katie sat up and caught hold of his arm. "Come on, darling, we shouldn't feel depressed about him just because he's having temporary difficulties; we've no right to expect him to become rich overnight. Let's go down and have a brandy with Chris and Liz."

"You're right, but I feel generally uneasy about things in the Transvaal. I got a report from Kruger that says the Volksraad finances are very low. If only we could settle this damned Saint Lucia Bay affair we could start exporting our produce so much more cheaply that we could sell three times as much!"

But the next day as Katie, Van Riebeck, Liz and Chris sat in the small drawing-room, a special coloured messenger brought a letter for Van Riebeck which shattered the South African Republic's hopes. It was from the Governor.

Dear Commandant Van Riebeck,
   It is my unhappy duty to inform you of the fact that news has just reached me from London as follows.
   "Inform President Kruger and his Volksraad that after much consideration Her Majesty's Imperial Government has decided it expedient to maintain possession of Saint Lucia Bay which was ceded to Great Britain by the Zulu King Panda in 1842."

"The bloody bastards!" Van Riebeck's clenched fist thumped the table, "Read it, Chris, for God's Holy sake!"
   Chris read the letter. "It's infamous! Damned infamous! Pure and unadulterated trickery!"
   "The bloody English have denied us the right to Saint Lucia Bay!" Van Riebeck's deep blue eyes blazed with an insensate hate—they were the eyes of a killer. "After we fought for the Zulus and had an honest treaty with them for the Bay in

payment. Great God! What a swindle for the English to revive a forty-year-old obsolete treaty. Now our only chance of having a port is to make the Portuguese let us have Delagoa Bay."

He swung around to Katie. "Pack! We'll trek at dawn. I won't waste another minute down here—I'm needed in the Transvaal."

"I'll help you prepare, Paul—see to the greasing of the wheels and the guns. You'll take Jantse of course as head boy," as Chris spoke he glanced at Katie and Liz. "You two had better start provisioning the wagons."

Katie stood in a half daze, then she nodded to Chris and grabbing Liz's arm she left on trembling legs. Outside in the hall she told Liz. "I *must* go with Paul, Liz! This is one of the worst blows of his life."

"But it's cruel for you to have to miss Terence's wedding."

"Yes, it is—but at this time I dare not fail Paul! He needs me! Will you start to stock the wagons. Oh Liz! I feel half dead with disappointment to miss Terence's wedding, but even more I feel for Paul.

It's so damned unfair of the English government, but they're mad if they believe the Transvaalers will lie down to this treachery! Watch my words, there'll be another war and this time I hope they'll drive the damned English into the sea."

"Shall I send word into town to Terence and John, telling them you are leaving?"

"No don't, we'll be gone before they can come. They'll understand when you tell them later. Now I'm going to find Maarje to start packing." Lifting the hems of her skirts she started to run up the stairs.

Liz watched her go thinking indignantly of what a slave her love for Van Riebeck had made of her. All Katie's private wishes had been swept away for her husband's interest. The Biblical words rang in Liz's head.

Whithersoever thou goest I will go,
Thy people shall be my people . . .

Wonderfully noble Katie. Then Liz swallowed back her sobs and hurried off to the kitchens to start organizing food supplies for the wagons.

15

THE two covered wagons, each drawn by a span of sixteen oxen, moved slowly, monotonously. They had traversed the great arid Karoo, climbed part of the dangerous Drakensberg Range that ran almost the length of South Africa and now they were crossing the vast mustard-hued veld with its far horizon where earth was starting to merge with red gold sky of approaching sunset.

The unrelenting scene was nothing but spewed up kopjes—great hostile-looking boulders, ant-heaps rising to eight feet or more, abortive looking thorn trees and low scrub bushes. Centipede and tarantula impudently lay about the oxen's and horses' hooves, for Van Riebeck and his faithful Zulu, Jantse, man and master for over thirty years, rode on either side of the wagons as protection from wild beasts and to hunt meat throughout the trek.

Seated on folding chairs at the back of the lead wagon as it swayed along on its high wheels, Katie and Eileen looked back at the veld. "Thank God it's cool at last," Katie said. "We can take off our masks, darling." She started to untie the supple goatskin mask.

"Oh, I'm glad, I hate wearing a mask, it makes me feel hotter," Eileen swiped out at the buffalo flies around her head.

"Long ago on my first trek, the Dutch women taught me to wear a goatskin mask as protection against the sun. You must *never* go without one—I've told you that since you were a little girl."

"I know, Mama, and if it keeps my skin as lovely as yours, it's worth being a bit uncomfortable."

From the front of the following wagon Franz called out to Van Riebeck riding alongside, "Papa, let's outspan soon, I'm so tired of being cooped up, I want to run about."

"Me too, Papa," Adrian cried.

"Be patient a little longer—a few more minutes then we'll halt."

Since leaving Abend Bloem Van Riebeck had forced the oxen to keep moving to the limit of their endurance in his eagerness to reach Lydenburg, and consequently had considerably reduced the children's playtime. But he told himself his young sons being of the South African Republic, must learn to endure hardship and so be strong, worthy citizens of their fine inheritance of freedom.

Before day began to die he shouted, "Halt!" to the coloured drivers and to the lead boys walking at the heads of the oxen. Even before the wagons were quite stationary, Franz and Adrian jumped to the ground.

"Hurrah! Hurrah!" The children shouted delightedly and started running wildly about but Katie cautioned, "Don't go too far away, boys."

"We won't, Mama."

"You play just around the wagons," Van Riebeck ordered as he dismounted. "This is lion country." As the boys suddenly stood still, staring up at him with wide blue eyes, he told them, "You've always got to remember wherever there are kopjes like those," . . . he pointed to the clumps of rocks . . . "you'll find lions, because there are caves in the rocks they can shelter in from the sun."

"But are we safe here, Papa?" Adrian

asked fearfully and Van Riebeck laughed with reassurance. "Certainly we are, the country has plenty of game for the lions to feed on. You remember we passed several herds of zebra and springbok today which means the lions can feed well. They don't deliberately go after man's flesh, only a wounded lion who's not fast enough to hunt animals becomes a man-eater. Now run around and stretch your legs while you have the chance."

Jantse was supervising the unharnessing of the oxen from the wagon shafts. They were allowed to crop around for a while, then still chained together the beasts were given water, then made by the drivers to squat down in a small circle to form a miniature laager around the two wagons that were lashed together. This was a small protection from possible attack of hostile Kaffirs or wild beasts.

Katie, Eileen and Maarje unpacked the food stores whilst Philip, Maarje's husband, a young English ex-sailor who had married the coloured nursemaid some years ago in Katie's London home, unslung the chicken coops that hung beneath the wagons and let the birds out to exercise and scrape around for food.

The coloured boys collected thorn bush and scrub, then fires were lit and Maarje started to cook vegetables, rice and eggs with which they would eat dried meat— biltong. Fresh meat would be a part of the next day's midday meal.

The Van Riebeck trek had covered eight hundred of the eleven hundred miles to Lydenburg and life had fallen into a routine. Each dawn, after breakfast of dried apple fritters and coffee, they inspanned. Katie rode in a wagon with Franz and Adrian where for a couple of hours she gave them lessons, just as she had given all of her children lessons when trekking with them.

At midday when the wagons halted whilst the oxen rested, the children played for a short while, then once more the trek was on the move. In the afternoons, Katie rode in a wagon with Eileen, and directed Eileen's reading. The works of Dickens and other classics were always on a book-shelf and all of Katie's children had benefited by them.

During the intense heat, Van Riebeck

sometimes rode in a wagon and refreshed his mind by reading his beloved Goethe's works which since a boy he had always carried in his saddlebags. When Katie commiserated with him about the loss of Saint Lucia Bay, he philosophically quoted from the great writer and thinker.

"Who never cuts his bread with tears, who never sat through the sorrowful night, weeping upon his bed, does not know You oh heavenly powers."

"You're absolutely splendid, darling, the way you've accepted this unfair defeat."

"I've not accepted it, Katje! But at the moment I must be patient until a time comes when I can act; for the Transvaalers will never forget this unfairness. Westminster has laid the cornerstone for future trouble for themselves."

And so they lived as best they could through the enforced monotony of trek life. Now one night when they had formed their laager, supped and washed in tin basins in the wagons, they retired. The family and Maarje to sleep in the wagons, the coloured drivers, oxen boys, Philip and

Jantse to sleep on the ground beneath the wagons.

The three camp fires were burning high, beside them two coloured sentries sat at watch. They would be relieved by another pair of sentries in three hours.

In Van Riebeck and Katie's wagon, they slept in the big double bed that ran the width of the wagon. He always wore shirt and trousers, with his veldshoen and gun at hand on the floor beside him. In the second wagon, Eileen and the small boys shared the bed, whilst Maarje slept on a lionskin covering the floor.

It was the middle of the night when screams of terror coming from Maarje awakened Paul and Katie who cried, "In God's name! What's happening!"

Paul sprang up, shoved his feet into his veldshoen, grasped his gun and rushed to swing the back flap open, then jumped across to the driver's box of the children's wagon lashed to his.

"What is it, Maarje?" he cried as he dashed in.

The girl was sitting up on the lionskin and the firelight coming through the open flap showed Paul the whites of her eyes rolling with fear.

"Murder—murder, *Baas*," she moaned. "All are dead."

The children were up now and Katie, climbing into the wagon, thanked God that they were safe. "No one's dead, Maarje!" She leant down and shook the girl's shoulders.

"Oh, Missus—Missus," Maarje screamed, "all are dead on the ground."

"That's rubbish!" Van Riebeck snapped, "You've just had a bad dream."

"She's having one of her prophetic spells," Katie muttered fearfully. "It's all right, Maarje—nothing terrible has happened."

"But why the hell don't Jantse and Philip look in here?" Van Riebeck barked as he lunged out of the wagon, then jumped to the ground his gun ready. Then he stood still—staring at the two sentries by the fire—assegais were sticking out of their slumped over dead bodies. He looked cautiously around so their murderers would not surprise him from behind then he called, "Jantse! Jantse! Philip!"

A low moan came from beneath a wagon

and Van Riebeck dashed to a fire to seize a burning brand and shine it under the wagon. Lying on the ground, Jantse's smoky brown eyes looked up at Paul. He was slashed across the chest and blood was pouring from the wound but he was alive. Beside him Philip looked dead from a spear thrust in his side that oozed blood. A frantic glance told Paul the oxen drivers and lead boys with throats cut were quite dead.

"My God, what happened, Jantse?"

"Basuto thieves—stole horses. They attack me in my sleep. Gone now, *Baas*—Hear Maarje screams—not return. Afraid of *Baas*' gun."

"Katje, Eileen, Maarje, come quickly!" Paul shouted.

In terror the women rushed off the wagon to Paul who told them what had happened; he was kneeling feeling Philip's heart. "Thank God, he's alive! Katje, you three women must carry him up to the wagon. I'll shoulder Jantse—but first I'll see if anyone is alive under the other wagon."

As the women were carrying Philip's slight body up into the wagon, Paul took the lighted brand to look under the second wagon. Four boys were dead and one driver bleeding from a stab wound in the shoulder was moaning. Paul left him to rush back to Jantse. He got the big Zulu across his shoulder, hefted him into the wagon and laid him on the bed beside Philip.

Katie was lighting the lantern as Paul said, "Bind up the wounds as fast as you can! For God's sake stop the bleeding! Now then, Maarje, don't go to pieces, but help the Missus save your husband's life."

Katie and Eileen already had the *huispoteck* open and were taking out medical supplies and bandages. Katie uncorked a bottle with her teeth and started pouring a solution of permanganate of potash to disinfect Jantse's wound, then she handed the bottle to Maarje to disinfect Philip's wound and took a roll of bandage that Eileen thrust at her and started to wrap it around Jantse's chest, with the help of Eileen.

Then Van Riebeck returned carrying the wounded driver and as he laid him beside Philip he ordered Franz who stood in a corner with Adrian, "Go for the brandy in my wagon quickly." The boy hesitated, his face puckered with terror of having to go out but Van Riebeck barked at him, "At once! Boer boys don't know fear!"

Tears streaming down her cheeks Maarje was helping Eileen to wrap bandages around and around Philip's body as Van Riebeck attended to the driver.

When the wounds had been cared for and Franz returned with the brandy, Van Riebeck held a tin mug with brandy to Jantse's lips whilst Katie and Eileen forced brandy down Philip's half-closed lips, he shuddered then swallowed and next they gave brandy to the driver.

"You will be well, Jantse," Van Riebeck told the Zulu whom he loved like a brother and with deep affection and assurance he gazed down into the smoky brown eyes.

"*Ja, Baas*—Jantse will be well." In turn he assured Van Riebeck who thanked God for the Zulu's indomitable spirit.

"You also will recover, your wound is not deep," Katie said consolingly to the driver who was swiftly regaining consciousness. "And you will get well, Philip," she said and was rewarded when the pale-faced Englishman forced a smile.

"Yes, thank you, Ma'am," then he managed a wink for Maarje who fell on her knees beside him, gently smoothing the damp hair from his sweat-laden forehead.

Franz and Adrian huddled together in a corner fearfully watching the scene until Van Riebeck glanced at them saying, "You two bring your mother a basin. Katje, there's water here in the wagon of course, so wash the blood off these men. I'm going to look around outside."

"I think, sir," Philip spoke feebly, "the murderers were from that tribe where we bought milk a few hours ago. In the fire's glow I recognised the man with a hair-lip."

"*Ja, Baas,*" Jantse said, "*ja,* he is right, they were those men and they came for the horses—they will not come back—I think."

"I hope you're right," Van Riebeck said, "but I don't understand why I didn't hear any sound of their attack or the horses riding off."

"Those skelm Basutos put daccha powder in the milk, *Baas,*" the driver was now fully conscious, "so we all sleep— even the boys on watch—they sleep too."

"*Magtig!* By God! We were all drugged!" Van Riebeck exploded at the revelation. "Those swine could have climbed aboard the wagons and murdered all of us if Maarje's screams hadn't scared them off."

"*Ja, ja, Baas*, the 'voices' told me in my sleep what was happening." Maarje nodded triumphantly, proud of her gift of second sight.

"Well, thank God they did, Maarje." Katie reached for two tin mugs hanging on the pegs below the shelf. "I think I need a brandy too, I think we *all* do. Eileen, give me some more mugs."

Still trembling with fright Eileen unhooked the mugs and held them out as Katie poured more brandy, then said, "Here's a sip for you, Eileen." Next Katie looked over at the solemn-faced Franz and Adrian. "Don't worry, darlings, I'll make you two some sugar water."

"Let's hurry, Katje." Van Riebeck tossed back a brandy, "I'll need all of you, except Adrian, to help me inspan the oxen. We must move off as soon as possible in case those swine return." Slinging his gun across his back he climbed off the wagon.

His first job was to build the fires high to give as much light as possible, then with the help of the women and Franz he started to drag the sleepy oxen to their feet. The clumsy brutes were obstinate and resisted, but eventually Van Riebeck and the others managed to get them up and to inspan them to the wagons, careful to be sure that the strongest animals were at the front of the shaft to do the heavy pulling.

"What shall we do about the dead?" Katie muttered to Paul.

"What *can* we do? Impossible for me to stay and dig a grave big enough to hold all the poor devils because those murderers might return! We'll have to leave them to the hyenas and assvogels. I'll move them closer together so that the wheels won't run over them when the wagons pull out. Will you be able to drive one of the wagons?"

"Of course I will," Katie answered firmly in spite of never having handled a span of more than four oxen; but if coloured drivers could handle sixteen so could she. "But the lead boys are dead. Can we manage without them?"

"No, the stupid brutes of oxen will go

astray or stumble into holes; we'll have to use Eileen and Franz as lead boys."

"Yes." Katie did not like the idea but the children must help. "It's not dangerous—only the closeness to the oxen's smell will be disagreeable," she told the wide-eyed children. "Maarje can care for the wounded and Adrian. Let's be off! The sky is lightening so we'll find the route."

"Katje, you are wonderful, by God!" Van Riebeck stood for a second to stare down at her.

"Darling, God has been so good to spare us. Eileen, quickly bring your clothes from your wagon and come and dress with me," she called out and was grateful for the girl's firm response. "Yes, at once, Mama."

Katie swiftly climbed into her wagon, pulled off her voluminous cotton nightgown, stiff with blood from the wounded men, then dressed rapidly. She flipped her wide frilled sun bonnet from its peg together with her goatskin mask.

Then Eileen came in with her bundle of clothes and as she started dressing Katie asked, "You won't be afraid to lead the oxen will you, darling?"

"Mama, don't worry, I'm never afraid when you and Papa Paul are with me."

"Thank you, darling. I'm very proud of you."

Katie found heavy gloves in a chest and pulled them on, for the rough leather reins, after a while would tear the flesh of her hands. A few minutes later she was seated on the driver's box, with her long gun beside her and ahead of her was Franz, his little body very straight as he stood holding the thong of the lead oxen.

Katie called out, "All right, Franz, I'm ready," then to signal the oxen, she cried, "*Voorwarts! Voorwarts!*"

As Franz pulled on the thong attached to the beasts to make them move, Katie whisked out with the eighteen-foot whip, making it crack over the backs of the lead animals, then the wagon moved forward and beside Katie's wagon, Van Riebeck with Eileen at the head of his span, started moving along.

After a few minutes of concentration in handling the sixteen span of oxen, Katie threw an apprehensive glance backwards to see if the murderers were trailing them. Thank God—no sign of humans, only the hideous assvogels with their long, featherless necks were dropping down from the pale pre-dawn sky to gorge on the bodies of the murdered men. Katie shuddered as it was borne in upon her that but for the mercy of God, her family might be lying back there to feed the evil birds of death.

16

THE following week was a gruelling experience for Katie, obliged to sit for hours driving the sixteen oxen, also for Eileen and Franz, forced to trudge over sandy, stony earth, leading the beasts. Van Riebeck had armed the children with long sheathed knives hanging from belts around their waists.

"They're a safeguard against tarantula or snakes," Van Riebeck said. "Don't worry; you won't have to fight Kaffirs; I'm here with my gun."

"I'd like a chance to knife a skelm Kaffir," Franz angrily assured his father.

The wagons moved slowly over the high veld, with grass so tall, Katie was filled with apprehension, for God alone knew what dangers were hidden in the greenery, but the wagons' actual path followed a beaten-down track scored by the wheels and animals of many treks coming and going from the Transvaal to the Cape.

They travelled non-stop from dawn until

noon, when Katie, Eileen and Franz helped Van Riebeck to outspan.

Maarje worked frantically caring for the three wounded men and little Adrian. Afterwards she cooked when the wagons halted and disposed of pails of slops and human waste which had collected during the travel time.

At night in one wagon Katie, Eileen, Franz and Adrian slept in the one big bed, the boys lying head to toe; but Van Riebeck never slept, he stayed on watch until dawn, when Katie relieved him, then he slept for an hour. In the second wagon the bed was occupied by the wounded men whilst Maarje rested on the lionskin on the floor.

At the beginning of the second week Jantse was strong enough to lead a team of oxen. This was an enormous relief to Eileen and Franz, who now halved the time of leading the second team. Eileen had the chance to rest her swollen feet and Franz the joy of sitting beside Van Riebeck on the wagon's driver's seat where he continuously asked his father questions about his boyhood. Van Riebeck revelled in this time with Franz, for these were the young years he had been denied with his eldest son, Paul, his love-child with Katje. Alas, Paul did not even bear the name Van Riebeck, but "Kildare" Katje's dead husband's name, for after one of his quarrels with Katje, Paul had left her and ridden further North and the letter she had written telling him she was with child by him had never reached him. The trader who was carrying it was murdered on the veld and the all important page had yellowed and fallen to dust in the great isolation.

Five years later in the Cape, Van Riebeck had accidentally met Katje again and still wildly in love with her he had decided that despite her fiery temper he would marry her; then, inadvertently, he had discovered that the small boy Paul was his son. Bitter and furious enough to kill Katje for having kept the truth from him, he had stormed out of her life and sailed for Holland. Years later on the Kimberley diamond fields where he had been sent with his commando to enforce law on the unruly mass of international diggers, he had seen Katje and Paul again and his son by then was a magnificent young man.

"Papa! Papa! You aren't listening to me!" Franz's complaining voice broke through Van Riebeck's reverie, and contritely he answered, "I'm sorry, son, but what did you say?"

"I asked you why did the Boers leave the Cape and trek North?"

"I thought you knew that, it was to escape from English rule. You see Holland had bartered the Cape to the English."

"But why didn't the Dutch fight the English off?"

"Because they were obliged to accept Holland's agreement. At that time the great farms in the Cape were worked by slaves and when the English freed the slaves it left the Dutch without labour to work their land. The English offered to pay us the worth of the slaves, but few Dutch people wanted to sail for several months to London to collect compensation and then back again. Anyhow, it wasn't only that but a great many of the Dutch hated living under English rule so they sold everything they could, packed their wagons and with their families and cattle they trekked North where there were great free spaces of land where they could rule themselves."

"Did you trek in the very first trek, Papa?"

"I was too young, but our President Kruger did, he was a small boy and very brave. My family left later, all but an older sister, who stayed behind to care for our estate—next to Abend Bloem."

"But what about your father and mother and brothers and sisters? Where are they, Papa?"

"Well when I was younger than you, I was out with my father hunting meat. Suddenly out of the high grass Kaffirs sprang up with raised spears and attacked us. My father was wounded in the chest but I shot the devil who speared him but with his dying strength my father whipped my horse's rump to make him bolt and cried to me, 'Fight on, Paul, never stop fighting for the Dutch Republic!'"

"And now you are the greatest Kaffir fighter in the Dutch Republic!" The words burst proudly from Franz.

"Well," Van Riebeck chuckled, "there are other great fighters in our fine nation, Franz."

"Yes—but you're the greatest! And I'm going to be one, too, Papa—just like you!"

The childish vow warmed Van Riebeck's heart. Franz was an answer to his longing for a son bearing the Van Riebeck name to fight for the Republic of South Africa. Paul had done just that at the battle of Majuba—but *Magtig!* his name was not Van Riebeck! This small boy beside him with little Adrian too— they were legitimate Van Riebecks—they would add honour and glory to the Van Riebeck name.

"Yes, yes, Franz, when we reach Lydenburg, I'm going to teach you to shoot and you have to learn to speak good Dutch."

"I will—I will, Papa, though Mama and Maarje and everyone always speaks English to me. But, Papa, tell me, when our people left the Cape why didn't the British leave us alone?"

"They promised to and did at first, but then diamonds were discovered in Kimberley and that made all the difference —they made an excuse to annex the place."

"Terribly unfair! . . . Papa, why did

they take the Transvaal? We had no diamonds up there."

"They annexed us some years ago to try to force us into a white man's federation, a sort of Union with the Cape, Natal and Orange Free State. They used the excuse that we were stealing Zulu and other Kaffir tribes' land, but thank God we fought the English and overthrew them at Majuba."

"Oh, that was a fine victory! I wish I could have fought in it."

"Well, Franz, let's hope by the time you're old enough to fight, the South African Republic will be allowed to live in peace. No-one wants to keep on fighting, there are better things to do with one's life. Now how's my pipe? Filled it?"

"Oh—I forgot—sorry." Franz swiftly stuffed tobacco into the pipe bowl, tamped it down with his small thumb then said, "Here it is. I hope I've done it well."

Van Riebeck took it. "It looks fine, son. You've packed it well." He was thinking that Franz should soon attend a Dutch school in Lydenburg, although he suspected that Katje would object to it.

As the wagons rocked along covering

miles over the wild isolation, both Van Riebeck and Franz cherished these conversations. Franz was learning a great deal of South African history which he presumed his mother did not know about and hitherto his father had been too occupied to teach him.

At the commencement of the third week after the Basuto attack the driver was strong enough to take over from Katie. Thanking God, she spent her time lying down, for she felt physically spent and was almost convinced she would never be rid of the ache in her back and shoulders or the cords of strain that had developed in her arms.

Soon the isolation was broken by desolate farmsteads that later gave way to tiny villages and then a day came when they reached the Lydenburg district. Never before had Katie thought she would welcome, as she now did, the sight of the 6,000 acre farm and the low spread-out white homestead.

As the wagons pulled up and Katie dismounted, she threw herself into Van Riebeck's arms crying. "Oh, dear God be praised! Darling—we're here! We are really here! You brought us safely back!"

He grinned down at her as black servants came running to meet them, wide smiles of welcome showing white teeth and the head boy in charge of the farm, Obsete, bowed to Van Riebeck.

"*Baas*, we worry for you, because for long we have watched for the *Baas* and Missus. *Baas* Breda come many weeks ago and say *Baas* send telegram to Pretoria and say *Baas* is coming."

"Good, Obsete." Van Riebeck clamped an affectionate hand on the faithful man's bare shoulder then, as the other Kaffir boys gathered round, he told them about the Basuto killers who had caused their delay.

"Skelm Kaffirs—skelm!" The blacks, muttering indignantly in Swahili which Katie and the children did not understand, told Van Riebeck they would castrate the bastards then kill them if ever they caught them.

As Franz and Adrian ran around Katie and Eileen started for the house and Joanna, the enormously fat cook, and half a dozen barefoot maids came running to welcome them.

"Quick, quick," Joanna ordered the maids, "get baths and hot water for Missus and open all the shutters."

As the girls went to obey Joanna said, "It is good you come home, too, Missie Eileen."

Eileen felt like kissing Joanna's blue-black smiling face, to hug the big lumpy shoulders, but she knew Papa Paul would not like that, so instead she squeezed Joanna's arm and said, "I'm longing for some of your tomato *brede* and your *mosbolletjies*—no one makes them like you do, Joanna. You're my good, good, dear Joanna." She turned from the delighted woman and asked Katie, "Shall I use my same room, Mama?"

"Yes, darling, it's all to yourself. No Nancy or Mary to share it with this time."

When Eileen had gone into the house Katie murmured to the cook, "Your daughter, Janga, is absolutely cured of smoking dacca and is very happy at Abend Bloem in the Cape."

Tears flooded Joanna's smoky brown eyes. "Oh, Missus, it is good you take

Janga away from here and she not smoke dacca any more. Now I go and make coffee for everyone. *Ja*, Missus, and brandy for the *Baas*."

As the cook waddled away Katie stood for a minute on the stoep looking out at the garden. Years ago she had planted the seeds which produced the now brilliant creeper of purple bougainvillaea, the blue morning glory, the pepper trees and weeping willows.

Van Riebeck was still talking beside the wagon and oxen, with the Kaffirs grouped around him and beyond him stretched the distant Mountains—layer upon layer of blue-grey heights poking into the sky and shutting out the world. Katie sighed and turned around to enter the house, glancing at the bleached oxen skulls used as chairs on the stoep. Ah, yes, she thought wearily, she was really back in the Lydenburg district, for her it was well named The Mountain of Sorrows.

She stepped into the living-room and saw that everything was the same; floor covered by lionskins; white-washed walls; the old upright piano which Van Riebeck, hoping to please her, at great expense, had transported from the Cape; the bookcase holding eighteen volumes of the *Encyclopaedia Brittanica* printed in 1788 and once belonging to her grandfather which she and Sean had brought from Ireland—all seemed like welcoming friends. She went over to examine the books, thank God her carefully made linen covers continued to spare the volumes from the ravages of white ants.

But what a sadly different room this was to her serenely beautiful drawing-room at Abend Bloem. Then she sharply upbraided herself; regrets must not weaken her on the very first hour of her return.

She went to supervise baths for Franz and Adrian, knowing that Maarje would be occupied in caring for Philip, whose wound was slow in healing. In the boys' room Katie knelt beside the round zinc tub where Franz was soaking in the soapy warm water as Katie washed his back.

"Oh, I'm so glad to be home, Mama!" Franz exclaimed. "It's much nicer up here than in the Cape Colony."

With amazement Katie stared at the small golden-haired replica of Van

Riebeck, "But however can you say that? The Cape is so beautiful compared with the dryness up here."

"But I don't have adventures there like the one on our trek and Papa has promised to teach me to shoot and to take me on leopard and lion hunts. I'm like Papa—I am a Transvaaler!"

It upset Katie to realize how deep the boy's feelings seemed to be. "But you always have such fun at Abend Bloem and Kenneth takes you to the beach to swim and fish."

"Oh yes, Mama, but up here I have to be a man—I must grow up to be like Papa." Franz's blue eyes, so like his father's, were shiny with admiration. "I want to be like my Dutch father." He suddenly smoothed her cheek with his soapy fingers. "Don't look so sad, Mama, but I hate the English." He spoke indignantly. "Just look how they cheated us of Saint Lucia Bay. Someday I'll help Papa fight them."

Upset by hearing the child's feelings, she soaped one of his arms and thought carefully how best to influence him.

"Please don't say you *hate* the English

—it's wrong to hate anyone, and just think, darling, of your stepbrothers; they're true South Africans and you must be like them, neither English nor Dutch but a good South African."

"No, no, Mama, I'm Dutch like Papa!"

She irritably sponged his obstinate-looking little face. "I'm much too tired to argue with you now. Come on, you've been in the bath long enough, out you go —it's Adrian's turn."

As Franz stepped out of the bath, Katie gave his bottom a playful slap, then Adrian stepped into the soapy water, making sounds of delight.

As Katie started sponging his brother Franz said, "You know, Mama, Adrian is Dutch too, like I am, aren't you, Adrian?" He towelled himself energetically. "You're Dutch like Papa."

"Like Papa—Adrian is like Papa." The child laughed delightedly whilst his dirty chubby hands slapped at the water thereby thoroughly splashing Katie's crumpled, soiled clothes.

"You're a little goose." She kissed the top of his thatch of golden hair. "You're a dusty little boy who's going to have his hair washed," and as he squealed she pushed his head back into the water.

A few minutes later she placed the boys in the care of one of the maids and wearily went to her own room to strip and bathe. She was surprised to find Van Riebeck already there, standing in clean under-clothes and pulling a suit from a mahogany armoire.

"You've bathed already," Katie exclaimed, "that was quick."

"And was it good to stand under the trees and have the boys pour cold water down on me. I'm going into Pretoria, darling. I can't waste a minute to see Kruger and the Volksraad."

She was not surprised, knowing his urgency to discuss the Saint Lucia Bay affair. "Have you any idea how long you'll be there?" she asked.

"It's likely to be a fairly long visit." He was buttoning the front of a white frilled shirt, his still wet hair dripping on to the shoulders. "I've so much to report and so much to hear and I hope policies to help with."

"I was just wondering when we might go to the Witwatersrand to visit Paul?"

"I simply cannot say at the moment." He stepped into trousers of pale cream serge. "But why don't you rest for a few days? God knows you need to after all you've been through, then as soon as I am back we'll discuss our visit to Paul." He tucked his gold watch into a waistcoat pocket and settled the heavy gold chain attached to it with a cigar-cutter on the other end across his flat stomach. "All ready, so I'll be off." He pulled a wide-brimmed cream hat from the armoire and bent to kiss Katie.

"Darling, you look smart enough to be received at Buckingham Palace."

"God spare me from that—unless it's to attend the Queen's funeral ceremony."

They kissed warmly; she liked the taste of brandy on his lips. "Sorry I'm still so dusty and dirty, darling."

"You're lovely—no matter how you are. Well, I'm off." He let go of her and strode out, his mind already absorbed with his political affairs.

For a moment she felt stupidly sad by his going but the separation was only for a few days so what was the matter with her? Then the maids carried in the zinc bath with pitchers of hot water and she swiftly undressed to sit crunched up soaking in the bath.

With relief Van Riebeck and his Kaffir boys cantered into the town of Pretoria that stood in a bowl encircled by low-lying hills. Though flat and dusty the solid-looking white buildings and tall church gave an air of stability. The wide streets were flanked by willow and mimosa trees which shaded the narrow canals running beneath them. Ox wagons, carts and some carriages ambled along with pedestrians made up of Boer women in voluminous cotton skirts and tight-fitting bodices, with wide-brimmed sun bonnets, shielding their faces while the men were in dusty-looking jackets and moleskin trousers. Many people recognizing Van Riebeck called out warm greetings to him.

He was glad to be obliged to keep on raising his hat in acknowledgement—these were his people, he loved them and he loved Pretoria, Capital of the South African Republic. The Transvaalers with supreme courage had fought, bled and died to reach the far North, and to create even this small mark of civilization from the isolated wilderness. The city was not much to boast of now, for it was only twenty-five years old, but in time it would grow into a splendid city with noble buildings housing a University, a modern hospital, a fine library, a theatre—even an Opera House. In his mind he could see it all, a city to admire and respect.

Reaching the grassy square where the solid Volksraad building stood Van Riebeck's eyes flew up the flagpole to gloat at the sight of the Vierkleur, the South African Republic's flag of green, red, white and blue.

Then he pulled up and dismounted; one of his boys sprang to take his horse, and Van Riebeck ran up the steps and strode into the building, making for Kruger's office.

17

IN an almost bare room with white-washed walls President Kruger and five of the Volksraad's council members sat around a rough wooden table. They were big, loose-limbed men, sun-browned from spending half their lives in the saddle. Their faded-by-many-washings shirts of blue or beige were stained at armpits and backs with perspiration, mole-skin trousers were clamped to their heavy legs, and veldshoen covered their bare feet.

The grey-bearded President alone was formally dressed in his customary black suit and on the table beside him he had placed his black stove-pipe hat with his bible. His men might dress as they pleased but he considered himself, not only their political leader, but their father; his burghers were part of his big family and it was his duty to give them a good example in all things.

When Van Riebeck entered, he received

a hearty welcome, the members standing up to slap him on the back, then energetically shaking his hand. Though he sensed that they disapproved of his smart cream suit, he cared nothing—it was his intention to illustrate to them that Volksraad members should dress like gentlemen and not farmhands.

"*Magtig!* But you've been a long time in coming, man," Kruger bellowed in his bull-like voice. "We've needed you badly. So much has gone wrong."

Van Riebeck told how the Basuto attack had caused his delay then hanging his hat on a vacant peg, he pulled out a chair and sat down. "I left the Cape the moment the Governor let me know of England's bloody decision about Saint Lucia Bay. I hope you haven't taken it lying down."

"*Ach*, you can be sure of that," exclaimed the red-haired, red-bearded Abraham Breda, an old colleague of Van Riebeck's. "We've sent two men to protest to Westminster, and if they get no satisfaction in London they'll go on to France, Holland and Germany to enlist sympathy for us."

"So far we've received no news," Piet

Joubert, the vice-president, dryly told Van Riebeck.

"And when you do—you know what it will be," Van Riebeck muttered.

"*Ja, ja,* we know that." Joubert's heavy fingers combed irritably through his long brown beard. "Have you any better suggestion of what we could have done?"

"No, man—no! Only this, as the bloody English have swindled us out of Saint Lucia—in recompense we must make them cancel our debt to them. Before God it was unjust of them to saddle us with a bill for £1,272,000 for civil expenses when England annexed us against our will."

"You're right, man!" De Vries thumped the table in agreement, "and also the bill of nearly £800,000 for repayment of old debts: England must cancel that too. Our victory at Majuba proved we can beat the English in battle so let's also insist that we change the conditions of the bloody Pretoria Convention we stupidly signed."

"*Magtig*—it was a mistake to have signed that! We should never have agreed not to deal with the Kaffir tribes over land disputes without England's sanction." Joubert pulled a pipe from his pocket and angrily started to fill it. "Nor to promise not to deal with overseas powers either, but in God's name what could we have done at the time? England had just landed 7,000 more troops at the Cape and the good God knows we weren't ready to take them on too."

"*Ach*, that's all over with." Kruger spoke impatiently then cleared his throat and spat loudly into a brass spitoon beside him. "We did what we had to do to regain independence."

"But de Vries and Joubert are right," Van Riebeck said. "We should *insist* that we break the Pretoria Convention! Don't worry; England will agree to our terms; she's got her hands full at the moment with Gordon in the Sudan and with Bismarck's greedy eyes on Africa: that's why she's keeping Saint Lucia Bay because she fears Germany's encroachment."

"Well, better the Germans for neighbours than the English," Breda said but Kruger bellowed at him. "You are *verdamnt*! We don't need *any* close neighbours to start pushing into the South African Republic—not English—not German!"

"Yes, yes, *mynheer*," Van Riebeck blurted out, "and we'll have to watch this mad Englishman, Cecil Rhodes. He's determined to control the 'Road North' as he calls it, not the 'Missionary Road', and we must keep it open for ourselves to travel to Delagoa Bay—that's surely our only hope of a port to replace Saint Lucia Bay."

"There's nothing for us but Delagoa Bay," Kruger muttered, "and we have to begin all over again to get the Portuguese to let our produce through."

Van Riebeck's mind flashed back to five years ago when he had trekked to Lorenzo Marques and negotiated for the Portuguese Governor's permission to start building a railway from Delagoa Bay to the Transvaal border. Finance for the project had come from the Netherlands Government but the project had died away and the railway materials now lay rusting and overgrown by brush.

"Something serious must be done soon! We must have help with our exchequer!" Kruger's mottle-skinned hand pulled on his beard. "You don't know it, Van Riebeck, but since you've been gone we've again become almost bankrupt." He spat into the spitoon. "We aren't able to raise a loan of even £5,000 from the Standard Bank in Cape Town."

"God in heaven!" Van Riebeck muttered and his flaming blue eyes swung around to take in the other men's solemn faces. "That means that none of our civil workers can be paid. But in God's name what about selling some more of our gold concessions?"

"*Magtig*—no!" Kruger's clenched fist thumped the table. "We've sold enough concessions and we don't want any more Uitlanders coming into the Transvaal; there are too many already and they are mainly English."

"*Ja, ja,*" the other men added their agreement, making Van Riebeck's temper rise at the Volksraad members' stupidity, at their insane insular attitude.

"But don't you see," he said as calmly as he could, "that while we are near bankruptcy and obliged to keep sending our produce all the way to Durban or the Cape we could be making money from the gold that the Almighty has given us! We *must* sell more concessions and charge heavily for them and also tax any gold that is produced. In the Australian and Californian gold fields the governments collect 40 per cent of all gold produced. If much gold is found in the Witwatersrand it could make us wealthy."

"*Ach, ja*, I suppose there is some wisdom in what you say, Van Riebeck," Breda nodded, "but we must be cautious or we'll find the Uitlanders will soon be overrunning us."

"That's madness! The Transvaal territory is larger than all of France; there's plenty of room here for decent men who mine on the Witwatersrand." Paul grinned at all of them. "There will be *some* decent men amongst them, who can later become citizens. God knows we've been trying to encourage people from Holland, Belgium and Germany to settle amongst us. Some Cape Dutch may also come up."

"Not *our* people—they won't! You know they're too smart to go in for mining," Oliphant, his cheek scarred where a lion had recently clawed him, said smugly. "They know that a man's true wealth is in land and cattle."

Van Riebeck groaned out loud.

"*Magtig*, Oliphant—in some ways you are right but in other ways you are bloody wrong! Just think of Kimberley and the Hottentot who found an 83 carat diamond and sold it for a horse, ten oxen and 500 sheep. After passing through many hands the Earl of Dudley bought it for £50,000 and it went on to earn more even than that. Before I left the Cape, Cecil Rhodes and Barney Barnato were amalgamating mining claims into a firm worth millions of pounds! Such men—starting with nothing—have become multi-millionaires —they outsmarted our people, bought their diamond lands for almost nothing!"

"That's not outsmarting our people," Oliphant burst out indignantly. "It's cheating them!"

"*Ja, ja*, but the Dutch were stupid," Van Riebeck looked challengingly around the tables. "The Almighty gave us brains so why the devil don't we use them? Let's sell concessions on the right terms."

"*Ach, ja, ja*, I think you may be right," Joubert said, thoughtfully staring at Van Riebeck as he sat back and mopped his perspiring face with a cream silk handkerchief.

"I know I've shocked you," Van Riebeck went on, "but, *magtig*—someone must wake you up." Now Paul was encouraged as he saw that in Kruger's eyes a greedy light had banished the first anger.

"Van Riebeck's advice is good." Kruger spoke reflectively. "He is broadly educated, been to University in Holland, lived amongst well educated Dutch in the Cape. He has travelled to England, Germany and France—he is our best man to advise us on our present problems."

"Thank you, Mynheer President," Van Riebeck answered humbly for he knew Kruger—the old fighting lion—did not easily capitulate. He threw a placating glance at the other men and said, "Of course like yourselves, I also believe that in land and cattle is a man's true wealth and I am not personally going to have any part in mining." He considered it expedient not to mention that he had a son on the Witwatersrand. "Our President said months ago, 'Leave the gold in the earth, it will only bring bloodshed', and at that time I agreed, but since we have lost all hope of Saint Lucia Bay I say let's sell as *many* concessions as possible on the

Witwatersrand! And as *fast* as possible to save ourselves from bankruptcy!"

Breda nodded. "You have convinced me that we must sell many concessions but we must also think up laws to protect ourselves in every way."

"*Ja, ja,* we shall not be made fools of like the Dutch were at the diamond fields," Vice-president Joubert said. "The Almighty has given us riches in our earth, for *our* benefit, to build up our nation. We must have good schools, hospitals . . ."

"A University with fine professors," Kruger interrupted. "Education for our young—this is very important but now . . ." he turned his deepset shrewd eyes on Van Riebeck . . . "How shall we sell new concessions?"

"To private prospectors, not to combines like Rhodes and Barnato, who have millions of pounds to buy everything up." He decided not to tell of his meeting with Rhodes about Saint Lucia Bay: it would infuriate the Volksraad. "Rhodes is a dangerous imperialist who wants Africa for the English from the Cape to Cairo."

"First the swine must kill all our

people!" Oliphant spat the words out; he was an intense English hater.

Van Riebeck continued, "He's so *verdamnt* he even hopes England will regain America."

They all laughed. "He's *verdamnt* all right," Breda said. "Look what a power America has become since her Independence only a hundred years ago."

"You're right, but let me tell you what Rhodes says to young Englishmen working for him, 'Remember you are an Englishman and have consequently won first prize in the lottery of life'."

Scornful remarks burst from all of them, then Van Riebeck said, "But why don't we circulate rumours that there are concessions to be sold along the Witwatersrand? That will bring prospectors to us."

"I agree," Joubert nodded. "Let's go for our midday meal to the Blesbok Inn and over brandy and coffee we'll talk loudly about concessions so that the owner will hear. He's such a gossip he'll spread the word all over town in no time."

As Van Riebeck nodded de Vries said, "That's clever—people will come to us—not us to them. Oliphant, let us eat at the 'Burgher' and talk loudly of concessions for sale."

"No, no! I'm against the plan!" Oliphant cried, "We don't want the redneck English here. Have you forgotten how that swine Sir Owen Lanyon, administrator up here when we were annexed, refused to shake hands with any Volksraad members?"

"Well, for now, let us forget that," Kruger said. "Join de Vries at the 'Burgher'; we must sell concessions to save our exchequer from bankruptcy."

Van Riebeck engaged a room at the Blesbok Inn and remained in Pretoria for another week. He was occupied with the State Attorney, a young Hollander, Dr. William Leyds; they were creating protective laws in connection with the gold fields. In the evenings Van Riebeck spent time with a young American engineer, a fellow guest at the Blesbok Inn. From him Paul learned all he could about the running of the California gold fields and applied many of the American ideas to the Witwatersrand's new laws.

He also managed to help make his fellow members in the Volksraad realize how essential it was to establish more schools with good teachers and to create a law that all children on farms be obliged to attend the nearest schools. But opposition to this idea was strong for the Burghers were not convinced that education was necessary for men to run tobacco and wheat farms.

When dining privately with Kruger at his home, Van Riebeck complained of the Transvaalers' ignorant attitude to education and was surprised when Kruger replied, "I know it and I've been obliged to overlook sons of the soil and engage educated men from Germany and Holland to fill certain posts. Unfortunately I dare not bring educated Cape Dutch up because it would create too much jealousy amongst our people here."

"This is one of our great weaknesses but we *must* concentrate on educating the young."

"*Ja, ja,* you are right, but even more important than that—we must send a good man to see the Governor in Delagoa Bay about starting a railway. I've been approached by an American, a Colonel

Edward McMurdo, who's trying to float a company in London to build a railway from Lorenzo Marques to the Transvaal border. He says he has a concession from the Portuguese Governor, but—*Magtig*, Paul, I don't know why but I don't trust the man."

"Well let's wait and see what he can produce. Of course I should prefer to interest German or Netherlands finance in the project, but that might become easier when we have more people on the gold fields which would warrant railway traffic. But first we must try again to make the Portuguese grant us the railway rights."

Kruger nodded eagerly. "It was you who cleverly obtained them a few years ago, so why don't you go back and fix them up again? Then we can try to raise capital from Germany or Holland to build the railway."

Van Riebeck felt his presence in the Transvaal at this time was more important than going to Delagoa Bay. "If you insist, of course I shall go, but I believe that any good man would do instead of me. Mynheer, if you don't mind my saying so, I feel I'd be more use on the

Witwatersrand to study the gold fields' situation in person."

Kruger was silent for a moment as he considered this, then he said, "You are probably right; your presence is needed in the Transvaal, especially as I must soon go to the conference to meet the British government officials about this question of us giving back land to the Bechuanaland tribes. The English are *verdamnt* to give the blacks so much land and with this talk of equal rights."

Kruger slurped a mouthful of coffee from his cup and loudly swallowed it.

"Do you approve of my visiting the Witwatersrand?" Van Riebeck asked.

"*Ja, ja.* I do." The President nodded and his heavy jowls wobbled. "The more intelligent information we can gather about the place the better. So far it doesn't seem that we'll make swift riches from the gold like the diamond fields did—but we shall see what the good Lord has willed for us."

"We need the advice of a first-class surveyor to gauge what hopes we have. I've heard of a man called Struben who is on the Witwatersrand now, so I'll go and question him, but first I must go back to my farm to see how my wheat harvesting is going along. I'll be on the Witwatersrand within three days and I'll send you word of my opinion as soon as possible."

18

KATIE was finishing writing a long letter to Mary. She had given her the news of Terence's and Elaine's wedding and promised that Aunt Liz would send photographs of the bridal pair to her soon. Then Katie ended the letter with assurances that she would return to Florence for Mary's confinement, and also begged Mary to write to tell her how she was and how her voice training was progressing. Katie deliberately asked nothing about Mary's marriage.

Her worried thoughts of Mary were broken into by the sound of galloping horses' hooves on the hard earth. Van Riebeck! No other man rode as he did. She swiftly folded the letter, slipped it into an envelope and pushed it down to the bottom of the small chatelaine holding her keys that hung from her waist. Anxiety weighed her being for God alone knew when the time came how she would be able to leave Van Riebeck and go to

Florence. But somehow she would manage it! Standing up she shook out her skirts and rushed to the front stoep to welcome Paul, as she always did.

He and his two Kaffir attendants were just galloping around a clump of bushes and, seeing her, Van Riebeck raised his hat high above his head waving it in circles in the gesture that for so long she had loved; then the horses slowed to a gentle canter and came up to the house. Excitedly she rushed down the steps as Van Riebeck swung a long leg over the horse's back, jumped down and caught her in his arms, just the sight of her had power that never lessened to raise his spirits.

They kissed, then she pulled away because of the Kaffir boys. "Darling, thank God you're back." Arms around each other they went up the steps as the Kaffirs led Paul's sweating horse off to the stables. On the stoep he sank into a big chair and tossed his hat on to a bleached ox skull. She hovered over him, and seeing his sweat-stained shirt she knew he had ridden hard.

"Coffee and brandy, darling?"

"In a minute—first let me tell you the

good news, beloved: we are going to visit Paul on the Witwatersrand!"

"Oh darling, how lovely! I've had itchy feet just waiting to be off. I'm longing to see him."

Then he told her swiftly of his commission to discover the true geological situation of the Witwatersrand and if the Volksraad could count upon receiving wealth from it.

"That knowledge is essential and let's pray that this geologist—Struben, will produce a favourable report," Katie said. "I'm selfishly thinking of Paul too—we don't want him slaving up there for nothing."

"I'd like to see him out of gold-mining altogether and back at Abend Bloem running the ostrich farm." Van Riebeck shrugged his wide shoulders. "One day when the vines start bearing grapes, he'll be needed to assist with the whole production of ostrich feathers—wine— dried fruits—too much for Ken and Chris to manage."

"Well don't worry about that now," she smiled. "I'll go and order your coffee and brandy."

The next day two Van Riebeck wagons were moving towards the Witwatersrand and Katie thanked heaven they were drawn by mules instead of the slow oxen. Eileen joined in Katie's excitement at the prospect of seeing Paul, her favourite brother. She was also curious to meet his new wife.

Franz and Adrian were anxious to see what gold mines looked like. "If you can pick the gold up off the earth, Mama," Adrian said eagerly, "I'm going to get handfuls of it."

"You silly," Franz retorted, "you've got to dig for it."

"Oh, that's all right, because I made Maarje pack my bucket and spade that Ken gave me to dig sea sand at the Cape."

"Adrian darling," Katie hugged the child's fat little body, "you sometimes have to dig *very* deep into the earth to find gold."

"I don't mind, Mama, I'm strong."

At that moment, Van Riebeck, riding beside the wagons, called out, "I don't like the colour of the sky ahead, Katje. It looks like a dust storm coming this way; the Witwatersrand is plagued by them. Better pull the canvas top over the slats and I'll tell Maarje to do so in the other wagon."

Katie looked out to the sky. In the near distance a heavy moving cloud of grey was blotting out the blue. "Help me pull the canvas over, Eileen," she cried. "Quickly!"

As they worked to secure the canvas top, Van Riebeck rode up to the drivers shouting, "Halt, Jong! We must cover the mules' heads with sacks. A big dust storm is coming."

"*Aa—ie, ja, Baas*—a devil-storm," one of the drivers shouted as he dragged on the reins.

Both wagons came to a halt and the Kaffirs, believing the storm was sent by evil spirits, worked swiftly to cover the mules' and horses' heads, tying the horses to the wagon sides. Then the Kaffirs huddled together under the wagons, with cloths covering their own heads.

Van Riebeck climbed into the wagon with Katie and the children and with the back and front flaps well secured they waited.

The great grey brown cloud came rolling forward and hit the wagons with terrible ferocity making them sway like boats. The animals' frightened cries joined with the Kaffirs' wails whilst billows of sand blew into the wagons through every crevice.

Dust blew into their eyes, their noses; it was embedded between their teeth; their hair was powdered by it and for twenty miserable minutes they sat and endured the torment.

Then the storm passed over the flat land, suddenly rolling away into the distance so that the wagons could again move forward, but dust remained inside the wagons. It was everywhere; in the tin mugs, the plates, the knives and forks, in boots and shoes, between people's teeth, in their hair. For hours, Katie, Eileen and Maarje wiped it off everything: they washed Franz and Adrian's faces and their own but dust still clung to everyone and everything, even the next day they were not completely free of it.

"Are such awful dust storms really frequent on the Witwatersrand?" Katie asked Van Riebeck as they sat in the wagon.

"Yes, they are a miner's special bonus." He grinned teasingly at her. "Do you

326

know there's even some of the damned stuff inside this brandy bottle?"

"But it was well corked, how on earth could it get in?"

"You know what the Kaffirs say—that it's evil spirits and they have access everywhere."

"Poor Paul, he didn't even mention dust storms in his letter. Do you think we'll easily find his wagon? I remember what terrible confusion there was finding people on the diamond mines."

"But it's not crowded at all here; there haven't been any great gold strikes to date."

"Perhaps Paul's will be the first." Excited that she was soon to see her beloved son, Katie went to look out at the side of the wagon. "We must be pretty close, darling. There's a group of wagons not far off and some tents—nothing but dust heaps."

Van Riebeck joined her at the wagon's opening. It was a God-forsaken scene, but he tried to cheer her. "Not so bad. Look, there's a farm house." He pointed in the distance to a low-lying shabby white homestead. "That might be Langlaagte Farm, that's near Paul's land so his wagon might be outspanned in the proximity of the homestead to make it easier to bring water from their well. I'd better get back on my horse. I can see more from there."

"But the sun is *blazing*."

"What do you expect, my love? We're on the Witwatersrand." He gave a dry chuckle. "If we come in winter we'll be knee deep in mud."

For another two hours they continued travelling through the great desolation of black undulating earth, passing huddles of brown tents and white covered wagons beside which groups of half-naked Kaffirs squatted in the dust. Occasionally they saw a neglected-looking homestead.

"Oh, Mama, what a hideous place," Eileen murmured. "I'm sorry Paul lives here. What a shame he left the beautiful Cape for this."

Guilt weighed heavily on Katie, for she was responsible for Paul being here. To placate herself as well as Eileen, she said, "The place won't be hideous if Paul finds gold enough to turn him into a millionaire."

"I do hope that happens soon; I'm sure he must hate it here."

When they approached the first well-kept looking farm, Van Riebeck decided they should stop and enquire where Langlaagte was. He rode up to the front stoep where a fat, elderly woman wearing voluminous cotton skirts and tight-to-bursting bodice rose from her chair and came to the top of the steps. With a suspicious expression on her face she peered at Paul as he dismounted and mongrel dogs rushed up to yap at his ankles.

"Good afternoon." He swept off his hat and in Dutch asked, "Can you tell me, please where Langlaagte farm is?"

"It's here and I'm the owner. My man is dead, I am the Widow Oosthuizen, but if you've come to try to buy the farm—I can tell you that I'm not selling! And I've told that to everyone who has been here!"

"Don't be worried. I am Paul Van Riebeck and I met your husband years ago; I don't want to buy your farm. I'm trying to find my stepson. He's prospecting on his land near here. Do you know him? Paul Kildare?" How it still riled him to voice the false name for his son.

Mrs. Oosthuizen's suspicious expression softened. "*Ja, ja*, I know the fine-looking young man and his pretty wife, they call here sometimes. His wagon is straight on the way your wagons are pointed, about ten minutes further on."

"Thank you. Would you mind telling me what kind of people have been trying to buy your farm? I'd like to know. The Volksraad is looking into all this type of thing."

"They were Uitlanders—English." She made a spitting sound as though to rid her lips of a bad taste. "The fools think there's gold here."

"They may be right, Mrs. Oosthuizen, and if you ever do decide to sell, don't let any speculators take advantage of you as they did with our people on the diamond fields."

She shook her head. "But I'm *not* going to sell! It's my home; twenty of my children were born here; they were married from here." She suddenly squeezed her eyes almost shut as she carefully studied Paul's face. "*Magtig!* Now I recognise who

330

you are! The great Commandant Van Riebeck! Many years ago you saved my whole family and many friends on a trek when thousands of Zulus attacked us. *Ach*, but you are a fine man! Come in—come in—and drink coffee and brandy, Commandant."

"Thank you very much—another day please." He waved toward his wagons. "My wife is longing to reach her son."

Mrs. Oosthuizen held out her hand, rough and calloused by years of hard work, and he shook it warmly. He would kill any bastards who tried to cheat this old woman. "Please don't sell your farm without legal advice. I'm a member of the Volksraad, so come to me in Pretoria and I'll see that the state attorney takes care of you."

She thanked him effusively and he left, promising himself to somehow keep a protective eye on her. When he told Katie what had happened she was elated.

"If the widow has gold on her land, it must mean that Paul also has gold. Ten minutes from here—I can't wait to see him."

Reaching a group of wagons where

Kaffirs were building fires for the evening meal, Van Riebeck asked if they knew Paul's wagon. They nodded and pointed to the edge of the cluster of wagons and Van Riebeck suddenly recognised the wagon he had bought for Paul in Lydenburg as part of his wedding present.

"Paul's wagon is here!" Van Riebeck called as he returned to Katie and the children who stood looking out eagerly from the back of a wagon and crying excitedly.

"Where is it, where?" Van Riebeck reached up and lifted Katie down. "Just on the edge of this lot." He pointed and, lifting the hem of her skirts, she started rushing toward the wagon calling.

"Paul! Paul! Herta! Paul!"

Suddenly her son's handsome face capped by thick gold hair was looking around the side of the wagon; then seeing his mother running and stumbling over the stony earth he jumped down shouting.

"Great Lord! Mother!" He rushed toward her and she threw herself into his outstretched arms. "Darling—darling Paul! At last!"

He held her in a bear hug as leaning down he planted kisses on her forehead and cheeks. "I can't believe it! I just can't believe you're here, Mother!"

"I came as soon as I could. Are you well, my love? Let me look at you."

She held her head back to look up at him. Even in her longing mind she had not visualized him to be as magnificent as he actually was. She loved him—loved him—loved him.

"Won't you allow the rest of us to say hello, Katje?" Van Riebeck's laughing voice came from behind her and she swung around then stepped aside to watch with joy as the two big men, so much alike, heartily shook hands and playfully thumped at each other's shoulders.

Then it was Eileen's turn for a bear hug from Paul who swung his young sister off her feet as he kissed her cheeks, then teased, "Hello, little gossip, so you're back again in the Transvaal—that's very good, I'll put you to work up here."

"Paul—Paul, are you happy in this hideous place?" Eileen could barely keep her tears back.

"Of course I am, silly." Now he looked down at his little brothers, who were calling up at him for his attention. "Hello, you Van Riebecks." He tousled their golden hair. "Have you come to help your big brother dig for gold?"

"Yes, yes, I have my spade and bucket," Adrian cried.

Paul caught the child up and hoisted him to sit astride around his neck. "You are just what I need, Adrian, and. . . ."

"Wherever is Herta?" Katie interrupted, knowing she could not have been in the wagon without hearing the excited greetings.

"She's ridden over to a little spring in the hope of filling the water buckets. We used up our water supply trying to wash away yesterday's dust storm. Shall we go to your wagon? Mine is crowded, almost everything I own is in it including my shovels and picks—not safe to leave tools lying about up here."

"Should you leave a note for Herta?" Katie said. "Telling her our wagons are over there."

"No need—I've got three Kaffir diggers. They'll tell her." He called out instructions in Dutch to three men lighting a fire. "*Ja, ja, Baas.*" They grinned with approval at sight of Paul's family.

When the adults were seated on folding chairs in Katie and Van Riebeck's wagon they shooed Franz and Adrian off to play with Maarje. Then pouring brandy into tin mugs, Van Riebeck handed them around to Katie and Paul—Eileen's refreshment was apricot Konfyt.

"This is almost too good to be true," Paul said, "having you up here." God in Heaven, how his mother reminded him of Nancy! It brought a terrible longing to him for his half-sister, but he told himself "to hell with the bitch"!

"We kept our visit as a surprise." Katie bubbled with happiness. "We've only been back in the Transvaal about ten days and as soon as your father had finished meetings with Kruger in Pretoria he returned to Lydenburg for us and here we are— hurrah!" She leaned over and squeezed his arm. "You look splendid, but thinner."

"That's all the hard exercise of digging." Paul sipped his brandy, "Gold mining is very demanding work."

"More than *diamond* mining?" Eileen asked. "I remember when I was very small on the diamond fields, you and Terence used to work like slaves."

335

"Yes and we found no diamonds, then you went along by the river's edge, picked out some weeds and there was a big diamond stuck to the roots. It didn't seem fair."

They all laughed, then Van Riebeck said, "You wrote that you were convinced that you have gold on your land. Why are you so sure of it? After all you knew very little about mining when you came."

"That's true, Father, but a blind man can see quartz in the stone. It's too late tonight, but in the morning I'll take you out to my diggings and show you so that you can see for yourself. It's not only *my* opinion about my land; there's a fellow called Struben—a fine geologist who agrees with me."

"Ah, you know him, that's good, I've got to talk to him; the Volksraad wants him to do a survey for us."

"The best man you could find—I assure you." Paul turned to Katie. "I'm sorry for you to find me looking so dirty, Mother, but water is scarce at the end of summer and what there is usually can't be used for bathing."

"Darling, that's the last thing that's

worrying me." She felt the wagon move and guessed Herta was climbing the step. The next second the blonde Dutch girl peeped in, her pretty face and bright blue eyes were framed by a pink frilled sun bonnet.

"Herta dear," Katie rose swiftly and went to kiss her daughter-in-law's cheek, then Herta quietly kissed Katie's cheek.

"You didn't let us know you were coming." Herta sounded reproachful, "Why not?" She nodded her head in greeting to Van Riebeck, then glanced indifferently at Eileen.

The girl's unfriendly attitude astonished Katie, but before she could answer Van Riebeck said, "If I didn't know you were a fine Boer girl, Herta, I'd be surprised by what you've just said." His voice was chiding. "It's customary amongst our people to drop in on each other, should we have sent word by a special messenger to announce our arrival to you?"

"No, no, it's not that—only I wish I'd known then I would have cooked some special foods and I could have been dressed properly to welcome you." Even after a journey Mrs. Van Riebeck looked well turned out and Herta hated her for it.

Herta looked so upset that pity made Katie say, "I know exactly how you feel, Herta, being taken by surprise, but don't worry, you look so pretty as you are."

"And, Herta, what special foods would you have cooked?" Paul teased. "We can't buy anything but stale beans until the new supplies arrive from Pretoria. Now sit down like a good girl and have a brandy."

He waved toward Eileen. "This is my sister Eileen."

Eileen was wondering whyever her wonderful brother had married this sulky Herta. But she smiled and said, "I've been longing to meet you, Herta."

"Thank you," Herta said and sat stiffly upright on the folding-stool that Paul placed for her.

"Is it true that you can't buy anything but stale beans?" Katie asked. "How awful. Thank Heaven we're loaded with supplies and can give you plenty of every-thing." She was sorry to see as Herta removed her sunbonnet that her lovely golden hair, worn with a heavy bun on the neck, was dull and in bad need of washing and her full-skirted cotton dress was stained. "I suppose the water shortage is very bad?"

"*Ja*, Mrs. Van Riebeck, most people stink because they can't wash; nearly all the men stink of sweat and beer." Herta was maintaining her bad temper and scowled in Paul's direction.

"My good little Herta," Van Riebeck said kindly, "I sense that you're not happy here."

"I hate it here! I don't *want* Paul to stop. It's a pig's life and. . . ."

"I've told you—you can go whenever you like!" Paul snapped at her. "I'll drive you the thirty miles to Pretoria and your father can call there for you."

"I didn't marry you to live with my parents," she flared at him. "I'll stay where you are—even if I die from heat and bad food."

Katie exchanged a worried glance with Van Riebeck, then said, "I suppose conditions are bad, Herta, but just think what dreadful hardships your grandmother suffered when they trekked from the Cape and not only that, they also had to fight the savage Kaffirs to stay alive."

"It wasn't so bad for them, their men were with them all day, riding beside the wagons, but mostly Paul is on his diggings from sunup to sundown and I'm alone."

"But aren't there any other young wives up here?" Van Riebeck asked, thinking the girl needed a good shaking.

"Nearly all of them are Uitlanders and I won't be friends with them."

"You should try to make yourself like the English." Paul spoke indifferently for he was tired of Herta's insular character. "I've made friends up here with some decent, amusing chaps, and their wives seem nice enough, but you won't . . ."

"You should go back where you belong, Paul, on the land! The Almighty didn't want His chosen people—the Boers—to dig in the earth for gold or diamonds. You'll never make a living up here!" Herta stood up, her face flushed with anger. "I'm going, Mrs. Van Riebeck, I have a headache, please excuse me."

She was gone in a flash before anyone could stop her, then Paul quietly said, "She's got a rotten temper, I found that out soon after we came here, but she'll be over it by tomorrow—I hope." He held out his mug to Van Riebeck for more brandy, "*Magtig*—this brandy tastes good, Father; I've had none for quite a while. It's an exorbitant price up here so I don't buy it. All my cash has gone on tools and paying Kaffirs to dig. But what's the news in the family?"

"Terence is married," Eileen burst out, "and Mary too."

"Jumping Jerusalem! There's a marriage epidemic in the family," Paul laughed, "and what about Nancy?" He hoped his voice sounded casual. "Has she married someone in Europe?"

"No," Van Riebeck swiftly filled in, sensing Katie's inner turmoil over Paul's and Nancy's incestuous love. "She very nearly married some French count, then at the last moment didn't, so that she could sail home with your mother."

"So she's back at the Cape?" Oh well, to the devil with Nancy, Paul thought savagely then said, "Tell me about Terry's wife—what's she like?"

From then on they spoke of Elaine, then Mary's artist husband, of Abend Bloem and the family in the Cape and Paul enjoyed every word he was told. He had not realized how homesick he had been.

Later when Maarje announced that she had prepared supper, Katie suggested to Paul, "Shouldn't you fetch Herta, darling?"

He shook his head, "No, at first I used to cater to her moods but now I let her stew in them. There's not much fun breaking my back digging all day, then returning to a bad-tempered wife. She's damned difficult; she won't even come with me to a drinking place-cum-café that a Chinaman runs in a tent near here."

"About Struben . . ." Van Riebeck deliberately changed the subject, "Any hope that I might meet him tomorrow? Does he frequent the Chinaman's tent?"

"Everyone does, that's where I met Struben in the first place. We'll go over tomorrow and I'll introduce you to him."

As the men were talking Katie was worrying about Paul and Herta; they seemed to almost dislike each other. Katie had known they were not suited when in Lydenburg—on an impulse—Paul had decided to marry Herta. Katie, though hating the marriage, had also been grateful for it believing that for Paul, having the voluptuous Herta in his bed, would help him to forget Nancy. Oh Lord, now it did not seem to be working well and what could she do to help her beloved son?

Then she decided to shelve the new worry as Maarje called them out of the wagon to sit around the cooking fire where she had made Sosaties, squares of mutton on wooden skewers baked in the fire's embers.

"Oh, oh, this is delicious!" Paul laughed as his white pointed teeth bit into the meat.

"Is fresh meat hard to come by?" Van Riebeck asked.

"Impossible sometimes, but a week ago I was lucky and flushed some plover and bagged a brace. That at least put Herta into a good mood."

The air was filled with the scent of smoke mixed with cooking odours and from a nearby wagon someone started to play a concertina, then from another wagon a violin played in time with it. Soon there was laughter and men's voices singing around the various camp fires.

As the sun sank suddenly and stars

silvered the black dome of the heavens, Eileen murmured to Katie, "In the darkness the camp fires look like rubies and with the music and singing it's quite nice now, Mama."

19

AT ten o'clock the music and chatter subsided. The diggers retired early for they rose with the first light, and Paul kissed his mother's and Eileen's cheeks then said, "See you at dawn, Father."

"I want to come too," Katie quietly told her son. "Darling—don't look so disapproving—I wouldn't miss seeing your diggings for anything. Eileen can keep Herta company."

"All right, Mother," Paul grinned, "if you insist." Then by the glow from campfires he made his way to his own wagon.

He climbed aboard, lifted the flap and, as he had anticipated, Herta was in the big bed that ran the width of the wagon. She was reading the Bible by the light of a candle in a lantern that shone on her abundance of golden hair fanned out over the pillow. Why the devil must she always read the Bible? Paul thought irritably.

Why can't she read some of the classics Mother gave her on our wedding day?

"At last you remembered that you have a wife?" Herta muttered as she put the Bible down to watch him undress. She revelled in the sight of his magnificent naked body.

As he unbuttoned his shirt he ignored her gibe. "Too bad you had to have one of your headaches just when my family arrived." He pulled his sweaty shirt off and tossed it on to a canvas chair.

"Well it was sneaky of your mother to come here without sending a message, I didn't even have a chance to wash my hair or any of my clothes."

"You're *verdamnt!* My mother wasn't being sneaky, she wanted to surprise us." He was unbuttoning his trousers and already she was growing so excited she hardly heard his grumbles. "You don't wash your hair or your clothes much in any case nowadays. You've grown so damned slovenly."

"That's because there's no one here to see what I look like. You're away all day —then most evenings you're getting drunk at the Chinaman's!"

"Drunk! What a lie!" He was out of his trousers now and stood naked staring angrily at her.

Then wildly impatient for him she suddenly threw the sheet off her bare body and the sight of her beauty immediately aroused him so that he climbed on to the bed, his hands closing roughly over her full tight breasts. A bitch she was, but what a woman for bedding—that and nothing else, and by God he would have all of that he wanted from the stupid cow.

Herta's passion for Paul was her food and drink, her compensation for being on the diggings. She stayed alive throughout the monotonous days by visualising the nights when their bodies rolled around in mad passion. Now her greedy hands ran over his splendid body, fastening on to his manhood, caressing him so wildly that he was immediately ready to enter her. He climbed on to her. She was like fire inside. Her being pulled at his strength, but even rising to exaltation he controlled himself so that she climaxed first. As she moaned aloud in delight he forced himself to pull out of her to come on her stomach.

For a few minutes they lay panting, his

head on her breasts, her fingers twined tightly in his thick hair which she always savagely pulled when climaxing. He was the first to move for he knew his weight could crush a woman—even though Herta was immensely strong. Then they lay side by side, not touching, for there was no tenderness between them and they seldom even kissed, theirs was raw passion. Paul thought caustically—a rich, spicy feast with only a main course—no delicate hors d'oeuvres, no delicious desserts.

"So you came again on the outside," she grumbled.

"Didn't I give you a good time first?" he asked nastily. "You thrashed around and moaned enough for a dozen women."

"I always have a good time. I told you how my older brother taught me to enjoy it—but he always waited for me to come first."

"Well, dammit—so do I." It never failed to disgust him to hear the incestuous details of her lusting with her brother. How different had been his love-making with the beautiful Nancy. Although also against God's law, it had been a merging of souls as well as bodies.

"When are you going to come inside me, Paul? Don't you ever long for us to have a child?"

He wanted to shout aloud, "Never—never—never! You cow!" but he clenched his teeth and muttered, "How *verdamnt* it would be for you to start a child up here. Wait until my land produces enough gold." Despite his satisfactory lusting with her each night he longed to be rid of her, he cursed himself for having believed that her young fresh prettiness would make him forget Nancy. Seeing his mother tonight—so like Nancy—had brought the mad love for his half-sister rushing back to him. "Herta, don't you think it would be a good idea for you to visit your family for a while?"

"No! I've told you a dozen times I'm not going to leave here without you. You think I want all my sisters and brothers laughing at me and saying I couldn't hold you? Why don't you give up these *verdamnt* diggings and go back to farm with your family in the Cape? Before I married you I thought you were going to take me down there, buy me satin dresses.

I wanted to look at the Ocean, I've never seen it!"

"I'll take you to the Cape when I've made a fortune up here. I know I can do it! Anyhow, you're better off up here than if you'd married a farmer in Lydenburg where you'd be working hard running the homestead as your mother always has and with a dozen kids by the time you're thirty and having to boss all the farm Kaffirs. At least with me you do damn well nothing."

"I wouldn't mind working like my mother and older sisters, at least that would be a decent life—but on the diggings. . . ."

"For God's sake, Herta! We've only been up here six months!" He caught her between the legs: it was the only way to stop her nagging. Within seconds she was squirming around, everything else was forgotten.

Hours later he muttered, "Let me grab some sleep." He gave her a playful push to her side of the bed and moved over to the other edge.

As she opened the lantern's little door to blow the candle out she giggled, "You see why you'll never make me go home, even for a week. I'd go *verdamnt* without you to lie with."

He breathed deeply, simulating sleep so that she would shut up. As he started to lose consciousness he thought whores in brothels must be like Herta who can climax every few minutes all night long. Herta could make a fortune running a pleasure house up here when the diggings became crowded.

They reined their horses in and stared out at a black expanse of undulating land. "There it is," Paul said, pointing to a long deep ditch with high banks of earth piled up along both sides.

Katie stared in amazement at the length of the ditch. "Paul—did you dig all of that?"

He dismounted and came to lift her off her horse. "I did most of it but then Struben advised me to hire three Kaffirs to help me." As Van Riebeck dismounted Paul told him, "Of course Kaffirs don't work as hard as I do; they won't own the gold that will be dug up."

The three of them walked to the head of the ditch as the Kaffirs, dismounting from a Capecart, started to unpack shovels, picks and buckets.

"When I started to prospect around here I found bankets like this." Paul knelt to pick up some pieces of rock, in his open palm he showed them to his parents. "You see the vein of quartz running through these stones?"

Katie was immediately excited. "That's the gold! Of course it is! It's like nuggets the hill Kaffirs brought me years ago at Hoffen. Just collecting piles of nuggets like these produced enough money to buy Abend Bloem."

"But you managed to get all the Kaffirs in the district working for you," Paul laughed, "and even then it took you five years, didn't it?"

She nodded, then suddenly realized these recollections might annoy Van Riebeck for Hoffen was young Paul's birthplace and from there she had vainly waited almost five years hoping for Van Riebeck's return.

"But if you found bankets like these on the loose earth why did you have to dig so deep?" Van Riebeck asked.

"Because there's not enough gold in

these. When I crushed them—for hours and hours—a hellish job—with pestle and mortar, they produced a negligible amount of gold dust, so I snooped around at other diggings and saw how people were digging down into the earth with better results." He pointed to the deep ditch where the Kaffirs were now pushing short, slender tree trunks into the earth. "That's Struben's idea to hold up the sides," Paul explained, "because sometimes when I'm digging the bloody earth slides down and almost buries me—Oh—sorry I swore, Mother."

"Go on, darling! Go on." She squeezed his arm.

"Well, once I was half buried for hours. After a while fortunately the Kaffirs missed me and came to dig me out."

"Oh God, Paul—it's very dangerous work," Katie murmured.

"It won't be, Katje," Van Riebeck assured her, "once he has those supports firmly wedged in. By the way, Paul, where do those small tree trunks come from. There's no sight of trees in the district."

"You're right, Father, everything has to be carted up from Pretoria. That not only makes the work so slow but the whole project so expensive. I would have been absolutely broke if I hadn't managed to extract some gold powder from the bankets I dug from this ditch."

"You've already sold some gold! How splendid!" Katie cried.

"Not much, just a few ounces to buyers in Pretoria, but I was able to buy my Capecart and more tools and have a little money in my pockets. Someday wealthy speculators will set up crushing machines and, poor devils like me will be able to hire them I hope."

"You've been here over six months and all you have to show for your labours is the Capecart and some tools," Van Riebeck said gravely. "You should remember that history has shown us that it isn't the men who are first to 'follow the Gleam', the discoverers in other words, who gain the prizes."

"Yes, Father, that's true, I've thought all about that but I've decided I'm going to stick with gold-mining. You see, this land is mine." Paul swung his arms out in a wide circle. "I fought for it as a soldier with the Afrikander Defence Corps and all this was my first payment. At Abend Bloem I'm working on a family estate and on your farm in Lydenburg, I'd be working 'your' farm." Paul grinned and raised his eyebrows—hoping for an understanding expression from his father; he already knew his mother was on his side.

"*Ja, ja*, Paul." Van Riebeck took off his wide-brimmed hat and slowly mopped his forehead with a cream silk handkerchief. "There's reason in what you say but don't let false pride make a fool of you."

"I won't, any more than Terence did by stepping out and making his way as a doctor. And what about you? You fought every savage tribe, you sweated and bled to help the Dutch trek North, your reward was 6,000 acres. You earned it, and I've earned my place." He shrugged wide shoulders, "Well if you don't mind riding back without me I'll start to dig."

"Yes, of course, we mustn't delay you." Katie was bursting with satisfaction at Paul's justifiable pride, and it shone in her eyes as she smiled up at him. "We'll see you for supper."

He nodded. "Then afterwards I'll take you to the Chinaman's to meet Struben."

The Chinaman's brown tent was larger than most, and in an attempt to give it a festive air he had covered the tin lanterns with brightly coloured Chinese lanterns. The floor was of earth stamped hard, the counter was made up of packing cases stacked together and on top of each other, there were several rough tables and chairs for patrons accompanied by ladies. The air smelled of a mixture of tobacco, lamp oil, beer and human sweat. The patrons were untidy-looking men who leaned against the "bar". At one table there were two men and a tired-looking woman.

Katie and Herta, whom Katie had persuaded to join them, sat down with Van Riebeck whilst Paul stood waiting for their drink orders. "I advise beer," he said. "Brandy is a terrible price."

They all decided upon beer, though Katie who disliked even the smell of it had no intention of drinking hers. "Good," Paul said, "I'll go for it and see if Struben has arrived."

They watched him moving to the make-shift bar where the Chinese owner, with his long black pigtail hanging over his shoulder to his waist, bowed a greeting to him.

"You see how well the Chinaman knows Paul!" Herta burst out in disagreeable triumph. "It's because he's always here of a night."

"I suppose that's because he wants to compare notes with other diggers." Katie spoke placatingly, thinking that the miserable place was a poor form of amusement for Paul.

Carrying a wooden tray holding tin mugs Paul returned with a middle-aged man wearing a well tailored black suit and he introduced Mr. Struben to the family.

"I'm delighted to meet you, Mr. Struben," Van Riebeck indicated a vacant chair for the surveyor who sat down beside him. "I've come to the Witwatersrand to see you," he smiled, "as well as Paul of course, but I'm a member of the Volksraad and President Kruger wants me to get your sincere opinion of what the gold potentialities are here."

"Yes, I had heard that he wanted a professional opinion and I'll gladly give it to you—free, gratis and for nothing."

357

"How very good of you, sir. A report from you will be invaluable to us."

Struben took a swallow of beer then continued, "I first heard about gold up here a couple of years ago so I came from Kimberley to look around and decided that gold was here without doubt. My brother and I—whilst not wealthy in the Cecil Rhodes or Barney Barnato class— still are men of means so we took a gamble and bought several farms . . . Sterkfontein and Swartkraus from Jacoby, Wilgesfruit from Dirk Geldenhuis who had already mortgaged it to my brother."

"But how right you were, sir, to buy them!" Paul said with enthusiasm.

"Ah, but we had some doubts at first I can tell you and all of our friends laughed at us—swearing we had made a bloomer."

"I was told you paid £2,800 for 6,847 acres," Van Riebeck said. "Excuse me for asking, but was that a fair price? You see, I'm very ignorant about these things but it's imperative that I learn about them."

"That's your job, I understand, Commandant Van Riebeck. Yes, I can truthfully say that a couple of years ago when so little was known about the

Witwatersrand, that we paid a fair price because we had to pour money into the land with machinery installations and labour. It took quite a time before we at last struck gold—not in great quantities you understand—but at least enough to convince us that gold is there."

Very excited Katie burst out, "Mr. Struben, on our son's land do you *really* think there is much gold to be found?"

Struben nodded as his shrewd eyes examined her lovely, flushed face. "I guarantee there is, but I can't say in what quantities or how deep he'll have to go. He needs machinery to work his diggings properly and that costs money. My brother and I ordered a gold-crushing battery from England. It should arrive any time now." He chuckled and looked over at Paul. "That will be a great day, you'll have to ride over to our place and watch us put it to work."

"I'll come and lend you a hand, sir." Paul's eyes held a deep longing look that made Katie venture the question. "If it's not a personal question, what does such a machine cost, Mr. Struben?"

"A great deal, I'm afraid, Mrs. Van Riebeck. £6,000."

"The machine costs £6,000!" Katie exclaimed in despair as she sank back against her chair.

Paul just nodded his head saying, "The price puts it out of reach for all the little fellows." He gave a shrug. "Still I'm grateful to own land that has gold on it! Even if it takes for ever to bring it out."

"You're right, young man, and later when speculators come along, offering to buy off part of your land or *all* of it, just you hang on to it," Struben advised. "Of course I'm lucky to have my brother for a partner."

"You are indeed, sir." Paul was envious. "I've three grown brothers, but one's a doctor, the other will be a lawyer and the third is on Cecil Rhodes' personal staff."

Struben burst out laughing. "With such a connection as Rhodes you don't need to look further. Tell your brother to let Rhodes know about the gold on your land."

"For God's sake!" Van Riebeck burst

out. "Let's keep Rhodes out of the Witwatersrand for as long as possible!"

"Don't worry, Commandant, I was joking," Struben said. "I've known the fellow for years in Kimberley and I'll wager he won't be up here until the land is really producing gold in quantities and the risk of failure no longer exists. It's Lobengula's land in Matabeleland that Rhodes is after and not only for the gold —he wants to spread the British Empire."

"He's dangerous in my opinion," Van Riebeck said. "With his mad ambitions to turn the world into the Queen's Empire."

Struben nodded gravely and glanced around to include Katie and Herta. "Commandant Van Riebeck is right: I've heard Rhodes say and I'll try to quote verbatim, 'I am wedded to the plan for the furtherance of the British Empire, for the bringing of the whole civilised world under British rule, for the recovery of the United States, for the making of the Anglo-Saxon race into one Empire'."

"As an Irishwoman," Katie's eyes blazed furiously, "I would like to punish him for his evil ambitions."

"Don't be upset," Van Riebeck spoke

quietly. "He hasn't a chance in hell of realizing his hopes. The South African Republic has proved that by beating England at Majuba."

"I was born in Pietermeritzburg of English parents," Struben said, "which makes me a true South African so I'm for Union—someday. Therein will lie our strength against England and don't let's forget Germany who has been casting too many longing looks at our country."

"*Ja, ja,*" Paul nodded, "but the trouble is—Union under whose flag—the South African Republic, the Orange Free State, the Cape Colony or Natal?"

"The South African Republic is quite satisfied with matters as they are," Van Riebeck said stiffly as he pulled his pipe from a pocket.

"But, Father, there are so many things that would benefit the Republic if Unionisation came: for example no more import and export taxes! And then railways built to connect all big towns to each other!"

"Perhaps you're right in a way, Paul; time will tell. About your report, Mr. Struben, when might I have it? Kruger is really anxious for your true opinion about gold on the Witwatersrand."

"In a couple of days or so. I must give serious thought to the wording of it."

"And you're already convinced that our son's land will produce gold, Mr. Struben?" Katie's eyes stretched wide with her longing for even further conviction.

Struben nodded. "I guarantee that gold is there; you've seen the quartz markings for yourself, but I'm not God, I cannot foretell how much will come out of Paul's diggings. In a few years he could be a multi-millionaire, only God knows that. But I do say—with studied caution—that if it were *my* son's land I would advise him to hold on to it for as long as possible." Struben looked for a moment into Herta's sulky face. "I'd try to find some honest, satisfactory partners to join him. Four or five young men together might be able to pool their funds and some day acquire their own crushing machine, otherwise it will be a long, hard job without a machine."

As the men went on talking and drinking their beer, Katie's mind was awhirl with excitement. Paul could some day be a multi-millionaire—those were Struben's very words! How could she help him? But £6,000 was an impossible sum for her to gather together—yet he just *must* have a crushing machine!

20

OR the next week, from dawn until sundown, Van Riebeck rode across the Witwatersrand, covering as great a spread as possible where prospectors were digging. He also called at isolated farms where it came as a shock to him to learn that the impoverished Boer owners were anxious to sell their land, consisting of 10,000 acres for a paltry £200.

"But why the devil do you want to sell, man?" Van Riebeck asked; "And for such a pittance?" The answers were always almost identical.

"Rinderpest wiped our cattle out some years ago and we had no money to replace them. Then we had several seasons of drought so there were no wheat harvests, now we want to get away. With a little cash we can buy some cattle and go to farm with some of our family in better districts."

"*Magtig!* But you must try to hold on to your land! Once the Volksraad is certain that there is gold all over the Witwatersrand we will let the whole country know it so that wealthy speculators will pour in and you'll sell your farms for ten times as much. There's a man called Struben who's paid over £2,000 for about 6,000 acres."

The farmers gaped open-mouthed at him but they had confidence in the great Commandant Van Riebeck and swore to him to hold off selling in the hope that a gold-rush would inflate the value of their land.

As he rode around he dismounted at places where diggers were at work, after introducing himself he would explain that he was making a rough survey of conditions for the Volksraad and the men of various nationalities willingly answered his questions. Many of them were from the diamond fields in Kimberley, where the amalgamations formed by men like Beit, Barnato and Rhodes were ousting small independent diggers.

Now a digger who gave his name as Reynolds, shook Van Riebeck's hand and said, "Of course these big chaps were right to buy up the little fellows to form great companies." The tall, thin Englishman stuck his shovel edge in the ground and leaned on the handle. "It's a protection for diamonds, otherwise if digging went on indiscriminately diamonds would flood the world and become valueless."

"*Ja*, diamonds are not a necessary commodity and how do you feel about gold? Are you convinced it's here?"

"I am. It's going to be hell to get it out but, by God, it's here."

"So it will be a long hard job." Van Riebeck handed his tobacco pouch to the digger. "Have a fill."

"Thanks, I will. Tobacco like everything else is an exorbitant price. The Volksraad in Pretoria should be very careful about selling concessions for supplies to honest men or you'll have all the blackguards in the world up here fleecing the diggers and most of us don't have much money. We made a little when the big combines bought us out in Kimberley but that won't last us for ever."

"Have you had any appreciable results here yet?"

"Not yet." The digger had filled his pipe and returned the leather pouch.

"Thanks, but I believe in what I'm doing, I believe it will pay off."

"Thanks for your help and good luck." Van Riebeck mounted and rode off.

After covering some miles he dismounted to talk to a big red-bearded digger, a German who spoke Taal, the low Dutch, which Van Riebeck had conversed in with Bismarck when visiting Germany.

"It's good earth," the German said in answer to Van Riebeck's question. "I mined at Pilgrim's Rest near Lydenburg for some years and here I see more veins of gold, but my God, what a job to get it out. All rock up here—no soft earth, no panning for gold here like at Pilgrim's Rest."

"Then why the devil did you come here, man?"

The German narrowed his eyes craftily. "Because I've an instinct that it's going to be richer up here—also it's easy to get to. Do you know the road to Pilgrim's Rest past Hell's Height and Devil's Kantoor? It's bad enough in fine weather but when it rains, every place becomes a sea of mud and a miner is imprisoned on his diggings. That's no life for a man or beast, but what you fellows in Pretoria must do is to guard the water!"

"What do you mean—guard the water?"

"Exactly that! Water is scarce up here in the summer and everyone just goes along in his wagon to the spring and fills up as many buckets as he likes so that the man who comes last gets hardly any. You've got to sell water concessions like you sell digging concessions, then you've got to put guards over it."

"That's very useful information—thank you." Van Riebeck pulled a small bottle of brandy from his saddle bag and gave it to the German who grabbed it with delight. "Good luck to you," Van Riebeck said and they shook hands.

Wherever Van Riebeck rode, he gleaned useful information and now at sundown when he returned to the wagon he told Katie, "It amazes me to see how optimistic these men are, I can't understand it and most of them are experienced miners." He started to wash his face in a small tin basin.

"Optimism is an absolute requisite to mining. I discovered that when we were on the diamond diggings." Her mind flashed back to that difficult period when she had persuaded Richard Eaton, her second husband, to relinquish his position on the Governor's staff in Cape Town and with their six small children together with Terence and Paul as youths, they had trekked to the diamond fields. After a year, almost in despair at finding nothing, Nancy had discovered a big diamond in the clay and Eileen a second large stone in the weeds.

Van Riebeck was drying his face when Katie suddenly said, "Oh, there's a letter for you from Struben." She handed him the letter.

He threw the towel on a canvas chair, eagerly opened the envelope, pulled out a sheet of paper and read the neat handwriting of the covering letter. "Ah, here's Struben's report." He unfolded the paper.

"Darling, do read it aloud." Katie settled on a folding-stool beside him.

"Are you really that interested?" Van Riebeck teased.

"You know I am, for the Republic's sake, of course, but truthfully, mainly for Paul's sake."

"I wish to God he'd sell his land—but I'm afraid there's no hope of that—well this is what Struben says," and he began to read aloud.

"That there is gold in great quantity on the Witwatersrand is my sincere conviction and I consider it the duty of the South African Republic's Government to foster and protect the mining interests. It will rest with the Government as to whether the resources are developed or smothered; it will not be the fault of the soil.

I intend to work to the full all the properties in my possession and I recommend that those who can possibly manage it, open up their properties, either individually, or else get up small workable companies of moderate capital, to exploit their lands, so as to keep the money as much as possible in this country, and not rush off with everything to speculators who will form gigantic companies financed by foreign capital; which it has now been proved (as in Lydenburg) did not pay dividends and brought the country into discredit.

My brother and I have sent for a

crushing machine; it is a 5-stamp portable steam engine of 10 HP and is made by Messrs. Ransomes, Sims and Jefferies Ltd of Ipswich, England. Cost £6,000.

My recommendation is that as many of these machines as possible should be brought to the Witwatersrand to start important mining developments for small companies as the rock is almost impossible to work by hand.

I also advise that you do not advertise too freely about the gold and so attract half the blackguards of the world to the Witwatersrand."

Elation brought Katie to her feet, "Oh thank God—Struben has really put it in writing! So there's absolutely no doubt about it! There's gold in great quantity up here! That's what he says."

"Struben seems to believe that." Van Riebeck spoke guardedly although relief flooded his being at the prospect of enrichment for the Republic. "I think we must pull out tomorrow so that I can show this to Kruger."

"So soon—oh, how disappointing."

"Sorry, darling, but I am up here on a mission and I must relay this good news as soon as possible, it can save the Republic from bankruptcy."

"Oh, couldn't we stay a little longer? I've really seen so little of Paul." Since hearing Struben's report her determination to help Paul had forcibly returned. "Just a few days."

"You know I must be honest and return at once! It's vital for the Volksraad to have this report but there's a group trying to run a stage-coach with horses between here and Pretoria so later on you'd be safe to come out in that to see Paul."

"Any charitable person here who'd offer a thirsty miner a brandy?" Paul called out as he climbed aboard the wagon and came in.

"Hurrah, darling!" Katie grasped his forearms and on tiptoe stretched up to kiss his cheek. "I've been waiting for you to come. Sit down," she laughed happily, "this wagon is really not big enough for both of you long-legged giants." She started to pour brandy into two mugs then gave one to each man.

Paul took a swallow of brandy. "I must tell you a joke I've just heard. Two fellows who want to sell their land brought some rocks to a friend of mine showing a definite proof of gold in them and, they tried to make my friend pay at once for the land but he sent the rocks to a Kimberley assayer who reported that gold dust had been fired by a cartridge into the rocks which have no natural gold in them." Paul laughed dryly. "What do you think of that for a swindle, eh?"

Van Riebeck looked disgusted. "That's the sort of rotten trickery that breeds in diamond or gold fields. Here, Paul—read Struben's report."

He handed the page to Paul who quickly scanned it then handed it back saying, "Splendid report, eh, Father? Make you feel happier about the entire project?" Paul tossed some brandy off, thinking triumphantly now his father could not condemn him for staying on the gold fields.

"Yes, it's a hopeful report for men with some capital. Through all my investigations I've come to the conclusion that to be successful a man needs a stake of £10,000." He hesitated, "I'm sorry, son, we just can't give it to you."

"But I've never expected you to,

Father!" Paul felt his anger rising. Why the hell had his father imagined that he wanted help? "But I don't agree with your figure of £10,000—it's too high."

"Oh no it's not! I've met Struben several times on my own and discussed things thoroughly for my report to the Volksraad. A crushing machine costs £6,000, then there's the cost for water rights, for timber, cement and dynamite, wages and food for your Kaffir boys, money for a claim licence and then you and Herta have got to live, no matter how frugally, and your food still costs money."

"All that's true if you want quick results but I know I can't get quick results. I'll just have to continue the way I've been going—with my hand-crushing and living from day to day on my small quantity of gold dust until some day I've saved enough for a crushing machine."

"That could take years! For God's sake be sensible, son, and sell out."

"For two bloody thousand pounds so that some rich bastard from Kimberley can come along and make a million out of my land! Oh, sorry I'm swearing, Mother." Paul forced himself to calm down. "No,

Father, I'm *not* going to sell out! I'll keep on working on my own until later other people's crushing machines arrive and I can hire them once in a while."

"But you'll have to *pay* for that and for amalgam plates and mercury to treat the powdered rock." Van Riebeck was growing furious at Paul's stubbornness. "For God's sake have some sense and give up the whole idea, Paul."

"Never, Father! Never!" Paul's blue eyes, so like Van Riebeck's, were blazing with fury. "Mother, I'm going for a beer at the Chinaman's, I'll see you later," and he swung out of the wagon.

"*Magtig!*" Van Riebeck muttered furiously, "Struben's report says that crushing machines are needed here and Paul knows that. I've seen hundreds of diggers from Pilgrim's Rest who marched here with hearts full of hope, then after one look at the hard rock they knew their sluice boxes and pans were useless, so sensibly they're leaving."

"Yes but hundreds more keep arriving!" Katie retorted.

"They'll learn, the poor fools, that no

man can make a fortune up here without machinery."

Greatly agitated but trying to control it, Katie twined her fingers through each other so tightly that the knuckles whitened. "Please listen to me and don't grow angry." She looked compellingly into Van Riebeck's stern face and spoke softly. "Have you ever thought that you and I owe Paul a great deal more than we owe to our legitimate sons, Franz and Adrian? They are *legal* Van Riebecks, they bear your illustrious name but Paul is known as Paul Kildare—he is no more than Commandant Van Riebeck's step-son. Political doors will not open for him, who knows who his supposed father was? Just an Irish gentleman who died years ago. What is Paul Kildare's heritage? None!"

Van Riebeck's sin of pride that had stopped him returning to know if she were with child by him so that he could have married her and given Paul his rightful name was suddenly resurrected like some heinous evil. "In the name of God! What the hell are you trying to do to me, Katje?"

"To make you realize that you've a *special* duty to help *him*—we both have."

"*Magtig!* So that's what you're after and where the devil do I get £6,000 for him to fritter away up here."

"He won't be frittering it! There's a good chance that he'll come out of this a millionaire."

"All right, you 'may' be right," he said with heavy sarcasm. "He 'may' come out as rich as Croesus, but that doesn't alter the fact that I haven't got any money to help him with! Even if I did have it, the last thing I'd do would be to finance him in gold-mining!"

His eyes that could be so warm, tender, loverlike, were now like blue glass and Katie almost hated him as she went on. "What about your Lydenburg farm, you could raise a mortgage on it."

"How stupid you can be. The Republic is almost bankrupt so do you think a bank would loan money on the property of a citizen of the Republic?"

"There's your estate in Stellenbosch; you could raise a mortgage on it." She would *make* him help Paul; it was his duty.

"Chris mortgaged that for me to buy guns and ammunition to fight at Majuba."

"You never told me that—but naturally for your precious Republic you found the money when you wanted to."

"It's *my* estate—have you forgotten? My ancestors built that house over two hundred years ago, I can do as I wish with it."

"Then sell it for God's sake and help Paul."

"Now you've really gone mad—that goes to my sons. . . ."

"Franz and Adrian! Van Riebecks—yes, of course." She spat the words at him.

"You are quite correct," he answered in cold fury. "That is if they *behave* like sons of mine." He flipped his hat off a peg. "I can tell you that Paul's behaviour, his bloody stubborness about this mining business, does not endear him to me and I haven't forgotten that it's not the first time he's crossed me. He knew damn well I was against his wasting three years elephant hunting around the Zambesi. I wanted him in Pretoria—studying law so that he could serve the Republic!"

"The Republic! The all-sacred Republic!" She glared at him and then at his hat in his hand. "For God's sake go wherever you intend going. I want to be alone for a while."

"For as long as you like; it might help you to forget your gold-fever madness and regain some common sense."

He swung off the wagon and she heard him ordering a Kaffir to saddle his horse, then she heard the horse trotting off.

Sick with rage at Van Riebeck's implacable attitude Katie sank on to the edge of the bed. She was grateful that Adrian, Franz, Eileen and Herta had ridden off in Paul's Capecart to see a spring and so she could have a few more minutes alone. She must think—think—think. Somehow Paul must have help.

Her clenched fists beat at her temples; she would devise a means to help him. There was gold on his land, but it was absurd! Ridiculous that he should spend most of his days digging then crushing out the gold dust by hand. Any money invested on Paul's land she knew would turn into profit; it would not be "frittered" away as Van Riebeck said.

380

He must have a crushing machine! £6,000! A huge sum—yet she would find it. How? How? Borrow from Howard? No, she could not place herself in such a position. Then she knew what she would do—she would mortgage Abend Bloem! Just as Van Riebeck had mortgaged his Cape estate to buy guns and ammunition.

A strangely calm elation came to her: she had arrived at the correct decision and it strengthened her. As soon as she returned to Pretoria she would see the manager of the Standard Bank there. He would not know the value of Abend Bloem, but he could telegraph the manager of the Standard Bank in Cape Town who had known her for years and also knew of all the money Abend Bloem had made in the past on wine, on ostrich plumes, and now dried fruit sales were coming along. She was convinced she would have no trouble in raising the loan.

The more she thought of her plan the happier she grew and wanted to ride to the Chinaman's to tell Paul, but a woman must not ride alone at this hour and be the cynosure of the diggers' eyes as they lolled about smoking, chatting or playing cards on upturned packing cases. Also Paul might refuse her help, not wishing her to mortgage the family estate. Wiser if she could order the machine, then write to tell him to expect it. But how could she do this? How?

Howard! Of course, he was the answer. In Pretoria she would cable him to order the machine and assure him repayment would come from the Standard Bank. But now—she must copy the maker's name and address for the machine from Struben's report, thank God Van Riebeck had left it on the little table.

Swiftly she found pen, ink, paper and wrote the necessary information, then tucked the piece of paper deep in her reticule. Now that her plans were made she was anxious to reach Pretoria to proceed with them.

Half an hour later the two men returned in apparently good humour and then Herta and the children arrived and the family sat around the camp fire eating *bobootie* which Maarje had spent hours cooking. Van Riebeck and Paul afterwards entertained Franz and Adrian by throwing small stones in the air which the boys tried to hit with sticks. Herta and Eileen chatted, Eileen answering Herta's questions about the Cape but Katie was almost silent, absorbed with her plans.

Then when Franz and Adrian were in bed, Katie and Maarje gave Herta nearly all their food supplies and Van Riebeck handed Paul three bottles of brandy.

"Thanks, Father," Paul grinned delightedly. "This is really a treat."

"Stupid of me not to have realized that supplies would be scarce up here; I should have loaded the wagons with things for you," Van Riebeck apologised, feeling that some brandy and food were poor presents.

"Next time please bring me some eau-de-cologne," Herta said feeling very worldly by using the French words. "When there's a water shortage everyone begins to stink."

The girl can't help being vulgar, Katie thought despairingly but said, "When the coach between Pretoria and here starts to operate, Herta, you should go in sometimes and buy things you need."

"Oh no! I'd never leave Paul by himself for a night, that's when he needs me." She giggled insinuatingly and shot Paul an intimate look that he loathed and was thankful it escaped his mother.

Soon afterwards "goodnights" were said and everyone retired to be awakened an hour later by a violent thunder storm that rocked the wagons like ships on a rough sea. Lightning slashed the heavens and hailstones large as eggs fell with such ferocity they cut through the wagons' canvas tops.

Van Riebeck went over to the children's wagon to see that they were all right whilst Katie mopped the lionskins and placed buckets and basins beneath holes made by hailstones. What a purgatory it was to live up here she thought despairingly and even after Paul had his crushing machine at work and his land was producing gold he must still live through this brutal existence! God willing not for too long though. God willing he would soon make a fortune!

Amidst the roll of thunder and battering of hailstones she heard laughter and shouting. What was happening? She pulled the flap open and was amazed to see bare-chested diggers, towels about their hips standing with the rain slashing down on their bodies. Poor devils, Katie thought, they've had no baths for months.

Just after dawn the Van Riebeck wagons were ready to pull out. As Katie kissed Paul's cheeks she ached to say. "You are going to have your crushing machine," instead she whispered so that Van Riebeck could not hear, "I believe you're right not to sell your land! I *know* in my bones you'll make a fortune in gold."

He grinned down at her, holding her shoulders tightly. "Thanks, Mother," he murmured suddenly feeling absolutely secure because of her belief in him, just as he used to feel when a small boy he suffered nightmares and she came in with a lighted candle to caress him and chase the bogies away.

21

LATE that afternoon as the Van Riebeck wagons were nearing Pretoria Van Riebeck said, "Katje, I'm going straight to the Volksraad to report to Kruger. I'll be there most of the day—so will you reserve rooms at the Blesbok Inn for a couple of nights."

As they had hardly spoken since their row the previous afternoon Katie now answered coldly, "I hope there'll be space at the Inn, judging by the streets we've passed through Pretoria suddenly looks pretty full."

"Let's hope they're all concession hunters from the Cape, the Orange Free State, Natal—oh, everywhere. Our Exchequer needs cash as fast as it can find it."

She had no intention of being drawn into a conversation with him over the Republic's finances; she was absorbed with finance for Paul. Standing before a small hanging mirror she busied herself in becomingly arranging her sunbonnet. She must look her best when she called at the Bank.

As the wagon neared the Volksraad building, Van Riebeck ordered the driver to halt, then told Katie, "Well, I'm on my way." Carrying his papers in a dark brown case he jumped to the ground, then the wagon continued following the children's wagon to the Blesbok Inn where they pulled into the big yard already crowded with wagons and carts.

Telling Maarje and the boys to wait, Katie took Eileen with her into the white-washed, spread-out building. The Dutch proprietor had known her for almost ten years, since her marriage to Van Riebeck and everything about her fascinated him.

"*Ach*, my dear Mrs. Van Riebeck, how nice to see you, and how many rooms will you be needing?"

"Two double rooms, please."

"We are crowded, but I'd turn even President Kruger himself out for you."

"Oh how kind you are."

"It's my pleasure—my pleasure. Four Englishmen have just arrived from Kimberley by the new horse-coach.

They're prospectors going to Witwaters-rand—they've got the gold-fever in their very eyes—I shall turn them out for you."

"I'm sorry you must do that."

"I'm glad to turn them out, red-neck English—for a good Boer family—you know, Mrs. Van Riebeck. . . ."

Katie interrupted, but with an ingratiating smile, "Thank you so much, I'll tell our drivers to outspan." She took Eileen out with her. "He never stops talking and I'm in a hurry. Darling, go and tell the drivers to outspan. I must go *at once* to the Telegraph Office next door so you bring Maarje and the boys to the Inn."

In the small Telegraph Office she did not care that there was a queue of eight people ahead of her because she was not quite ready to be attended to. She dug into her reticule hanging from her wrist, pulled out the paper with the message she had composed in the wagon and re-read it. Then she went to a little writing-shelf against a wall and on a clean sheet of paper started to print.

"Duke of Rotherford, Belgrave Square, London

Please purchase my behalf from Messrs Ransome, Sims and Jeffers, Ipswich a five stamp portable steam engine of ten horse power stop Use your influence obtain immediate delivery and ship fastest way care Liz Abend Bloem stop Price six thousand pounds stop Repayment coming from Standard Bank stop Please confirm care Post Office Lydenburg. Love Katie."

As she queued up to receive attention she was trembling with excitement; then handing the clerk the message she hoped that Howard's title would not interest him, also the order to purchase a crushing machine, but already people were crowding up behind her and the clerk, unaccustomed to such activity, merely read her telegram swiftly, counted the words and told her the cost.

She paid, then left and standing outside on the dirt pavement she heard a clock strike four. "Damn!" she swore silently, the bank was closed so she must wait until morning to be sure she could obtain the mortgage. But absurd! Ridiculous! To harbour any apprehensions. Then she went back to the Blesbok Inn to be sure the children were comfortably installed.

A few hours later a Kaffir boy brought her a message from Van Riebeck saying he was dining at the President's house, so Katie ate with the children, bathed the boys and put them to bed, then she and Eileen accepted an invitation to play whist in the drawing-room with a middle-aged Welsh couple, Mr. and Mrs. Steele, recently arrived by horse coach from Kimberley.

"We're hoping to buy a concession in Pretoria to open a dormitory house in the Witwatersrand," Mrs. Steele told Katie as Mr. Steele and Eileen shuffled the cards.

"We've just returned from there," Eileen burst out, "and it's very ugly, I don't think you'll like it, Mrs. Steele, will she, Mama?"

"Well, it's not very pretty countryside." Katie did not wish to sound depressing.

. "Can't look worse than the diamond fields did to begin with . . ." Mr. Steele laughed showing gaps in his upper teeth . . . "but the dormitory house we built there made a tidy sum for us until people started to build houses and our corrugated dormitory wasn't needed much."

"That's why we thought we'd come up here and get in early," Mrs. Steele nodded at her husband.

"That sounds very sensible of you." Katie tried to sound enthusiastic. "Do tell me about your trip from Kimberley." She was excited about the introduction of the horse-coach which drastically cut the journey to Kimberley.

"It was shocking, my dear—just shocking," Mrs. Steele said. "Five days passing through the most dreary country-side and sleeping in poor Boer farmhouses. I chose the bare floor in preference to the beds which were infested by vermin and I was never out of my clothes all the time."

"I slept out most nights with the other male passengers," Mr. Steele said. "It was pretty rough but look how quickly we got here. It was worth the hardship; the journey was cut by weeks."

His words lifted an enormous invisible weight from Katie. "Yes, it would be worth the discomfort and cheaper, too, than taking your own ox-wagon with people to guard you. Thank goodness for progress." So one could go to Kimberley in five days and from there catch the train for the Cape. That's how she would travel to go to Mary. Soon she must write to Howard asking him to cable her about Mary's pregnancy, supposedly by her new husband.

"That's right, Mrs. Van Riebeck, you said you'd been on the gold fields, has your husband got a claim there?" Mrs. Steele's sun-dried face was full of interest.

"No but my son has."

"Oh my—you don't look old enough to have a son who's a digger," Mrs. Steele said.

"Why don't you dig for gold, Mr. Steele?" Eileen asked enthusiastically, "like my brother—wouldn't that be better than the dormitory?"

"Perhaps yes, perhaps no, but you need plenty of cash to work the claims so I've heard. You see in Cardiff, where we were born, we ran a boarding-house and did quite nicely, then we heard about the diamond fields, so we sold up and sailed for the Cape, then we joined a trek up to the diggings. By that time we hadn't too much cash left so we looked around but saw plenty of fellows who'd been digging for months and were absolutely wiped out —some poor devils committed suicide. Nasty business that—so the Missus and I decided to do something we know about like the boarding-house. That's why we opened a dormitory and, believe me, it paid well. That right, Martha?"

"You know it, Jeff." She flashed a triumphant smile at Katie and Eileen. "We've been sending money back to Cardiff for our old age and now we've come up here to make some more."

"Of course corrugated iron is expensive and to drag everything up here costs a fortune . . ." Mr. Steele started to deal the cards . . . "but then we'll have to charge more for accommodation than we did on the diamond diggings."

Katie suddenly thought what an improvement it would be for Paul if he and Herta could sleep under corrugated iron, instead of a wagon top or a tent when winter came. "Does it take long to put up a house with corrugated iron?"

Steele shook his head. "No, I'm experienced, but I've been here three days and

I can't even get in to see the Minister of Concessions and it's expensive hanging around like this, so I don't want to wait much longer, I'd rather go back to the Cape and sail for Cardiff."

"I'll ask my husband to arrange for you to see the Minister of Concessions tomorrow—my husband is a member of the Volksraad, you see."

"Now that's a bit of jolly old luck, thank you very much."

They played whist then, until about ten o'clock, when a row broke out between a couple of half-drunk Englishmen who accused a couple of half-drunk Boers of cruelty to the Kaffir tribes.

"I hate these stupid racial rows," Katie told the Steeles, "so I think we'll be off to bed," and she and Eileen retired.

She was asleep when Van Riebeck returned but the following morning she asked him to arrange for Mr. and Mrs. Steele to see the Minister of Concessions and he promised to do so. As soon as he left she arose, washed and dressed carefully, then, after some coffee, left to go to the Standard Bank where after giving her name she was almost immediately ushered into the manager's, Mr. Turner's, office. She gave him her most charming smile, hoping to secure his immediate co-operation and when greetings and hand-shakes were over she sat facing the middle-aged Englishman across his desk.

"Mr. Turner, first of all I must ask you to treat the purpose of my visit in absolute confidence."

"But of course, Mrs. Van Riebeck." He bowed his head with its salt and pepper coloured hair. "Without your request, in any case, your confidence would be strictly observed."

"Thank you, I was certain of that, but the important thing is. . . ." She hesitated for a second, not liking what she was obliged to say. "I do not wish my husband to know about it."

His expression did not alter. "If that is your wish, Commandant Van Riebeck shall certainly not hear of it."

"Thank you, the fact is that I wish to raise a mortgage on my estate in Stellen-bosch. You may know it—Abend Bloem?"

"I certainly know of it. What amount do you have in mind?"

"£6,000."

"That's quite a heavy loan."

"Not on Abend Bloem. Your Mr. Perkins in Cape Town is familiar with the estate and all that it produces. It's one of the richest estates in the wine district. Mr. Perkins knows how we recovered from our losses when phylloxera ruined our vines by developing our ostrich farms and dealing in ostrich plumes."

"Yes I see." Mr. Turner sat back and pursed his lips. "I'm afraid that I'm utterly helpless to assist you from up here, I would advise you to write to Mr. Perkins about a loan. By the way where are the deeds of the estate?"

"In my safety deposit box at your Bank in Cape Town, but I can't wait for a letter to go back and forth between Mr. Perkins and myself; time is important to me, that's why I've come to you to ask you to telegraph my request to Mr. Perkins. The Bank surely has a code for telegrams, hasn't it?"

He gave a little smile, she was such a beautiful woman and intelligent too. "Indeed we do have a code."

"Good, then would you be so kind as to telegraph on my behalf? You see, if I did it, in this small place, my message to Mr. Perkins would be common gossip all over the town—everyone will know I want to borrow that sum. It would look very bad for my husband."

"Yes, I appreciate that." He pulled a sheet of paper toward him, dipped his pen into the silver inkwell and looked up at her. "Now you want to borrow £6,000 immediately—correct?"

"Exactly."

His pen started to scratch on the paper. "And to be paid—to you—where?"

"Oh not to me, it's to be transmitted to the Duke of Rotherford, Belgrave Square, London."

Although amazed by this information Turner never looked up, his pen went on scratching over the paper and he repeated, "Duke of Rotherford, Belgrave Square."

Katie felt instinctively that an explanation was essential. "He's a cousin of my late husband, the guardian of my children."

"Ah yes. Are you prepared to pay whatever interest the Bank wishes to charge on the loan?"

"I think so, Mr. Turner," Katie said

hesitantly. "I'm sure that Mr. Perkins would treat me fairly about that."

"You need have absolutely no qualms about that, I can promise you." His grey eyes enjoyed examining her face. "And what provision have you in mind for repaying the loan?"

"Oh, I . . ." she gave a nervous little laugh . . . "well, I hadn't really thought of that."

"But that's a very important point when trying to raise a loan, I'm sure you realize that."

"Yes, I suppose it must be." Once Paul owned the crushing machine he would make a fortune and help pay the loan back, she had no doubts about that. "Do you think I could have—say—two years to repay the loan?"

"Two years? Hmm . . . I take it that Abend Bloem is a very valuable estate so that should unforeseen difficulties arise in repaying the loan, the Bank could always dispose of part of the estate to collect their £6,000, together with interest owed?"

Katie's eyes blazed with fury at the quiet, calm man. How dare he suggest that part of her beloved Abend Bloem should be sold? But she warned herself that Turner was only doing his job. "You can assure Mr. Perkins that the loan will be promptly repaid on the arranged date, and possibly sooner."

She stood up and gave a little shake to her skirts as he swiftly rose to his feet. "Mr. Perkins' reply will probably be here by tomorrow afternoon, Mrs. Van Riebeck. Shall I send it to you?"

"No thank you, I'll call—if that's convenient to you."

"It will be my pleasure, Mrs. Van Riebeck."

They shook hands, she thanked him and left.

Outside she stood for a moment under a mimosa tree. She was trembling all over; it had been quite an ordeal in a way. She decided to go into the "Pioneer Coffee House" across the road for a coffee and a chance to think before returning to the Blesbok Inn and the children.

In the café with its whitewashed walls decorated by stuffed heads of leopard, buffalo and rhinoceros, she sat at a corner table sipping the strong coffee. She was suddenly filled with apprehensions at mortgaging Abend Bloem. Supposing by some evil chance Paul could not refund the £6,000? What then? Supposing the bank claimed a part of the estate? Had she robbed her other children for Paul? Well, Terence would be well cared for by his own brilliance and also Elaine was Sir Daniel's only child and his heir. Her five children by Richard Eaton would inherit Lady Eaton's fortune and also Howard had told her they were mentioned in his will. Franz and Adrian were Van Riebeck's legitimate heirs but Paul—her beloved Paul—he could look to no one but to her. Yes! A million times yes! She had been right to seek a loan on Abend Bloem for Paul. She owed it to him.

In any case the estate was worth a great deal. Even should she default on repayment and the bank sell part of it, there would still be a good deal left for Liz and Chris—who must be cared for and also their offspring for Liz and Chris had faithfully run Abend Bloem for ten years on Katie's behalf.

Feeling more at peace with herself she left the "Pioneer Coffee Shop" and returned to the Blesbok Inn, but now she began to worry about Mr. Perkins' reply: Would he agree to the loan? Had she been wrong in cabling Howard to purchase the crushing machine before she knew if the money were secured? Her whole being revolted at the idea that Howard should be left unpaid. That was unthinkable!

That evening Van Riebeck again worked late with Kruger, so Katie was absorbed with thoughts of the £6,000, but for Eileen's sake she played whist with Mr. and Mrs. Steele who were filled with gratitude because Van Riebeck, true to his promise, had arranged for them to see the Minister of Concessions and they had been able to purchase the right to erect the dormitory.

"So we'll be leaving tomorrow afternoon," Mr. Steele told Katie, "when we've made our necessary purchases."

Katie could only think of her appointment tomorrow afternoon at the Bank and wonder if Mr. Perkins' answer would be favourable.

Filled with trepidation, lest she meet with Mr. Perkins' refusal, Katie was ushered into Mr. Turner's office and at first sight of his smiling face her fears were dissipated.

"Mr. Perkins is happy to accommodate you, Mrs. Van Riebeck, I'm glad to say, so I've prepared the necessary documents for you to sign, also a letter giving Mr. Perkins permission to open your safety deposit box."

"Oh? But why open it?"

"Well you see, the bank must keep possession of the deeds of ownership of Abend Bloem."

"Really—they're very old, written on sheepskin, I hope they'll take care of them."

"I can assure you they will."

"Ah yes, well, where do I sign?" It pained her a little to be signing part of beloved Abend Bloem away but then as she continued to sign her name at designated spots on different pages, the depression suddenly slipped away, like shining brilliant light into blackness and she felt an almost hysterical joy to be able to give Paul the help he needed at this difficult period of his life, for might this time not be for him a "floodtime"? As Shakespeare said, "There is a tide in the affairs of men, which, taken at the flood, leads on to fortune."

It made these moments some of the finest of her life and she thanked God.

When she had finished at the Bank she rushed back to the Blesbok Inn and sat down to write to Paul. She would then take the letter to the Steeles to deliver to him.

Paul Darling,

Wonderful news! I have cabled Howard to order you a crushing machine like Struben's and asked him to insist upon immediate delivery so if all goes well, you should have the machine within three months, but I am giving you the good news at once so you will know that your days of slavery, of mining by manual strength—are not for long.

In case you are worried that I robbed a bank or borrowed the money from Howard, be at ease: I have taken a Bank loan on Abend Bloem. The loan must be repaid within two years and I have every confidence that your land will be yielding a fortune by then. But don't worry, darling if it does not, for we shall find other means of repaying the Bank, but I know you will make your fortune on your land.

No one knows what I have done and I would rather the secret remain between the two of us, so please destroy this letter. I cannot wait for the day that you have your "crusher" at work.

All my love and God bless you,
Mother.

As she folded the letter and put it into the envelope, her eyes grew misty as she imagined her beloved son's great joy when he read it.

22

"I'VE been thinking that the swiftest way to spread word about the Witwatersrand gold is to let the *Independent* know in Kimberley," Van Riebeck told Kruger, "The newspaper is read by most of the 10,000 population and diggers who sold out to the big amalgamations will still have gambling fever in their blood."

"*Ja, ja,* and have been well paid by those skelm millionaires Rhodes, Beit and Barnato, who have made millions of pounds themselves on the small men," Kruger spat in disgust and the spittle landed into his brass spitoon.

Van Riebeck busied himself with filling his pipe, he could never become accustomed to Kruger's rough manners. "I've nothing against Alfred Beit. He's a German who doesn't give a damn about enlarging Germany's possessions as Rhodes wants to enlarge England's. Beit just wants money and it's the same with

Barnato—he's a smart Hebrew from London's East End. I wouldn't object if they invested in the Witwatersrand."

"*Ja, ja*, the Almighty has willed it that we must encourage Uitlanders to our Republic and so we must do it, we need their money."

"I thought of writing a small article telling about Struben's finds, 5 ounces of gold to the ton with the possibility of 8 ounces, then sending it to the *Independent*. Of course I won't use my name on it."

"A good idea, let the article go by today's coach."

"Better to telegraph it; it will be there in five hours—instead of five days."

"Right, man." Kruger's small eyes lit up with enthusiasm. "We need the gamblers up here as soon as possible, but when they come let us be sure that we sell them only concessions for *mining*, no other privileges. You and the State Attorney work out the laws. Now send a Kaffir off with the telegram."

Kruger turned around to his desk to sort through piles of papers whilst Van Riebeck sat at a table to write the telegram. As he finished the message an idea came to him and he signed, "Paul Kildare, Camp 23, Witwatersrand". The Editor of the *Independent*, pleased to receive the news, might engage Paul as the *Independent*'s journalist on the diggings. Tonight he would write an explanatory letter to Paul and send it by Mr. and Mrs. Steele.

When the telegram had gone, Kruger looked up from his papers at Van Riebeck pacing the floor, "So what's next?"

"I'm worried by those poverty-stricken farmers, spread over the Witwatersrand who want to sell 10,000 acre farms for £200."

"*Magtig*—they need cash like the Republic does!"

"But we must stop them selling so cheaply!"

"*Ach*, man, but how? We have no money to help them with."

"Not yet but we will have pretty soon, I'll wager. If those poor devils sell for such a pittance, we'll be to blame. We should make a law at once that no man sell a farm without Government permission."

Kruger's fat fingers combed thoughtfully through his grey beard as he considered the idea. "I don't know about that; it's something like Pretorious' old law forbidding people to say if they found gold or copper on their land—Burghers was right when he broke the law."

"But this law would only be temporary to protect the people. I grow fighting mad when I think of the bloody Uitlanders who are going to buy those farms for £200 then turn the land into diggings with millions of pounds. We *must* do something to help our people to hold out for fair prices."

"No good sending them letters of advice," Kruger muttered. "Most of the doppers can't read, but in the sight of God they are all my children and as a good father I must protect them. I will send a man to them telling them that *I* say they must somehow wait to sell and as soon as possible the Government will help them."

"That will be something anyway. And why not instruct them, as I tried to, that they must never sell without consulting the State Attorney's office? That will be some protection for them."

" *Ja, ja,* I shall do this tomorrow, I have work here . . ." he pointed to his desk . . . "to last me for months and all the

Volksraad members are busy, trying to save our bankrupt exchequer."

" *Ja*, and I'm off to work with our State Attorney." Van Riebeck grinned at Kruger for whom he had a great respect as an able leader. "But we're going to be a lot busier when the *Independent* prints our news. I'll wager the town will be bursting with Kimberley's diggers within the next five days."

"*Magtig*, it's not what we wished for: we wanted the South African Republic for the Dutch, that's what we trekked for, that's what our ancestors bled and died for and now here we are almost begging the Uitlanders to come in, but we need their cursed wealth."

"Our laws will be so tight they won't be able to harm us—don't worry, but I wish to God we had more educated young men amongst us. Every German I met on the diggings spoke English and Dutch as well as their own language. We must concentrate on educating our people as soon as we have money for it."

"*Ja*, the ignorance of most of our Transvaalers is one of our weaknesses." Kruger was thinking if only he had more men like

Van Riebeck he could spread the South African Republic from the Cape Colony, Natal, the Orange Free State and up to and including Delagoa Bay. "Have coffee with me, man, after dinner at my house, the rest of the Volksraad will be there."

"Good, mynheer, I'll join you," Van Riebeck flipped his hat from the peg and left.

Late that afternoon at the Blesbok Inn he showed Katie the letter he had written to Paul. She read it swiftly.

Dear Paul,

Today I telegraphed a report to the Editor of the *"Independent"* in Kimberley giving news of Struben's find, five ounces of gold to the ton, with the hope of eight. I signed your name to the telegram hoping the Editor might employ you as his reporter on the diggings. If they communicate with you, you will understand why.

I hope, son, that you will approve of my action, sired by my desire to aid you, although only in a small way.

All my best wishes and love,
Father.

410

Katie was trembling as she finished reading the letter; she felt rent by emotion at Van Riebeck's attempt to help Paul, but almost hysterical at the paucity of the gesture. Yet she must try to sympathise with his position: he was weighed down with Governmental responsibilities and distracted by a bankrupt exchequer.

She looked up at him with truce in her eyes and she saw the stern lines of his face soften. "That was a clever idea, darling. I think Paul will be pleased. What kind of money might the *Independent* pay?"

"God knows, I'm ignorant about newspaper work, but whatever they pay, it will help Paul. You know, Katje, I realize that you've probably been blaming me for not attempting to finance him but I'm in the most hellish fix."

She turned away to button the clean bodice she had just put on. She was so secretly elated at her arrangement for Paul's crushing machine that she felt quite forgiving toward Van Riebeck. "I do realize that everything is very difficult for you at the moment," she murmured.

"Difficult! My God—it's impossible! We haven't money to pay our Governmental employees, from the highest down to the lowest street sweepers, the sewage collectors. Members of the Volksraad are paying all small expenses from their own pockets. I even paid for that telegram today—if money doesn't start to pour in right away we'll all have to help with our own money or Pretoria and all the other towns will come to a standstill."

She pitied the Transvaalers the distances of transportation for their produce; the import and export taxes at the ports had ruined them and to top it all the English had denied them Saint Lucia Bay. "I'm sorry, darling, I remember once before when you had to pay the Post Office workers with stamps, but I'm sure people will start rushing in to buy concessions for digging and your financial worries will soon be over."

He stepped up to her and caught her by the shoulders and pulled her to him, he adored her in this soft encouraging mood. "Katje—Katje, God knows how I love you." He crushed her to him and kissed her lips with all of his tired being.

With great warmth she returned his kisses, glad that they were once more reunited in spirit. Years ago a row such as they had had the previous evening would have caused them to part. Thank God with maturity had come wisdom.

In a few minutes she pulled herself out of his arms saying, "Your letter, darling, to Paul, and I've also written one, I must take them to the Steeles and say goodbye to them."

Longing to lie with her he said, "Don't stay long with them. Please come back quickly."

She smiled and nodded, for she understood his meaning. "Don't worry, I'll only be a few minutes."

She found the Steeles in their room. They looked tired, hot and anxious as they finished strapping their portmanteaux. She gave them the letters and told them how to find Paul's wagon near Langlaagte's farm and they promised faithfully to deliver the letters the next day.

"We've bought a tent," Mrs. Steele told Katie, "at a most exorbitant price, but the

Dutch shopkeeper said he only had a few. He's afraid to order more from Durban in case there aren't enough people coming to buy them."

"That's one of the troubles about Pretoria," Mr. Steele grumbled. "All the shopkeepers have such small stocks; a tin kettle, plates and mugs were so hard to find and lots of other camping necessities aren't here. I'm going to have to bring everything up from Natal, corrugated iron for the dormitory's roof—there's none on sale here, or wood for the sides of the hut." He looked very harassed.

Pitying them Katie said, "Don't worry, supplies of most articles will be coming up soon. I'm not supposed to say so but one of the big surveyors says there are five to eight ounces of gold to the ton on the diggings."

"That's splendid news!" Mr. Steele winked encouragingly at his tremulous looking wife. "See, Martha, you'll have nothing to worry about. People will be flocking up here and we'll be the first with a dormitory."

"I'm so glad, Jeff." Mrs. Steele smiled and looked at Katie with a woman-to-woman expression. "It's not so easy being the wife of a pioneer, is it? And that's what Jeff really is—a sort of pioneer and that's what I've become."

"Indeed it is not easy," Katie commiserated, then smiled widely, "but the most important thing in life is to be with the man you love, isn't it?"

Martha's dried up face flushed, she found it embarrassing to discuss such intimate affairs.

Guessing this, Katie swiftly shook hands with them saying, "Have a good journey and do find my son first. His name and address—such as it is, is on the letters. He'll help you with everything."

She left them, hurrying down a narrow corridor to Van Riebeck.

At the bedroom she lifted the latch and went in to find Van Riebeck lying on the bed in the shadows for he had partway closed the shutters.

"Back at last, darling—but you were a long time."

"Sorry, but of course I couldn't bounce in and out in one breath saying I must go at once because my husband wants to make love to me."

He laughed with her and excitedly watched her stepping out of her full skirts, then she bolted the door. "The Steeles were complaining about not finding supplies for camping in the shops. The shopkeepers' stocks are very low."

"That's natural, the poor devils don't know what the future holds for them, but we must instil confidence in them and make them stock up. Hurry up, darling, or do you need my help?"

She went to lie beside him still wearing her muslin camisole and long drawers. "All right, my love, you can do the rest."

He chuckled as, naked, he sat up and undid the blue ribbon bows on her camisole and took it off. At sight of her beautiful full breasts he started to kiss them and she clasped his head tightly, running her fingers through his thatch of golden hair. The sight of his head on her breast stirred deep feelings of happiness in her, of wonderful memories as well as the present, this is what for years she had loved almost most in their love-making. Then his hands moved down to untie the ribbons at the waist of her long drawers and he dragged them off.

Arms around her naked body he gathered her to him, his mouth on hers. Then her hands smoothed over his big back, down to his tight buttocks, and her fingers squeezed the flesh. Then he rained kisses all over her and within a few moments was ready to enter her. As always their bodies were absolutely in tune and together they reached a summit of ecstasy.

As they lay side by side in complete lassitude she thought of what she had said to Mrs. Steele. "You know, darling," she murmured, "I tried to cheer Mrs. Steele up when she was feeling sorry for herself, by saying the most important thing in life is to be with the man you love—poor woman, I really think I shocked her."

"You probably did!" He chuckled at the absurdity. "She's English and they don't speak about such things—not as you sentimental Irish do. But thank God you still feel like that."

"Why 'still'—you know I'll never change. I just hope that *you* won't, you're a magnificent-looking man and lots of young girls could fancy you." She was too wise to say what she was thinking. Now that I'm middle-aged you might prefer a young girl.

He rose on an elbow to stare down at her and he spread her red-gold hair out like a fan on the pillow around her face; this was the way he always loved to see her, her naked body still so beautiful despite having borne ten children.

He said softly, "Well, my love, God hasn't created the young girl, or any kind of female, who could take me from you." He leaned down and kissed her smiling mouth.

"You don't feel like that when we're quarrelling," she teased him. "Do you?"

"Damned true! I could choke you when your wild temper is let loose."

You very nearly did once when we were quarrelling, she thought as she twined her arms around his neck and pulled his head down to hers. "Lucky—aren't we?" she said aloud. "We've been blessed."

He started to fondle her breasts, already excitement was mounting in him. "I can never have enough of you." He gently bit her breast as he threw a leg over both of hers. "Sometimes you make me feel like Chaka—the best of the Zulu Chiefs—he used to eat the hearts of his enemies believing he would have their greatness inside of him."

"Darling, darling, don't swallow me altogether," she chuckled, "but bite me to your heart's content."

"You're a lovely—lovely devil, Katje," he murmured, playing with her body, turning and twisting her around as if she were an India rubber doll and she revelled in it all, caressing his manhood with joyous abandon where once she had been too shy to touch him.

"Now, darling, now," she whispered, then he climbed on top of her and entered her.

There came a banging on the door but they ignored it until they had reached their summit, then Van Riebeck rolled off her and called out.

"Who is it?"

"Maarje, *Baas*, come quickly, Massa Franz has locked himself in the outhouse and can't come out. He says it stinks very bad in there and is full of flies."

Van Riebeck laughed aloud. "I'm coming, Maarje" then he told Katie,

"Good of Maarje not to have knocked two minutes sooner."

"Yes," she laughed, "but I do wish I could make her use the word 'smell' instead of 'stink', I don't want the boys to pick it up."

23

VAN RIEBECK was obliged to remain working in Pretoria whilst Katie and the children went back to the farm from whence she had driven into Lydenburg and at the small Post Office found Howard's cable.

"Crushing machine your specifications leaving this week aboard steamship *Lancaster Castle* Love Howard."

In a state of euphoria, Katie wrote to tell Liz to expect the machine and asking her to arrange to have ox-wagon transportation ready to have it immediately transported to Paul. She added that the project must remain a secret between Liz and herself. She deliberately did not mention that she had mortgaged Abend Bloem, considering it would be wrong to burden Liz. She then wrote joyously telling Paul that "his" machine would soon be on the high seas, and his letter of heartfelt thanks was one of the most wonderful missives she had ever received.

A couple of weeks later he again wrote.

Dearest Mother,

The Struben Bros. crushing machine has arrived and is at work. In what seems like a magically short time it has crushed 61 oz of gold dust so you can see what we have to look forward to when "our" beauty arrives.

At the moment the Strubens are using their crusher full time so there's no chance of hiring it but I am buoyed up knowing that I shall have one. I am contemplating naming my mine "Madre" after the finest mother any fellow ever had and as soon as I have a chance I intend to see a lawyer in Pretoria and to sign over to you fifteen per cent of any profits the "Madre" will produce.

All my love and gratitude,
Paul.

A wonderful man—her love-child, born out of such a profound love. A love that had been unselfish and all-giving between

Van Riebeck and herself. Of course she would not accept his gift of fifteen per cent of his mines.

Being alone on the farm with just the children made Van Riebeck's absence almost a physical pain but she tried to fill her days in giving lessons to Franz and Adrian. Wishing to please Van Riebeck, she was teaching them all that she knew of Dutch history since the first Dutch sailors had been shipwrecked at the Cape more than two hundred and fifty years earlier. She also spoke to them in broken Afrikaans, to help them to become bilingual.

To Eileen, she devoted several hours a day reading the classics aloud and instructing her in the piano, Katie was delighted that her young daughter showed a definite talent for music. Then in the cool of the late afternoon, with Adrian astride a pony, they would all ride around the farm. Their favourite stop was at the sight of blue mountain peaks emphasising the gold of the wheat fields where Kaffir men and women, wearing bright bandanas to cheer their drab clothes, worked rhythmically scything the wheat as they sang softly in a mixed tongue of Swahili and Zulu. The following morning Katie would note the quantity of wheat cut and how much was baled ready for transportation day.

Later when the boys were in bed and Eileen sat reading, Katie wrote long letters to her family and nostalgically re-read Liz's letters describing Terence and Elaine's wedding and telling that Nancy appeared to be interested in several young Captains who were utterly enamoured by her. She also told of the family pride when Kenneth had received his law degree with honours. John as usual was all-absorbed in Cecil Rhodes' employment.

One of Liz's postscripts troubled Katie, for she believed in the saying that a woman's most important message is left for the postscript. Liz said, "Don't let it worry you but lately orders on our ostrich plumes have fallen off rather badly. Chris and I believe this is a temporary state for most exports are poor at the moment."

But this postscript certainly nagged at Katie. She had of course anticipated a time when the fashion for ostrich plumes might change, hence her interest in dried fruits.

Anyhow, once Paul made a fortune in gold, Katie was confident she would have no more financial worries. She had also received two short letters from Mary which she now re-read.

Darling Mama,
　　All is well at home I hope? Thank you for your letter giving me the news of Terry's wedding. Elaine sounds very nice.
　　You will be happy to know that my singing coach is very pleased with the progress I am making and I enjoy my lessons. I also like Florence and am learning Italian quite fast, I suppose because in Cape Town, Madame Visele taught me Italian songs.
　　　　　　　All my love,
　　　　　　　Mary.

How unsatisfactory! Not a word about her physical condition and by now she was entering her fifth month of pregnancy. Dear God! What difficulties lay ahead for Katie because even when she received the cable Howard would send saying Mary was pregnant, it would not warrant her going to Florence. To a Dutchman like Van Riebeck who was used to Boer women delivering themselves when alone on their farms, and Kaffir women dropping babies by a stream, washing them, slinging them on their backs, then trotting off to work in the fields, to such a man it would seem madness to go thousands of miles to be present at a young daughter's confinement. God! Oh God, she could not tell him she wasn't going for that but to see the colour of the child. Well, go she must and God would help her to somehow manage it all. Sighing, Katie opened Mary's second letter and read.

Darling Mama,

All goes well with my singing lessons and Cosimo has painted a life-size portrait of me which makes me look far too beautiful, but people think he has great talent and will be a famous artist one day. He is a nice person and very kind to me.

All my love,
Mary.

"He is a nice person and very kind to

me." "Thank God for that," Katie prayed, 'Oh God, let Mary fall in love with Cosimo! Let her tragic memories and experience with poor Sannie all die. Oh Lord—Lord—Lord!" But Mary's baby! What would be the colour of the unfortunate mite?

Van Riebeck's telegraphed report to the *Independent* in Kimberley, which they had immediately printed, had created a furore and experienced diamond miners, spurred now by gold fever, had rushed to Pretoria, travelling the fastest way by horse, or mule or horse-coach. Pretoria overflowed with noisy, eager men who grouped around the door of Vice-President Joubert's office waiting for their turn to buy claims. Once they were in their possession they went roaring off to the Witwatersrand to commence "making their fortune".

It all infuriated the Volksraad for the buyers were all Uitlanders, but the members calmed each other's rage, reminding themselves that the Uitlanders' money was killing the monster of bankruptcy and daily their exchequer was swelling with money.

"Do not fret," Kruger told his Cabinet in a solemn voice, his hand lying flat on the Bible. "Remember the words of Job—'All that a man hath will he give for his life'."

"*Ja, ja,*" Breda nodded heavily, looking into Kruger's rock-like countenance, "and the Lord knows that like Job we have been sorely tried—the last blow was being denied Saint Lucia Bay."

"Now that the good Lord is caring for His Chosen people . . ." de Vries gave a wide smile showing a gap in the row of his fine upper teeth . . . "isn't it time we started to plan ways of protecting our people in Goshen and Stellaland."

"The fate of those little republics is hard to decide," Van Riebeck said warningly, "because some of the Kaffir tribes in the district are for the Dutch, but some are for the English and it's these who keep causing us trouble."

"But we must keep Goshen and Stellaland no matter what happens!" Joubert threw a challenging glance at the others. "We've got to incorporate them in the Transvaal."

"*Ja, ja*, but they straddle the Missionaries Road and so block the Cape's trade and that's the root of the trouble," Breda argued, "and I don't believe those places with only one hundred Boers living there are worth much trouble to us."

"But we didn't start all this argument," Kruger reminded Breda. "It's Van Nickert and his Kaffir puppet, Massonu who asked for Transvaal protection."

"*Ach Magtig!*" De Vries burst out angrily, "all that land was ours before the *verdamnt* English annexed us and I say we should keep it. There are Boer homesteads there. It's part of the Transvaal."

"Rhodes spoke in the Cape Parliament persuading the House to annex Goshen and Stellaland with the whole of Bechuanaland as a British Protectorate," Van Riebeck warned, but said nothing of his meeting with Rhodes on the subject. Now that Saint Lucia Bay was a dead issue it was of no importance.

"*Ja, ja*, Rhodes has his dreams for the British Empire." Kruger's eyes moved craftily over the others' faces. "But I have my dreams for the South African Republic. We shall spread from Zambesi to Simon's Bay at the tip of the Cape—then shall it be truly Africa for the Afrikaaners. We must secure vast spaces in Central Africa so that the Lord's Chosen People shall not be encircled by her enemies—we must secure space for our descendants!"

My God, Van Riebeck thought despairingly, Kruger sounds like Rhodes in reverse. Their dreams of empire are wild, impracticable.

"But," he said aloud, "now one of our main tasks is to establish the Delagoa Bay Railway. Without a port we shall remain bottled up and unable to ship our produce to the world. I've been thinking that once Americans come to look over the Witwatersrand we might find finance in America for the Railway. Even if Germany would help us, the British would think up a way to block the enterprise."

"Van Riebeck's right," Breda nodded. "The British are terrified by the way Germany is spreading in East Africa. Already she has seized Mamaqualand and Damaraland." Breda knocked his pipe out on the heel of his shoe. "Britain therefore imagines Germany intends to march overland and annex the South African Republic . . ." he gave a nasty laugh . . . "and as we all know Britain would rather have us herself."

"Even now the red necks don't understand us," Joubert said. "Not she, nor Germany, nor Belgium, Portugal nor the French or any other bloody nationality who've stuck their feet in Africa will ever best the South African Republic!"

"By the God above us! That is right!" Kruger swore.

"*Ja! Ja!*" came the vehement mutters from the others.

For the past three weeks they had all been working from dawn until midnight and being exhausted they were not making the best of decisions.

It was therefore a relief to them all when Kruger said, "*Mynheers*, now that it is nearly the end of the week, let us return to our farms and in peace keep the Lord's Day at our district churches. Let us meet here again on Tuesday to carry on with the Lord's work."

One afternoon as Katie with the children

were returning from the wheatfields they saw two covered wagons drawn by spans of eight mules turning a kopje and heading for the house.

"Visitors, Mama," Eileen cried, "I wonder who they are?"

"Let's hurry and see." Katie dug a heel into her horse's flank and cantered up to the house where a young man was jumping off a wagon.

"John! It's John, Mama!" Eileen cried with delight at seeing her brother.

"But that's impossible!" Then Katie laughed happily as she recognised the slim figure in English riding breeches and tweed jacket. "It *is* John!" Katie pulled up beside her son just as Cecil Rhodes was descending from the wagon.

The loose-limbed man in dirty white trousers and shabby jacket politely raised his wide felt hat to her, then Katie recovered from surprise and smiled at him.

John reached up to lift her off her horse and catching at his shoulders she planted kisses on his cheeks, then words burst from her.

"What a heavenly surprise! I can't believe it is really you, John darling!"

"It's splendid to see you, Mother." He was proud of her before Mr. Rhodes—she looked so beautiful, so youthful and rode so well. "Here's Mr. Rhodes, Mother."

Turning to Rhodes whose watery grey eyes were examining her, Katie proffered her hand. "How nice to see you here; you gave us a delightful lunch at your wonderful Groote Schuur home last time we met."

"Yes, yes, I remember." His falsetto voice was incongruous with his heavy build. "Come on out, Jack and Leslie," he called cheerily over his shoulder and two good-looking young men, attired much as John, jumped from the second wagon.

"Mother—Leslie Drood and Jack Masters," John said, "we three share Mr. Rhodes' secretarial work." Then to Rhodes he said, "And this, sir, is my sister, Eileen, and half-brothers, Franz and Adrian."

When everyone had met Katie said, "Come in, please."

She started for the house with Leslie Drood falling into step beside her saying in a very English voice, "John's been so excited about coming here, Mrs. Van Riebeck."

"Really? I'm astonished; when he was about thirteen he hated the place."

In the living-room as the adults were being seated, Katie told Eileen to take the children to Maarje and come back, then she ordered a coloured maid to bring brandy. She was grateful it was too late for tea for she had no good china on the farm and would have hated offering thick cups to Rhodes, although she had grown accustomed to them in the wilderness.

"Mrs. Van Riebeck, you must be wondering what we are doing up here—so far North," Cecil Rhodes said.

"Actually I'm amazed," she laughed, pulling off her sun bonnet and tidying her hair as best she could.

"Well, it's a sort of holiday, combined with work. When I was ill as a young man, my brother thought a trek up in this dry country would be good for me and it was." He smiled benignly at his good-looking secretaries. "I am showing these young men the Missionary Road or as the Dutch call it the 'Road North' and as John wanted so much to see you, we've come some miles off our route to do so."

"That was very good of you. I can't tell you what a marvellous surprise it is," Katie glanced at Jack and Leslie. "And do you like the country up here?"

"Oh indeed!" "Oh yes!" they replied in well bred English accents.

The maid brought a tray with glasses and a decanter of Cape brandy and John started to pour it as he said, "We've heard all the optimistic reports about the gold on the Witwatersrand. Mother, has Paul had any luck yet?" John asked eagerly, handing brandy around.

"Well, of course Paul hasn't started to make a fortune yet." Katie gave an attractive little shrug. "It's still too early, but when we were there he had excellent reports on his land and I'm convinced he's going to be very successful."

"Ah, the optimistic attitude is quite the right one." Rhodes gulped his brandy down and held out his empty glass to John for a refill. "I always felt optimistic when I was a youth on the diamond diggings and that's how I still feel about life."

"And how right you always are, sir,"

435

John said beaming with obvious admiration for he cherished wealth and respected the ability to acquire it.

"Never give up! That's what I told myself and that's what I tell everyone." Rhodes gave a cackling little laugh.

"That's excellent advice," Katie nodded, "I do hope that you will spend a little time on the farm—it's not luxurious by any means, but we shall make you comfortable."

"Very kind of you, Mrs. Van Riebeck, but we are a little pressed for time. Is the Commandant not here?"

"No, alas, he's detained in Pretoria and. . . ." She broke off as the sound of galloping hooves thundered on the hard-baked earth, "But that's him now! I always recognise his horsebeats. No one else rides like that. Excuse me, I must go to meet him." She jumped up.

She reached the stoep and Van Riebeck was dismounting and leaving his horse to the Kaffirs with him he took the stoep steps two at a time. Katie was apprehensive for she was well aware of his dislike of Rhodes.

When they had kissed she murmured,

"Rhodes is here—he brought John as a surprise."

"*Magtig!* What the hell is Rhodes doing here!" Very irritated he unslung his long gun from his back.

"Come in and hear all about it. The 'great' man seems in a very jovial mood."

Van Riebeck followed her in, fitted his gun into the gun rack, hung his hat on a peg and went deeper into the room. He gave John a warm welcome, then shook Rhodes' hand, then the young secretaries'.

"You must forgive my dusty appearance, but I've been riding hard," he said, sitting in a deep chair and gulping down some brandy which Katie gave him.

"I hope you don't mind us dropping in like this, Commandant?" Rhodes said affably. "But we're here on a sort of working holiday. Work for the boys to learn about the country up here and holiday for me."

"But it's our pleasure, Mr. Rhodes, to have you visit us. You know, of course, that it's a Boer custom to welcome callers." What the hell was the shrewd bastard doing in the Transvaal? Van Riebeck did not believe a word of Rhodes' explanations for being up here. "I suppose you're on your way to Gubulawayo to see Lobengula," he continued and grinned at Rhodes' mock astonishment as in a falsely naive voice Rhodes replied.

"Well, actually I had not thought of doing that, but now that you suggest it, I'll think about it as we're not far off. But we've only two coloured boys with us and they can't shoot straight so that means we are only four guns. Do you believe it would be safe for us to go to Matabeleland?"

"Why not? I've never heard that King Lobengula is out to kill anyone who comes merely on a visit, although his Matabele warriors are fond of dipping their spears in blood. What frightens Lobengula is the thought of white men coming in to settle on his land." Van Riebeck, with three Volksraad members, had visited Lobengula a few years ago to warn the King the British were coming to obtain digging rights for gold.

Rhodes looked down at the glass in his hand and slowly swilling the brandy around, asked in an indifferent tone, "And what did you learn about his feelings with regard to selling gold concessions?"

That's why the bastard is here! Van Riebeck suddenly guessed. To discover what we know.

"I'm afraid I can't help you," Van Riebeck lied easily. "We've not communicated with Lobengula." He smiled. "As you know we seem to have plenty of our own gold."

Everyone laughed. "No one can deny that, Commandant Van Riebeck," Rhodes said, "and actually it would be a stupidity to look for other gold. You see since we met in Cape Town I've changed my mind about the Zimbabwe gold, because it seems the Witwatersrand has all the gold that's needed. We must be careful not to flood the world with gold, a mistake that was very nearly made with diamonds, until we controlled the output by amalgamation."

Van Riebeck nodded. "I agree with you, if the Witwatersrand opens up into even bigger finds, added to the California and Australian gold fields, I should think there'll be more than enough gold in the world." He unfolded his great height and stood up. "I wonder if you'd excuse me for a few minutes whilst I have the Kaffirs throw water over me and change into clean clothes."

"Of course, of course. We could play cards or something, eh, Mrs. Van Riebeck?" Rhodes enquired.

As Van Riebeck left, John explained to Katie, "Mr. Rhodes loves games, Mother," and he commenced to organise what Katie thought were childish games but which they all played amidst great laughter.

As Van Riebeck stood under the big tree and Kaffir boys sitting in the branches poured bucketsful of water down on him, his mind was racing and he concluded that Rhodes intended to bluff Lobengula by offering to buy gold concessions, then offer them in England and so have the English flocking out as Colonists *not* miners to settle in Matabeleland, or if the Matabele proved too bloodthirsty, the Colonists would then settle in adjacent Mashonaland where the people were peace-loving. In any case Rhodes would buy or barter land for a new English settlement. His scheme was brilliant. Would Lobengula fall for the catch?

Everything must be done to circumvent Rhodes' scheme. Van Riebeck left his makeshift shower and wrapping a huge towel around himself he went into the house to his bedroom and immediately sat down and wrote a detailed letter to Kruger about Rhodes. He also suggested that a telegram be sent to the Portuguese in Lorenzo Marques to warn them the English were moving in on Lobengula and must be stopped by the Portuguese going at once to alert Lobengula to the danger. Van Riebeck also suggested that a Boer trek leave at once travelling as fast as possible to call on Lobengula to confuse him by offering to buy concessions. In his perplexity the King would throw Rhodes and all whites out.

Van Riebeck sent his fastest horseman with the letter to Kruger on his farm. Whilst dressing, Van Riebeck's mind was racing to find a way of detaining Rhodes, so a Boer trek could get a head start on Rhodes and reach Matabeleland before the Englishman. Then an idea came to him and returning to the living-room he smoothly lied.

"My head boy has just told me that there are lions on the outskirts of the farm. Some of the women were washing clothes at a far off stream when a lion snatched one and carried the poor creature off alive: you could hear her screams coming from deep in the bush."

"Oh, Papa, how awful!" Eileen covered her face with her hands and Katie shuddered. "But in God's name why were the women so silly as to launder in an out of the way stream?"

"Because the farm streams are pretty low after the blazing summer and we're waiting for the rains, remember."

"Good heavens, sir, what a terrible story," Jack said. "Will you go after the lion?"

"Yes, in the morning." Van Riebeck turned to Rhodes. "Care to join in the 'lion hunt'?"

"Oh, please *do*, sir!" Leslie begged Rhodes. "I've never had a chance to get close to lions and in the Cape. . . ."

"But you've seen the two lions in my

zoo at Groot Schuur dozens of times."
Rhodes looked a little irritated.

"But, sir, that's not the same," John
assured him, "I've been on lion-hunts and
it's a deuced exciting business."

"Oh yes, sir, please don't let's miss it!"
Jack said. "It really would be something
to write home to Sussex about."

"It looks as if you'll have to stay, Mr.
Rhodes." Van Riebeck grinned in a
comradely fashion at Rhodes who gave a
wide shrug.

"I'm afraid I'm out-voted by the boys."

"Splendid! Splendid!" Van Riebeck felt
triumphant on the succcess of his lie and
hoped he would be able to easily pick up
a lion's spoor somewhere or other in the
morning.

24

AFTER dinner in the living-room as Rhodes and Van Riebeck were chatting it suddenly occurred to Katie that whilst the young men were perfunctorily polite to Eileen, such a beautiful golden-haired girl, their attention was given wholly to Rhodes; it seemed as if they were determined not to miss a word or gesture of his. This absorption was unnatural, it somehow made her feel uneasy and she suddenly determined to try to pry John loose from Rhodes' employment.

To create an opportunity of being alone with John, she murmured to him, "Do come and see old Joanna—she used to adore you when you were up here years ago."

An annoyed expression swiftly crossed his thin, aristocratic face but then he smiled tolerantly as if he must humour her silly request and they left the room.

Katie led the way to the front stoep

instead of to the kitchen and when well out of hearing of those in the living-room, she faced John under the light of the hanging lantern.

"Darling, I've been longing to talk to you. I've a splendid idea—why don't you join Paul and work with him on his claim? I feel instinctively that you'd make a fortune together."

"You mean that I should leave Mr. Rhodes!" he asked in awed shock, his steel grey eyes stretching with amazement at her stupidity. "I'd *never* leave him."

"Whyever not?" she snapped, "You talk as if you were one of the Apostles following Christ."

"And that's exactly how I feel. He's the most marvellous man alive."

"Just what is so marvellous about him?"

"His vision, his plans, his ambitions for South Africa. He's an idealist, I'm afraid Mother, that you've never known anyone like him. He's going to change the map of the entire country."

"And do you think that would be good for the country?" She hated John's superior manner and wanted to shake him.

"Really, Mother, as a woman you don't

understand these matters, but I'll try to explain some of Rhodes' dreams to you." He spoke in a hushed voice. "Instead of South Africa continuing to be a country of little inefficient republics and the Cape colony that relies on Westminster's Government, Rhodes wants a *Union*. Surely you see the wisdom of that?"

"No, I don't! These little republics *are* republics because that's what they wish to be!" She must not quarrel with John, the most difficult of her children, yet if Rhodes was a danger to him she must fight to save John, but wiser to try flattery, not argument with him. "Darling, I am very proud of you, you are extremely intelligent and at Eton and Oxford you learned *so much*, but why not consider taking time off from Rhodes—oh—I mean only temporarily—and join Paul on the gold mine. Together you might become millionaires." She was thinking of Struben and his brother.

"Utterly out of the question, Mother, and in any case, I'll make a fortune serving Rhodes. He not only pays handsomely, but he gives us a chance to buy early shares in the Diamond Amalgamations as well as his other ventures, but that's not why I want to stay with him—it's because of his spectacular brain and character. You should hear him address Parliament or his board meetings—he's absolutely brilliant!"

Looking up at John's face flushed with fervour and his eyes like those of a religiose, Katie lost some of her apprehensions over him; it was Rhodes' mental powers that fascinated John, not anything physically unnatural.

"I think I understand how you feel, darling, I'm so glad you've found such happiness in your work."

The tense expression suddenly left his face and he planted a kiss on her cheek. "What about Ken joining Paul, instead of me?"

"Splendid idea! There's a great strength in brothers working together. You try to persuade him to join Paul when you return to the Cape." She saw immediately that her reliance upon him flattered him, as she intended it should. "He'll listen to you."

"Yes, leave it to me. I'm learning a lot from Rhodes about the art of handling people. It will be good for Ken to leave off helping to run the ostrich farm—now that he has his law degree. And that will be useful to him and Paul if they form a company on the mines."

"You're right, John! I'm sure you are."

"I'm anxious for Ken to get to some place where there's a chance to develop into greatness. Diamond mines did it for Rhodes, for Beit, for Barney Barnato and dozens of others—so why shouldn't gold mines do it for Paul and Ken?"

"Darling John, you've become so wise." She was a little awed by the determination tightening his jaw, but then he smiled. "Well, we've settled matters so let's go and say 'hello' to old Joanna."

Later when they returned to the living-room Katie was at peace about John. Studying Rhodes she thought perhaps the gossip about him was all malicious lies prompted by people who envied his phenomenal success. Because he preferred bachelorhood to marriage proved nothing. Weren't Catholic priests normal men who devoted their lives to God and chose a life of celibacy?

Seated near Van Riebeck and Rhodes, her full skirts spread out about her feet she thought. One is the epitome of an Englishman, the other the epitome of a Dutchman, yet they instinctively seem to be in accord—tragic that it so seldom happened like this between the races.

"I give a great deal of thought to the North of Africa." Rhodes was saying, "to the great plateau and the Equatorial Lakes, on up to the Sudan. The climate there is suitable for white men and I dream of model villages and cities, all connected by railways."

"And an all-English population?" Van Riebeck asked quietly.

"No, not necessarily." Rhodes had a habit of rolling around in his chair. "Why shouldn't such a colony from the start be made up of citizens of different nations, all benefiting by a benign English rule?"

Van Riebeck chuckled good-humouredly, "Ah, I think you start running into difficulties as soon as you say that."

"But why? The English want trade and the Dutch want land, so there must be a meeting place between them, but I've been told that Kruger is obstinate and stubborn as a mule, as immovable as a rock—that he's like a Neanderthal man."

"His enemies may think that, but to his own people he seems like a prophet from the Old Testament." Van Riebeck slowly unwound his long legs and sat upright, "How much do you really know about our President?"

"Only what I've heard in the Cape from English people who've had dealings with him."

"Well, I'll tell you a few facts about him. He was a child on the great trek and you've got to try to imagine what that was like. The trekkers had to cross wild spaces where white men had never been. Nowadays you can travel without much risk of being murdered, that's thanks to the pioneers but things were different when Kruger was a boy. At fourteen he shot his first lion and also fought with the men on Commando against the savage Malikazi and until you've fought with only a handful of your own people surrounded by thousands of blood-lusting warriors—you don't know what 'courage' means." Van Riebeck's jaw had tightened, his eyes were like blue grass catching fire. "Kruger's youth was just one battle after another."

Van Riebeck pulled on his pipe, then

slowly exhaled as everyone sat silent, waiting for him to continue. "It was the same for all the treks that followed that first one, all were attacked by Basutos, Zulus, Amatongas, oh, dozens of savage tribes who were determined to annihilate the white invaders. Time and again we fought the greatest warriors of them all— the Zulus. My wife," he shot a smile at Katie beside him, "can tell you all about that. She came to Africa at seventeen and trekked North; she fought in laager on her wagon-board and shot as well as a man; she accounted for quite a few of the Zulu impi."

"A courageous lady." Rhodes gave a brief deferential nod to Katie.

"Necessity, Mr. Rhodes," Katie said.

"And the pioneers lived under fear of constant attack," Van Riebeck told Rhodes.

"We were attacked here in the *very* house," Eileen's grey-blue eyes were wide with remembered terrors. "The wild Batlapins suddenly rose up one night and swept over the country killing all whites. Luckily a lot of friends had come for a party here and with their wagons and oxen we could form a laager. All the women and children. . . ." She suddenly broke off, embarrassed at being the centre of attention. "Papa, I'm sorry, *you* must tell Mr. Rhodes about it."

"No, no, carry on." Van Riebeck considered it a good thing for Rhodes to hear the young tell of how the pioneers had fought and died to civilize the Transvaal. "You tell the story, Eileen."

"Well, the men and boys were on the wagons ready with their guns, the women and children were crowded into the house, with furniture barricading the windows and doors. The mothers had long knives ready and we children were praying that God would send us help, for Papa had sent messengers to other districts. The worst of all was the waiting—I can still remember that. Then at dawn we heard the sound of thousands of warriors, it was. . . ."

"Like low rumbling thunder," John interrupted excitedly. "The stamping of thousands of feet and the hoarse war cries. Then we made out this huge black wave that seemed to sweep over the earth to engulf us." John jumped to his feet. "Throwing assegais they rushed forward screaming, '*Bulala! Bulala!* Kill! Kill! Our guns barked and the first wave of mad warriors fell but they kept on coming, jumping over piles of their own dead. It seemed to last for ever—our guns kept barking but nothing could hold back the thousands of Batlapins. At last they reached our wagons and our ammunition was exhausted. With a long knife I stabbed at their faces, slashed at their hands as they tried to jump aboard. Then there was an awful cry from one of our people—'The devils are in the laager! They're attacking the house' and we. . . ."

"Yes, yes, we heard it inside this room," Eileen cried. "The Batlapins were banging on the shutters, pushing the furniture from the windows and door and the black bodies poured in, assegais raised. 'Kill, Kill the white man's vermin!' they cried. And they did." Her voice broke on a choking sob. "My little sister—they stuck an assegai through her body."

"No more! No more, for God's sake!" Katie cried. "It's all wrong to deliberately recall those horrors."

Rhodes and the English boys looked

distressed and Rhodes asked Van Riebeck, "But how on earth did any of you escape?"

"A strong Commando from Chriqstad came in answer to our message and they brought plenty of ammunition and between us we drove the Batlapin off. But we suffered heavy losses." He threw a little smile around the room. "I must say that John, only a boy of fourteen or so, showed marvellous courage."

John had recovered something of his calm and sat down. "Sorry I got so excited, I didn't realize that the experience was so strongly buried in me, I suppose being up here again brought it back."

"Such memories will never leave you, I fear," Rhodes said understandingly, "but you must look upon it all with pride, old man. You found nothing to match that battle at Oxford, eh, John?"

"No, thank God." John forced himself to laugh as Leslie and Jack stared at him with open admiration on their young faces.

Van Riebeck turned to Eileen saying in a tender tone, "I'll wager some day you'll terrify your grandchildren with that tale and they won't believe that such awful things happened in South Africa's Republic."

"Oh no, Papa—I'd *never* tell that story to children, it would terrify them. I'm afraid I shouldn't have told it tonight."

"I'm glad you did, it will help Mr. Rhodes understand what the Transvaalers have endured and why they value the freedom they've fought for."

John refilled everyone's brandy glass as Rhodes said, "To return to Kruger, I've the feeling he and I will never be able to talk policy; he's too prejudiced against the English to listen to me, but you are not. How is it that you get along well with the English?"

The remark, meant as a compliment, did not please Van Riebeck. "I'm originally a Cape Dutchman and still have interests there. I've mixed with the English a good deal and I've half English stepchildren, so I'm not as prejudiced against them as Kruger is."

"Yes, I know that from our last meeting, so that's why I came here to talk to you."

"Ah!" Van Riebeck burst out laughing.

"But I thought it was pure altruism so that John could see his mother."

"That was a facet of the call," Rhodes smiled. "You see, I was devoted to my own mother and I wanted to please John. Now, as man-to-man, what is your *true* feeling about a railway from the Cape to the Transvaal?"

"Oh, that would be wonderful!" Katie cried.

So that's why the bastard is here, Van Riebeck told himself. At last it's out. "There would be advantages for the Transvaal of course," he said aloud, "but you obviously are aware that some years ago Kruger appealed to the Cape Parliament to continue the Kimberley line to Pretoria and Uptington refused to. But now since the discovery of gold Kruger has changed his mind and doesn't want a railway to the Cape."

Rhodes waved his arms about impatiently. "I know, Kruger doesn't want it, but he's being stupid. But you have great influence over him as well as the members of the Volksraad: you could make them realize how such a railway could benefit the Transvaal, and could make them accept the scheme."

"I'm not sure I could and also I'm not sure that I would wish to try to." Van Riebeck spoke thoughtfully, his eyes studying Rhodes' heavy-jowled countenance. "Actually our farmers dread the idea; they're afraid a railway would bring competition up here for their business; and there's another aspect: the Transvaal transport people are violently against it because they're convinced that a railway would make their wagons and oxen absolutely obsolete and put their drivers out of work."

"For God's sake! Such stupidity should not be tolerated to halt progress. Think, man, when you have a real gold rush up here you'll *have* to have a railway and the Transvaal hasn't the money to build it so why don't you be sensible and agree to let my company finance and build it?"

"Because Kruger and most of the Volksraad believe that it would give the Cape open access to the Transvaal and then in no time there'd be Britishers pouring into Pretoria. They think it's bad enough that half the scum from the Kimberley mines are coming up."

Rhodes blurted out, "But against that surely *you* see the advantages to your country of having all the supplies you need delivered in no time as well as having all your produce travelling to the ports—also in no time."

"Yes, yes," Van Riebeck nodded, knowing Rhodes was right, "But give me time to consider it and then I'll talk to Kruger about it—not that I can promise he'll accept my advice. Now, let's have a nightcap and turn in."

As they sipped a final brandy Rhodes said, "You and I get along like Jan Hofmeyer and I do in the Cape. I'd like *us* to be friends."

"That would be nice," Van Riebeck smiled, but not trusting Rhodes for a second.

As they all stood up to retire Katie suggested that they went to stand on the front stoep, "To look at the stars."

The purple-blue dome of the heavens was silvered by myriads of stars that seemed to be joined together by their radiance. In the distance the dark hulks of mountains were sinister monsters and the earth's blackness was made less frightening by the encirclement of camp fires that Kaffir farm-hands would keep burning until the first light chased night from the world.

"The fires are to discourage curious leopards and lions," Van Riebeck said then puffed comfortingly at his pipe.

"It's a fine sight," Rhodes murmured, "makes a man believe that there really is an Almighty Spirit."

From far off came a leopard's cough, then within seconds a lion roared and the sound seemed to shake the stoep.

"Perhaps that's the killer, Papa," Eileen shivered, "who carried the poor woman off into the bush."

25

BEFORE it was quite light, Van Riebeck awoke and gently leaving the bed so as not to awaken Katie he moved quietly through the kitchens and left by the back door, crossed a clearing and went to Obsete's hut. There he instructed the head Kaffir to send out riders to try to pick up lion spoor and return to privately inform him. Then Van Riebeck went back to bed where he slept for a further couple of hours.

After breakfast Obsete brought him the information he wanted and about ten o'clock the hunting party mounted their horses, with guns across their knees, hats pulled low on their foreheads against the sun's rays. In their saddlebags they carried their lunch of biltong, freshly baked bread, water and brandy.

As they trotted off Katie, Eileen and the small boys stood watching them go. Although Katie had ridden with Van Riebeck on a dozen or more lion-hunts, she was always apprehensive for guns could jam as young Paul's once had and a treed leopard had sprung on him, almost killing him; or a horse's hoof could catch in a rut and throw the rider as an offering to a lion. Her thoughts were interrupted by Franz's complaints.

"It's unfair of Papa not to take me! I'm big enough to hunt with him."

"Me too! Me too!" Adrian shouted indignantly.

"How silly you are—you can't shoot yet." Eileen tousled Adrian's wheat-coloured hair. "Supposing a lion sprang at you and carried you off?"

"Come on, boys, time for your lessons." Katie herded the children into the house to the schoolroom and sat them down at their little desks Van Riebeck had made for them. She then put books before them and left them for a few minutes whilst she went to the kitchens.

"Good morning, Joanna—good morning, everyone." She nodded to the fat cook and coloured scullery maids who were peeling big yellow marrows. Lifting her skirts she stepped carefully around naked babies crawling over the hardened dung floor, reddened by oxblood and always swept scrupulously clean.

Katie leaned down to pat several little round black bottoms then reached Joanna's table, where the black woman, her head wrapped in a snowy white doek had her hands in a bowl of dough.

"The *Baas* says our guests will be here for dinner again tonight, Joanna, so what shall we give them?"

"*Ach ja*, Missus. *Babootie?* Missus like?"

"Yes, that would be good, I'm sure they eat curry in the Cape but in case they don't like it, let's also have a cauliflower *brédé*, made with lamb." Katie wanted John to be proud of the cooking if nothing else up here.

"*Ja, ja*, Missus, cauliflower *brédé*—very good."

"And your very best *mosbolletjies* with lots of sour wine in them." Joanna was an artist at cooking the spongy buns, "then an apricot tart with thick cream, let the girl really whip the cream well and fresh coffee afterwards *not* coffee from the pot that's always standing on the stove." She laughed to soften her complaint. "This *Baas* says that tastes like mud."

Joanna laughed with Katie and her big body bounced all over. "The *Baas* is funny, very funny, but best *Baas* in all the country."

"I'll tell him you said so."

"*All* the *Baas*'s people say that—he the best."

"Thank you, Joanna, and don't make a big lunch for the children and me, just stewed chicken and spiced rice and some of those Zambesi bananas that I bought in Lydenburg yesterday and what about the jam making? Will you start tomorrow?"

"*Ja, ja,* now that Missus bring plenty sugar from Lydenburg."

Having finished in the kitchen, Katie went back to Franz and Adrian and hearing the piano being played she was pleased that Eileen was practising. Someday she might be a great pianist and accompany Mary a great singer—poor Mary! God watch over her!

They had been riding for several hours, but had not picked up lion spoor. One of Obsete's messengers had traced lions near a certain stream, but Van Riebeck had deliberately taken another course as he was determined to delay Rhodes on his trip to Matabeleland to give the Boer trek a chance to take off and with luck reach Lobengula ahead of Rhodes.

At one o'clock in a blazing blue sky the sun was punishing so Van Riebeck called a halt and the men dismounted beneath the shade of a baobab tree, whilst the horses cropped at any greenery they could find. Glad to be out of the direct sun, the men sat cross-legged on blankets as they chewed on stringy dried meat. No Boer ever travelled without biltong in his saddlebags. They drank some water and brandy then stretched out on the hard earth and although sand fleas were troublesome, they all fell into a doze excepting Van Riebeck who, back propped against a tree trunk, sat smoking his pipe.

He would have liked to let them sleep well into the afternoon, then bring them back here tomorrow and so delay them by another day but he had no intention of appearing like a fool and returning home without bagging a lion. After an hour he awoke them and they swung on to their horses and started off. Now Van Riebeck led them in the right direction.

Within another hour they reached a vast expanse of bush edged by low lush greenery.

"Those clumps of reeds mean we're near water," Van Riebeck said quietly. "It's a favourite spot for lions to lie in—they enjoy the coolness—so keep a sharp look-out because they are the very devil to spot amongst the reeds and remember what I told you: when you shoot, aim for the brute's nose, a lion has no forehead, it's all hair. Now I suggest no more talking."

There was a terrible tenseness in the three younger men and their hands sweated as they held their guns before them across their horses' backs but Rhodes felt no apprehension only excitement, for he was well aware that with Van Riebeck they were safe; he was one of the greatest hunters in South Africa.

Suddenly Van Riebeck muttered, "Halt!" and reined in and the others did the same, "Look! Lions must be near us." He pointed to the body of a dead impala; its stomach had been savagely ripped open, its entrails had spilled out, and its hind quarters had been chewed away.

"The lion must have killed some time ago but got bored with the impala and went after bigger game, but he'll probably come back later."

The nervous horses started to make shrill frightened cries, but the men patted them, trying to quieten them.

As they moved slowly toward the reeds again Van Riebeck muttered, "See how the reeds are flattened down over there. There were two lions—I can tell that by all the flattened reeds."

"Where do you think the lions are now?" Leslie's hushed voice was tremulous.

Van Riebeck silently dismounted and peered down at the sandy earth. "Those are pug marks—see them? They go all the way into the bush. The lions have gone in I imagine after bigger game."

"By God, sir, are we going in there after them?" Jack muttered staring apprehensively at the tangled impenetrable-looking bush.

"If you want to track them we've got to go in after them—but listen!" Van

Riebeck held up a cautionary hand. "They're near here."

From not far off came a low moaning sound that was repeated several times; these were then followed by great deep sighs.

"Good lord! Do lions moan like that?" Rhodes murmured.

"They do! They are very close; they'll probably come back for their abandoned kill. Dismount everyone, spread the horses out in single file and tie them together by their bridles. Stay behind them and rest your guns across their backs. Aim for that opening just ahead, the lions should break through just about there."

Rhodes and the young men, with sweat pouring down their faces, dismounted, tied their horses together and stood with guns across the quivering animals' backs. The men's eyes were glued to the opening in the bush about fifteen yards ahead of them.

"A lion can charge 100 yards in a few seconds so for God's sake be ready," Van Riebeck whispered.

Then came a great terrifying roar that seemed to shake a nearby tambooti tree and sent birds screeching from the branches to the sky.

The next second a huge lion, with almost black mane, broke quietly into the clearing and stood unconcernedly looking around. The men's guns in their sweating hands were all pointed at the great beast.

"He hasn't spotted us yet or got our scent," Van Riebeck whispered hoarsely.

"Why don't we shoot him, for God's sake?" The urgent whisper came from Rhodes standing beside Van Riebeck and he answered, "Because I don't want to alert the second lion; I'm waiting for it to come out."

Then they heard the sound of crackling twigs and in a moment a young lion, smaller than the first, came gracefully out of the bush moving silently on its huge cushiony paws and stood beside the senior lion.

"They'll have our scent in a second," Van Riebeck warned, "then they'll charge us—Rhodes, you and I will take the big brute—you boys take the other. Get ready!"

Almost immediately the big lion raised his head and held it sideways as he sniffed the air and at that second the younger lion caught sight of the men. For terrible seconds men and beasts stared at each other. Then with blood-chilling roars the lions crouched, then charged.

"Shoot!" Van Riebeck cried. "Shoot!"

Four shots cracked out. Van Riebeck's bullet caught the old lion right between the eyes, penetrating the brain, he swayed for a moment then collapsed—dead, but the young lion, wounded in three places, by the boys' poor aim, stood for a second with blood flowing from both shoulder and a leg, then maddened by rage he let out an enormous roar and charged at Jack, smashing down the boy's horse and clawing at Jack, as he fell beneath the horse. Van Riebeck grabbed Rhodes' unused gun and taking careful aim shot the lion between the eyes and the beast collapsed half over the boy.

"Quick, lift the brute off Jack," Van Riebeck ordered and they all tugged at the huge body and dragged Jack free. He was clawed around the shoulders, though nothing serious, but he suddenly collapsed with shock.

"By God—if the horse hadn't been

there, Jack would be dead," Leslie said as he pulled his brandy flask from his saddlebag and forced some through Jack's lips.

"He'll be all right." Van Riebeck examined the wounds. "The claws didn't go deep, but what bloody rotten shots you fellows are! And Rhodes, for God's sake, why didn't you even shoot?"

"I never interfere with experts." Rhodes said coolly. "I was confident I was absolutely safe with you. It was polite of you to offer me a shot with you, but if I were judging diamonds I wouldn't ask for your advice. We're both experts in different fields. I know all about the Boers' crack marksmanship and that a bullet is never wasted."

Van Riebeck guessed Rhodes had heard about the Boers' superb marksmanship at their victory of Majuba. "Well let's be off; we must disinfect Jack's wounds. Too bad about the horse being killed but he saved Jack's life."

"I think you did that, Commandant," Rhodes said and Van Riebeck gave a little smile. "All right boys, let's mount Jack on my horse, I'll double up with him."

The following morning as Rhodes' party were preparing to leave, John pulled Katie aside saying, "Let's just stroll in the shadow of the house for a few moments."

She tucked her fingers into the crook of his arm. "Your visit was really wonderful for me, darling."

"It has been for me, too, Mother, and I wish we could have stayed longer. But before I go I wanted to say I've been thinking—as my father's oldest son it's my duty to care about his other offspring. You see, Mother, I intend to enhance the Eaton name. I can't inherit an illustrious name like the Duke of Rotherford, but I can do such useful work that someday I'll be created a baronet."

Whilst Katie wanted her sons to be successful and wealthy, she thought that John's ambitions were too strong. He almost revered titles and riches and years ago had begged her to divorce Van Riebeck and marry Howard. "I'm sure you'll succeed in gaining a title, John," she said.

"I *know* I shall, Mother! But I can't allow myself to be dragged down by my family." At her scandalized expression he

471

swiftly added, "Oh, I mean by Nancy's wild escapades! Eloping with a penniless musician . . ." he spat the words out . . . "then divorcing him and becoming a Faro hostess in a club on the diamond fields."

"Of course that was terrible for all the family." God! If John knew about Sannie and Mary he would kill her.

"Why the deuce doesn't Nancy marry that French count in Paris and repair her mistakes? But I think Ken will be all right if he joins up with Paul, and Mary might be a credit to the family if she really becomes an opera star, or if this Italian painter husband becomes a famous artist; then there's Eileen—she must marry well."

"Darling, she's still so young." Katie gave a nervous little laugh; he was behaving like a middle-aged man. "Anyhow, Terence is a credit to you."

"By jove yes, old Terence certainly is." The tautness left his face. "I'm proud of my stepbrother and his father-in-law. Sir Daniel Musgrove is most highly regarded, not only in the medical world, but socially as well and Elaine is a sister-in-law *par excellence*." He patted Katie's hand on his arm as if with approval. "Mr. Rhodes takes a fine view of those three—he's entertained them to dinner at Groot Schuur and they reflect very well on me."

Katie had heard rumours that Rhodes courted titled people and she despised this in him. "Mr. Rhodes liked Cousin Howard, I suppose."

"His Grace the Duke of Rotherford! Rather! Being Howard's cousin was my entré to Rhodes. You know it's too bad that Uncle Paul," . . . John had always refused to call Van Riebeck "Papa Paul" . . . "doesn't like Mr. Rhodes, because Rhodes likes him."

"John, are you being a diplomatic go-between?" Katie laughingly teased.

"Nonsense, Mother, I just want to help Uncle Paul to see the English viewpoint."

"I hope you also make Rhodes see the Transvaal's viewpoint."

"But he does, Mother, that's why he wants Union between the races."

She was on dangerous ground so instead of demanding, "Yes, Union, under whose flag?" she said, "Since seeing Rhodes up here I like him. He seems a mixture of brilliant man and simple child."

"He's certainly brilliant." John started walking her back toward the wagons where the rest of the party were talking to Van Riebeck. "Looks as if we're ready to leave." He planted a kiss on her cheek. "I'm glad we had this chat and do try to control Nancy. Don't let her do some mad thing and disgrace us all."

"Well, I can't influence her much from up here, but don't worry—now that there's a horse coach from Pretoria to Kimberley, I'll probably come down to the Cape before too long."

"Lord, I hope so—it's a sort of sacrilege wasting you up here." He thought impotently of how different her life would have been as the Duchess of Rotherford.

"But I'm happy, darling—don't forget," she smiled reassuringly into his questioning eyes and he murmured, "I'm glad."

As they walked toward the wagons Van Riebeck was saying, "Leslie and Jack, I shan't forget to send the lionskins down to you. Take care of those wounds, Jack. Keep pouring the permanganate of potash solution on them to keep them clean."

There were "thank you's" and "goodbyes" then the wagons moved off and Van Riebeck, Katie and the children stood waving to the departing men. Katie could not help but feel miserable. John's visit had given her such a short space of concentrated happiness, rather like the concentrated beauty a highly coloured butterfly gives flying around for a day and then it dies.

"What a brilliant rascal Rhodes is," Van Riebeck murmured to Katie, so the children would not overhear.

"A rascal? I thought you seemed quite friendly, especially after the lion-hunt."

"On the surface yes, but did you notice that he never expressed a personal interest to invest in the Witwatersrand?"

"Yes, that thought did occur to me, but I think he *is* interested in the Witwatersrand because John wants Ken to go and join Paul; he thinks they'll make their fortune there and surely John is re-flecting Rhodes' thoughts."

"Yes and I'll wager Rhodes already has some of his men in secrecy looking the land over, but instead of going himself he's making for Matabeleland so that Kruger and the Volksraad will think he's trying to buy gold concessions there when in reality he wants to establish a British Colony there to close in on the Transvaal and to stop us having an outlet to the sea."

"That's terribly devious." Katie wondered if in Van Riebeck's near-fanaticism to keep the Transvaal free he could be exaggerating.

"He's as devious as Machiavelli; saying he came here to please John. What he actually came for was to try to twist me around his finger to help establish his Cape to Transvaal railway."

"But wouldn't that be a good thing?"

"To hell with *his* railway! We've got to have our *own* railway but not from the Cape. We want a railway from the Transvaal border to Delagoa Bay; it's a distance of fifty-seven miles—and the Cape to Pretoria is eleven hundred miles! Our railway to Delagoa Bay! I'm going to pound that into Kruger's head! We've got to work on that!"

Now the wagons were disappearing around the kopje and the family gave a final wave then started for the house.

Eileen caught at Katie's arm murmuring, "Aren't Leslie and Jack nice, Mama."

"Indeed they are."

"They asked me to write to them and they want to see me next time I go to Abend Bloem."

Heavens! Katie thought, Eileen is blushing, so she's started to be interested in boys. I must arrange some more parties for her up here. "That's very nice, Eileen, and you must write to them. It was a shame that Jack had such a fright during the lion-attack."

"Oh he doesn't mind now that it's over. He only hopes the claws will leave some marks that he can show off to people. I like him, he's nice."

"Yes, he seems to be. And you like all the young Bredas and Oliphants, don't you, darling. Their farms are quite close; we must ask them over."

"Of course I like them, I've known them since I was little. The Dutch boys are just as nice as English boys and I love what they call their 'hops'—dancing to the Hottentots' violins."

Thank God Eileen was blessedly free of racial prejudice. She was a love—

uncomplaining, adaptable, affectionate and so easily pleased. Oh why couldn't Nancy and Mary have been like Eileen?

A little later, Katie went to her desk in the living-room, sat down and wrote invitations to the Breda and Oliphant families, inviting their young, of Eileen's age, to come on a week's visit.

26

FOR the next two weeks Van Riebeck was occupied in Pretoria which was already crowded with new prospectors seeking concessions.

The problem of finding finance to build a railway connecting the Transvaal borders with Delagoa Bay had to be temporarily shelved for all Volksraad members were coping with the extra work created by the Witwatersrand, but the "railway" was constantly in Van Riebeck's mind and the moment there was a slight lull in the Volksraad's hectic working days he spoke of it.

He was seated on the stoep at Kruger's house, drinking coffee with the President.

"The railway is the most imperative of all our tasks," Van Riebeck burst out as Kruger pulled on his pipe.

"*Ja*, man, I haven't forgotten it, but even though the concessions we've sold have saved us from bankruptcy, we still don't have money to spare to even think of helping finance a railway of our own—you know that as well as I do."

"Of course I do, that's all the more reason we must start looking for finance."

"Some time ago you suggested trying America."

"Yes, and I've questioned the surveyors who've come here from the California gold fields: they all think we've a good chance of raising the money in New York, so we should send a representative as soon as possible."

"*You* must go, Van Riebeck. You are our best man to deal in English and you know about all the fancy ways of the outside world. *Ja, ja*, you are a match for any man."

"Well, thank you, *mynheer*," Whilst he did not want the job, Van Riebeck knew Kruger was right. "I will go, but when?"

"Next week, we should have papers ready for you to prove to any backers how our concessions are selling."

"Yes, that is essential to show that with increased population here a railway would be a profitable venture. You can always let me know in New York how much the sale of concessions has grown. If I leave next week, take a horse coach to Kimberley, then another horse coach to Wellington and a train from there to Cape Town, I could be sailing for Southampton in two weeks. As soon as I land there I'll sail for New York. The whole journey shouldn't take more than eight weeks."

"Good, good." Kruger gave a guttural laugh. "And for the first time, man, the exchequer can pay your expenses, thank the good Lord."

Van Riebeck felt like saying, "And it's about time too," but that would shock the religious Kruger, "*Ja*, the South African Republic's prospects are bright, I'm anxious to hear if our trek reached Lobengula before Rhodes did."

"We should know before too long. Your stepson never tells you anything useful about Rhodes? *Magtig*, that's a pity."

"He's a very honest boy: he would never willingly betray his employer and of course I never tempt him to." Van Riebeck got to his feet and knocked the bowl of his pipe on his heel. "I'll be off now to my farm, *mynheer*, to prepare for my departure—I'm not looking forward to telling my wife that I'll be travelling for four months or so—but she will understand the importance of my mission."

"She's a good wife, even though she's not a Boer." Kruger spat into his brass spitoon. "Give her my respects . . . I'll see you then when you return from your farm?"

They said goodnight and Van Riebeck left, with Kruger's deepset eyes following the tall, well tailored figure down the steps of the stoep. He was a fine man, Kruger was thinking, he might in years to come have been President in Kruger's own place, had he married a Boer woman instead of an Uitlander. Kruger spat with vexation into his spitoon, picked his big bible off the table, took up his stove-pipe hat and went into the house.

During Van Riebeck's absence, Katie occupied herself with her usual tasks in addition to caring for a crowd of young visitors who were keeping Eileen happy, but Katie's anxiety about Mary was growing. However was she going to Florence? What sensible excuse could she produce? She had informed Van Riebeck and the family in the Cape that Mary was with child so she must arrange with Howard to cable her when it grew close to the time for Katie to leave saying there were complications in Mary's pregnancy and Katie must come at once.

It seemed an unlucky lie, as if tempting Fate to make it a reality, but thinking of John and his ambitions for himself and his brothers and sisters, Katie was more deeply determined than before that they must not be disgraced.

Then coming like a direct answer to her prayers Van Riebeck returned and told her he must leave for America. She was so astonished at what seemed like this demonstration from God that she just stared at Van Riebeck, her eyes filled with the far-off look of a prophet, a seer.

"Darling! Katje! In God's name why are you looking at me like that?"

She was recovering herself swiftly. "I . . . I suppose I was so surprised . . . America—you've not been there before."

"And you don't mind my going?"

"Mind!" She gave an hysterical little laugh, wondering what he would say if she said, "I'm delighted, it frees me to do what I *have* to." "Darling, you know how

I loathe being separated from you," . . . she was speaking quietly almost to herself . . . "but all human beings have duties laid upon them." Hers was to decide the fate of a possible black grandchild. "Your duty is to go to America."

"Are you feeling well, Katje?" He grasped her shoulders as his eyes anxiously examined her face. "You're not going down with malaria again, are you?" He laid his hand across her forehead. "No, you seem quite cool."

By now she had herself under control. "Don't worry, darling, I'm perfectly well. I know it's your duty to go. That railway is vital to the South African Republic. When do you go?"

Greatly relieved at her sensible acceptance of his departure he said, "Next week, by horse-coach to Kimberley and from Kimberley ride inland to Wellington and I just heard that the train there to the Cape has started running so I'll travel by it to Cape Town."

"That cuts the journey by months. Oh Lord, how wonderful! I'd like to take the children and go to the Cape whilst you're gone. You wouldn't mind that, would you?"

"No, the rainy season up here doesn't agree with your health." He felt the old indignation flare in him that she never considered the farm as her home but left whenever she got a chance, but he did not talk of it any more. "How do you wish to travel? It's not safe by ox-wagon without me, I wouldn't trust your life, or the children's, without white men and guns. But for all of you to go by coach and train would be a terrible expense and. . . ."

"Don't worry about all that, I'll make the arrangements when you're gone." She would telegraph to Liz to wire money to her at the Standard Bank in Pretoria and of course she would go by coach and train. Never again would she suffer the hellish journey by the damned ox-wagon. "Come on, darling, and I'll help you sort out the clothes you'll need for America. Aren't you excited about going to New York? Will you sail from Southampton?"

"I expect to." He was surprised by what seemed like her detachment. He supposed that was thanks to maturity. He followed her into their bedroom saying, "I've already told the servants to bring a leather trunk from the sheds."

"Good, I hope they turn it upside down to shake snakes or tarantula out." She opened his stinkwood armoire and lifted out a suit that had been tailored for him some years ago in London when he had been there. "This one you'll take for sure, won't you?"

He stood right behind her so that as she swivelled around she looked straight up into his wonderful blue eyes and a dry sob almost choked her. "Oh, darling—darling —it's going to be so horrible without you."

His arms went around her and he crushed her to his hard body but at that moment there was a knock on the door and Katie pulled out of his arms.

"Come," he called and two Kaffir boys came in. They were carrying the big leather trunk and placed it on the floor. "Open it, Jong," Van Riebeck ordered, "and let's see if you swept it well." They lifted the lid and he examined the inside. "It's good," he smiled and they left grinning happily.

Katie brought the suit over and kneeling

beside the trunk carefully spread the trousers on the bottom. The musty smell of the leather reminded her of other times when she and Paul had packed to travel together. Now he brought another suit and knelt beside her to help spread it out.

As she watched his long sun-tanned fingers with the light golden hair growing on the backs a terrible nostalgia overwhelmed her—for so many years she had loved to watch his fine hands at work, holding the reins of his horse, in the vats at Abend Bloem helping her to sort grapes, carving toys for the children, filling his pipe, patting a nervous horse, aiming his long gun—untold pictures of his hands kaleidoscoped through her harassed mind.

She reached over and caught one of his hands and buried her lips in the palm as she prayed. "Dear God, don't let anything happen to him on this, his longest voyage." Her tears were warmly wet on his hand.

"Katje, Katje—beloved, you're crying." He swept her up in his arms and in a stride he was at the door, dropping the wooden bar across it then he carried her to the big four-poster bed and started to unbutton her bodice.

Van Riebeck had been gone ten days before Katie could leave Pretoria. The money had come promptly from Liz, but the difficulty was obtaining five vacant seats in one coach to Kimberley. At last with great excitement, not only from the children and Maarje, but also from Katie, they were off.

The journey turned out to be much more uncomfortable than an ox-wagon for there was little space in which to move. Remembering Mrs. Steele's grumblings of vermin infested beds, Katie had come prepared with plenty of paraffin to douse on the beds, so that the family slept, but like Mrs. Steele, they were never out of their clothes for almost six nights and six days.

At Kimberley, grown into a small town since she had been on the diamond diggings eleven years previously, they stayed at an hotel where they bathed and ate fairly well and slept in clean, comfortable beds. Then another horse-coach took them the forty miles inland to Wellington where they boarded the train for the Cape, much to the excitement of Franz and Adrian.

At Cape Town they changed to the Stellenbosch train and when they arrived at the small station they were joyously welcomed by Liz, Chris and Ken.

When the kissing and embraces were over Katie cried, "Liz, oh darling—how blessed a thing is progress, the journey took seventeen days and when I first did it so many years ago it took nine months! Now you and Chris can visit us up there."

Chris and Ken went to collect the luggage as Liz said, "It's wonderful, thank God, and Paul's journey was faster: he got here on the fourteenth day. Chris met him in town and drove him straight to the ship: he was just in time to board it. Oh I do pray he raises the American finance for the railway."

"If anyone can do it, he will!" Katie said proudly then looked around the platform. "Where's Nancy? Why didn't she come to meet us?"

"But she's not with us, she's left."

"Left! For where? England?"

"No, for the Witwatersrand, she said

she'd write you from there—she wanted to surprise you."

"Oh God!" Katie grabbed at Liz's arm with a terrible grip. "Was she going to see Paul?"

"Oh yes, she telegraphed him to meet her in Pretoria, she must be there by now. But, darling, whyever are you so upset?" Liz stared in surprise at Katie's face gone a sickly pale. "You know, Nancy, she wants to see all the excitement of the gold fields. She swears she wants to open a casino up there, but I suppose she'll be back before we know it."

"All right, you two lovely sisters," Chris called to Katie and Liz. "We've got the luggage piled in the Capecart so if you'll climb into the carriage we'll be off home."

In a sick daze Katie let Ken hand her up into the carriage, then leaned back against the leather upholstery. Too horrible to believe that Nancy and Paul intended to renew their incestuous affair. The thought was intolerable!

Liz was now seated beside her talking to Eileen so in a voice difficult to control Katie asked Ken, sitting opposite her,

"What happened to the two captains Nancy was supposed to be interested in?"

"Oh, they're nice fellows and she enjoyed herself playing them along like fish so that they even saw her off at the Cape Town railway station, poor fools," Ken gave an indulgent smile, "and with their arms filled with flowers."

The carriage moved forward and Katie waited a few seconds then asked, "Was Paul surprised, do you know, when he received her telegram?" Surely he had not wished to continue the heinous sin.

"Yes, I believe so. In fact, he tried to stop her coming, he telegraphed that the diggings were pretty grim and she would hate the place."

Thank God for that. "But she went just the same?"

"Oh yes, she does as she likes, you know that." He moved forward on the seat to talk directly to Katie, "Mother, I had a letter from John . . ." Ken's grey blue eyes lit with excitement . . . "and he said you and he thought I should join Paul."

Oh Lord, yes! Ken must go at once! Ken's presence might be a deterrent to Nancy and Paul's terrible liaison, for

Herta lacked the worldliness to deal with someone like Nancy.

"Hey, Mother—why don't you answer me? Shall I go?"

"Of course you must go! And *at once!*" She forced a smile to tone down her desperate vehemence of a moment ago. "You see Paul needs your help. Together you'll make a fortune up there."

"Jumping Jerusalem! What an adventure—I can't wait! But we'll have to fix things up with Uncle Chris and Aunt Liz —I mean about running the ostrich farm"

"Yes, yes," Katie murmured, so upset by shock she felt her heart might stop. "We'll make plans—after dinner— tonight."

Later when the carriage turned into Abend Bloem's long drive flanked by giant oaks with the beautiful white homestead at the end of it, for the first time a homecoming brought Katie no elation. Her grief was crushing her. Telling Liz that she felt exhausted, she went to her room, took her shoes, bonnet and dress off and lay down.

What could she do? Who could help her? Van Riebeck, who suspected the incest, would have somehow fought it—

but with him at sea—there was no one to turn to. Impossible to lay this burden on wonderful, virtuous Liz or to betray Nancy and Paul to Chris. What bad seed was in Nancy and Mary?

They would excuse their actions by saying they were in love. Love! What a ragged, shabby word they had made of it. Well, so far she had coped with Mary's problem and she would soon have to cope with Mary's child. But how could she help to save Paul and Nancy? Perhaps Paul would have strength to withstand Nancy and force her to leave. Katie's mind went around in an agony of frustration until Liz knocked at the door.

"May I come in, darling?" she called.

"Yes, yes, Liz."

"It's almost dinner time, did you sleep well?" Liz closed the door softly behind her.

Wonderful, kind, pure-souled Liz. "Yes, darling, I'm feeling much better. I'll wash and change and come down."

"You seemed so disappointed to learn that Nancy had left, but it was impossible for me to restrain her. She had grown very irritable for quite a while then suddenly she burst out with the idea that she *must* visit the gold fields and I don't think Paul wanted her to come. Oh well, darling, I'll see you downstairs."

Liz left, wondering if she had been right in not letting Katie know about Nancy's increased liking for brandy, so that she was often in a condition bordering inebriation, making Liz almost glad to see the departure of her beautiful niece. But poor Katie did not look well and she had endured so much. Now she was undoubtedly missing Van Riebeck.

After dinner Katie discussed with Chris and Liz the prospect of Ken going to the gold mines and with their usual co-operation they agreed that he should go and that their sons, Jan and Cornelius could replace him on the ostrich farm.

It came as a relief to Katie to help Ken in his preparations for the journey and two days later she went with the family to wave her excitedly happy son off at Stellenbosch Railway Station. With Ken's departure she felt that for the moment she had achieved all that she possibly could to help save Paul and Nancy.

She was to spend the next week-end

with Terence and Elaine at Sir Daniel's eagle-nest house by the sea, so on Friday afternoon she met Terence at his consulting rooms and he proudly drove her off in his newly acquired one-horse jig to Seapoint. Happiness was bursting from him as he told Katie almost non-stop of Elaine's virtues.

Katie revelled in all he said and was delighted at the way her thin, aesthetic looking first-born had filled out into a handsome, imposing-looking young man.

Before reaching the house she asked him, "Tell me, darling, what did you and Elaine decide to do about little David? Of course I've been able to cuddle my darling grandchild at Abend Bloem where he's always around Aunt Liz's skirts, but I didn't ask her about him—I thought I should speak to you first."

"Well, Elaine and I discussed the problem of what was best for him with Aunt Liz and between us we decided that to take him from Abend Bloem to live with us would be doing him an injustice. He not only adores Aunt Liz but he is adored by her and all her family as well as by all the staff. If he came to us he'd be lonely

—no matter how much love Elaine and I gave him."

"Yes, yes, that's true and also it seems to me it would be an unfair responsibility to put on to Elaine."

"It wasn't that which influenced us, I swear it, but Aunt Liz pointed out it would be wronging David because when he was old enough to understand these things, he'd ask why he had Nancy's name yet called me Father?" Terence flushed with shame. "And later he might discover the truth that he had been born illegitimate."

"There would always be that chance. Yes—you've made a wise decision, I'm sure of it. You mustn't worry about it any more. You can always be David's favourite uncle and naturally throughout his life you'll watch over him and care for him. It's still obvious that Marie wants absolutely no part of her child?"

"None whatever, she wrote to Aunt Liz that she's going to become a missionary and teach somewhere in India."

"Extraordinary girl—poor Aunt Liz hasn't told me a word about her."

Katie's week-end with Elaine and

Terence was so happy that for long intervals she was able to wipe Nancy and Mary from her mind. Learning to know Elaine more intimately Katie revelled in discovering that the beautiful girl was even kinder, more intelligent, more loving than Katie had found her to be on their first meeting and she thanked God for Terence's wonderful marriage.

Back again at Abend Bloem, Katie started to become agitated because the cable which she had arranged with Howard to send at this date was overdue. Had he forgotten to send it? Had he mistakenly despatched it to the Lydenburg Post Office instead of to Abend Bloem?

Every time she heard hoof beats cantering down the avenue of oaks, she ran to see if it were a messenger with the cable. When at last it came, she read it aloud to Chris and Liz. "Complications Mary's condition advise you come love Howard."

"Dear God, what can be wrong?" Katie hated acting the necessary lie to Liz and Chris.

"It can't be serious, darling," Liz said,

trying to sound reassuring, "or Howard would have said so."

"Oh, I shouldn't worry, Katje," Chris spoke soothingly in his deep voice. "I imagine that Mary being with child in a foreign country has probably got nervous about it all."

"Yes, yes, but I must go to her—it's my duty."

Liz backed her up completely. "You're right. Of course you must go, Katie. Anyhow the sea voyage will do you good; you're not looking at all well."

"I'm all right—of course I'm missing Paul, he should soon be in Southampton I suppose."

Liz nodded whilst Chris said, "If you sail this week, Katje, Stephan can accompany you." Chris gave a little dry laugh at Katie's surprised expression. "Yes, last night your dear sister finally twisted me around her little finger."

"Whatever do you mean, Chris?"

"I agreed to allow Stephan to go to Rome."

"It's true, Katie. Stephan is going to be a priest; he's going to enter the Sacred College." Liz's big grey eyes were swimming with happy tears. "Chris has agreed at last."

"That's really the best news I've heard for a long time. Chris, how good of you." Katie leaned over to squeeze his arm, she understood a little of his sacrifice.

"Well, Stephan went into town this morning to book his passage on the *Norfolk Castle*, she sails on Friday." Chris occupied himself in filling his pipe; it was a difficult time for him. "If you wish it, Katje, I'll go into town and book passage for you too."

"Thank you, Chris, it would be a great comfort for me to sail with him." Katie felt a little awed by Chris' unselfishness in giving up his eldest son to the Church to please the boy and Liz. A wonderful man, Chris, he and Liz deserved each other.

On Friday afternoon, Katie stood on the deck of the *Norfolk Castle* beside her tall nephew, both of them holding the rail as they stared down at the little family group standing on the dock gazing up at them, as the throbbing of the ship's engines increased and the vessel started to edge slowly away from land.

Liz held a handkerchief to her eyes, for

she was crying. Poor Liz, Katie thought, she would sorely miss her eldest son, but lucky Liz! She had borne a son who would devote his life to God. Liz could be so proud of Stephan. Katie was proud of her sons too. God, oh God, make Paul be strong against the temptation of Nancy!

"Don't weep, Aunt Katie, Mary is going to be all right, I'm sure." Stephan placed a comforting arm around her shoulders.

Dabbing at her eyes, she glanced up into Stephan's serene-looking face, already there was an intensified aura of Godliness about her young nephew. She was grateful to be travelling with him, to be able to lean on his spiritual strength.

"Thank you, Stephan, I feel Mary will be all right, but it's your mother I was crying for—she will miss you so much."

"Mother has great fortitude and we are close in spirit; she has wanted me to be a priest as much as I've wanted it. It's Father I'm sorry about; he's such a wonderful man, but he can't understand yet that I've been blessed with a vocation. Later I pray that he will."

"Yes, Yes, he's such an unselfish man."

Katie turned her head to look back at

her family on the dock but the *Norfolk Castle* was gaining speed and the distance from shore was lengthening so that voices calling out goodbyes and nonsense-messages were fading, but the ship's band continued to blare out *Auld Lang* Syne thereby sustaining the pain of parting.

How shall I feel when next I see those beloved faces down there? Katie wondered. When I return to gaze at Table Mountain shall I be grandmother to a child as black as Sannie? Oh God, Thou who knowst the secrets of all hearts aid me to act fairly and wisely in this my greatest trial, help me to protect Terence and lovely Elaine, Paul, John, Eileen—all my beloved children as well as my beloved husband, help me to shield them from shame so that Mary's sin is not visited upon them.

GUIDE
TO THE COLOUR CODING
OF
ULVERSCROFT BOOKS

Many of our readers have written to us expressing their appreciation for the way in which our colour coding has assisted them in selecting the Ulverscroft books of their choice.

To remind everyone of our colour coding—
this is as follows:

BLACK COVERS
Mysteries

★

BLUE COVERS
Romances

★

RED COVERS
Adventure Suspense and General Fiction

★

ORANGE COVERS
Westerns

★

GREEN COVERS
Non-Fiction

ROMANCE TITLES
in the
Ulverscroft Large Print Series